W9-BLI-567

THE
KILLING
HABIT

MARK BILLINGHAM

THE KILLING HABIT

Atlantic Monthly Press
New York

First published in Great Britain in 2018 by Sphere,
an imprint of Little, Brown UK

Printed in the United States of America

First Grove Atlantic hardcover edition: June 2018

Library of Congress Cataloging-in-Publication data is available for this title.

ISBN 978-0-8021-2824-9
eISBN 978-0-8021-4623-6

Atlantic Monthly Press
an imprint of Grove Atlantic
154 West 14th Street
New York, NY 10011

Distributed by Publishers Group West

groveatlantic.com

18 19 20 21   10 9 8 7 6 5 4 3 2 1

For Claire, Katie and Jack. It's a good job that Kevin and Stan can't read . . .

I have absolutely no pleasure in the
stimulants in which I sometimes so
madly indulge. It has not been in the
pursuit of pleasure that I have periled
life and reputation and reason. It has
been the desperate attempt to escape
from torturing memories . . .

EDGAR ALLAN POE

The sea hath fish for every man.

WILLIAM CAMDEN

The party was in full swing, the cash-and-carry booze flowing freely and the buffet his wife had slaved over taking a hammering, when Andrew Evans spotted the Duchess, and thought, for a second or two, that he was going to shit himself.

That, or throw up on the spot.

He was in the garden, watching the son he hadn't seen in eighteen months creep carefully down a plastic slide, when he caught sight of her. She was standing at the open back door with a serviette in one hand and a drink in the other. She smiled and stood aside to let a teenage boy past, then turned to look at Evans.

She waved and raised the paper cup she was holding.

'It's going pretty well, isn't it?' Evans's wife helped their son up from the bottom of the slide and shook her head as the boy immediately ran around for another go. 'Good turnout.'

'Yeah ...'

'Lucky with the weather.' She looked at him. 'You all right?'

'Yeah, I'm fine,' Evans said. 'Why wouldn't I be?' He reached across to stroke her bare arm then downed what was left of his beer and crushed the empty can in his fist. 'Just going inside to get another drink.'

The WELCOME HOME banner that had been strung across the small patio had begun to droop a little and he was forced to duck beneath it on his way towards the back door. The old woman in the doorway stood aside for him and he walked past without acknowledging her. In the kitchen, he grabbed the beer that he now very much needed and hugged his sister who had clearly needed several already. Collared on his way back out by a couple of people he used to work with, he thanked them for coming, told them it meant a lot and said he would catch up with them properly later. Then, though it was the last thing he wanted to do, Evans walked back outside, laying a hand on the old woman's mottled, fleshy arm as he passed, to let her know that she should follow him.

A minute or so later, she pushed through the side gate and joined him at the front of the house.

'What are you here for?' He took another drink, half the can gone already.

'Well, that's not very nice.' She sounded genuinely hurt. 'I mean, why wouldn't I be here?'

'This is family. Friends.'

'Don't be like that,' she said. 'It's a special occasion, isn't it? And I was a very good friend until yesterday, wasn't I?' She stepped across and touched her plastic cup to his beer can. 'Congratulations.'

Evans stared and fought the urge to back away.

The Duchess . . .

It's what they all called her, the ones she came to see, what they thought she looked like. Always nicely dressed, with her hair up; smelling of something sweet and with a bit too much old-lady make-up, as though she could just have been somebody's grandmother. Probably was, because she played the part well enough. Grandmother to God knows how many blokes on visiting day.

She smoothed down the front of her party dress, looked up and saw him staring. 'Like I said, special occasion . . . so I made an effort. I always do.'

Whatever they called her, whatever she was trying to look like, the accent was pure Essex.

He said, 'You should go. We can do this by phone.'

'I just wanted you to know how things stood, that's all. It's my job to make sure you know what the situation is.'

'It's about two grand, right?' Evans took another drink. 'Obviously I haven't got a job yet, I mean it's only been a day, but as soon as I do, I'll start paying it off.'

The Duchess nodded, smiled. 'That's nice,' she said. 'But you're forgetting about the interest, my love.' She shook her head, laughing softly as though the mistake was one she was very familiar with. 'The interest *on* the interest.' She reached down to prod at the earth in a terracotta plant pot. 'That needs a bit of water, that does. Dry as a bone.'

'How much?' The hand that was clutching the beer can had begun to shake a little, so he held it against his chest.

'It's around twelve, I think—'

'*What?*'

'Don't worry, because that's why I'm here, isn't it? There's no need to panic, because you can work it off. That's the beauty of it.'

'Work it off how?' Something bright caught Evans's eye, and he looked up to see a WELCOME HOME balloon rising up and away from the back of the house. He could hear his friends and family laughing in the garden.

'Oh, I couldn't say for sure, love. Bits and bobs, that's all. Just a few bits and bobs. They'll let me know, and I'll let you know, see?'

'What if I don't want to do it?'

'Now, don't be daft, love . . .'

This time, when the Duchess moved towards him, Evans did step back and found himself against the side of the garage. She reached for his hand, and when he finally gave it she pressed a package into his palm then wrapped her own fingers around his. 'There you go.' She patted his hand. 'I bet you need this, don't you?'

For those few seconds, before Evans slipped the package into his pocket and pushed himself away from the wall, he could smell her: sickly and cloying, the lacquer and the skin cream.

'And this one's on the house,' she said. 'Like a whatever you call it . . . a goodwill gesture.'

3

As he pushed back through the gate into the garden, he could hear her chuckling behind him. 'A welcome home gift from Granny.' Then: 'Do you mind if I stay for a bit, love? Those sausage rolls are bloody lovely.'

Evans's wife was coming towards him across the grass, the smile slipping from her face, and she was saying something, but he began walking faster and cut hard left on to the patio and into the house. Into the noise and the crush of bodies. Immediately, arms were outstretched towards him, but he pushed past them and hurried quickly into the hall and turned on to the stairs.

He took them two at a time.

The Duchess had been right. He needed what she had given him, but first he needed to be sick.

PART ONE

NINE LIVES,
TWO DEATHS

He was always amazed at how easy it was.

Part of that was down to him of course, and it was no more than common sense: the thorough preparations, the thought he put into it. The care taken each and every time and the refusal to get lazy.

That was what *they* were, after all. So trusting and desperate for affection.

Victims had never been hard to find, quite the opposite, but still, each night's work needed to be treated with caution. Best laid plans and all that. There were basic measures that needed to be taken, things to steer clear of, cameras and that sort of carry-on. He was no expert when it came to forensics, but he knew enough to avoid leaving any sorts of traces. The gloves were thicker than he would have liked, but that couldn't be helped. It took away some of the feeling at the end, which was a shame, but he wasn't going to risk getting scratched, was he?

Enough feeling, though. There was always enough left, and each time it was as though things were starting to . . . even out inside him.

A lifting, of sorts.

Funny old word, but it sounded right.

He shook his head and drank his tea, one ear on the radio, as he sat and thought about who he was.

He knew there were some who would declare that this business of his was all about hate, but that kind of nonsense wasn't even worth considering. It was never about that, never would

be. Certainly not about sex, either, because that would be ...
ridiculous.

He smiled, shook his head, just thinking about it.

Did it really have to be about *anything*? Was it worth making a fuss about in the first place?

Not when you actually stopped to think, not if you sat down and put what he was doing into perspective. When there were bombs going off and plane crashes and kiddies getting cancer right, left and centre, did pathetic creatures like these really matter? What was the point of them, anyway, in the scheme of things? At the end of the day, how many people were really going to miss them?

He turned off the radio and carried what was left of his tea out into the hall. He watched himself in the mirror while he downed it. He checked the front door was locked, then turned and walked back into the living room, such as it was.

He stopped and stretched, then rubbed a hand across his belly.

It felt as though it was time to go looking again, not that he would need to look very hard, of course.

He decided that he might even treat himself to a new pair of gloves.

ONE

'Cats?' Thorne shook his head. 'Are you serious? I mean they're just . . . cats.'

DCI Russell Brigstocke gathered some papers on his desk and straightened them. 'Yes, but there's a good few of them. Fifteen more that we know about in the last ten weeks.' A tone sounded from his mobile phone. He picked up the handset, swiped and stabbed, then laid it back down on the desk.

'It's a lot of dead cats, I get that.' Thorne had followed the case in the papers and seen the coverage online and had known straight away what Brigstocke had been talking about. 'Obviously, people are upset, and I know you're getting it in the neck from the Chief Superintendent, but surely there's someone else who can handle it. For now, at least. I mean, we're Homicide. We're not . . .'

Brigstocke grinned. 'Tomicide?'

Thorne smiled in spite of himself.

'See? You've even got the perfect name for it.'

'Look, maybe whoever's doing this just doesn't like cats. Some people don't. Think they're a bit creepy.'

'We have to take it seriously, Tom.' Brigstocke sat back and ran fingers through hair that seemed to be getting greyer by the day. 'I don't have to spell it out, do I? Not for *you*.'

Thorne didn't need to answer. He knew very well that he was fighting a losing battle; that fighting at all was no more than a reflex. A degree of bolshiness that was usually expected of him, especially this early in the week, still not quite up to speed after a weekend trying and failing to relax with his partner Helen and her overactive four-year-old.

On top of which, he knew exactly what Brigstocke was talking about.

It had long been received wisdom that the corpse-littered career path of the common or garden serial killer – despite the fact that there was no such thing – more often than not began with the killing or torture of animals. Cats, dogs, birds. Together with fire-starting and persistent bed-wetting beyond the age of five, it was one of the telltale traits that made up the so-called Macdonald triad: a set of three behavioural characteristics suggested by an American psychiatrist in the early sixties that might help to identify nascent serial offenders. A common or garden copper, and there were plenty of *those* about, might be lucky, or *un*lucky, enough to come up against such an unusual killer once in a career.

Thorne had certainly dealt with more than his fair share.

He thought about a man who had suspended his victims in comas, incapable of movement and trapped, helpless within their own bodies.

He thought about a man who had targeted the children of those murdered many years earlier.

He thought about a man called Stuart Nicklin, whom he had eventually seen convicted of the most depraved murders imaginable, but whose whereabouts were now unknown.

He thought about Stuart Nicklin a great deal.

Thorne let out a long breath. 'So, you think there are going to be murders?'

'There's always murders, Tom.' Brigstocke was beginning to sound a little irritated. 'It's what pays the mortgage, isn't it?'

'You know what I mean.'

'Well, we hope not, obviously, but we have to consider it a strong possibility. We need to be prepared for it.' Brigstocke took off his glasses and began to clean them. The smile was icy, a warning. 'So, why don't you stop complaining and go and do your job?'

Thorne held out his arms, a picture of wronged innocence. 'I'm raring to go, Russell. In fact, I'm already thinking that maybe we should try to trap whoever's doing this. We could set bait.'

Brigstocke put his glasses back on and folded his arms. He said nothing, but his expression made it clear that he knew, more or less, what was coming.

'It's genius, now I come to think about it.' Thorne got to his feet. 'I know a great fancy dress shop where I could get the perfect outfit. Then all I need is a collar with a little bell on . . . '

Brigstocke shook his head and held out a piece of paper; waved it until Thorne stepped across to take it. 'Make sure you know what's been happening. The SIO on it right now is based at Kentish Town, so when you've finished being a smartarse, get down there and introduce yourself, because I've already told him you're coming. Your old stamping ground, isn't it?'

Thorne winced a little at the 'old'. He was still spending ninety-nine per cent of his time with Helen and her son in Tulse Hill, but he was not entirely comfortable in south London and doubted he ever would be. He hated the daily commute to Hendon. He missed what he still thought of as his local pub and curry house. He missed running into fellow Spurs fans on match days. Yes, the living arrangements were ideal for his other half in terms of work and childcare, and the rental income on his old flat came in more than handy, but he still lived in hope that Helen would one day see sense and the three of them could decamp to God's side of the river.

'Tom?' Brigstocke had his phone to his ear, having already put a call through. 'Anything else you want to give me a hard time about?'

Thorne shook his head and stepped away. He folded the piece of paper into the pocket of his leather jacket, lighter on his toes than he had been half an hour before. He felt excited suddenly, not just because of the back and forth with his boss and the welcome opportunity to pick up a takeaway from the Bengal Lancer, but because common or garden was not what got his blood jumping. Never had been. Because there was always the chance, slim but still compelling, that his cat-killer might just turn out to be something altogether more appalling.

He mumbled a 'sir' as he walked to the door.

But he could not resist a murmured 'miaow' as he opened it.

The remark had been characteristically cynical, but Russell Brigstocke was telling the truth. It was murder that paid the mortgage, that brought Thorne and his colleagues into work every day. More often than not, though, it was the humour, dark as all hell, that kept them there. Oiling a machine that was fuelled by violence and loss; the bad jokes and the banter that were necessary to quiet a brimming fury, or hold despair at bay.

It didn't work for everyone, of course.

Thorne had spent the rest of the morning working through a backlog of paperwork, but by the time he returned from lunch, word of his latest assignment had clearly spread around the office and been gratefully seized upon. There were the predictable smirks on the faces of those walking past him and a few off-colour remarks about 'pussy'. He casually raised two fingers at DI Yvonne Kitson, who he guessed was responsible for the can of Whiskas left on his desk. It became *one* finger when the 'who, *me*?' expression confirmed his suspicions. Had their roles been reversed, it was the kind of thing Thorne might have done himself, but he didn't think he would be finding it funny for very long.

He read through the notes Brigstocke had given him and the email attachment that had quickly followed.

The details were suitably horrific.

Looking at what had been done to so many helpless and innocent animals, Thorne could only hope that, terrible as these killings were, they were not merely a curtain-raiser. That he wasn't reading the early chapters of some trashy true-crime book waiting to happen.

He looked across at Yvonne Kitson and her smile died when she saw the expression on his face.

He ignored the grin from a pimply DC on a coffee-run.

If a killer this brutal decided that he was ready to expand his repertoire, he would not be the only one shifting gears. The machine in which Thorne was one tiny cog would need to race instead of merely turning over; flat out and fast enough to do some damage.

Then, any number of jokes might not be enough.

TWO

When the man he'd been sent to see opened the door, Andrew Evans waited a second or two before slowly taking his motorbike helmet off. It was what he'd been told to do. What they'd told the Duchess and the Duchess had told him.

'Scares them before you even start,' she'd said. '*Then* you take it off, so they get a good look at that big ugly mug of yours. Puts them on the back foot, so they don't try and do anything stupid.'

The woman clearly knew what she was talking about. He watched the man take half a step back and saw the colour drain from his sunken cheeks, having realised that Evans wasn't there to ask directions or deliver a package.

'There's no need for this,' the man said. 'To come round.'

'Yes, there is.'

'I'm paying, aren't I?'

Evans glanced along the landing, then back over the balcony towards the street below to check that nobody was watching. 'Don't want busybodies,' the Duchess had told him. 'In and out before anyone can stick their beak in.' He took off his leather gloves and pushed them inside his helmet.

14

'Not fast enough,' he said. 'Doesn't even cover the interest.'

'You winding me up?'

The shocked expression was probably much the same as Evans's had been that day at his coming home party, but it was replaced a few seconds later by something else. A drop of the head. A setting of the jaw, when the man realised just how stupid he'd been to think it would be any other way.

Evans recognised that reaction as well.

'You need to give me whatever you've got in the house,' he said. 'Now.'

He had no idea how large the man's debt was. Bigger than his own, or smaller? It was drugs, he figured – the man on the doorstep had that look about him – but he thought the people he was now working for probably dealt in all manner of merchandise. He still wasn't sure why there weren't people knocking on *his* door, why they'd chosen to let him work off what he owed, but he already knew better than to ask any questions. Just keep his head down and get the job done. It wasn't as though he'd been given a great deal of choice in the matter, but whatever his employer's reasons, he guessed he was better off being the one doing the knocking.

Though, looking at the man on the doorstep, he wasn't sure which of them was the more afraid.

'I've got nothing in the house,' the man said. 'A few quid, you know? What's left of my benefit money. Food for the kiddies.'

'You're a liar.'

'I swear to you. You think I wouldn't give it you if I had it? You think I want this?'

'I think you've probably spunked most of what you've got on buying more of whatever got you into this, but that's not my problem.' Andrew leaned closer to him and dropped his voice. 'I'm just here to collect some cash and if I don't, then I'm the one that's in trouble. I don't like being in trouble.'

'Come back on Monday when I get the next benefit cheque.' The man tried to fabricate a smile. 'Before it's gone.'

'I won't be nearly as nice if I have to come back,' Evans said.

The man just shook his head and kicked a training shoe softly against the door jamb. 'I've got bugger all, mate, and that's the truth.' He raised his arms then let them fall against his sides. 'It's gone. There's a couple of tenners or something in my girlfriend's purse and that's it, but like I said, we need it.'

Evans said, 'You need to shut your mouth now and give it to me,' because he had to. He said it with the necessary amount of menace, but even as he narrowed his eyes and reached into his jacket pocket, he was fighting back a surge of sympathy for the man in the ratty sweatshirt, with skin like old plasterboard and a swarm of spots around his mouth. Mistakes made that he didn't need to guess at and tics he recognised only too well. Someone who, in all respects except the one that counted, was exactly where he had been not very long ago.

The man opened his mouth to say something and then he saw the gun in Evans's hand.

The gun that had been delivered to him the night before. Handed over on the corner of the street by someone dressed much the same as he was now, while his wife was putting their son to bed.

Food for the kiddies . . .

The man raised his hands and shouted 'Jesus' or 'Christ' or something, but Andrew struggled to hear clearly above the buzzing in his head. The tinnitus of panic and terror.

He grasped the butt of the gun a little tighter and pointed it, as casually as if it were a finger. He somehow managed to say, 'Money.'

'All right, mate.' The man stepped back further. 'No need for that.'

'Not if you stop pissing about and get me some money—' Evans froze as a young woman appeared behind the man in the doorway. It was only when she saw the gun and screamed that he became aware of the toddler whose hand she was holding, staring up at him, wide-eyed.

16

'Shut up, all right?' the man shouted.

'Please,' the woman said.

The man rounded on her. 'Go and get your purse.'

The woman just stared and pulled her child, who had begun to cry, closer to her.

'Get the fucking *purse.*'

When the woman had shrunk back into the house, Evans and the man he had been told to frighten stared at one another for a few too many awkward moments. Evans saw fear in the man's face, certainly, but he saw something else, too. Something like disgust. It was the look of someone who knew a fellow victim when he saw one and was quietly appalled. The look one prisoner might give to another who is earning brownie points by rounding up his comrades and marching them away to be punished, or worse.

Andrew Evans was still thinking about that a few minutes later as he climbed on to his bike. As he tucked what turned out to be forty pounds into the same pocket as the gun and pulled his helmet on.

He wrapped his hands tight around the throttle and clutch levers. As much to stop them shaking as anything else.

He put his son to bed while his wife, Paula, made dinner. Once they'd eaten, they sat in front of the TV together and Evans told her lies. The fictitious job interviews he'd been to that afternoon, the trips to various building sites to see if they were hiring.

'You'll get something,' Paula said. 'You're a hard worker, someone's going to see that.'

'Yeah,' Evans said. 'Hope so.'

'We just need to be a bit careful with money, that's all, but it's working out OK.' She had struggled while he was inside, he knew that. He hated the fact that she still was, that she was working two part-time jobs to top up his benefit money.

'Don't worry, I'll keep looking.'

17

While the work he was actually doing, if you could call it that, wasn't bringing in a penny. In truth it was barely keeping his head above water.

'You feeling all right?'

He looked at her. 'I'm fine.'

She reached across to lay a hand on his forehead. 'You're still not a hundred per cent.'

'I just can't seem to shake this bloody cold.' He picked up the remote to change the channel, and if she saw the tremor in his hand, she didn't comment. 'Stupid thing is, eighteen months inside, I was fit as a fiddle.'

Ultimately, there was nothing he could do to disguise the shakes and the night sweats and he was only grateful she hadn't seen the vomiting, couldn't hear how fast his heart was beating. He had managed to hide what he was up to when she'd visited and he was doing his best to keep it that way. It was difficult, because now she was with him for more than an hour one day a week, and Evans knew his wife wasn't stupid.

'I'll go to the chemist again tomorrow,' she said.

'Thanks,' he said.

'Make you another appointment with the doctor.'

Aside from that first time at the party, whenever he'd got his hands on new stuff, he'd left the house to use. Suddenly he'd become the one who volunteered to take the dog across to the park, or make trips to the local shops that took far longer than they should have done. He'd got away with it so far, but he wasn't sure how long he could keep it up.

Any of it.

Unless he was being the stupid one and Paula knew exactly what was going on. Perhaps she had known what he was up to from the kick-off and was refusing to judge him for it; allowing him to pretend. Had such a thing been possible, each time he looked at her and those sour bubbles of guilt rose up and burst in his throat, he would have hated himself even more.

There were moments when he felt like using that gun on himself.

'You should get an early night,' Paula said.

'Actually, I might take the dog out again.'

'It's a bit late, isn't it?'

Evans stood up and stretched, then walked out into the hall. 'I think the fresh air helps a bit,' he said. There was still a little left of the last ten grams that had been delivered; an envelope at the bottom of the plastic bag the gun had been in. His wage packet. 'Exercise is good, too.' He came back in, pulling his coat on, and leaned down to kiss her. 'I need to get fit again.'

'Yeah, well you've certainly been doing a lot of walking since you got out.' His wife smiled and turned off the TV. She reached down for the newspaper that was lying on the floor. 'One good thing.'

THREE

Kentish Town station was one Thorne knew very well. Though he had never been based there, he had lived five minutes' walk away for many years and two of the local beat officers were currently renting his old flat. Still, the familiar voice that greeted him when he entered the squad room was the last one he'd been expecting to hear.

'Fuck me, sideways . . . look what the cat dragged in.'

He smiled. 'Oh, God help us.'

Thorne had last seen Sergeant Christine Treasure a few years before, when he'd been briefly – and unhappily – back in uniform, as inspector on a borough team in Lewisham. With a temper every bit as filthy as her mouth, Treasure was certainly capable of putting backs up, which was probably why she ended up being one of the few genuine allies he had managed to acquire at the time. At any time, come to that. She was a good skipper and one Thorne quickly came to trust, but that was not to say teaming up with the woman had been a *wholly* pleasant experience. The investigation Thorne had worked on back then had left him in hospital with serious injuries, but now – hearing

20

that characteristically generous greeting and seeing Christine Treasure grinning at him – the horrific memories of those occasions when they had shared a patrol car made a gunshot wound seem like a minor inconvenience.

Treasure, rampant, at the wheel of what she called the 'fanny-magnet'.

The bad impressions and the heavy-metal singalongs. The championship-level farting. The sexually explicit monologues that would inevitably follow a sighting of anything with two legs and tits, and which made Donald Trump seem positively sensitive in his appreciation of the female form.

Now, displaying a turn of speed that was rarely seen off duty, Treasure bounded across the squad room and threw her arms around him. An officer nearby looked up from his newspaper and whistled. The radio and stab-vest and a belt adorned with baton, cuffs and mace ensured that it was not the most comfortable embrace Thorne had ever been pulled into, but it felt good, nonetheless.

'What the hell are you doing here?' Thorne asked.

'Nice to know you've missed me.' The last time he'd seen her, Treasure's dyed-blonde hair had been short and teased into spikes. Now it was longer and swept back. She saw Thorne clock the new look and smiled. 'Going for the fifties matinee idol thing,' she said. 'The ladies love it.'

'Well you've always been idle, certainly.'

The punch on his arm was a painful reminder that she was not someone to mess with. He remembered the straight jab that had laid out a drunk who'd been foolish enough to take a swing at her in Catford shopping precinct.

'Seriously though,' he said. 'Long way from Lewisham.'

She led him back into the tea-room and flicked the kettle on. The smell of what was no more than a glorified cupboard took him back again to those few, uncomfortable months of demotion, when he'd been one of the 'lids'.

'You were always talking about how great it was up here,' she said. 'So I thought I'd see what you were banging on about.'

'I was right, wasn't I?'

'Yeah, I suppose.' She threw her belt down on the table and undid the vest. Just after lunch and she was clearly coming off the early shift. 'Slightly better class of shit, I'll give you that.'

The 'shit'. Treasure's decidedly un-PC collective term for any and all offenders who had the audacity to cross her path and give her paperwork to do. Drunk-drivers, thieves, rapists. She despised them all equally.

'Plus my girlfriend lives in Tufnell Park, so it's handy, you know?' She grinned again, the gap between her front teeth making her look deceptively girlish. 'I should say wife-to-be.' She held out a hand to show Thorne the ring and waggled her fingers like a princess. 'Getting married in a couple of months.'

'Congratulations,' Thorne said.

'I went to her fitness class and proposed over the PA. Good, eh?'

'Classier than I would have expected.'

'You want to come?'

'Do I have to wear a hat?'

'You can wear a fucking tutu for all I care.' She picked up a mug and raised it. 'Want one?'

'I should probably crack on.' Thorne looked at his watch. He was already twenty minutes late for his appointment. He also needed to pop into the flat to check out a possible damp issue and there was that takeaway to pick up.

Treasure mashed her tea. 'You here to see Uncle Fester, yeah? The cat thing.'

'You involved with that?'

'I'm involved in everything, mate, one way or another. Knocked on a few doors.'

'Anything I need to know about the boss?'

'He's all right. He might think you're a bit underdressed, but

22

he won't piss you about.' She took a fast slurp of tea. 'Come on, I'll take you up.'

Thorne followed Treasure up the stairs and along a carpeted corridor to the part of the station where CID was based. A nest of small offices and an open-plan incident room. He asked her if she'd be around when he'd finished, but she told him she was keen to get away; there was a hot body waiting for her in Tufnell Park.

They stopped outside the detective superintendent's office.

'What about a wedding present?' Thorne asked.

'You don't have to.'

'Oh, all right then, I won't.'

Treasure punched him again, but not as hard this time. 'I'll send you a link to the wedding list.'

Thorne shook his head. "You've definitely got a lot fancier since you moved up here. Harrods, is it?"

Treasure grinned and turned to walk away. "7-Eleven," she said.

Thorne understood the nickname, and Treasure's remark about clothes, before he'd even sat down in Simon Fulton's office. The man was as bald as an egg and the care he'd taken over the rest of his appearance led Thorne to guess that, lack-of-hair-wise, he had made the decision to jump before he was pushed. He did not look like the kind of man who would be able to live with a comb-over, but then Thorne could never understand anyone who did. Fulton's dove-grey suit was not off any peg Thorne could afford, the white shirt was pristine, and if he hadn't had his teeth straightened it would only have been because they didn't need it.

He looked like that actor in *Kingsman*, but Thorne couldn't remember the name.

'I'd ask if you found us all right,' Fulton said. 'But then I don't need to, do I?'

The detective superintendent was clearly someone who did his homework and was keen to let people know he had. Who liked to know as much about those he'd be working with as possible. Thorne hoped he hadn't done *too* much digging.

'No, I used to live round here,' Thorne said. Mark somebody, he thought. That actor.

Fulton nodded and straightened a picture on the corner of his desk. His family? Thorne couldn't see a wedding ring. His car? 'Nice part of London,' he said. 'Well, maybe not if you're a cat lover.'

'So, where are we?'

Fulton did not react to the 'we', at least not visibly, which Thorne took to be a good sign. With those rather less secure in their abilities or authority, it might have rankled.

'You know the basics, I presume.'

Thorne nodded. 'The numbers, whatever.'

Fulton told him anyway.

'The truth is that even the numbers are all over the place. Look . . . a local animal welfare charity brought these killings to our attention over a year ago, and obviously we're very happy they did.'

Thorne said, 'Of course,' but he had begun to sense that the only thing Fulton was remotely happy about was handing this case over.

'The charity says there are *this* many victims, the RSPCA reckons it's another number altogether, and despite the scare stories in the papers, the truth is it's probably somewhere in between. A lot of the time, killings are being reported when animals have simply gone missing or been hit by cars. Even if it *is* something more deliberate there's always the possibility it's just someone getting fed up with next door's ginger tom crapping in their flower bed or some thug taking advantage of all the media coverage.'

'A copycat?' Thorne tried hard not to smile.

Fulton did the smiling for both of them; just a glimpse of those perfect teeth. 'So . . . our estimate is somewhere north of three hundred that we believe to be the work of one individual, and the majority of those are in and around north London.'

'I thought it was wider than that,' Thorne said. 'Some of the papers are calling him the M25 cat killer.'

'There've been plenty a little further afield,' Fulton said. 'We think so, anyway. As I mentioned, it's hard to be precise about all this. We took everything to a geographical profiler and she's convinced our offender lives locally.'

'How's he doing it?'

'A number of the animals have been examined by a veterinary pathologist and in every case the stomach contents were the same, suggesting that he lures the cats to him with chicken. The actual cause of death is always strangulation or blunt head trauma, so the animals are all stunned or already dead before the removal of body parts. Heads or tails, usually. Some limbs. All very clean cuts, so we're thinking garden shears.'

'What about forensics or prints?'

Fulton shook his head.

'Can you *get* fingerprints off a dead cat?'

'Yes, but we haven't and no DNA either. We're guessing he wears gloves, because he doesn't want to get scratched to death. He's clearly someone who doesn't like to take chances, because he's never been seen. No CCTV, no ANPR. He likes to stick to residential areas where there are fewer cameras. We certainly don't think he's . . . impulsive.'

'So, what *do* you think?'

Fulton sat forward. 'At one time or another we've had three distinct theories.' He counted them off with raised fingers. 'Initially, we brought in a forensic psychiatrist, a . . . profiler from the National Crime Agency.' The hesitation was enough to make the man's feelings about such 'experts' abundantly clear. 'She considered the possibility that our offender might just be a disgruntled teenager, but eventually suggested we were probably looking for a white male between forty and fifty.'

'With unresolved mummy issues.'

'Exactly, so without much else to go on, we based our inquiry around that profile for a while. Then . . .' another finger, 'we began thinking more specifically. Outside the box, you'd probably say.' There was another smile, and Thorne wondered if the theory he was about to hear was one Fulton had come up with himself. 'Do you know how many birds are killed by domestic cats every year?'

'Not a clue,' Thorne said. 'A lot?'

'Fifty-five million.' Fulton sat back. 'Sounds ridiculous, I know, but there's nine million cats in this country, so that figure's just based on one cat killing one bird every two months. So, we began to consider the possibility that the individual we were looking for had a particular grudge. A specific agenda.'

'Seriously? A crazed ornithologist?'

'Why not?'

'I take it you brought Bill Oddie in for questioning.'

Perhaps Fulton did not understand the reference, but if he appreciated the attempt at levity, he decided not to let his face know about it. 'As of now,' he said, 'it's still an active line of inquiry.' Finally, the three fingers were up. 'And, obviously, we have the step-up theory, which is certainly the one our profiler was keen on, and which is where you and your team come in.'

'Right,' Thorne said. Thinking: Cavalry or sacrificial lamb?

'So far, thankfully, that's not happened, but we'd be stupid if we didn't consider it a real possibility. Whichever theory's right, if *any* of them are, we need to catch him. Oh, and you should know that a couple of the charities have clubbed together and put up a ten thousand pound reward.'

'Nice.' Thorne was not surprised. The animal welfare organisations were usually pretty well heeled, most of them raising more money every year than the charities which protected children.

He was not sure what that said about those who donated.

'Doesn't show a lot of faith in our abilities, but I suppose it might help.'

'A number of the animals,' Thorne said.

'Sorry?'

'You said a number of the animals were examined by the veterinary pathologist. Why not all of them?'

In the few moments of obvious discomfort before Fulton answered the question, and from the earnestness of his response, Thorne finally understood the real reason this case was being handed over.

'Well, as I'm sure you can appreciate, unless and until this becomes a murder case, we can't really justify every resource we would otherwise be throwing at it.' Fulton shook his head and tried to look disappointed. 'To be honest, the profiler was about as high-end as we were able to go. Now we've got a specialist homicide unit looking at it, those resources shouldn't be subject to quite the same scrutiny.'

'I get it,' Thorne said.

Not your problem any more. My problem . . .

He guessed that the detective superintendent was fighting the urge to punch the air, thrilled to be finally passing on such a poisoned chalice. After all, if the killings did not escalate, his team would be lumbered with a case he was unequipped to solve, while if the man they were after *did* make that step up, Fulton would then have a very dangerous murderer to catch, which no copper in their right mind would relish.

Though there were one or two who would, naturally.

There were a few minutes of amicable natter after that: anything I can do, happy to help, you should seriously think about moving north again, your other half's Job, isn't she?

Thorne stopped at the door. 'Bill Oddie's a birdwatcher.'

Fulton blinked. Said, 'Yeah, of course. I knew that.'

FOUR

'It is better. This is *still* better . . .'

Lying beneath a thin, stained duvet on a sofa his neighbours had been throwing away, Adnan Jandali nodded and spoke to himself out loud. Whispered, as he so often did these days, in those moments when he was not shaking or doubled up. A few moments of comfort; spluttered when he could not stop weeping, or chanted – low and broken – as he wandered aimlessly from room to room.

A few scraps of wreckage to cling to.

Things were not as bad; how could they be? He thought this and a weak smile briefly cracked the pasty mask of his face. *Bad* had been one of the first words he'd learned in the detention centre, because it was simple and had said everything he wanted. Those first few weeks, when hope had made him talkative and he'd been keen to pass it on to others. When he'd tried to tell anyone who would listen what things had been like in the place he'd travelled so far from.

'Trust me, this is not so bad . . .'

However terrible he felt now, however awful things had

become – he had *allowed* them to become – Adnan had to keep reminding himself why he was here; why a life in this country was so much better than the one he'd had at home. A life, such as it was, that he'd endured until there had been no choice but to leave. Back when he'd first arrived, when he and his children had stepped into a city that was not being bombed out of existence, there had really been nothing to think about.

The rain was wonderful.

The language he could not speak sounded magical.

This was home now, he had told himself. This was where, God willing, he would raise his children and keep them safe. They would grow, be healthy and prosper, and in time perhaps they would forget their mother, or at the very least she would become no more than the memory of a beautiful woman in a story they had been told when they were very little.

They would forget, even if Adnan could not.

Those long weeks in the centre had been where it had all started. Weeks that had become months, while they checked his documents and made their decisions. While his children stayed with strangers. Confused and frustrated until he was offered something he was promised would make things easier for him, make the time go faster. He had no money to pay for it, but that wouldn't be a problem, they had said.

Smiles and laughter and pats on the back.

Once you're out of here and settled, you can pay for it then.

It had made things better, they'd been right about that. It was as if what was in those little packets just shut down the part of him that remembered, or cared. It put blinkers on him and wrapped him in a blanket. Of course, *of course*, once he was out of there and back with his boys, he had not stopped needing it and there was never enough money.

And now his boys had been taken away again.

Now he had the debt and the pain and a craving that would not stop for something he could not afford.

29

This is still better.

There was a saying here about frying pans and fires. He knew what it meant because there was a similar expression in his own language. Bad to worse, something like that. When things were the other way round there were no words for it, but it was still a blessing. It had to be, didn't it? When you had escaped from a fire, watched it burn and felt the heat of it, surely anything was preferable, however terrible. Lying here now, with a stinking bucket on the floor and a hole inside because he did not know where his children were, Adnan was still grateful.

Another thin smile . . .

Because he still gave thanks to the Almighty for the frying pan.

The volume on the television was so loud that it took him a minute or more to register that the doorbell was ringing. Long, insistent. It was another minute before he had wiped his face and buttoned his shirt, walked slowly to the door and opened it to find himself staring at the man in the dark motorcycle helmet.

The rain outside was not quite as wonderful as he had once thought.

He said, 'I have nothing.'

He raised his arms to ward off the punch, then saw too late that it wasn't a punch. The noise was like someone coughing behind their hand, and before he sank to his knees and watched his visitor walk away, Adnan felt the blood leaking through his fingers and thought: There are fires everywhere.

FIVE

After visiting his flat to check that his tenants weren't trashing the place, and collecting his takeaway, Thorne drove down to Camden and parked outside a gym behind the Electric Ballroom. A few minutes later, he sat waiting in the gym's sleek and shiny reception area, watching an assortment of Lycra-clad men and women on their way in or out, and trying not to get too depressed at the fact that this was as close as he was ever likely to come to a fitness regime.

Much as Thorne loved football, and enjoyed watching almost any sport on TV – through he drew the line at the mind-numbing boredom of Formula One – he had never been the most enthusiastic of participants. A few years before, he had been talked into turning out one evening for a Serious Crime Directorate five-a-side team, and had not exactly covered himself in glory. After ten minutes of being made to look and feel silly by a bunch of coppers half his age, he had thrown in the towel and spent the rest of the game in goal, fighting to get his breath back and deciding there and then that he was better off at home in front of his Samsung.

With a beer in his hand.

And a kebab . . .

Eventually, Phil Hendricks appeared, coming down the bleached-wood stairs two at a time. A spiked leather kit-bag was slung over his shoulder and the absurdly tight black T-shirt showed plenty of intricate tattoo work.

'You're late,' Thorne said.

'Sorry, mate.'

'I've been sitting here ten minutes. I'm knackered.'

Leaning against Thorne's chair, Hendricks raised his foot, grabbed his ankle and bent his leg behind him to stretch out the muscle. 'Had to cool down properly, didn't I?'

'Eh?'

'Gets your heart rate back down.' Hendricks straightened up and moved away towards the exit. 'Stops your blood pressure dropping because it's pooled in the large muscles.'

Thorne got to his feet and followed his friend out through the revolving door. 'If you say so.'

Hendricks was standing on the pavement, continuing to stretch. 'Gets rid of the lactic acid, all that bollocks.'

'All right,' Thorne said. 'Don't start throwing fancy jargon at me.'

Despite the less than medically precise turn of phrase, Hendricks knew what he was talking about. As a forensic pathologist, he knew exactly what could be done to the body by things an awful lot worse than lactic acid.

'You need to cool down after a workout, mate.' Hendricks grinned at him, then began to walk. 'It's like you throwing the empties away.'

They went to the Spread Eagle on Camden Parkway and Hendricks offered to get the drinks in. Thorne feigned shock, then asked for a pint of Guinness. 'I'll enjoy watching you drink your orange juice.'

'I like keeping fit,' Hendricks said. 'I'm not mental.' He ordered two pints, then pointed to a selection of home-made sausage rolls and Scotch eggs on the bar. 'Fancy one of them?'

Thorne explained that he was only staying for one drink and that he had a takeaway from the Lancer in the boot of his car.

'Nice,' Hendricks said. He picked up the drinks and carried them across to a table by the window. 'So, what's the plan? Helen going to take one mouthful of the rogan josh, decide you need to move back up here and stick her flat on the market?'

'I can dream, can't I?' Thorne said.

They touched glasses and drank. On an adjacent table, a pair of media types discussed some exhibition they'd both seen recently, while clearly taking part in a 'who's wearing the stupidest glasses?' competition.

'So, what's with this gym business?'

Hendricks stared at him, wiped the froth from his top lip.

The assorted bits of metal decorating almost every part of his body imaginable meant that Hendricks was probably a damn sight heavier than he might have been otherwise, but he had always been muscly and fit. He might have been mistaken for a somewhat exotic-looking bouncer, though this had never seemed to require much in the way of conventional effort. For most of the time Thorne had known him, his friend's idea of a workout had involved dancing himself stupid in a darkened club, followed, if he was lucky, by a marathon bout of sexercise with whoever he managed to pick up. Since settling down a year or so ago with his partner Liam, however, he had become something of a gym bunny.

'Those nice arses in tight shorts, is it?'

Hendricks shrugged. 'Not interested,' he said. 'I mean, don't get me wrong, that's a bonus, but I go to the gym because I care about staying with Liam.'

'What, you reckon he'd bugger off if you put a few pounds on?'

'No chance. He knows he got lucky.'

'So, what then? I thought once you'd settled down with

33

someone you could sort of . . . give up. You know, if you weren't on the pull any more.'

'He likes that I'm fit, that's all. *I* like that I'm fit.'

Thorne grunted, took another drink.

'That what *you've* done then, is it? Given up?'

'No—'

'Does Helen know that?'

'No . . . it's just she doesn't mind if I don't look like an underwear model, that's all.'

Hendricks nodded. 'She told you that, has she?'

Thorne said nothing.

'Well, there you go. Would you say anything to *her* if you thought she was getting a bit chunky?'

'Don't be daft.'

'Right. But you'd be thinking it.'

'She doesn't have to say anything,' Thorne said. 'I know she's not that shallow. Anyway, she doesn't need to totally love my body, because she's got my amazing mind and my winning personality.'

Hendricks laughed. 'Blimey, you really are in trouble.'

Thorne muttered, 'Piss off' into his Guinness.

'Seriously, though, I'm asking. You think she prefers it that you've let yourself go?' Hendricks leaned towards him. 'Obviously, I'm using that phrase loosely, because it implies you had hold of yourself to begin with, but you know what I mean. You really reckon Helen likes having you bouncing around on top of her, that she wouldn't prefer a six-pack to a Watneys party seven? I'm telling you, mate, she's started eyeing *me* up lately, and that means she must be desperate.'

'Yeah, all right.'

'You could start by throwing that curry away.'

'Not going to happen.'

'Or you could give it to me. Luckily, I'm gorgeous, *and* I've got an amazing metabolism.'

'Can we change the subject?'

'Not to mention what you're doing to your heart and your blood pressure ... the risk of diabetes and stroke. I cut open a bloke who looked a bit like you the other day. He had a layer of fat all over him thicker than Lurpak, a liver that might just as well have been pâté and a heart like a bag of melted lard.'

'You done?'

'Wasn't pretty, all I'm saying.'

'What part of "change the subject" didn't you understand?' He watched as a barman delivered huge plates of posh fish and chips to the pair on the next table. However stupid their glasses were, they were both as skinny as sticks and Thorne guessed that neither had much to worry about as far as body mass index or cholesterol went.

Hendricks smiled and said, 'Touchy.' Then, 'So what are you doing back up here, anyway? I know the Lancer's good, but ...'

Thorne told him about the cats.

'The sort of thing that could get nasty,' Hendricks said.

'That's the worry.'

'You ever thought it could be more than one killer?'

Thorne waited.

'You know, a team of angry mice, working together?'

'Hilarious,' Thorne said, though it made about as much sense as Fulton's psychotic bird-fancier. 'Like I haven't had the jokes up to here.'

'Not as good as that one though, I bet.'

As was so often the case in these situations, the words coming out of Phil Hendricks's mouth – the perfectly timed punchlines, the flat Mancunian accent – suggested a glibness and lack of concern that were in stark contrast to the grace and skill with which he worked daily upon the bodies in his care. These had included the victims of several serial killers and Thorne knew he understood the implications of the case they were discussing perfectly well. It was simply Thorne's turn to be the straight man, that was all. The grown-up. While Hendricks provided the same kind of smartarse remarks he himself had already made, Thorne was there now to shake his head and look serious.

Because it *was* serious, he was certain of it.

He had known before he'd walked into Fulton's office in Kentish Town and now realised he'd had a fair idea what lay ahead even when he'd been sitting in Russell Brigstocke's office the day before; complaining and making the same jokes.

Whistling in the dark.

'The forensic psychiatrist that Fulton's been liaising with seems to think it's pretty clear-cut,' Thorne said. 'She's not quite staking her reputation on it, but near enough.'

'Well, she wouldn't,' Hendricks said. 'I mean, they can get it wrong, you know.'

'Textbook step-up, she reckons.'

'Yeah ... have to admit it looks that way.' Hendricks nodded slowly and stared at his glass. 'I thought that months ago, when the papers started covering it. Some nutter flexing his muscles, seeing how he likes it.'

'Oh, I think we can be fairly sure he likes it,' Thorne said.

'When was the most recent one?'

'Last one for definite was a couple of weeks ago, but it's hard to keep track. Sometimes it takes a while for someone to be sure their pet's missing and even if it is, it might just be because it's run away. Sometimes it turns out the cat's just been run over.'

'Well, if he *is* still warming up, it sounds like we might have a chance.'

'Let's hope so.' Thorne was pleased to hear the *we*. The answer to a question he had not needed to ask. He and Hendricks had worked closely together on almost all those cases where Thorne had been hunting a serial offender, and he did not want this one to be any different.

For all the wind-ups, there was an understanding between them that generated results. A spark and a shorthand.

36

It was more or less what Hendricks had said the previous evening, though it had been couched in rather gentler terms. A few sarky remarks as he put his second pint away. He had said he was simply playing devil's advocate and had seemed more concerned that Thorne might make a fool of himself than anything else.

'It's certainly counter-intuitive,' Perera said. 'But that's not necessarily a bad thing. It's often the way to come up with a thesis that changes everything.'

'If you say so.' Thorne decided it was probably best not to mention that his 'thesis' had popped into his head while he had a drink in his hand, though something in the woman's tone suggested that she might not altogether have disapproved of that.

'Look, if there's one thing I know about this somewhat ... niche area of the profession I've mysteriously ended up in, it's that you need to keep an open mind. Obviously we have *guidelines*, but there's no real ... orthodoxy. How could there be? Every killer I've studied or interviewed has brought something different to the table.'

'One way of looking at it,' Thorne said.

'Yes, and quite literally, in the case of at least one individual I can think of. What I'm saying is, they're never the same, not completely. Yeah, there are usually certain common factors or signifiers, I mean that's how the Macdonald triad came to be so widely accepted, but these kinds of killers always have something that marks them out as different. That's the point. They don't *want* to be the same as anyone else. They need to feel they're special.'

'Don't we all?' Thorne continued to doodle; faces and shapes he decided he would not have wanted the likes of Melita Perera to see. He was not too keen on the idea of anyone rummaging around in *his* twisted psyche. He said, 'I was ready for you to shoot me down in flames.'

The woman chuckled. 'I had a patient who did that once.

Ex-army bloke up in Scotland, got hold of a military-grade flame-thrower and barbecued his mother.'

'Bloody hell.'

'Listen, Tom, I could sit here and piss on your chips if I felt like it, and there are probably plenty of others with letters after their names who would have done, but they aren't the ones who are good at the job.'

'To be honest, part of me wanted you to.'

'I get that.'

'Like this thing isn't messed up enough as it is.'

'You have to be ready to adapt your thinking, that's all I'm saying. You never know what's around the corner, do you?'

'I suppose not.'

'Or *who*.'

'OK, well thanks,' Thorne said. 'That's good to hear, I think.'

Perera laughed again, high and easy, and Thorne decided that when this was all over he'd happily offer to buy the woman a drink or two, if she fancied it; spend an evening listening to a few more of her nightmarish war stories. 'Yeah ... I know what you're saying. Obviously, if you're right, if our killer's in a cooling down period, it's because he's already had his workout. It means there are some murders that you've missed.'

Thorne drew a big, fat question mark. 'Yeah, some,' he said. He screwed up the piece of paper and lobbed it just wide of the bin. 'Murdered women, you think?'

'Well ... '

'You said you thought our cat killer was almost certainly male, so what does that tell us about his human victims?'

'If there are any.'

'Yeah, obviously,' Thorne said. 'Female?'

'You want an expert opinion?'

'Look, I'm not going to hold you to it, but we need to start somewhere.'

'Probably,' Perera said, eventually. 'Best I can do.'

'Thanks.'

'But let's not ignore the elephant in the room.' Another laugh. 'Well, the giant cat in the room.'

Then, as though she was stating what any child would understand, Perera said something Thorne had known to be true when Hendricks had casually thrown it into their discussion the night before. Something Thorne had blithely skated over in his excitement, but which now lodged in his head like a dreadful image from a nightmare he thought he'd forgotten.

Something he would not forget again any time soon.

A few minutes later, the psychiatrist's words were still clattering round his brain, like an angry rat in a bucket, as he walked towards Brigstocke's office.

'I'll have to run it by Fulton,' the DCI said.

He explained that, going forward, they, or rather he, would have to run everything past the detective superintendent at Kentish Town. Though they had been tasked with picking up a case that had become too unwieldy for one team, Fulton remained the nominal SIO. 'We'll run an incident room here, and we'll probably have several members of the original team joining us, but Fulton needs to be kept in the loop. Fair enough?'

Thorne nodded, letting the logistical details wash over him, as they usually did; impatient for Brigstocke's reaction to what he had told him. The suggestion that their killer-in-training might not actually be training at all. He had decided against running his 'thesis' past Brigstocke first thing, but as soon as it had been validated – or at least not dismissed out of hand – by the forensic psychiatrist attached to the investigation, he had felt more confident about voicing it. Brigstocke had plastered on a look Thorne had seen plenty of times before, but his senior officer's naturally defensive instincts had begun to weaken as Thorne recounted his conversation with Dr Melita Perera.

The DCI had nodded and made unfamiliar noises of approval.

He had scribbled notes while Thorne used words like *orthodoxy* and dropped *counter-intuitive* into the discussion whenever he had the chance.

'I always knew that's what you were.' Brigstocke leaned back. 'Only I just call it "being an awkward bastard".'

'Well, now you know there's a proper term for it,' Thorne said.

'So ... we're going to have to go back a bit,' Brigstocke said. 'Presuming Uncle Fester's OK with all this.' He ran a hand through his own, relatively luxuriant head of hair.

'I'm sure he will be,' Thorne said. 'Especially now the psychiatrist's approved it.'

'She said that?'

'As good as.' Thorne watched Brigstocke scribbling again and said a silent prayer that his well-intentioned exaggeration would not come back later to bite him on the backside.

'Well, *if* you're right, we need to find out what our killer's been up to already,' Brigstocke said. 'And as you've been fully briefed on the cat killings, I'm sure you understand that won't be easy.'

Thorne nodded again. Logistics. Though this time he had something up his sleeve. Some*one*.

'If the way he's expanded the area of these cat killings is anything to go by, we'll have our work cut out.' Brigstocke shook his head. 'Have we even got any idea where to start looking?'

Thorne said nothing.

'Or how many we're looking for? Maybe we'll be lucky and discover this bloke needs this cooling off period after each murder.' He looked up at Thorne. 'Might only be one.'

'No chance,' Thorne said. 'The number of animals he's killed, I think we might be looking at several human victims already.'

Brigstocke nodded and let out a slow breath, well aware he'd been clutching at straws. 'OK ... let's start looking closer at the cat killings, the various areas and methods he's used. See if anything corresponds with unsolved murders.' He leaned back. 'Talking of which ...'

'Unsolved murders?'

'Looking closer at the cat killings.'

'I thought that's what we were doing.'

Brigstocke shook his head. 'Let's forget about where they might lead, just for a minute.'

'What's led to them, you mean.'

'Perhaps ... but either way I've still got the brass all over me, because the media are all over *them*. We need to do something.'

Thorne nodded. 'Be seen to do something, you mean.'

'Come on, you know how this works. We've got to show that we're making every effort to catch this bloke. Something positive to keep the *Daily Mail* happy, a horrified nation of animal lovers. I know you've got this new angle on it and I'm happy to let you run with it – happy-*ish* – but you need to find time to do something a bit more ... visible.'

It was Thorne's turn to lean back. He guessed he was not going to like what was coming. 'Such as?'

'Just basic coppering, nothing fancy. Go and talk to one of the victims.'

'*What?*'

'You know what I mean.'

'You want me to hold a séance for dead pets?'

Brigstocke waved a hand. 'One of the victims' *owners*, more than one preferably. Get a few statements, something the press office can use, the impact ... usual stuff. Come on, it's not asking a lot, is it? Certainly a damn sight less than you marched in here asking for.'

Thorne could see there was little point arguing. 'Right ...'

'And you'd be doing everyone a favour if you could squeeze it in before the end of the day.' Brigstocke waited a few seconds. 'Good. Sorted.' He picked up his pen again. 'So where do you want to start with these theoretical homicides?'

'We'll work the computers, look for patterns.'

'Really?' Brigstocke's slightly dubious expression returned. 'Not exactly your strong point.'

'No, but we both know someone who's very good at it,' Thorne said.

Brigstocke shook his head. 'Not going to work,' he said. 'She just caught a very nasty murder.'

'Oh, right.' Thorne tried his best to look as though this was the first he'd heard of it.

'I don't want to put too much on her plate. You know, considering.'

'Come on, Russell, she can multitask in her sleep.'

Perfectly on cue, there was a sharp knock at the door and DI Nicola Tanner walked in. She looked suitably surprised to see Thorne, then waved a piece of paper at Brigstocke and stepped towards the desk. 'We just got lucky on the Jandali homicide, sir. A match on the fingerprints from the murder weapon.'

'Nice one,' Thorne said.

'Just thought you'd like to know I'm rustling up a couple of firearms officers, then I'm away to make an arrest.'

'Good news,' Brigstocke said.

'Can you send someone else?' Thorne asked.

'Hang on,' Brigstocke said.

Tanner looked from Brigstocke to Thorne and back again.

'Yeah, OK ... send Dipak to do it.' The DCI removed his glasses and squeezed the bridge of his nose, as though his first hour at work had done him in for the day. 'Tom's got something he needs some help with.'

'It's a piece of piss,' Thorne said, turning to her. 'I swear.' He summoned his sweetest smile; the one that was usually reserved for bedtime or, occasionally, the interview room. 'I can't think of anyone else better ...'

Brigstocke ran Tanner quickly through what was needed and why she was the ideal officer to oversee it. A search through nationwide force databases for patterns of offence; her invaluable expertise when it came to correlating and organising information. Then he told them both to clear off and get on with it, while he made the necessary call to Fulton.

44

'Sir,' Tanner said.

As they were on their way to the door, Brigstocke spoke again, and the panic that Thorne had been feeling since he'd spoken to the psychiatrist was kicked up another notch. 'You don't just need to go *back*, of course ...'

What the psychiatrist had said on the phone.

I mean, your theory's interesting, but at the end of the day it doesn't change much, does it? Not when it comes to the suspect's activities speeding up, which almost everyone accepts to be the normal way of things. It's not a pleasant thought, but it makes sense, when you think about it.

Now, Thorne could not stop thinking about it.

Once you've had your workout and cooled down, you have another workout, don't you? Melita Perera had sounded matter-of-fact, but the implication was anything but.

You get your kit back on and do it again.

SEVEN

'How was that for timing?' Tanner asked.

'Pretty much faultless,' Thorne said. 'Were you listening out-side the door?'

Tanner smiled, giving nothing away, then leaned across to help herself from the canteen's salad bar. She spooned coleslaw and tomatoes on to her plate, while Thorne moved past her and asked for the shepherd's pie.

'Nice big portion,' he said. 'Oh, and if you could manage some of those lovely crispy bits round the edge, that'd be great.' The woman behind the counter did not bother looking up and, without saying a word, served him a normal-sized spoonful from the middle of the dish. 'No, thank *you*,' Thorne said, taking the plate. He was tempted to say something a little more industrial, but gave her the benefit of the doubt and decided that sarcasm was probably as much as the woman deserved. He could only guess that a close family member had just died, or that the ludicrous netted trilby she was required to wear every day had resulted in serious self-esteem issues.

He caught up with Tanner, who was waiting for him at the till.

'You go ahead,' he said.

'After you.' Tanner stared at him. 'I think the least you can do is pay for my lunch.'

Thorne watched the meals being rung up and shook his head. 'Three pounds seventy-nine? You'd better be worth it.'

'Keep the receipt,' Tanner said. 'Just in case.'

They carried their trays across to a table in the corner. From the top-floor wraparound windows of Becke House, Thorne had a good view across the seventy-acre grounds of the Peel Centre. It had once been an RAF base and had become the Met's cadet college in the 1930s, but was now one of several regional training centres, where officers could attend courses in everything from crime-scene analysis to advanced driving skills. The parade square and the running track were – thankfully – no longer considered important, and these days trainees were more likely to be spending their time at the firing range or in a state-of-the art HYDRA suite, developed for real-time critical incident training. Looking out past both these buildings, Thorne could see the memorial garden, built to honour those officers whose lives had been lost on duty, and struggled to remember ever being quite as keen as some of the eager young things he saw making daily use of the new facilities.

He wondered if the powers that be should think about instigating a few new courses, that more accurately reflected a career wearing the Queen's Cloth.

Keep Calm And Step Away From The Bottle.

Relationship Counselling For The Terminally Job-Pissed.

Don't Get Too Excited, It's All Downhill From Here.

There had been some genuine excitement a couple of years before, when sequences for a new *Avengers* film had been shot at the centre and for a week or so the grounds had been home to camera trucks and catering wagons, and the occasional permatanned movie star had stepped from an absurdly large trailer. Even Thorne had not been immune to the buzz around the place. Unlike several of his colleagues, he did not volunteer for work as an extra, but instead just had a quiet word with several of those who did; asked if anyone fancied trying to 'liberate' the odd prop or costume when nobody was looking.

'That bloody big hammer would come in useful,' he'd said.

'Tom . . . ?'

Thorne turned from the window to see Tanner looking across the table at him. She was already tucking in to her salad. She said, 'You're a lucky bugger.'

Thorne took his first mouthful. '*I'm* lucky? I've got to spend the rest of the sodding day talking to old ladies about dead cats. You're the jammy bugger who caught a nasty one, then got a fingerprint match off the murder weapon.'

'Yeah, but it's done you a big favour, hasn't it? Got you what you wanted. I don't think Russell would have gone for this otherwise, you and me working together.'

'I'd have talked him into it,' Thorne said.

'You reckon?'

Thorne grinned. He knew very well that he'd been fighting an uphill battle until Tanner had arrived like the cavalry and saved the day. 'Actually, when you marched in there telling him your murder was all but done and dusted . . . for a second or two I thought you might be making it up.'

Tanner looked at him, open-mouthed. Thorne held up his hands.

'I'm joking.'

It had taken a major charm offensive, first thing that morning, to persuade Nicola Tanner to 'interrupt' his meeting with Brigstocke, so that they might try to double-team the DCI. That in itself, Thorne knew, was very much at the limits of her personal and professional code of conduct. The day she lied to a senior officer's face about an investigation would be the day pigs flew in formation across Scotland Yard and Piers Morgan went on a women's march.

Tanner glared, only half joking herself, and speared a cherry tomato. 'You owe me a damn sight more than three seventy-nine,' she said.

Thorne had first become aware of Nicola Tanner a year or so before, when he'd been brought in to work undercover on a case for which she had done all the legwork. At the subsequent trial, he had been surprised when she had asked for his help again, this time in trying to catch two men she suspected were involved in a series of honour killings. The case they went on to work together had almost cost Tanner her life and, back then, Thorne had seen her break plenty of rules. She had done things that even he had been uncomfortable with, but at the time it had been unavoidable and made a twisted kind of sense. Something new and terrible had been driving her, and she was working 'off the books', on an investigation that, in accordance with standard Job protocol, she had no right to be part of.

Because she had been trying to catch the men she believed had murdered her partner, Susan.

'I hope it *is*,' Tanner said now.

'What?'

'Done and dusted. The Adnan Jandali murder.'

'No reason to think it shouldn't be, is there?' Thorne said. 'I mean, it'll be interesting to see how your man explains that fingerprint on the murder weapon.'

Tanner nodded. 'Right.' Dipak Chall had already texted her to let her know that he had made the arrest and was on his way back to the station with their prime suspect in custody. 'Should get the DNA back before close of play today, and I'm pretty sure that's going to match as well.'

'There you go, then.'

'Just saying. We've all seen cases that looked open and shut go tits up at the last minute, haven't we?'

Thorne told himself that, experienced and thorough as she was, this murder was probably the biggest case Tanner had caught since she had made the move and joined a new team. That

49

she was just understandably nervous. He said, 'Yeah, but not this one,' and went back to his tepid shepherd's pie again, glancing up every few seconds to watch Tanner polishing off her lunch.

She ate ... efficiently, and it was hard to tell if she was enjoying it.

He still had a clear picture of her lying broken in a hospital bed, drugged up to the eyeballs and talking to her murdered lover. Tender one moment and ranting the next. He could still remember the vehemence with which she'd sworn at him and a certain pathologist both of them knew well.

And you can fuck off as well, Philip ...

When Tanner had finally returned to work, after the compulsory compassionate leave and a prolonged period of physical therapy for her injuries, it had been to a homicide team based at Belgravia. She and Thorne had stayed in touch for a while, gossiped and moaned a little, but eventually the texts and emails had become no more than sporadic. Then stopped altogether.

He had been amazed when, only three months earlier, she had rung to tell him that she fancied a change of scene and was pushing to join the team at Becke House. The fact that she knew such a posting was up for grabs at all, when Thorne did not, was a perfect illustration of the difference between them. As was the confidence with which she announced that, were she to be making the move to Becke House, she would be bringing DS Dipak Chall – who had also been part of that original investigation – with her.

As was usually the case, she had got exactly what she wanted.

'I think they felt I was owed a favour,' she had told Thorne back then. 'After everything, you know.'

'Maybe,' Thorne had said, watching her smile falter a little. 'Who cares why, though. You're here now.'

It was still somewhat strange, seeing her every day; a little disconcerting, but overall Thorne was glad of it. The good memories – the blood and the bullets and the end result – just about outweighed the bad.

When Tanner had finished, she pushed her plate away and dabbed at her mouth with a paper napkin. 'Well let's hope I *can* put this murder to bed on the hurry-up, because I'm not sure what you need me to do is quite the "piece of piss" you seem to think it's going to be.'

'I was saying that for Russell's benefit,' Thorne said.

'Obviously.'

'Exaggerating a bit.'

'A bit? I hope you've got the say-so for a *lot* of overtime.'

'But I can't think of anyone better to give it a go.' He looked at her, long enough to let her know that he had not been stretching the truth when he'd said that, at least. That he needed her. Long enough to be reminded that in ways that were rather more obvious than some, Tanner was not quite the same woman he had first encountered twelve months before.

Six weeks ago, on her first day in Hendon, Thorne thought that she had perhaps lost a little weight. Her face certainly seemed thinner and her hair was different, the somewhat severe bob now a little stragglier than it had been before her life had been turned upside down. The clothes were not quite the same either; a series of typically unfussy skirts and blazers, though in colours a little brighter than Thorne had remembered her wearing when they'd first worked together. Powder blue and pillar-box red.

Stripes . . .

'Because I'm anal, yes?'

'Well, I prefer *organised*,' Thorne said. He smiled, remembering the pathological neatness of Tanner's front room and the colour-coded paperbacks on her bookshelves. He thought about the meticulous way she prepared material, gathered and collated everything from crime-scene photographs to coffee-shop receipts. 'I know how good you are at putting together information and at not pissing off the dozens of different people – different *forces* – you might need to provide you with it. I know you can tell when something's important and when it isn't. Most of all, I know that once you've done all that, you can see what the information *means*, while the likes of me are stumbling around like idiots because we can't see the wood for the trees.'

Tanner nodded slowly and looked at him for a few seconds. She shrugged and said, 'Anal. No need to dress it up.'

It wasn't quite a smile, but Thorne could see that she was pleased. Not that he had buttered her up, he knew that, because Tanner was not the sort to succumb to flattery. It was simply because he had acknowledged the facts. He had never known her to be remotely cocky, but much as she understood her weaknesses, she knew her strengths.

The fact that, sometimes, they could be one and the same.

'I hope you're wrong,' she said. 'About what this bloke's up to. I hope there's nothing there for me to find.'

Thorne pushed his own plate away, the meal only half eaten. He knew that if the theory he had run past Perera and then Brigstocke were to be borne out, this case would turn out to be a damn sight bigger than the straightforward murder Tanner appeared to be so nervous about. It would make the fatal shooting of a man on his doorstep look like a minor shoplifting incident.

Thorne did not think he was wrong.

Tanner had turned to look out of the window, in the same direction as Thorne had been staring when they'd first sat down. She might have been looking down at the memorial, as he had, or further, over the rooftops of Colindale and following the winding grey ribbon of the M1. But Thorne saw that her eyes were raised a little higher up, towards a sky that was rapidly ceding ground to banks of dirty-white cloud; the early promise of the spring sunshine no better than a junkie's vow to stay clean.

'I hope so, too,' Thorne said. 'But if I'm not wrong, I need you to help me catch him, Nic.'

Tanner stayed silent for just long enough to make Thorne think she might not have heard him. Then, without turning from the window, she gave the smallest of nods.

EIGHT

As Thorne drove away from the house in Gospel Oak, he glanced at the rear-view mirror and saw that the woman was still standing on her doorstep, one hand raised and the other still clutching the picture she had dug out from a leather-bound photo album half an hour before. Studied with a sad smile then passed across to Thorne. She had made him tea and fussed over the kitten she had bought to replace the cat she'd lost, and the tears had only welled up once, as she talked about the morning a few months before when she'd come out of the house and almost stepped into what had been left of her pet.

Sodden scraps of blood-soaked fur and flesh.

'I'm certainly not letting this one out.' She'd picked up the kitten and pulled it to her chest. 'Not until you catch whoever's doing it.'

'Probably sensible,' Thorne had said.

'Even when she's bigger ... I don't care if she does her business all over the house.' Her face had hardened before she set the kitten down again, her mouth twisted. 'It's sick, is what it is. The fact that he so obviously enjoys it. Creeping around in the dark with his hammer and his knives. Well, you'd better get hold of him before we do, is all I'm saying. Anyone who's lost a pet. We've all got hammers and knives as well.'

'Right,' Thorne had said.

She was certainly not the 'old lady' type he had joked about with Tanner, and neither was the forthright young couple Thorne had spoken to an hour earlier at their flat in Archway. In retrospect, Brigstocke had not been wrong when he'd asked Thorne to interview the victims. Thorne still believed that the cat killings were part of a pattern that already involved human casualties, but there was no doubt that the slaughter of animals on this scale, the ritualistic display of the corpses, was aimed every bit as much at the people who had loved them and would be left to mourn.

Their pain was part of it.

Thorne had once adopted a cat of his own, inherited, iron-ically, from a murder victim, and named before Thorne had discovered that he was actually a she. The name Elvis had stuck, the favour for a dead woman turned out to be a blessing, and Thorne found himself remembering the sing-song yowling as he'd torn at a pouch of food or poured treats into a bowl, the cat nosing urgently at his shins. He remembered his return from work feeling an awful lot more pleasant than it had before.

He stopped at the end of the road and waited for a gap in the traffic. He selected a CD, turned it up, thinking about the woman he'd just left, hosing blood from her path.

Elvis had died relatively young, but her death had been a good deal more peaceful than those afforded the unfortunate animals like the one in the photograph. Buried in the back garden, as opposed to being laid out, headless, on a front lawn, or displayed in pieces beneath the owner's bedroom window.

He/she was like one of the family . . .

It's what Thorne had expected them to say, and, when it was said, they meant every word.

He had got the statements Brigstocke and those above him so desperately needed. A few soundbites to feed to the press, that all-important impact. There, in the owner's words, crackling with anguish while they scrabbled for a tissue, and later etched across their faces when Thorne had shaken their hands and assured them that he would be doing everything he could.

When *he* had meant every word.

When a Willie Nelson song kicked in, Thorne thought immediately of Helen and her persistent, if inaccurate, complaint that country songs were all about dead or dying dogs. He tried to imagine the outcry if it were dogs being butchered rather than cats, and decided there would have been riots in the streets long before now.

He pulled out into slow-moving traffic heading south.

That kitten had been cute, no question about it. Ginger and white. Same colouring as Elvis.

NINE

By the time the necessary paperwork had been completed, the forensic samples taken and the detainee declared medically fit for interview, it was almost seven o'clock when Nicola Tanner sat down to talk to the man she believed was responsible for the murder of Adnan Jandali.

A man who had already been in custody for almost five hours.

She turned on the digital recorder and cautioned the man sitting opposite her. She announced the attendance in the interview room of herself, DS Dipak Chall and Angela Hooper, the duty solicitor. Then, after half a minute glancing through her notes – for effect as much as anything – she looked up at her suspect and shook her head.

'Only three months since you were released, Andrew.' She turned to Chall, who tutted theatrically. 'Not going very well, is it?'

Andrew Evans sat with his arms folded and his head down. 'No.'

'A little louder please,' Tanner said. 'For the tape.'

Evans slowly raised his head. 'No. It's not going very well.'

Tanner looked at him. He was tall and well muscled, with cropped hair and craggy features which would have been enough to scare Adnan Jandali even before he'd seen the gun. The man's appearance now, unshaven in trackies and T-shirt, was startlingly at odds with the image she had carried into the interview room with her: the sleek, high-flying city trader she knew that Andrew Evans had once been.

That had been a long time ago, before the crash.

Before two crashes . . .

Chall looked up from his own notes. 'Eighteen months of a three-year sentence for causing death by dangerous driving. You were lucky.' He looked for a reaction, but saw none. 'Fourteen years is the maximum sentence now, but they're talking about bringing in whole life tariffs for people who did what you did, same as manslaughter. You were certainly a damn sight luckier than the kid you ran down while you were sending messages on Facebook.'

Now, Tanner saw Evans's face change. A tightening of the jaw and a tremor in his cheek. He swallowed, and she wondered if he was about to be sick.

Hooper leaned forward. 'I'm sure we're all very grateful for the update on sentencing guidelines, but, with respect, this is ancient history. What's any of it got to do with the offence for which my client has been arrested?'

Chall shrugged. 'It's useful background.'

'In what universe?' Hooper said.

'I think Miss Hooper's probably got a point,' Tanner said. 'Clean slate, right?' She reached for a sheaf of fresh documents and straightened them in front of her. She tugged down the sleeves of her blazer. 'Do you know a man named Adnan Jandali, Mr Evans?'

The solicitor turned and looked hard at Evans.

'No comment,' he said.

'Really?' Chall sighed and folded his arms. 'We doing that?'

'Have you ever *met* Adnan Jandali?'

'No comment.'

'Have you ever visited Mr Jandali's home at 42, Athlone Gardens, Wanstead? It's the ground floor flat, if that helps.'

'No comment.'

'Mr Evans, you're perfectly entitled to sit there and say "no comment" until you're blue in the face, but you do know we're entitled to draw an adverse inference from your silence, right?' Chall looked at Hooper. 'You did mention that?'

'Of course I did.' Hooper said it casually, but did not look best pleased at having her professionalism questioned. 'My client is simply exercising his right to silence, as enshrined in the Police and Criminal Evidence Act of 1984 and protected by the European Court of Human Rights. Fair enough?'

Chall nodded, as though impressed.

'OK then, Mr Evans,' Tanner said. 'I'll tell you all about Mr Jandali, shall I? It's quite a story.' She sat back. 'Adnan Jandali came here as a refugee from Syria, just after his wife was killed and right around the time you were getting banged up, as a matter of fact.' She pulled a photograph from a plastic wallet and slid it across the table. 'Here he is. Now I can't tell you exactly how Mr Jandali got here, but you can be sure it was a hell of a journey. Selling his house for peanuts to buy a flight from Beirut to Istanbul most probably, then using what little money he had left to pay some smuggler with a dodgy boat to get him across to Greece, then on to a refugee camp in France. Him and his two children.'

Chall produced another photo and pushed it across the table. Jandali, smiling; two small boys wearing football shirts, one on either side of him. Hooper cleared her throat and appeared keen to say something, but Tanner's look seemed to change the solicitor's mind.

'When he finally arrived here as an asylum seeker, Mr Jandali's children were taken into care by social services, while he spent the best part of three months in a detention centre in

Harmondsworth. Things started looking up when he was finally released, reunited with his children and given accommodation at the address I've already mentioned. The one you may or may not be familiar with.

'But this isn't a story with a happy ending, unfortunately. Because a couple of months ago his children were taken away again, as a direct result of the drug habit Mr Jandali developed during his time in the detention centre.'

Tanner stopped to look at Evans, at the sheen of sweat across his neck and forehead that she had noticed as soon as he'd been brought in. She wasn't sure exactly what the custody nurse had needed to give him, but she recognised a dependency of some sort when she saw it.

'You'd think things couldn't get much worse for Mr Jandali, wouldn't you?'

'You'd hope,' Chall said.

'As it was, they got a lot worse, because in the early hours of yesterday morning he answered the door to someone who promptly shot him in the neck. He bled to death on his doorstep.'

She looked at Evans, but he refused to meet her stare. Pulling a bottle of water from her bag, the solicitor looked uncomfortable, though it was hard to tell if she was sickened by the story or by Tanner's emotionally manipulative telling of it. She might just have been thirsty.

'Does that last part ring a bell, Mr Evans?'

Evans shifted in his seat, pushed a hand down the neck of his T-shirt and rubbed at his chest. 'No comment.'

'My client's assertion is that he was at home with his wife at the time of the alleged offence,' Hooper said. 'And that his wife will be happy to confirm it.'

'That's good to know,' Tanner said. She nodded to Chall. 'We will obviously be talking to Mrs Evans at the earliest possible opportunity.'

'All right, so why don't we go back a bit?' Chall glanced down at his notes. 'Three weeks ago, officers were called to a flat in Mercer Road, Tottenham. Is that familiar?' He looked at Evans, then shook his head. 'No? Never mind. A woman had called the police after hearing screaming, then witnessing a violent altercation on a neighbour's doorstep. A man in a motorcycle helmet waving a gun around, by all accounts. Now initially, the man she claimed had been threatened denied all knowledge of the incident, but finally his girlfriend told officers that there had been such an argument and gave us a full statement.'

'Gave us a very good description of the gun,' Tanner said. 'One that matches the weapon used to kill Adnan Jandali.'

'Now you're being ridiculous.' Hooper put her water down and leaned towards Tanner. 'A very good description of the gun? A small black one? How many guns do you think that might be describing?'

Tanner nodded. Hooper had been given full disclosure as to the evidence against her client. She was only doing her job, but her objections now were half-hearted at best.

Because she knew there was far worse to come.

'Do you ride a blue Yamaha YZF motorbike?'

'No comment.'

'A lot of people ride motorbikes,' Hooper said.

'It's a rhetorical question really,' Tanner said. 'We know you do, because we seized it shortly after you were arrested and it's now being examined, together with your motorcycle helmet. It's the same bike ... I'm sorry, the same *model* of bike that was ridden by the man who murdered Adnan Jandali.'

Evans stared at her. He suddenly looked terrified.

'And the reason we know about the gun that was used to murder him is because we have that, too.' She reached inside the wallet again and slid a photograph of the gun across the table. 'The killer got careless and dropped it when he was speeding away from the crime scene. Have you seen that gun before, Mr Evans?'

60

'No comment.'

'Really?'

Chall leaned across. 'You forgot about the print, guv.'

Tanner rolled her eyes. 'See, any one of us can forget things, Mr Evans. I somehow forgot to mention that we got a fingerprint off the gun that was used to shoot Adnan Jandali.'

'Several fingerprints,' Chall said.

'Your fingerprints.'

Evans was breathing heavily now and blinking fast. He bent his head to wipe his face on the sleeve of his T-shirt. He said, 'No.'

'Just "no"?' Chall looked confused. 'Do you not want to add the word "comment" on to the end of that?'

'We were able to get a match so quickly because your prints are on record, thanks to all that ancient history.' Tanner flashed a smile at Hooper. 'We should have the DNA results back at any time and obviously we've got all that on record, too.' Tanner had been a little optimistic when she'd told Thorne that the DNA results would be back before the end of the day, but she was still confident that when they did arrive they would provide a match for Andrew Evans.

Tanner looked at Hooper again. The solicitor had nothing to say.

'Listen, Mr Evans. The truth is that Miss Hooper has given you advice which in certain circumstances can certainly be to a suspect's advantage. On this occasion, though, *I* would advise you to seriously reconsider.' She left it a few seconds, watched him squirm. 'Now, bearing in mind everything I've just told you, all the evidence I've now disclosed and the further evidence we're expecting any time, I'm going to ask you a very straightforward question. Did you kill Adnan Jandali?'

Evans shook his head, kept on shaking it.

'This interview is being filmed,' Tanner said, 'but for the benefit of the sound recording?'

Evans glanced at Hooper. Whispered, 'No comment.'

Tanner exchanged quick nods with Chall. She checked her watch, announced the termination of the interview, and turned off the digital recorder.

'We're done,' she said. 'For now.'

Outside the interview room, Tanner moved close to Evans as a uniformed officer stepped across to take him by the arm.

'You might want to sleep on it, Mr Evans. See if you feel a bit more talkative in the morning.'

He looked at her, wincing a little at the officer's grip. 'You think I'm going to *sleep*?'

Tanner didn't care a great deal either way. 'Be just like old times for you.' She took a few steps away, then turned back to look at him. 'Anyway, it'll be worth trying to get used to a cell again. Because I don't think your story's going to have a happy ending either.'

TEN

Coming through the front door into Helen's flat, Thorne heard voices from the living room and was not overly thrilled to recognise one as belonging to Helen's younger sister, Jenny. He thought he'd come in quietly enough, so half considered turning round again and waiting in the pub down the road until she'd gone. Then Helen called his name, so, after a few whispered curses, he plastered on a smile he hoped would do the trick and went through to say hello.

He didn't bother sitting down.

Alfie ran across for a hug, which made Thorne feel slightly less miserable, but the four-year-old was clearly not in the mood for chatting and quickly moved back to his spot on the floor in front of the sofa.

To his urgent appointment with the Gruffalo on Helen's iPad.

Jenny's greeting was no more effusive than Thorne's had been, so he spent a couple of minutes talking to Helen about his day while her sister carried a glass of wine across and sat with Alfie, who – much to Thorne's delight – seemed entirely oblivious of Auntie Jenny's company.

Thorne told Helen about his meetings with victims of the cat killer and about the scam he and Tanner had worked on Brigstocke. She warned him that the DCI was a lot smarter than Thorne sometimes gave him credit for, that he'd probably known exactly what was going on and that Thorne should probably stop feeling too smug about it.

Thorne agreed, with part of it, at least. Smug was the last thing the day had left him feeling.

He ran through a few of the day's other highlights, which took no time at all, as he couldn't think of much beyond his phone conversation with Melita Perera and his exchange with the surly server in the canteen. It took Helen even less time to talk about her own day, but that in itself was not unusual. It was rare for a shift on a child abuse investigation team to provide the stuff of banter or idle conversation.

If Helen talked about her work at all, it would certainly not be in front of her sister. Her team colleagues aside, it would not be to anyone but Thorne, and when she chose to do so, it was often at an hour when she had to wake him up first.

There were some things best talked about in the dark.

Thorne looked across at Helen's sister, who was necking her wine and pretending to be fascinated by the Gruffalo's on-screen antics. He pulled a face that only Helen could see, like he'd sucked a lemon then swallowed a turd, and announced that he was going for a shower.

Beneath water almost hot enough to take his skin off, Thorne stood and thought about those moments of the day that were rather more mundane and far more depressing than the events he'd recounted to Helen. The two hours spent with Tanner at the computer before he had set off for Archway and Gospel Oak, while Tanner had been waiting to question her murder suspect. The two of them looking again at a spate of killings that might have followed another of a very different sort.

The workout and the cool down.

64

He moved the soap around where necessary, closed his eyes and let the water wash across his face. He thought about white and ginger fur matted with gore and those whose loved ones could never be replaced. The ones he had yet to find, the missing wives and daughters – because the earlier victims would be women, almost certainly. It was something else he had talked to Melita Perera about. Whatever this individual *thought* he was doing, and however much pleasure he derived from doing it, his actions were about power, and like most of his kind he would have chosen to target those he believed to have less of it than he did.

After drying off in the bathroom, Thorne hurried through to the bedroom with a towel wrapped round him and listened to 5 Live while he got dressed. Driving home, he had envisaged an evening in tracksuit bottoms and perhaps a faded Hank Williams T-shirt, but, for reasons he wasn't clear about, he did not want Helen's sister seeing him dressed quite that casually, so he pulled on jeans and a clean polo shirt. He put his shoes back on.

Ammunition, that's what it was. He did not want to give her any more ammunition, knowing that at some point she'd find some way to use it against him with Helen.

Is he always such a slob?

Why's he still wearing T-shirts like that at his age?

It's probably because you're that much younger than he is. Mid-life crisis kind of thing ...

Turning the radio off, Thorne could hear voices from the living room, so he leaned close to the bedroom door and was just able to catch snippets of the women's conversation. Jenny's voice was far louder than Helen's, more strident. He couldn't hear everything, but he heard enough.

'Well, there's bound to be trouble if that woman's involved.' And, 'If it's anything like last time.'

He could not make out Helen's response, if there was one.

After a few minutes of prowling the bedroom, quietly seething, he was delighted to hear the front door opening, the sounds of goodbye. He pictured the sisters hugging at the door, Jenny whispering that she was always around if Helen needed to talk about anything.

You know, like how unhappy you are.

Then he heard Jenny shouting through to him: 'See you then, Tom.'

Not if I see you first.

'Yeah, see you, Jenny ...'

The moment the front door had closed, Thorne opened the bedroom door and followed Helen back into the living room.

'Nice to see Jenny giving us the benefit of her wisdom about Nicola Tanner,' he said.

Helen dropped on to the sofa and looked up at him. If she was confused about what he was wearing, why he wasn't dressed as he would usually be by this time, she didn't say anything.

He knew that Helen would never have discussed Tanner with her sister, or the details of any inquiry that Thorne had been involved with. But the dramatic conclusion to the case he and Tanner had worked on together the previous year had made most of the papers. Armed police, a car chase; an officer in hospital and a dead suspect. The coverage would have been more than enough to make Helen's sister an expert.

'She might have a point,' Helen said.

'What?' Thorne joined her on the sofa and looked down at Alfie. He did not want to be the one instigating raised voices before the boy's bedtime. 'I thought you liked Nicola.'

'I did,' Helen said. 'I felt sorry for her. I *do.*'

'So ...?'

'I still think she went back to work a bit early.'

'Come on. It was a while ago now.'

Helen looked at her watch and groaned, seeing how long it was past her son's bedtime. She leaned down to him and gently prised her iPad away. She said, 'Right then, matey. Teeth. Pyjamas.'

She watched Alfie slope disconsolately out of the room, then turned back to Thorne. 'I didn't go back that soon after Paul was killed. Not officially, anyway. And *I* didn't spend months on crutches after somebody tried to kill me. She's still ... fragile, if you ask me, and that's not good for anyone working with her, is it?'

Thorne took a few seconds, the way he always did after Helen's ex was mentioned. The man who was probably Alfie's father and had been murdered before he was born.

'I think Nicola knows what she's doing,' Thorne said. 'She seems fine to me, honestly, and she's *so* the best person to help out with this.'

Helen got up and began clearing away assorted toys and games. 'She's worried, that's all. Jenny.'

'About you, maybe. I don't think she gives a toss about me.'

'Let's not have a stupid argument about that.'

'I don't want to have an argument about anything,' Thorne said.

'Am I going to have to start arranging for her to come over when you're not here?

'No—'

'You know she gets on my tits every bit as much as yours.'

'I doubt that,' Thorne said.

It was certainly true that Jenny often annoyed her elder sister intensely and that Helen tried not to show it because she wanted to avoid the confrontation and, more important, because she needed the babysitting. But Jenny's obvious dislike, or *distaste*, for Thorne was something else entirely. When he was feeling generous, he put it down to the fact that she thought Helen, having had one relationship with a police officer that had ended so unhappily, was unwise to embark upon another. Or perhaps she simply disapproved of the age gap.

There were other times, though, when he just felt Jenny plain didn't like him, for reasons he could never fathom. And it seemed to be getting worse.

'Maybe she secretly fancies you,' Hendricks had said once, when drink had been taken.

'She's only human,' Thorne had said. 'At least I think so.'

'This isn't like the case last year,' he said now. 'Nothing like that.' The truth was that he had no idea what it was going to be like, and there was still the possibility that there might yet turn out to be no case at all. He didn't say that to Helen. He wasn't fooling himself, so there was no point trying to fool her. Instead, he said, 'Look, I'll keep an eye on Nicola, if it makes you happy, but nothing's going to kick off. She's gone back to being the sensible one, I swear.'

'You need to be sensible, too,' Helen said.

'Goes without saying,' Thorne said.

'Does it?'

They both looked up as Alfie reappeared and neither was hugely surprised to see that he looked no more ready for bed than he had a few minutes earlier. Thorne got another hug, the boy veering suddenly away from Helen and rushing across as she tried to usher him back towards the door. Welcome as it was, Thorne knew well enough that this show of affection was a trusted and effective time-wasting manoeuvre.

He saw through Alfie's scam every bit as easily as Brigstocke had quite probably seen through his.

He said, 'Sleep well, Trouble.'

'*You're* trouble.' Alfie grinned and punched him on the leg. 'You're *big* trouble.'

Helen said, 'Now,' running out of patience.

When they had gone, Thorne thought for a moment about getting undressed again and putting on the things he'd wanted to wear in the first place, but he couldn't really be bothered. Instead he sat back and pointed the remote.

Flicked through the channels and wondered if someone some-where was taking the piss.

An old episode of *Juliet Bravo*.

A true crime documentary about Ted Bundy.

Garfield: The Movie.

ELEVEN

Oddly, she felt less pain in her hips and ankles walking upstairs than when she was sitting still. Less than when she was lying down even, waking in the night with it and needing to get up and move around. Overall, it was better than it had been, and Tanner was content to grin and bear it, because she was no fan of pain-killers. Hadn't addiction to painkillers done for Elvis and Michael Jackson and Prince? She'd read all sorts about it and wasn't quite sure what to believe, but she didn't want to take the risk, because she'd seen dependency up close and it had not been pleasant. She was not someone who sought to abandon control, as others did.

As Susan had done, for reasons Tanner had never understood.

So she got on with it, because she didn't have a lot of choice. The limp had almost gone and she doubted anyone who did not know her well would ever see that there was a problem. Once or twice, she was aware Dipak Chall had caught her wincing as she climbed out of the car, or seen her face whiten on a very bad day, but he knew better than to mention it.

Thorne too had said nothing, but perhaps he simply hadn't noticed. She couldn't be sure.

Once she had finished in the bathroom, Tanner walked into the bedroom and closed the curtains. It was dark outside anyway, but the view down to the patio, the York stone slabs on to which she had crashed from this very spot, was not one she was particularly fond of any more. Gardening, if you could call it that, was not something she had done since Susan's death and the events that had followed, so a few weeks before she'd asked one of her brothers to come round and tackle the weeds when they had been threatening to take over. They'd done so much for her after the fire; rebuilt and redecorated, done their best to turn the house into a home again. Though there was little they could do, of course, about the thing she missed the most.

She carefully laid out her outfit for the following day before getting undressed. She folded back the duvet and reached for the book on her bedside table. She'd done a lot of reading since Susan died, more than she'd ever done, now that there was no longer anything better to do in bed. Not that she and Susan had been at it like rabbits or anything, they'd been together far too many years for that, but there had always been puzzles to argue over, conversations to be had.

They had been ... comfortable.

She put the paperback down when she realised she'd been reading the same paragraph for several minutes. Her eyes were already tired after two hours sifting through documents relating to what had now been christened Operation Felix, and from a file she had brought home, crammed with Police National Computer printouts on unsolved murders nationwide.

She turned on the radio and switched off her bedside light.

These days, it was the conversation on Radio 4 that helped her sleep or kept her company when she got up in the night and spent long hours walking around the house. *Rattling* around. That's what it was now, she knew that; rattling around, in a house that was far too big for one person.

She had been thinking about moving for a while, had taken the first few steps more than once and then put it off, but only because she was busy and certainly not because she was sentimental.

Never that.

You took memories with you wherever you went. These were just rooms; too many walls to bounce off, too much air.

No ... not *comfortable*.

It had not been like that, not towards the end, anyway. It had not been comfortable clearing up the mess, physical and emotional, after Susan had been on a binge. It had not been comfortable being screamed at for interfering, for trying to impose standards – so she had been less-than-politely informed – that nobody but a robot could ever live up to. It was not comfortable to be told by the woman you loved that her alcoholism was your fault.

Some memories you would not want to take with you.

On the radio, they were discussing the day's proceedings in parliament and, as the bickering, braying voices distorted into background noise, Tanner found herself thinking about Andrew Evans.

He certainly had the look; the face of someone well used to intimidating others, or worse. Nothing that had taken place in the interview room had caused Tanner to question that initial impression, and despite an alibi provided by the man's wife, the evidence already gathered had left her in little doubt as to his guilt.

And yet ...

She had interviewed many people accused of murder. Plenty had looked her in the eye and sworn they were blameless as babies, when she'd known them to be guilty as sin. Some had crowed happily about their crimes and a few had broken down and confessed them. She had seen every variety of fear written on the faces of men and women in those interview rooms; from those who knew that only prison lay ahead, and from one or two so unfortunate as to genuinely have no idea what they were doing there.

Today, her suspect had barely spoken, doing exactly as his brief had advised, but he had looked as if he *wanted* to. Hard

71

as that face was, it had been easy enough to read. It niggled at her, because whatever the evidence suggested, Tanner could not shake the impression that Andrew Evans had been afraid to say he was innocent.

Andrew Evans was not sleeping.

Many hours earlier, being marched in handcuffs to the police car, he had turned to see Paula watching from the front door. An expression he had last seen nearly two years before and had tried hard to forget. He had shaken his head and said, 'I swear, I've got no idea what this is all about,' and he had not been lying. He had kept on saying it; on the journey to the station, as the cell door closed and was locked behind him, while the nurse had done what she'd needed to.

Then the solicitor had arrived and explained what was going on, and those protestations had died in his throat.

And all he could do then was fall for a while; a numbness creeping across his body as he went down, and a scream so loud inside his head that he could barely hear himself speak from that point on. Meaningless words tumbling from a dry mouth.

No comment.

No comment.

No . . .

Saying it and saying it, like a button was being pushed; because he'd been told to and because there was really nothing else he *could* say. Because he was still falling and because he was trying to make sense of the things he was hearing or being presented with.

Guns and photos and witnesses.

I swear I've got no idea . . .

He turned on the thin plastic mattress and lay on his side. He stared at the wall and shivered. More than anything he wanted to get high, but he knew that was not going to happen, much as he knew that the same need was what had led him here.

He punched the wall, once, twice, until he felt his knuckles split.

No, the drugs had come later, and there was nobody to blame but himself for the reason he'd needed them.

One glance too many at the phone in his lap, a second too late on the brake, and his life had been turned upside down.

He licked at his bloodied fist, the flap of skin shifting and the raw flesh tart beneath his tongue, and thought again about what he'd told Paula. When it was still the truth and he had no reason to believe he would not be home in time to put his son to bed. The words he'd said on the phone from the police station after they'd booked him in; shouting to be heard above the sound of her sobbing and the boy crying somewhere in the background.

What would she tell him, now? How could she even begin to explain?

Now, he'd finished falling and he finally understood exactly what was happening; what it was all about. He knew what had been done to him and he knew who had done it. Try as he might, though, he still had not got the faintest idea why.

His eyes did not leave the screen as he bit into toast that was darker than he would have liked and thought how pitiful it was sometimes; how *needy* some people were.

That craving for a hand to hold or a shoulder to cry on. A body to rub up against when you wanted other things.

It had been handy for him, obviously, but even now he found it baffling, that overwhelming desire to be *appreciated*. Why should that be anyone's right? You had to earn appreciation and those with plenty of good company to call on usually deserved it, because they were good company themselves. How hard was that to understand? Like with most things, you got back what you gave out. When it came to those whose own company was not enough for them, he thought he knew better than most what he was talking about, and believed that though there were certainly plenty of people who were lonely and unable to find companionship the traditional way, there was usually a very good reason for it.

Even if some people couldn't see it themselves; deluded as wannabe pop stars, setting out their stalls like some chancer in a dodgy market who was knocking out antifreeze and calling it Chanel No. 5.

Outgoing meaning *loud and annoying.*

Educated meaning *dull as ditchwater.*

Sensitive meaning *mental.*

And nobody needed telling what *attractive* really meant, did they? Or *Rubenesque,* for pity's sake. People lied to themselves all the time, but there was no excuse for lying to others. Not that he felt even a little bit sorry for those on the receiving end of such shoddy goods, because (a) they should have known better and (b) nine times out of ten they were doing much the same themselves.

Liars and losers, the bunch of them.

So needy, so unlikely to be mourned, and all of them making what he wanted to do nice and simple.

After checking to make sure there had been no last minute changes to anyone's plans – he had been caught out by that before – he printed out the pictures he would need the following day. He closed the computer and studied the faces one more time; popped them into his satchel, together with everything else he would need for the journey.

Not as long as some had been, but he did not want to have to make unscheduled stops. There, done, and back in a few hours, which was how he liked it.

He brushed crumbs from his shirt and walked towards his bed, thinking how wrong it was; the idea that nothing worth having came without hard work. That getting what you wanted should be a struggle. These people might have been difficult to understand or sympathise with, but they were easy enough to find.

TWELVE

Tanner was already working at a desk in the incident room when Thorne arrived a little after nine. She raised a hand as he walked past on his way to the kitchen. Clocking the empty mug and sheaf of notes gathered neatly in front of her, he guessed that she'd already been at it quite a while.

He brought his coffee across to the desk. 'Any joy?'

Tanner looked up at him. '*Joy?*'

'You know what I mean.'

Her eyes returned to the screen. 'I'll get back to you.'

Thorne wandered into the office he shared with DI Yvonne Kitson, who arrived a few minutes after he'd sat down. She looked flustered.

'Psychopaths.'

Thorne glanced towards the incident room. 'Yeah, the place is full of them.'

'I'm talking about kids,' Kitson said.

'Ah.'

'Little bastards. Teenagers, specifically.'

Thorne nodded and slurped his coffee. Kitson was a single

mother of two boys, though he couldn't remember their ages. Seventeen, eighteen, around there. 'Which one?' he asked.

'Both of them.' Kitson dropped her bag on to her desk and dropped into the chair. 'I'm serious. Teenagers are basically psychopaths with acne.'

'It's not pulling their trousers up properly that bothers me.'

'It's like nothing matters outside their own little worlds, nothing else is remotely important, you know? They're totally selfish, they've got no empathy. Like I said, psychopaths.' She sat back and sighed. 'Talking of which, Tanner the Planner's hard at it out there.'

Thorne could only presume that Kitson was referring to the case Tanner was now busy working on, and not casting aspersions on her psychological make-up.

'I'm not even sure she went home,' he said.

Kitson logged on at her computer, moved the mouse around for half a minute. 'You've been to her house, haven't you?'

'Just the once,' Thorne said. 'Before the fire.'

'What was it like?'

'It was ... nice.'

'Nice?'

'Like you'd expect.'

Kitson nodded. 'Yeah, I wonder how she'd cope if she had to pick a teenage boy's dirty pants off the bathroom floor.' She grinned suddenly. 'She'd probably file them.'

Thorne smiled and downed what was left of his coffee.

Seeing Tanner hard at it first thing had confirmed Thorne's belief that she was the right person to work on the case, though there had been a momentary pang of guilt at the fact that she was already proving rather more diligent about it than he was. He'd told himself that his time would come; that this phase of the inquiry was best left to those who knew one end of a spreadsheet from another. Who knew if spreadsheets even *had* ends.

Anal. No need to dress it up ...

'You got much on?' Thorne asked.

'About average.' Kitson ran him quickly through her current caseload. A hit-and-run in Crouch End, what looked like a gang-related stabbing in Kensal Green. 'Nothing that can't be handed over, if need be.'

'Right.'

'Hoping not, obviously.' She understood that if Thorne's worst suspicions were confirmed, she and many others would suddenly find themselves drafted in to help.

'Obviously.'

They both looked up as Russell Brigstocke marched past their open door, glancing in as he did so, but clearly with little time to stop and chat.

'Got his serious face on,' Kitson said.

Thorne stood up and asked her if she wanted tea. She was still telling him in which cupboard she'd stashed a box of Earl Grey teabags when he left to follow the DCI and find out why he was looking so serious.

A few seconds later, he poked his head back round the door. Said, 'This whole cat/serial killer thing. If either of your boys should come up as likely suspects, do you fancy doing the interview?'

By the time Thorne arrived at Tanner's desk, Brigstocke was already in full flow.

'... well, I wasn't expecting it to be straightforward, because it never bloody is with them, is it?' He became aware of Thorne lurking at his shoulder and turned. 'CPS.'

'Oh,' Thorne said.

Liaison with the Crown Prosecution Service was rarely some-thing a senior investigating officer looked forward to and, by a good stretch, the most popular topic when it came to moaning about the job. There was a time when the CPS had kept an office one floor above where Thorne was now standing, but that had long gone and these days it was a matter of endless phone conversations, or ferrying paperwork through London traffic and even, on one memorable occasion, to a CPS office on the south coast.

As Brigstocke had said, never straightforward, but like most who knew how tedious and time-consuming the process could be, the DCI had started it good and early this time. He had briefed a CPS lawyer just prior to Andrew Evans's arrest. He had let them know how much evidence they already had and how much was yet to come, and he had been quick to send the necessary paperwork across as soon as it had been completed.

'You get your retaliation in first, right?'

'Best way,' Thorne said.

'So ... we've had Nicola and everybody else working their arses off, pulling extra shifts to put it all together on the hurry-up, and, to be honest, it got to the point about half an hour ago when I lost it a bit and told this idiot in the CPS office that I really didn't know what else he was expecting. How many other hoops he wanted us to jump through.' He began counting off on his fingers. 'We've uploaded and sent across the fingerprint evidence from the murder weapon, a printout of the DNA evidence from the murder weapon ...'

Thorne looked at Tanner.

'Came in overnight,' she said.

'They've got a detailed description of the motorbike which matches the one owned by Evans and positive identification, based on photo ID, from the woman who says he threatened her boyfriend with a gun three and a bit weeks ago. We've had a "no comment" in interview and the only thing our suspect has got going for him is an alibi from his wife, and we all know that's as reliable as an inflatable dartboard.'

Tanner nodded.

'Eventually, I said, "Look, aside from coming over there and giving you a hand-job, I really don't know what else I can do to get you to sign off on this."' He looked from Tanner to Thorne, milking it. 'So, he calls me back ten minutes ago, and would you believe it?'

'Would I believe what?' Tanner asked.

She and Thorne exchanged a look. The effort to make whatever was coming nice and dramatic was endearing, but the DCI's timing was about as good as could be expected from someone whose experience of working an audience consisted of a few magic tricks in front of a group of pissed coppers.

Brigstocke shrugged, then grinned. 'We're on.' He laid a hand on Tanner's shoulder. 'So, get yourself down to Colindale and charge him.'

Tanner began to gather her things together.

'Good news,' Brigstocke said. 'Nice way to start the day, putting this one to bed.'

'Nice one, Nicola,' Thorne said. It was certainly good news as far as he was concerned. A quick result on the Jandali murder would mean that Tanner was able to devote more attention to Operation Felix while others handled the nuts and bolts of bringing Evans to trial and securing a conviction.

Tanner looked at him. 'Fancy coming with me, Tom?'

'Well ...'

'We can talk on the way.'

'You found something?'

'I'm working on it.' She stood up. 'My turn to ask a favour, that's all.'

Brigstocke smiled, seeing Thorne's face fall. 'Fair's fair, mate.'

Tanner walked past Thorne towards the stairs, as though expecting him to follow. She said, 'I told you this was going to cost you more than three pounds seventy-nine, didn't I?'

THIRTEEN

Alice Matthews stared down at her bed, the clothes laid out like a high-end jumble sale, and felt every bit as ridiculous as she was excited.

The excitement was heady and familiar; that same buzz-and-flutter she'd first felt almost forty years before, getting ready for her big night out at the pictures with Simon Phipps. It had not ended well for either of them, but the memory still made her smile.

Simon in his Oxford bags and beetle-crushers, faux-Bowie hair and stinking of Clearasil.

He'd taken her to see *Earthquake* at the Gaumont, with Charlton Heston and that black actor who'd played Shaft. He'd paid for her ticket and bought her popcorn and Coke. He hadn't tried to put his arm around her for at least twenty minutes. Unfortunately, the film had some weird gimmick, so that you *felt* the earthquake when it happened. Alice still wasn't sure how it had worked – extra speakers or something vibrating beneath the seats – but whatever they'd done, she'd started feeling sick almost immediately and poor old Simon had rushed her out of the cinema just in time. He'd held her hair back, because he was a nice lad, while she'd puked all over his shiny new beetle-crushers . . .

She took a pair of shoes from the wardrobe, set them down next to the others at the foot of the bed.

Stupid . . . so *stupid*, that she should be this excited about a date with a man at her age. Laying out blouses and jackets, most of which she'd already tried on, when she wasn't even meeting him for – she looked at her watch – *seven* hours. Christ, was she that desperate?

She took one last look in the mirror, still unsure about the hair she'd had done first thing, then walked downstairs, thinking how much simpler things had been when she was sixteen.

Which jeans, which top? Wedges or DMs?

How much simpler *she* had been . . .

A snogging session and maybe a quick fumble, and someone to hold hands with at lunchtime in the sixth-form block. Now, she wasn't sure what she was after. It was more than just sex, certainly, because it wasn't like she'd been living like a nun since the divorce. There'd been a couple of blokes she'd met at work; backed away from when they'd hinted at something more per-manent, because they might have scratched an itch but neither of them was exactly an attractive prospect long-term.

She straightened the photos of her sons pinned up on a cork board in the kitchen. One of them grinning on graduation day, the other only twenty-three and already holding his baby.

Was that the reason she was feeling quite this foolish?

A grandmother, for heaven's sake, flapping like an ado-lescent girl.

It was her boys who had told her to get back out there and get stuck in. To have a look, at least. They'd both said how attractive she still was, told her she was definitely not the type to sit around with puzzle books and watching gardening programmes.

Come on, Mum, you're a glamorous granny. You're a GILF . . .

It had been fun those first few weeks, dipping her toes in the water, getting a feel for it. Facebook had been the obvious place to start and she'd spent long hours searching for anyone she'd once had a thing with, or better still who'd carried a torch for *her*. Men she'd lost touch with long ago; men and boys. A lad she'd gone out with at university who she was shocked to discover had died at forty-three. A man who had got her pregnant before she'd met her husband, then fled, leaving her to sort out the mess. Even good old Simon Phipps had turned up eventually; a balding stockbroker on his third marriage, with three kids as old as hers and two more under ten.

It had become rather depressing in the end.

And yet, standing in the kitchen now, unable to remember what she had come downstairs for, that lovely, scary buzz-and-flutter was still there. Because she had to admit that Gavin ticked all the boxes. Well, nearly all, but she couldn't expect someone to share every one of her interests, or for her to share his, and perhaps those sorts of differences were no bad thing. In a relationship at her age, she would still want a little space of her own, some time to herself.

He was arty and clever and she wanted that. He was nice-looking too, considering his age, which couldn't hurt.

Considering his age . . .

She shook her head and rubbed at the finger where her wedding ring had once been. He was three years younger than she was.

He had a serious face, but there was definitely a twinkle in his eye that suggested he knew how to have fun. He was a dog-lover. He liked the same music she did and she was pretty sure he'd hold her hair back if she ever puked up.

She hadn't done that for a very long time.

Smiling, Alice drifted out of the kitchen and found herself hurrying back up the stairs. There was one more skirt she needed to drag out and try on, and she still hadn't decided what jewellery to wear.

FOURTEEN

Careful to avoid the panic strip, Tanner leaned back against the wall of the narrow corridor and watched the uniformed officer unlock the cell door before pushing it open with the tip of a highly polished Doc Marten. He said, 'Up you get,' then stood aside when Tanner stepped forward.

Andrew Evans was sitting on his bunk.

'Come on then, Mr Evans.'

Evans did not move, did not acknowledge her.

'Look, I'm having quite a good day so far,' Tanner said. 'So let's not play silly buggers.' She turned to look at the officer, but he was already walking away.

Evans spoke directly to the floor. 'I want to talk.'

'Fair enough,' Tanner said. 'Politics? Films . . . ?'

'You know what I mean.' Now, Evans looked up. Save for the dark stubble and crescents of shadow beneath his eyes, his face was grey; his lips were dry and pale. 'I want to talk to you about all this. Why it's . . . wrong.'

'Well, you had every chance to talk yesterday and you decided to say nothing. That's your right, obviously, but things have moved on since then, so I'm afraid it's all a bit late.'

'It's a mistake.' Evans shook his head. 'No, not a mistake, exactly ... *you* haven't made a mistake. You've done what you were expected to do. It's how all this was supposed to happen.'

'How what was supposed to happen?'

'I didn't kill Adnan Jandali, that's the first thing. I didn't kill anyone.'

Tanner sighed, the news about the CPS approval already looking like it was going to be the high point of her day. 'Right, if you want to get that down on record before you're charged, I can arrange for you to make a statement, but we can't talk about this here and I strongly advise you to get your solicitor back.'

'No.' Evans shook his head again and shifted forward on his bunk. 'I only want to talk to you. I don't want a solicitor and I don't want anything going down on record.'

'That's not going to happen,' Tanner said. 'I can't do it.'

'Five minutes, that's all. I just need you to listen for five minutes.'

'Where?' Tanner pointed behind her. 'The minute we step out into that corridor, everything is recorded, audio and video. Same in the custody suite or in an interview room. And that's as much for your protection as it is for ours.'

'Protection.' Evans chewed at the inside of his mouth. 'Right.'

'OK, I've told you what the situation is, now I need to crack on. So—'

Evans stood up quickly enough to make Tanner take half a step back. She looked along the corridor to see the uniformed officer deep in conversation with a colleague.

'Yeah, I threatened that junkie, OK?'

'You can put that in your statement—'

'And yeah, it was the same gun, I'm not saying it wasn't, but that was the whole point. I get the gun, I give it back after. That's how it works.' He looked down, breathing heavily. He slid his

84

hand beneath his T-shirt and rubbed his chest as Tanner had seen him do in the interview room the day before, the cell light catching the sheen of sweat, just for a second, as he turned to look at her again. 'It felt horrible putting the wind up that poor sod, taking his money off him, because I'm basically a junkie too, like you didn't know that . . . but me waving that gun around was all part of it. That was their plan. You're in someone's pocket deep as I am, it's not like you've got a lot of choice, but I never banked on any of this, I swear.' His shoulders sagged and he dropped back on to his bunk. 'You've got to let me tell you what's going on, because I know you'll put it all together, same as I have. The bigger picture or whatever they call it. If you still want to charge me after that, then go ahead, because I'm pretty much screwed either way.'

Tanner looked up at the camera on the cell ceiling.

'Five minutes, that's all I'm asking.' The anger and urgency had gone out of the man's voice. He sounded exhausted. 'I just need five minutes.'

It was simple, because it was procedure; escort Andrew Evans from his cell to the custody desk, charge him and move on. It was what her senior officer had told her to do, what the rules of conduct she swore by demanded of her.

It wasn't even worth thinking about.

Tanner stepped off the cliff and pointed towards the camera high in the corner of the cell. 'Video, but no audio,' she said. 'Not in here. All right?'

Evans turned his eyes up to the camera then back to her, nodded.

She looked along the corridor again. This time, the uni- formed officer was looking back at her, arms outstretched, palms upwards. His expression asking the question. *What's taking so long?*

'You'd better talk fast,' Tanner said.

*

Thorne had known the custody skipper at Colindale for a number of years, so they chatted at the desk while they were waiting for Tanner to bring Evans out. Football and family, a car thief who had bitten off a PC's earlobe while being booked in the week before. Thorne laughed or shook his head in the right places, though he was still thinking about his conversation with Tanner on the ten-minute walk from the Peel Centre.

Frustratingly little of that time had been spent discussing Operation Felix, though, in truth, there had not been a great deal to talk about, as at this stage it was all about number-crunching. Thorne had done at least some of the groundwork, so knew just how daunting the job was.

Even for the likes of Nicola Tanner.

The geographical scope of the cat killings meant that they might have to look nationwide, but in terms of a timescale their search parameters were no better than a best guess. Even if their suspect was behaving in the way Thorne suspected, it did not necessarily mean a clean break between the workouts and the cool-down periods. There could easily be some overlap. As the cat killings appeared to have begun around six months earlier, Thorne had decided – somewhat arbitrarily – to go back as far as eighteen months when searching for possible human victims.

With somewhere around seven hundred homicides in that period, of which approximately a third of victims had been female and almost a fifth had gone unsolved, they were already looking at fifty or so possible cases.

'Fifty-three,' Tanner had said. They had left the grounds of the Peel Centre and turned on to Aerodrome Road. 'It's way too many . . . well, it is unless they want to throw a lot more resources at us. We need to narrow it down. We need to focus on a particular type of killing.'

This was the key decision and, by far, the most difficult.

It was clear that not every animal killed had been the victim of the same individual, but those they did believe to be the work of one man had involved strangulation or the use of a blunt instrument. Garden shears or perhaps a machete had been used many times, both pre- and post-mortem.

In her report, Melita Perera had expressed a degree of doubt that a similar range of methods would have been used on any human victims. There was time and location to be taken into account as well as the fact that cats were less able to protect themselves and fight back. It would be unusual, she had said, based on her experience in studying similar serial offenders. Though the psychiatrist had fought shy of making a definitive prediction, her money had certainly been on the killer having a more clear-cut MO when it came to humans.

'We can probably rule out the shootings,' Tanner had said. 'Any victims who died in fires or were poisoned ... anything drug-related. Still leaves us plenty to choose from though.'

Still plenty for Thorne to be thinking about, but as they had walked on towards the station, Tanner's main concern had been the favour she needed from him.

'I'm putting the house on the market,' she'd said.

'Oh, right.'

'It's time.'

'So what, somewhere smaller?'

Tanner had nodded, then, barely breaking stride, had bent to pick up a discarded plastic bottle. 'We had a policy, you know? It paid off the mortgage when Susan died. So I can get somewhere decent and still have enough left to mean I don't have to worry.'

Thorne was not surprised to hear that Tanner had made provision should the worst ever happen. Practical, as opposed to pessimistic. He was yet to see though, what any of this had to do with him.

'So, want to come flat-hunting with me?'

'Me?' He watched her drop the plastic bottle into a litter bin, wipe her hands on her jacket. 'I'm not going to be any use.'

'Come on, I just need another pair of eyes, that's all.'

'Not mine, you don't. Trust me, I'm rubbish at that kind of thing.'

'Your flat is pretty nice.'

'It's Helen's flat. That's all down to her.'

'What about your own place?'

'Not quite as *nice*.' They walked on, turning into Grahame Park Way, the station a few minutes ahead. Thorne knew he did not have very long to wriggle off this particular hook. 'I don't have any ... imagination when it comes to that stuff. Honestly, I'd just take one look and go, "the walls are a horrible colour" and yeah, I know you can paint walls, but I can't see beyond that, or if the furniture's crappy or if I don't like the owner's face. Seriously, you'd be better off asking someone else. What about Phil?'

Tanner shook her head. 'It's about company as much as anything else and there's only so much of Phil's I can take before I want to slap him. Look, I just need someone to tell me I'm being too picky, that's all. Someone else to deal with slimy estate agents.'

Seeing that his arguments were falling on deaf ears, Thorne took one last shot. 'I'm not sure you'll have a lot of time anyway. With all this, you know? The extra work.'

'Oh, I can manage time,' Tanner said, waving his concerns away. 'You know I'm good at that. An hour or two here and there to go and look at a few places, that's all. Just come and see a couple with me and we're quits.'

Now, the custody sergeant leaned across the desk. 'Talking about biting off more than you can chew ...'

Thorne stared. 'Sorry?'

The man tugged at his earlobe. 'Our lugless PC.'

'Oh, right.'

'Word is, you've taken over this cat thing. Trying to find out if it's more than just a cat thing.'

'Yeah, well, we'll see,' Thorne said.

Tanner had been right. If they wanted to make any progress,

they needed, at the very least, to prioritise one set of victims, one method of killing. Someone had to make a choice and decide which way to jump.

Thorne took out his phone.

Fulton probably knew as much as anybody about the case thus far, but Thorne doubted Uncle Fester would be brave enough to make the call. Or rather, to live with the flak if it turned out to be the wrong one. Thorne was certainly brave – or stupid – enough, but even he wouldn't do so without seeking a bit of advice first, and he knew just who to ask.

While the custody skipper returned to the ear-biting incident and made some crack about *Reservoir Dogs*, Thorne sent the text. Putting his phone away, he turned to see Tanner emerging alone from the corridor. The sergeant craned his neck to look, as though Andrew Evans might simply be taking his time, ambling along behind her.

'What's going on?' Thorne asked.

Tanner shook her head and strode past him. She raised a hand to the bemused custody sergeant and made quickly for the door.

'You done, then?' Thorne hurried to catch her up. They pushed out into the car park and walked towards the main road. 'We heading back?'

Tanner nodded. 'I need to see Russell.'

'That doesn't sound good.'

The wind had picked up a little. Tanner took a scarf from her handbag and began to wrap it around her neck. 'Mr Evans has got a very interesting story to tell.'

Thorne waited, looked at her. He raised his voice above the noise of the wind and her heels clattering on the pavement. 'Nicola . . . ?'

Tanner gave him the headlines.

Perhaps the jungle drums had beaten them back from Colindale, or maybe Russell Brigstocke was just good at reading the expressions on his officers' faces. Whatever the reason, when Tanner and Thorne walked into his office ten minutes later, he did not look as though he was expecting good news.

'We've got a problem.' Tanner took off her scarf. Brigstocke was already nodding when she said, 'With Andrew Evans.'

'Which is why you haven't charged him.'

'It's complicated.'

The DCI sat back and looked up at the clock. 'We're already pushing the twenty-four hours, so I'll get on to the superintendent, get her to sign off on another twelve. Shouldn't be a problem.'

'I don't need any more time,' Tanner said.

'Right.' Brigstocke sighed and took his glasses off. 'Well, I don't really need to tell you that as things stand, and that includes muggins here not having the first idea what you're playing at, we've only got two options.'

He glanced at Thorne. Thorne shrugged.

'We charge or release.'

Tanner dropped her shoulder bag on the floor and pulled back a chair. She said, 'I don't want to do either.'

FIFTEEN

Melita Perera had suggested a bar in Holborn, just north of Lincoln's Inn Fields and only a street away from her office. She would be working late, she'd told Thorne, before assuring him it was a nice enough spot for a rendezvous. Thorne thought it should have been an awful lot nicer, considering the prices, though making the place look like the inside of a disused warehouse had probably cost a small fortune. Bare brick walls, wooden benches and dusty industrial lighting; a line of battered metal stools along the bar that reminded Thorne of many uncomfortable hours in his school chemistry lab.

A pain in the arse, and plenty more elsewhere.

Standing at the bar, he thought about the teacher who had caught him dicking around with a Bunsen burner. Every bit as formidable in the lab as he was on the rugby field, he had seized Thorne's hand, sought out the usual cuts and scrapes, then taken great delight in pouring neat wood alcohol into them.

Probably best not to get into childhood trauma with a psychiatrist ...

Thorne spent five minutes perusing the bewildering array of

craft beers listed on a chalkboard above the bar, then ordered a Guinness. Perera asked for a glass of red wine.

They sat at a table beneath a thick, tubular heating vent, which might have been a design feature and might simply have been a heating vent. Perera was willowy, her long dark hair tied back with a simple red band. The dark skirt and jacket were not surprising as she had come straight from work, yet she somehow managed to look both smart and casual, striking Thorne as a woman whose appearance would be effortlessly stylish whatever the surroundings. They talked about nothing for a few minutes. Then Thorne said, 'So, how did you get into this game?'

'Game?' The woman seemed to find that funny.

'Mysteriously ended up in it, you said. Something like that.'

She put down her large glass of Merlot. 'God knows. You don't always have much of an idea where you'll end up when you're training. You read a few studies, take a few courses and suddenly you're specialising. It wasn't exactly planned.'

'Fair enough.'

'To be honest, I'm always a bit suspicious of the people who *want* to work in this . . . area. Who know early on, I mean. Same as dentists. Why would anybody want to do that?' She sniffed and took a sip of wine. 'Did you always want to be a policeman?'

Thorne considered it. 'Pretty much,' he said.

'Right.'

'When the rock-star thing didn't work out and Spurs hadn't come knocking.'

Perera smiled and nodded.

'You must be interested in it, though?' Thorne shifted his chair a little closer to the table. The legs scraped against the concrete floor. 'These sorts of individuals.'

'Yeah, absolutely, when I'm working. I try not to take too much of it home with me, though. Doesn't go down too well across the dinner table. Same for you, I'm guessing.'

Thorne suddenly found himself wondering who might be

sitting on the other side of the woman's dinner table. There was no wedding ring, but then again, he wasn't wearing one either. He nodded. 'Yeah, course.'

'It's not like you can turn it on or off, obviously. You can't unthink things. You have to compartmentalise, that's all. Cases stay with you, though. Certain people.'

'Who was the worst one?'

She looked at him, clearly well used to this sort of question; the ghoulish enquiry at a party, the invitation to share horror stories. Her casual response, though, suggested that she knew Thorne's curiosity was not simply a morbid one.

'It's the ones that say nothing that are actually the worst. The details tend not to bother you after a while, not once you've heard enough of them. But the subjects who want to hold on to their power by staying silent are the ones you end up thinking about for a long time afterwards.'

'Like Shipman.'

'Absolutely. Two hundred and eighteen *identified* victims, so almost certainly more than that, and he never said why. Refused to talk about it. Gave the police nothing and then topped himself.'

Thorne nodded, drank. He remembered the *Sun*'s less than subtle headline after the doctor's suicide.

Ship Ship Hooray.

'I suppose it's the same for you,' she said. 'It's the cases you never solve that stay with you.'

'Most of the time.'

'Well, I'm sure there are exceptions.'

'You remember a man called Stuart Nicklin?'

She thought for a few seconds, then nodded. 'There were two of them, weren't there? Working together.'

'Nicklin was running the show,' Thorne said. 'It was all down to him.'

'It's not common, but with killers working in tandem that's usually the way. There's an alpha.'

93

'I did . . . solve it, and we put him away eventually, but now he's out again.' Thorne looked across and met her eyes for just a second. 'He *got* out, and that was down to me, more or less.'

The psychiatrist waited as though keen to hear the story, but Thorne wasn't keen to tell it; to relive it. He'd already given her as much information as was needed.

'I just wondered what he might do.'

'Do?'

. 'If you had any thoughts . . .'

It was something Thorne thought about a great deal.

'Well, if he's got any sense and he doesn't want to go back to prison, he'll do nothing at all. He'll disappear, start again somewhere else. Go abroad, maybe? If he's clever, he'll stay well away from you.' She looked at him. 'If that's what you're worried about.'

'Oh, he's certainly clever,' Thorne said. 'Ran rings round everyone, me included. But I'm not sure he's got too much common sense, not the way you mean, anyway. He's driven by something a bit more . . . basic.'

'They usually are.'

Thorne blinked away an image of dead flesh in a plain brown envelope. The scars on Phil Hendricks's back. He downed what was left in his glass and said, 'So, what about our man then?'

Perera leaned back, laughing.

'What?'

'I wondered when you'd get round to that. I thought I was going to have to start charging you.'

Thorne found a thin smile from somewhere.

'Why don't I get us another drink?'

When she sat down again a few minutes later, Perera said, 'You're worried about what to start looking for, yes? The method. I've been thinking about that since you texted me.'

'In the report you said that if he stepped up to murder, there would probably be just one method.'

'Yes, *if*. And *if* our offender is a he.'

'Surely.'

'Probably. Nothing's ever one hundred per cent when it comes to these types of offences. I've certainly learned that much.'

'OK, noted. But . . . you said it would be one method.'

She quickly raised a hand. 'I didn't say that. It was . . . educated speculation.'

'Well, I need you to speculate some more,' Thorne said.

'Look, it's still my professional opinion that the diversity of methods used on the animals would not necessarily be reflected in any homicides, if there were any. I simply haven't come across that kind of . . . variety before. I know that when we spoke on the phone I said these kinds of killers do their best to be different, but I can only tell you that in my experience there does usually tend to be a fixed MO.'

'Right—'

'To begin with, at least.' The woman's voice dropped a little. 'I'm not just saying this to cover myself, but there's always the possibility the killer might change things up with each spate of murders. Each theoretical spate, obviously. If we can stretch your exercise analogy a little further, they might decide to introduce a new component to their workout.'

Thorne thought about that for a few moments. 'In terms of possible historic offences, though . . . ?'

'One method. *Probably.*'

'OK, so let's start from that assumption. We've narrowed our causes of death down to three, but it's still too many. Strangulation or asphyxiation, stabbing, or the use of a blunt instrument.'

She nodded. 'The cats were strangled or bludgeoned to death and obviously a blade of some sort was used on them afterwards.'

'So, what about with people? With women?'

Perera puffed out her cheeks, took a few seconds. 'So . . . knives are silent, *intimate*, and the penetration of the flesh would

95

obviously tally with any sexual element. Then again, our offender might want to get up even closer and put hands on them. A blunt instrument is quicker, but often messier than a knife . . .'

'So, which one would your money be on?'

'I'm not sure I'd put money on any of them,' she said. 'And I certainly wouldn't risk my career.'

'Not asking you to,' Thorne said. 'This doesn't go on any kind of record, OK? We're just having a drink.'

The psychiatrist stroked the stem of her wine glass.

'It goes down as my decision.'

Melita Perera leaned back and shook her head. 'This is like some weird game show. I feel like the contestant who's got to decide which box the jackpot's in.'

'Stabbing, strangulation, blunt instrument.' Thorne picked up his glass and stared at the woman across it. He said, 'Pick one.'

SIXTEEN

Alice stared up, the fight all but gone from her and thought, Stupid, and Who the hell ticks every box? and Christ, oh Christ, he's strong, and she kicked out one last time and thought: Somebody will come.

She thought about dinner and singing in the car and the clothes laid out on the bed. That serious face across the table. The numbers exchanged and the buzz-and-flutter . . .

Somebody will come.

The light faded, closing in around her, and she remembered how quickly the blackness had come a long time ago, when everything shrank until there was just a dot. When she was little and her dad switched the TV off. Pictures, then nothing and that whoosh to a tiny white dot and she always refused to go to bed until the pinprick of light had gone.

She thrashed and spat as they swam through her head: all the people she had loved and all those who had loved her in return. Her boys, her parents, her friends, her useless lump of an ex-husband . . . and her tongue felt so thick and useless between her lips.

The silent scream she knew that nobody would hear, that this was not fair, this was so *unfair*.

And a stockbroker in funny shoes.

Pulling back her hair and saying, *Shush, shush* . . .

Looking up through bulging eyes, all she could see at the end were twin images of someone like herself. Flickering as he blinked; two tiny pictures of a woman who could not possibly be her, distorted and disfigured. Her own face, cracked and wet and ugly, reflected in the eyes of the man who had his hands around her neck.

A doll's eyes, Alice thought. Dead. No sign of a twinkle.

She heard something snap, like a wishbone.

Then there was no light.

PART TWO

THE PICTURE
ON THE BOX

SEVENTEEN

Thorne took the M25 south and drove towards the M3, heading for Salisbury. The traffic had eased a little by the time he was past the Heathrow turn-off, when he glanced across and saw that his passenger had her eyes closed.

'Nicola . . .'

Tanner opened her eyes immediately. 'I wasn't asleep.'

'Wouldn't be surprised if you were.'

'I wasn't, though.'

'Fair enough.' Thorne knew that Tanner had spent most of the weekend making the arrangements for Andrew Evans, as well as trying to make inroads into the data she had amassed on eighteen months' worth of unsolved murders. He knew she had earned whatever overtime she would be due, and knew equally that, unlike most other officers – himself included – she would be claiming no more than she was owed. 'People don't usually snore when they're awake though, do they?'

Tanner ignored him. She was already pulling papers from her bag and arranging them in her lap.

'And you've dribbled a bit.' Thorne drifted across into the

inside lane and slowed a little. The person they were on their way to see wasn't going anywhere, and Thorne wanted time to discuss the progress, if any, that Tanner had made.

She spent another few moments arranging the papers to her satisfaction, then stabbed at the top sheet. 'So, just looking at homicides where the cause of death was strangulation, we've got six unsolved.'

'That's not too bad,' Thorne said.

'Gets better, actually.'

'Really?'

'Up to a point.' Tanner removed another sheet. 'Now, I'm not totally discounting the one eleven months ago in Aviemore, but I'm setting it aside for the time being, because the north of Scotland is way further afield than he's gone with any of the cat killings.'

'Sounds reasonable.'

'Just for the time being, like I said. He might have found himself up there for whatever reason and couldn't help himself. Maybe he's got family in that part of the world or maybe he just likes walking in the Highlands. We shouldn't rule out anything.'

'Obviously.' Thorne was already growing frustrated with the lorry doing less than fifty in front of him and moved out to overtake.

'I'm setting aside two more. One because the team investigating it were convinced it was domestic, even if they still can't prove it, and one because the pathologist says the killer's female.'

'Perera said that might be a possibility. That we shouldn't rule it out, anyway.'

'Really?' Tanner looked at him. 'I can't see it.'

'Me neither.'

'She's covering herself, that's all.'

'So, we're down to three,' Thorne said.

'Right. Fairly widespread geographically, no one location

within a hundred miles of another, but all in the final few months of last year.'

Thorne looked at her.

'And the most recent one was just a few weeks before the cat-killing started.'

'That's great,' Thorne said. He shook his head, slammed a palm against the wheel. 'You know what I mean. Great work, Nic . . .'

If Tanner was bothered by Thorne's unfortunate choice of words, she didn't show it. 'We've got a botched burglary, what looks like a homicide carried out by someone the victim knew and one that sounds like a dead end. Like I said, promising up to a point.'

'Tell me about the victims,' Thorne said.

Tanner shuffled her papers again, put those she was finished with back into her bag in the footwell. 'Patricia Somersby, a fifty-eight-year-old widow and retired librarian from Bristol. Annette Mangan, twenty-six, a mature student at Kent University, and Leila Fadel, a doctor.' She checked her notes. 'Thirty-one. She was murdered in Norwich.'

'Someone who travels for work, do you reckon?'

'Maybe,' Tanner said. 'Or wants us to think that.'

'That's a big variation in ages.' When Thorne glanced across, Tanner was holding up three pieces of paper, fanned out; the photos of the three murder victims next to one another. 'Completely different physical types, too.'

'If the person responsible for the cat-killing is also responsible for these murders, I don't think he's bothered about types,' Tanner said. 'I mean, it's not like he only targets ginger toms, is it?'

Thorne waited.

'*Women* are his type.'

'No obvious connections between them?'

Tanner shook her head. 'We've got similarities, though. All the

103

victims were single, for one reason or another, and all of them were killed at home.'

'Right.'

'I know . . .'

A domestic crime scene in itself was probably not significant. They both knew that the vast majority of female murder victims died in their own homes, and Thorne supposed that, in the end, it didn't much matter whether you were face down on your own carpet or the dirt of a rutted back alley. He doubted that a familiar photograph or kitchen cabinet was of much comfort to anyone when the life was being squeezed out of them.

'It'll have to do for now,' Tanner said.

There was clearly a long way to go, but much as he would have liked a little more to be excited about, Thorne still felt as though he and Tanner already had plenty to work with. He pulled across into the fast lane, thinking it through. The fact that these three murders had taken place within a few months of one another had to be significant.

He said, 'I wish we could get stuck into this *now*. Start digging around.'

'Yes, me too, and we will.' She turned in her seat to face him. 'Russell's gathering the troops. Yvonne and Dipak are on it right this minute. I told you, we've got the time to work both these cases.'

Thorne nodded ahead. 'How long do you think we're going to be there for?'

'I don't know. Not all day. Look, for a few hours at least; we need to focus on a murderer we *know* is out there. On what else the people who organised the killing are capable of.'

Frustrated as he felt, Thorne couldn't argue, because Brigstocke and those above him had already set out the guidelines. Since the Adnan Jandali case had taken its surprising turn a few days earlier, it had become clear that it could turn out to be an inquiry every bit as important, in its own way, as the hunt for an as yet theoretical serial killer.

If Thorne wanted Tanner's help, he had to help her in return.

Tanner put the rest of her notes away and sat back. 'Right, let's find out how Andrew Evans has settled in, shall we? See what else he has to say for himself.'

EIGHTEEN

Long Barrow Manor sat in six acres of its own land, a mile or so south of Salisbury. The front of the house overlooked fields and parkland, but on a good day any resident staying in a bedroom at the back could gaze out across water meadows to the River Avon beyond and just make out the tallest cathedral spire in the country. Provided the occupant was in a fit state to get out of bed and gave two stuffs about the view, which was never guaranteed.

During the remainder of their drive down, Tanner had given Thorne a potted history of the place.

Once a grand manor house, and later a privately owned asylum, it had been taken over by the NHS in the mid-fifties and run as a psychiatric hospital before it was finally closed down thirty years later and left abandoned. Nobody was quite sure whose idea it had been to turn Long Barrow Manor into the somewhat peculiar establishment it was now, but since it promised to be useful to several forces, including the Met, raising the funds necessary to buy and renovate the place had not been a problem.

Thorne was doubtful such a scheme would be approved today.

The drastic budget cuts of recent years meant that the acquisition of a new kettle for a squad room was seen to be pushing the boat out.

'Makes sense, when you think about it,' Tanner had told Thorne in the car. 'You've got witnesses who are likely to be in danger and need protection, so they have to be kept out of the way. If they also happen to have addiction issues, you need to get them clean if their evidence is going to stand up. So, you need somewhere that can do both.'

'Part safe house, part rehab.'

'It's a clever idea.'

'Counter-intuitive,' Thorne had said.

Tanner told him about the friend, an officer from the Gangs and Organised Crime team, who had first mentioned the place to her a year or so before. 'He said it was a bit like the Priory, only with tattier furniture. A few more armed robbers and not quite so many pop stars.'

'Sounds lovely.'

'The countryside's nice.'

'Do they take bookings?' Thorne had slowed a little, the turn-off only a mile ahead. 'I'll see if Helen fancies a weekend away.'

Tanner had laughed, then pointed out the sign for the exit, just in case Thorne hadn't noticed the three previous ones. 'I'm sure it isn't the sort of place where you'd want to go for a romantic mini-break. But once it started to look like we'd got the Jandali inquiry arse about face, I thought this might be just the place to stick our star witness.'

'Let's hope that's what he is—'

'It's this exit,' Tanner said, pointing again.

'I know,' Thorne said.

They skirted the town centre and followed handwritten instructions to an unmarked road that wound for another half-mile or so; rattling across cattle grids, tall hedges looming on either side. Just past a flaking sign for fresh farm eggs, they turned sharply on to a narrow track and stopped. The car had presumably triggered some kind of alert, because a uniformed officer appeared within half a minute and carefully checked their ID before opening the gate.

The copper pointed the way, then smiled, rueful. 'I don't know about lunatics taking over the asylum—'

It was presumably some clever line the officer had come up with and trotted out for each visitor, and Thorne felt a little guilty at driving away before the man had a chance to finish it.

Five minutes later they drew up in front of the house.

Two more officers in plain-clothes checked their ID a second time and took them through to a small office in the entrance hall to sign in.

'How many guests?' Tanner asked.

The chattier of the two said, 'Just the one, believe it or not. There's a couple more coming in a few days, but it's all pretty quiet at the moment. Between us and the security team, doctors and therapists and what have you, there must be twenty-odd people here playing nursemaid to your bloke. Makes you wonder, doesn't it?'

'Does it?' Tanner made a show of looking at her watch, before the officer took the hint and led them back out into the hall and along a corridor to a pair of tall double doors.

'I'll leave you to it,' he said. He knocked gently, then eased the doors open, though he looked very much as if he'd have preferred to kick them in.

'Bloody hell.' The room was probably as big as Thorne's flat. Ahead of them windows ran the length of one wall, a pair of French doors opening out to a covered patio with plastic tables and chairs and, beyond that, an overgrown lawn sloping away towards a thick line of trees. There were seemingly dozens of mismatched armchairs and small sofas, which together with the collection of side tables and standard lamps made the whole room resemble a freakish, down-at-heel furniture showroom. Moving further into the room, Thorne could see that almost everything else was bland and utilitarian: dark brown corduroy curtains; an industrial grey carpet with fresh hoover tracks; a few crappy prints in clip-frames above a large oak fireplace and a large TV on a dusty glass and metal stand.

A few DVDs scattered beneath. *100 Great Premiership Goals, Michael McIntyre Live & Laughing, Fast & Furious 6.*

There was a smell too – a sharp tang of cleaning fluid and something musty – and Thorne realised that what it reminded him of, above all, was the day room in an old people's home.

Andrew Evans was sitting on a sofa in the corner, next to a middle-aged man in a suit, who stood up as Thorne and Tanner came in. He mumbled something to Evans, then smiled at Thorne and Tanner as he walked past them and closed the doors behind him.

'Counsellor,' Evans said. 'Load of old toss, but it's not like I've got anyone else to talk to, is it?'

'Well, you've got us, now.' Tanner introduced Thorne and the two of them drew a pair of ratty armchairs closer together.

Evans watched as Thorne took off his jacket and continued to stare around the room. 'It's all right, isn't it?'

'Better than a cell, I should imagine,' Thorne said. Though the furnishings left a lot to be desired, the room itself remained impressive, and he found himself wondering what its original function had been. A room that had probably hosted balls or banquets, he guessed. Back before it had become home to those locked away because their behaviour offended Victorian sensibilities. Men who were suffering from stress or had perhaps liked a drink too much and women with post-natal depression or whose infidelity was labelled 'moral insanity'.

'Worth a few bob, I reckon,' Evans said, nodding. 'Sort of place my company used to snap up, when I was a city-boy wanker. That was back in the day, obviously, when there was still plenty of money sloshing around. You know, before . . .'

'We know,' Tanner said. 'It's all in your file.'

'Before you decided to check Facebook at fifty miles an hour,' Thorne said.

Evans lowered his head and tugged the sleeves of his sweat-shirt down to cover his hands. 'That was my joke, when I was inside,' he said. 'That I didn't know which I was more ashamed of. What I did to that lad I hit, or the fact that I used to work in the city.' He looked up, reddening. 'Stupid joke . . .'

'You're looking better than the last time I saw you,' Tanner said.

'You think?' His face was still drawn and pasty, and the heel of one foot bounced almost constantly against the grey carpet. Along with the baggy blue sweatshirt, he was wearing faded tracksuit bottoms and training shoes, all presumably provided from a collection of clothes on site.

'Well, a bit.'

'Don't feel it.'

'How's it going?'

'Oh, apart from not sleeping or eating properly, chucking up once an hour and shitting through the eye of a needle, it's cracking.'

'The treatment, I mean.'

'Well, the counselling stuff's started, for what it's worth, but they can't really start the detox until I get through this bit.' Evans smiled, showing surprisingly good teeth. 'Ten times worse than heroin withdrawal, they keep telling me. Coming off Spice. Makes me think I should have taken heroin instead, but that was even more expensive inside.'

'Yeah, it's shocking some of the prices these days,' Thorne said.

Evans ignored him, still looking at Tanner. 'I'm on something to make sure I don't have seizures, something else for what they call my *discomfort* and another one I can't even pronounce to try and calm me down. I'm rattling.'

'Got to be done,' Tanner said.

'I've got this counsellor talking to me about how I need to sort my life out and I keep telling him that I want to.' That foot was still bouncing off the carpet. 'It's why I'm here, isn't it?'

'It's only part of the reason you're here,' Tanner said. 'You understand what's going on, right? Why *we're* here?'

Evans nodded. Said, 'Course I do.'

'Good.' Tanner leaned forward. 'So, I know the story.' She nodded towards Thorne. 'And obviously I've told my colleague, but I'd like him to hear it from you. So, tell it again.'

Evans took a deep breath and described his first few, terrible weeks in Her Majesty's Prison, Pentonville. He talked about the weeks and months afterwards that had seemed far better at the time; that had passed more quickly, thanks to the drug on which he'd quickly developed a dependence, and the woman who had delivered it.

'The woman you called the Duchess?'

'She knew that's what we called her,' Evans said. 'I think she liked it.'

Thorne knew very well that drug use in prison was at an epidemic level, and that smuggling in everything from heroin to mobile phones was seriously big business. He was still shocked, though, to hear of the ease with which such things were done.

'Drones are the big thing now,' Evans said. 'The Duchess is probably into all that too, but she wasn't quite that high-tech with us. She'd bring in these phones that were small enough to hide up your arse, two or three at a time if you wanted to. Small enough for her to bring into the visiting area inside a Mars bar. She could do that with the Spice too, but she had plenty of other ways. She'd get it as a liquid and spray it on to kids' drawings then let them dry. Easy enough to hand them over, then you just tear a piece off, roll it into a fag and you're away. You just had to call her and she'd bring in whatever you wanted.'

'What about after you were released?' Thorne asked.

Evans did not describe the latter part of the journey that had brought him so low quite as easily. He stumbled over his words and the pauses grew longer as he tried to gather his thoughts. He seemed close to tears several times as he talked.

'The people who'd been supplying the Spice made it clear that if I wanted to pay off my debt . . . if I wanted more of it . . . I'd need to . . . do things for them.'

'And you really didn't have any idea what these *things* might be? What, you thought you might have to do a bit of DIY for somebody? Help out with some paperwork?'

Tanner threw Thorne a look. *Go easy . . .*

'You think I had any choice? You think I wanted to?'

Thorne said nothing.

'They gave me stuff to look after for them, bags I hid in the loft . . . drugs or cash, I never looked. Then there were jobs . . . just putting the wind up other poor sods that owed them money. Nothing too heavy at first, then this bloke brought a gun round.'

'What bloke?'

Evans shook his head. 'I never saw his face. He had a crash helmet on, same as mine. That was the gun I used to threaten that sad case in Tottenham; the same one that was used to kill Jandali. The bloke came round to collect it after that first time . . . that's why it had my fingerprints on.' He looked from Tanner to Thorne and back. 'That was obviously their game all along, but I still don't understand why.'

'Because you're expendable,' Tanner said.

'Right,' Thorne said. 'It's the way they do business. Maybe Jandali had threatened to go to the police, or just told them that he wasn't going to pay them any more. Either way, they decided that killing him would send a message. And I'm betting they didn't want to risk losing the man they sent to deliver it, who's obviously very good at his job. So they set you up for it, because sending that message to others was more important than the money Jandali owed or whatever you owed.' He shrugged. 'You came in handy, that's all.'

Tanner nodded. 'Just a bit of business.'

'These are dangerous people,' Thorne said. 'Which is why we need to catch them and why you're going to help us.'

For a few seconds it looked as if Evans was ready to jump up and bolt.

'What are they going to think's going on, though?' He licked his lips and swallowed hard. 'That's what worries me.'

'I'm not with you,' Tanner said.

'Well, they did a pretty good job of putting me in the frame, laying on plenty of evidence, and they would think I'm too scared to talk, so they're expecting me to be charged and go to prison, aren't they? I mean, don't get me wrong, I *am* scared of them . . . but by rights, I should be on remand by now. What if they work out that something's up?'

'That can't be helped,' Thorne said.

'This is still your best chance, Andrew.' Tanner stared at him. 'And it's not like you've had any other choice.'

No choice or not, Evans looked as though he was ready for his hourly appointment with the toilet bowl.

'Look, you could have said nothing and gone to prison for a crime you didn't commit. Or, knowing full well you didn't kill Adnan Jandali, we could have stuck you in a remand cell for appearances' sake, because it's what they'd be expecting. Either way you'd be in prison, and if the people doing this think there's even a chance you might have told us something before that happened, we all know they can get to you inside.'

Evans nodded slowly and pressed both hands against his thigh to control the tremor in his leg.

'Our best bet is to track down the Duchess,' Tanner said. 'And that won't be easy, because with you arrested she'll have gone to ground or moved away. That number you called her on was a pay as you go and it's already dead, but we knew it would be. She may know about the plan to frame you and she may not, but either way she's the only connection we've got to them.

113

Obviously we'll be talking to any other prisons where she might have been doing business, but I'm not holding my breath. From what you told me back at Colindale, she uses different aliases and has various fake IDs.'

'We need names,' Thorne said. 'Her other customers.'

Tanner took out her notebook while Evans thought about it, then wrote the names down when he began to list them.

'Are these people who are still inside?' she asked.

'Yeah, I think so.'

Thorne shook his head. 'No good. What about people who are out?'

'What difference does it make?'

'We've got to think ahead,' Tanner said. 'And juries don't tend to trust statements made by people who are doing time. Think they'll say anything to get a few months off their sentence.'

'Which they usually will,' Thorne said.

'Is there anyone you can think of who's out and who knew the Duchess?'

Evans thought again. Thorne looked up as an officer walked slowly past the window and moved close to peer inside. Thorne nodded sharply and the officer walked away.

'There's a couple ... a bloke called Mason, who I've talked to on the phone once or twice. Kyle Mason. Lives up near Caledonian Road, I think.'

'We'll find him,' Tanner said.

'And Graham French. He's cut my hair a couple of times since I got out.'

'Sorry?'

'He's a barber ... hairstylist, whatever. He did everyone's hair inside. In for fraud, I think ... something like that.'

Tanner took down the details and put her notebook away.

'How long do you think all this is going to take?'

'We'll try and keep you informed.' Tanner stood up. 'And we'll be back if we need anything else.'

114

The nosy officer had reappeared outside the window. 'At least you've got a bit of company,' Thorne said.

Driving back, Tanner said, 'You were a bit hard on him.'

'Not easy to think of him as a victim,' Thorne said. 'That's all.'

'I don't see why.' Tanner leaned back and turned to look out of the window. 'He committed an offence and he did his time. Now he's just someone with an unfortunate drug habit who's been falsely accused. Seems pretty clear-cut to me.'

Thorne said nothing, because there was no point. With Tanner, there were very few grey areas. Innocent or guilty. The correct thing to do or ... well, as far as Tanner was concerned, there wasn't usually an alternative.

When he looked across a few minutes later, her eyes were closed again.

'Put some music on if you want.'

'I thought you didn't like music,' Thorne said. 'You told me once it was just background noise.'

'I'll probably nod off in a minute anyway.' She leaned her head against the glass. 'So, go ahead. What have you got?'

Thorne flicked through the list of CDs on the multi-changer and listed them for her. George Jones, Patsy Cline, Merle Haggard and Gram Parsons. Margo Price, in case anyone thought he only listened to people who were dead.

'Haven't you got anything decent? What about Billy Ray Cyrus?'

'What?' Thorne turned and saw the grin.

'They were right,' Tanner said. 'You are *so* easy to wind up.'

Thorne knew who *they* were. Kitson, Brigstocke, Hendricks. Maybe even Helen. He and Tanner might not have been part of the same team very long, but she had already got her feet under the table. He chose Merle Haggard, turned it up nice and loud and put his foot down.

NINETEEN

Half an hour's sleep in the car had not helped a great deal and Tanner was exhausted by the time she finally got home after a fourteen-hour day and locked the front door behind her. She poured some food into the cat's bowl, showered, and came back downstairs in a dressing gown. She threw away the day's junk mail and wiped down the kitchen surfaces, then, without quite being able to recall how she'd got there, she stood staring through the glass door of the microwave, watching a ready-meal revolve.

Two major inquiries to think about, to formulate as they took shape.

Information to examine and prioritise.

Actions . . .

She had already followed up on the names Andrew Evans had provided and made plans to interview the first of those who might give them a lead to the Duchess. She had spoken to the deputy governor at Pentonville and arranged for visits ID and security information to be sent across, though, as she'd told Evans, that line of inquiry was not one for which she held out a great deal of hope. Whoever this woman was, she was clearly an experienced operator, who had been able to bypass standard security protocols at any number of places. The Duchess could smuggle herself into prisons as easily as the drugs and mobile phones she carried.

Watching the plastic container turn slowly beneath the orange light, Tanner thought about Andrew Evans, how pleased he would have been to see that woman on the other side of the table, back when he was inside. To take whatever she had brought him. Had he really been naïve enough not to realise that, further down the line, he wouldn't be quite so happy to see her? Thorne clearly did not think so. Tanner remembered their conversation in the car, her insistence that Evans was as much a victim as anyone else. She was not sure she really believed that deep down, but she was equally convinced that what she believed wasn't important. Yes, Andrew Evans had threatened someone at gunpoint, but now he was working for them, so it didn't matter, or at least it mattered less than it had. The bigger picture, all that. Sympathy, or a lack of it, was simply not relevant. Besides, sympathy had never been something Tanner had been overly burdened with.

Certainly not since Susan, when so much of it had been used up, wasted on herself.

She had no shred of sympathy for the man at the centre of the other inquiry, however damaged he might be. Was. His issues were for the likes of Melita Perera to worry about.

Much of the afternoon had been taken up with a full-scale briefing on Operation Felix, focusing a much-enlarged team on the three unsolved murders she had highlighted. Interviews had been arranged with a friend of Annette Mangan's and with the parents of Leila Fadel, though making contact with anyone close to the third victim would be a little slower. Patricia Somersby's nearest relative was a sister in the US, so in the meantime Tanner had made several unsuccessful attempts to connect with the SIO on the case.

Another case that, as of now, was being run by her and Tom Thorne.

Dream team. That's what Hendricks had said the year before. Taking the piss, naturally, but still. That had been something much closer to home, though, and this was a very different test. Now they would both find out exactly what sort of team they were.

When her food was ready, she carried it through on a tray to the sitting room and turned on the TV. As usual, after a few minutes, whatever programme she had tuned in to had begun to drift over her. She had never watched much television, even before Susan, but these days it was just there as background, and what little she did catch convinced her that was what it was probably designed for. Cookery, antiques, people getting off with each other on islands, whatever. Sitting there, she wondered if she should make the effort to watch one or two of the umpteen property shows on offer, now she was actually looking for some- where. *Homes Under the Hammer. Location, Location, Location. Property Ladder.* She quickly decided not to bother. She wasn't sure there was a programme called *Decent Two-Bedroom Flat In London That Wasn't Going To Bankrupt You* . . .

An hour later, the cat fast asleep on the sofa next to her and Tanner about to go the same way, the phone rang.

DC Terry Jackson said, 'Sorry, pig of a day. Patricia Somersby, that right? Sounds like it might be part of something bigger . . . '

Tanner told him exactly why that might be the case and, in as collegiate a manner as she was capable of, why the case was no longer his. Jackson didn't sound particularly upset about it, or perhaps it was just the soft West Country burr.

'Botched burglary, then,' Tanner said.

'It looks like it.'

'Looks?'

'Just an expression. There's nothing to suggest that it's any- thing else. We did bear other possibilities in mind, but there's

118

sod all so far to indicate it's not exactly what is says on the tin.' There was a pause. 'Your team think it might be something else?'

'Was there much of a mess?'

'No, not really,' Jackson said. 'Drawers opened, usual stuff . . . I mean it definitely wasn't kids. No turds on the bed, nothing like that. All the predictable items taken, the small valuables. Phone, laptop, handbag.'

'Stuff he could carry.'

'Right.'

'Tell me about the forced entry.'

'A broken window at the back.'

'You think that could have been done afterwards?'

'Well, it *could* have been—'

'What about prints and forensics?'

'Sod all. Have you not seen the file?'

'Everything's on its way over,' Tanner said. 'But I wanted to get your take on it first, as you know it best.' She already knew there had been no more forensic evidence found at the Somersby crime scene than there had at any of the others, but she was canny enough to know that a little buttering up would go a long way. Nobody on the homicide team at Avon and Somerset would be very sorry to get an unsolved murder off their books, but there was usually a degree of professional pride, so it didn't hurt to pay it the appropriate lip service.

'No prints that weren't hers to get excited about,' Jackson said. 'From what we can gather, I don't think she had a lot of friends round, anything like that. No forensic evidence on the body, either. Looks like he wore gloves, but a professional burglar would have done that anyway. Patricia just came back unexpectedly.'

'Possibly.' Tanner had already begun to wonder if the victim's return *had* been unexpected. Or perhaps she had already been in the house when the killer arrived and had let him in. Had Patricia Somersby been expecting the man who had murdered her?

'This is the cat thing, isn't it?' Jackson asked. 'These unsolved cases you're looking at. My burglar.'

The man was clearly not stupid.

'That inquiry has been widened out, yes.'

The man laughed softly. 'So . . . cat burglar, then.'

Tanner could summon no more than a non-committal hum. She was staring across the room at the four framed prints she and Susan had bought from Camden Market years before. Simple pencil drawings they had both fallen in love with, spent far too much on. Along with almost everything else on the ground floor, the original frames had been damaged in the fire, the glass cracked and blackened, but Tanner had managed to salvage the drawings themselves and have them reframed.

She remembered Susan making a balls-up of trying to hang them first time around; standing on a chair and swearing. She remembered taking measurements, then drawing a diagram for her, so that she could get the spacing right.

'Listen, I'm sure you'll be wanting to come down,' Jackson said. 'So just let me know and I'll try and make sure I'm around.' His voice lowered as he turned on the charm, such as it was. 'I mean you'll probably have to stay the night, so I'm more than happy to take you round if you want. Show you what Bristol's got to offer.'

Tanner swiftly revised her opinion of the man. 'Thanks, Terry.'

Very stupid.

TWENTY

'Obviously, there's always one good thing comes out of having a row.' Thorne inched across the bed towards Helen. 'The make-up sex afterwards.'

'In your dreams,' Helen said. 'Besides which, it wasn't a row.'

'Wasn't it?'

'Not really.'

'OK, so can you still have make-up sex after a healthy and forthright discussion?'

'Not a row with you, anyway. I was only pissed off with you afterwards, because you kept sticking up for Phil.'

'I wasn't sticking up for him,' Thorne said. 'I was trying to tell you he wasn't being serious, that's all. He was just winding you up.'

They had eaten at a Turkish place in Camberwell. Thorne and Helen, Hendricks and Liam. It had all been going well – great food, cold bottles of Efes and idle chat – until Thorne had brought up the Andrew Evans case and they had begun talking about drugs in prison.

'They found three hundred and fifty thousand quid's worth

121

in two cells at HMP Northumberland,' Thorne said. 'And that's only what it's worth inside. Worth ten times that on the street.'

'How's it get in?' Liam asked.

Hendricks leaned across and rubbed his partner's arm. 'Bless him, he's so innocent.'

Liam smacked the hand away. 'I know *how* it gets in, obviously.' His work as a forensic entomologist had brought him into contact with the police often enough to be more aware of such things than the average civilian. 'But how does that much get into a prison?'

'At least some of the guards must be in on it,' Thorne said.

Hendricks nodded. 'Right, and plenty who aren't actually making money from it are turning a blind eye.'

'Bloody hell,' Liam said.

'They prefer it when the cons are out of their heads,' Thorne said. 'Makes their lives a bit easier.'

'These days it's the cons who run prisons, not the guards.' Hendricks spooned yoghurt on to his plate. 'They don't give a monkey's.'

'That's serious money, though,' Liam said.

'Yeah and these are serious drugs. This new synthetic stuff is properly nasty.'

'Spice, right?'

'You're *so* down with the kids,' Hendricks said.

'I read the news.'

'Yeah, well, Spice, or Genie or Black Mamba or whatever they're calling it this week is killing more people every year. A good few every month and I know, because I've worked on several of them. And that's not counting the people who die because someone else is off their tits.'

Thorne and Liam ate and nodded along.

'I'd make it legal again,' Helen said suddenly. 'It was much safer when it was just another legal high and people could buy it from head shops or a stall on Camden market or whatever. Same old story, isn't it? Now it's controlled by criminals, and surprise

surprise, it's *way* stronger and way more dangerous. People walking around like zombies, getting robbed or sexually assaulted. I'd do it with all drugs.' She tore off some bread and popped it into her mouth. 'I'd legalise the lot of them.'

Thorne looked at her. 'Eh?'

'Or at least decriminalise them. It's a load of bloody nonsense.'

This was not something Thorne had heard Helen say before. He knew that, like him and most other coppers, she believed that prosecuting weed smokers was a waste of time and money and that it was surely only a matter of time before cannabis became legal. This was an altogether more ... radical stance.

Hendricks turned to her. 'You seriously saying you'd legalise all drugs? Heroin, acid, whatever?'

Helen nodded, chewed.

'I think that's a bit over the top.'

'Is it?'

'Yeah, and you probably shouldn't say it in front of your DCI. Not if you want promotion any time soon.'

'I'm entitled to an opinion.'

'He's winding you up,' Thorne said.

Helen wasn't listening. 'They did it in Portugal,' she said. 'They decriminalised all drugs over fifteen years ago, and the results were amazing.'

'Yeah, well that's Portugal, isn't it?'

'What?'

'It's sunny, so nobody's that bothered about drugs anyway.'

'I'm telling you, addiction levels dropped like a stone, violent crime is way down, the incidence of AIDS is as low as it's ever been ... and all the money they saved by not waging a pointless war on helpless junkies was spent on creating jobs and building rehab centres. I just don't understand why people aren't shouting about this from the rooftops.'

Hendricks looked at Thorne. 'Or in Turkish restaurants.'

'I wasn't shouting.'

'Helpless junkies, you said. *Helpless*? Really?'

'Yeah, some of them. *Most* of them.'

'I don't know about that—'

'And we're sitting here pouring booze down our necks.' She picked up her beer bottle. 'A nice *legal* drug, which kills far more people every year than all the illegal ones put together. It's the hypocrisy which pisses me off more than anything.'

Hendricks shrugged and took a swig of his nice, legal drug. 'Anyway, just because something worked in Portugal ... and besides, I'm not convinced—'

'Look it up—'

Thorne said, 'Ignore him, Helen.'

'Who's to say it would work anywhere else? I just think it might be a step too far, that's all.'

'Well, I think you're wrong.' Helen raised her bottle in a mock toast.

'Why have you got such a bee in your bonnet about it, anyway?'

Helen stared at him for a few seconds. 'I can't believe you're asking me that. You haven't drunk so much that you've forgotten what I do?'

'I know what you do,' Hendricks said.

Thorne was shaking his head. Liam was staring at the table.

'So, for a kick-off, you've got kids being raised by drug-addicted parents, often placing them at physical risk, which is abuse in itself. I'm not going too fast for you, am I, Phil?'

Thorne glanced across and saw that two people at the next table were staring.

'More importantly, there are any number of studies showing that, as well as causing serious mental health issues, childhood abuse can drive people to use drugs in later life. Trauma, then self-medication, I mean it's not rocket science, is it? So, it's not bad enough that these kids I see at work every day are abused, because now, thanks to our stupid attitudes towards drug addicts, some of them are going to grow up and be treated like

124

criminals.' Helen took a swig of beer, reached to tear off a piece of flatbread. 'So ... '

Hendricks nodded slowly, then looked across at the couple on the next table and shrugged apologetically. 'What can I tell you?' he said. 'She's high as a bloody kite.'

'Piss off, Phil.'

Thorne leaned across the table. 'He's joking, Hel ... '

Now, lying in bed, Thorne said, 'He was just saying all that because Liam was there. I mean, back when he was clubbing every night of the week, Phil probably took every drug known to man. In fact I *know* he did. Maybe he doesn't want Liam to find out he was into all that stuff.'

Helen hummed, non-committal.

'You know, now he's all loved-up and trying to be well behaved. Now it's all about keeping fit and I don't know ... spending Sundays at the garden centre.' Thorne moved closer to her. 'He was just messing about. You know what he's like.'

'Yeah,' Helen said. 'I didn't mean to sound so bolshie.'

Thorne was still hoping that the slim possibility of make-up sex was on the table. Or in the bed, at the very least. 'Nothing wrong with you being bolshie,' he said. 'It's quite hot, actually.'

'Last week this kid nearly died on the Alton estate,' Helen said. 'Just because his mum thought it was a good idea to keep her methadone in Fruit Shoot bottles. He was OK in the end, but it was touch and go.'

'Jesus ... '

She pulled the duvet up, then stretched across to pick up her book from the bedside table. 'Same age as Alfie.'

Thorne said nothing. He sighed and stared at the light fitting for half a minute, and when he closed his eyes the bulb continued to glow behind them.

As though she was able to read his thoughts, Helen turned a page and said, 'You're welcome to make up with yourself, if you want. Won't bother me.'

TWENTY-ONE

He'd spent the last hour or so browsing Facebook; clicking on profiles at random and looking at strangers' photographs. Their friends, their partners, their pets. It was something that often helped him to unwind at the end of a stressful day, but none of the pictures could compare with those that had been in his head for the last three days.

It was quite the album.

His Friday evening had certainly been one to remember, probably the best one yet, he decided. He could not be sure though if that was simply because he was getting better at what he did, learning how to relax a little more and enjoy himself, or if it was down to her. He'd known it would be special from the moment he'd seen her, known he was not going to be disappointed. That dress and those fancy shoes, the trouble she'd gone to with her hair and make-up.

She'd looked as good as she was ever going to.

And he very much appreciated the effort.

He had guessed that Alice would go to a lot of trouble, had worked that much out about her already, seen how keen she was.

She could have had no idea about the trouble *he* had gone to. None of them did. The thought he had put into it, the time and effort lavished. She might have got a sneaking idea right at the end, of course, put two and two together, but by then there had been other things for her to think about.

As ever, he could only guess at what those things might have been.

Regrets, if he had to put money on it.

Would have, should have, could have . . .

There was no question he had made a good choice and that pleased him enormously. These days, there was too *much* choice, if anything. Too many options when it came to all sorts of things. You couldn't buy a cup of coffee without half an hour to kill and a degree in Italian. He remembered trying to get breakfast in America once, when it had taken the waitress five minutes to list the different types of bread available just because he'd been stupid enough to ask for toast.

Who needed the aggravation?

It was the same with everything. There were far too many channels on his TV, too many products on the shelves whenever he went shopping, and he still hadn't worked out some of the things he was able to do on his phone.

Not that he had any issue with technology. Making his choices would have been almost impossible without it.

He clicked on a photo of a young boy playing with a puppy and 'liked' it, because he was in a good mood. A few moments later, he was looking at a picture of a frail-looking old man who had recently passed away. He posted a sad-face on the bereaved daughter's page, because it felt like the right thing to do.

In the end, he decided, it wasn't the number of available options that really mattered, it was all about going at things properly and making an educated choice. Doing your homework. Any idiot could go '*that* one', but that was how people came unstuck, wasn't it? Besides, when you got it right, it was the best feeling ever and the pictures afterwards were so much better.

It wouldn't be long, he reckoned, before he'd have to start checking out some new possibilities. Not quite yet, but he was already looking forward to it, and why the hell wouldn't he?

Choosing them was almost half the fun.

TWENTY-TWO

Kyle Mason worked in the service department of a car dealership in Holloway, less than a mile away from the prison in which he had once done time alongside Andrew Evans. He was in his early thirties and – Tanner supposed – handsome, though there was no trace of the winning smile she had seen in his photograph when he walked out to meet her in the reception area. Tanner introduced herself and he nodded, pushing his hands a little deeper into the pockets of blue overalls emblazoned with the company logo.

A 'can-do' raised thumb with a nice, smiley face.

Tanner followed Mason up a narrow stairwell to a viewing area the manager had told her they could use for fifteen minutes. As interview rooms went, it was suitably grim, with curling carpet tiles and a single, dusty strip light. They sat in moulded plastic chairs next to a drinks machine with an OUT OF ORDER sign taped to the front, while in front of them, on a low table, somebody had taken the trouble to artfully arrange dog-eared copies of *What Car?* and *Auto Express*.

Doing her best to ignore the music from a tinny speaker

on the wall, Tanner laid her bag on the floor and stared down through a dirty window at the service workshop below; a four by four on a vehicle lift and three or four mechanics moving beneath it.

'I don't see the point,' she said. 'I mean you can sit here and watch people working on your car, but you've got no idea what they're doing, have you? Well, I certainly wouldn't.'

'Is this going to take long?' The man's voice was deep, the accent pure south London. 'The boss took a punt, giving me this job, you know? It doesn't look great when you lot come bowling in for a chat.'

'I've already spoken to him,' Tanner said. 'It's not a problem. He knows you'll be helping us with an investigation and that's only going to look good, right? Good for everyone. So, let's hope you can.'

'What?'

'Help us.' She watched Mason shift awkwardly in his chair and reached to take her notebook from her bag. 'Must be a bit strange, Pentonville sitting there on the doorstep.'

Mason sniffed. 'I cycle past it every morning on the way to work. I like looking at it.'

'A reminder of old times?'

'A reminder of *shit* times. Something I don't want to go back to. That I'm never going back to.'

'What was it you were in for again?'

'Assault.'

Tanner nodded. 'Sexual assault, wasn't it?'

Mason sat back and sucked his teeth. 'What's the point of asking if you already know?'

'I wanted to see what you'd say, that's all. If I'm looking for information from someone, I like to know how upfront they are. I'm not trying to catch you out.'

'I did a stupid thing, I paid for it.'

'*Stupid?*'

130

'A bad thing, OK? I'm not that person any more. I'm nothing like that person.'

'Pleased to hear it,' Tanner said.

There were shouts and a peal of throaty laughter from the workshop below. A pneumatic hiss and the scream of a drill in short, angry bursts.

'What kind of information?' Mason asked.

Tanner opened her notebook and nodded towards the door; the streets beyond. 'For at least some of the time you were over there in Pentonville, you were on the same wing as a man called Andrew Evans.'

'Yeah, that's right. Andy was a mate. Stayed in touch, like.'

'Right, and you and your mate Andy were both using Spice when you were inside.'

Mason hesitated.

'I don't care about that.' Tanner looked hard at him, made sure he understood. 'I'm only here because I'm trying to find out a bit more about the woman who delivered it to you.'

He folded his arms, grimaced. 'Her. The *Duchess*.'

'Well, this woman may not be someone you think of very fondly now, but I'm sure it was different when you were inside. According to Andrew Evans, she visited you dozens of times.'

'Yeah . . . probably.'

'So, what did you talk about during those visits?'

Mason shook his head slowly as though he was struggling to remember.

'Look, we know she used different names and we know none of them were real.' Tanner leaned towards him. 'So as of now, all we've got is a picture on a bunch of fake IDs and anything you can tell us would really help. I did tell your manager that you were going to help, remember?'

'She talked about all sorts,' Mason said eventually. 'The weather, the news, anything. Just so it looked like the visit was kosher, if a screw walked past or whatever. Most of the time she

131

asked how I was doing, what the food was like, how my classes were going.' There was a flash of that winning smile. 'I did car maintenance, you know, which was how I ended up getting this job, but there was all sorts. Computers, foreign languages, all that.'

'And she never said anything about herself? Her family? Where she was from?'

'I don't think so.'

'Did she have an accent?'

He shrugged. 'Just ordinary, you know. I mean, not northern or Scottish or anything foreign.'

'A London accent?'

Mason snapped his fingers. 'She had a kid.' He nodded. 'Yeah, she definitely mentioned that.'

Tanner scribbled. 'Boy or girl?'

'I don't think she said. I was just talking about missing my son and she said she couldn't imagine what that was like. How she'd go mad if she couldn't see her kid. Something like that.' He watched Tanner writing. 'Is that any good?'

'It's something.' Tanner finished writing and looked at him. 'Anything else you can remember? Some comment she might have made . . . '

Mason was looking through the window. One of his work-mates had clocked him and was waving while another was happily making 'wanker' signs. Mason turned back to Tanner. 'She said something about the seaside once.'

'What about it?'

'That she liked it, you know? That it was a good place for kids to grow up and all that. Said that when I got out I should take my son down there, get him out of London for a bit.'

'You think that's where *she* grew up?'

'Yeah, could have been, I suppose.' He turned to the window again. 'I mean, a lot of the time I was talking to her I was out of it, so it's hard to remember. You know what I mean?'

Now, the men below them were making even less subtle gestures; tongues lolling, thrusting their hips.

Tanner nodded and closed her notebook.

'We done, then?' As Tanner reached for her bag, Mason stood up, looking hugely grateful that he could be on his way. 'So ... how's Andy doing?'

'What do you mean?'

'Well, I saw him after he came out and it was pretty obvious he was still caning the Spice.'

'He's doing better.' Tanner stood up, too.

'That's good. That's good ... '

Tanner walked past him and stopped at the top of the stairs. 'How did you manage to sort yourself out, Kyle? I don't mean getting the job.'

'Listen, I had plenty of friends who did time before me, people who used the same stuff, so I knew how that shit worked, OK? What you come out *owing*. Soon as I was out and I was clean, I paid it all off.'

'You make it sound easy.'

'No, it was not easy, but it had to be done. I sold my car, sold anything I could think of. I scraped the cash together and got those animals off my back.' He smiled again and this time it lingered a while. 'I even managed to get a little bank loan once I'd got my job.'

'I'm impressed.' Tanner wondered why Andrew Evans had not been able to take similar steps to get his life back on track. Whether he might have done, had the people he owed money to not generously offered him another way out.

Had he been as streetwise as his friend.

'I'm not stupid,' Mason said. 'I know you still have to pay a bank loan back.' He nodded, the smile gone. 'But if you can't, the bank don't come after you with guns. You know what I mean?'

*

133

In the dealership car park, Tanner sat in her VW Golf and took a call from Long Barrow Manor.

'I need to see Paula,' Evans said.

He was trying to sound calm, but Tanner could hear the effort in his voice. She said, 'That's not going to be possible, Andrew.'

'I need to see my wife. What's the big deal? Why can't I see my wife?'

'We went through all this—'

'Yeah, but I don't get it.' He wasn't making an effort any more. 'I get that *they* don't know what's going on and I know it has to be like that, but why can't Paula know? It's not fair.'

'She knows you're safe. She's been told.'

'Yeah, but she needs to *see* I'm OK. And my little boy needs to see.'

'I can't do it.'

'Just for an hour or something, yeah?'

'Look . . . maybe I can arrange for a phone call, but I'm not promising anything, so—'

'I don't want to talk to her on the phone. Why can't she come and see me?'

'*They* don't know what's going on or where you are, but that doesn't mean they might not try to find out.' As soon as she stopped talking, Tanner knew that she'd said the wrong thing.

'You saying she's in danger or something?'

'No, I'm not saying that.' In the rear-view mirror she watched herself shaking her head. 'I'm really not saying that, Andrew. I'm just trying to make you understand why nobody can know where you are, that's all.'

Glancing up, Tanner could see the manager of the dealership staring at her from the doorway to reception. He saw her looking and waved. Tanner listened to Evans breathing for a few seconds and said, 'I'll go and see her, OK?'

Evans muttered something, low and fast, but Tanner couldn't make it out.

'I'll go and see Paula,' she said. 'I promise.' The tone sounded on her phone to let her know that another call was coming through. 'OK, Andrew?' She looked at the screen and saw the number that was waiting. 'Listen, I'm sorry, but I really need to hang up now.'

TWENTY-THREE

'Leila was so busy,' Mina Fadel said. 'I think that was the trouble.'

Next to her, Leila's father, Barin, nodded. 'Very busy, but that was because she was so popular. Most popular doctor at the surgery, because she was the best.'

'Are you sure I can't get you something to drink?'

'No thank you,' Chall said.

'But you've come such a long way.'

'We had something on the train,' Kitson said.

A bacon roll for Kitson and a skinny muffin for Chall, grabbed from a bakery at Liverpool Street station, just before they boarded.

'So, come on then, tell me about Nicola,' Kitson had said, once their breakfasts were finished.

'Tell you what?'

'Dish the dirt. Come on, you've worked with her long enough.'

'There really isn't any,' Chall said.

'You're loyal.' Kitson sat back and nodded. 'That's good.'

'So what about Thorne? You've worked with *him* a long time.'

Kitson said nothing.

'That makes two of us then,' Chall said. 'Loyal.'

'Nothing to do with being loyal,' Kitson said. 'Just that there's nothing to tell you he wouldn't tell you himself. Plenty to tell, mind you, but we haven't got enough time.'

'It's the best part of two hours to Norwich.'

Kitson shrugged. 'Like I said ... '

'So.' Barin Fadel shuffled forward on the sofa and reached for his wife's hand. 'Why have you come such a long way? Is there any news?'

'We're looking at the case again,' Kitson said. 'Which is not to say that other officers ever stopped looking at it.'

'Just coming at it from a slightly different angle,' Chall said.

Mina shook her head. 'We already said everything to the police afterwards. We said it lots of times.'

'I know,' Kitson said. 'But that was four months ago and we were hoping that you might have remembered something. Anything.'

The husband and wife looked at each other. He had a full head of silver hair and, though retired, was still dressed as though he would be going to work. A shirt and tie, a brown cardigan. If the man's clothes were perhaps a little drab, his wife's were anything but. She wore a red trouser suit over a white blouse, the jacket decorated with an enormous brooch which complemented the gold bangles around both thin wrists. Her highlighted hair was perfectly coiffured, *Dynasty*-style, and her pink fingernails looked recently manicured. A woman who clearly took pride in her appearance and was unaware, or unconcerned, that she looked somewhat overdressed in her suburban sitting room.

'Too busy to have friends, you said?' Kitson looked from one to the other.

Leila's father shook his head. 'No, no ... of course she had friends, because people liked her.'

'She was the most popular doctor at the surgery,' Mina reminded them.

'Too busy to socialise, I meant. Not the same thing at all.'

Both still had strong Iranian accents, despite the fact that they had moved to the UK in the mid-eighties. They had lived in the same house for the best part of thirty years, no more than a mile from the surgery at which their daughter had worked and only a little further from the flat in which she had died.

It had all been in the case notes, which Chall and Kitson had studied on the train. Both looking out every few minutes at the dirty browns and greens of the flat farmland rushing past, before dragging their eyes back to the pictures of a strangled woman: froth at the corners of her mouth, a black and bloated tongue that was virtually severed, clenched between perfect white teeth.

'Leila was smartly dressed when she was . . . found.'

'Of course,' Mina said. She spun one of the delicate gold bangles around her wrist.

Chall nodded. It was possible that Mina Fadel's commitment to a highly polished appearance had simply rubbed off on – or been drummed into – her daughter. But he doubted it. He glanced across at the framed photographs arranged on a cupboard near the television: Leila posing proudly with her degree certificate; sitting somewhat formally between her parents; arms wrapped around her younger brother. 'Could she have been going somewhere, perhaps? Or do you think she might have been somewhere?'

'The police asked us this before,' Mina said.

'Yes, I know—'

'We can only tell you what we told them.' Still clutching his wife's hand, Barin Fadel thumped both into the sofa cushion for emphasis. 'Leila was a professional person and she took her appearance very seriously. These were the sort of clothes she would have worn to work every day.'

'This was a Saturday, though,' Kitson said.

'Yes, I know that.'

'Leila hadn't been at the surgery that day.'

The old man could not mask the twitch of irritation. 'My daughter was *always* smartly dressed.'

A hundred and sixty miles away, Tom Thorne sat in the kitchen of a shared house in Canterbury, watching a young woman drink tea that was green and smelled like fish.

Fish that had been recently shampooed.

Herbal tea aside, his expectations of the student house in which Zoe McCausland lived had been largely confounded. Based purely on old episodes of *The Young Ones*, Thorne had prepared himself for multicoloured bikes in the hall, mushrooms blooming in a freezing toilet and a sign on the fridge saying DON'T EAT MY CHEESE! As it was, the kitchen, like everywhere else he had seen, was spotless, with washing folded neatly into a wicker basket by the door and a dishwasher chuntering behind him. It certainly appeared to be a far cry from the heady student lifestyle Phil Hendricks and others claimed to have enjoyed; one Thorne often regretted having missed out on himself.

The university of life was all very well, but there were early starts and taxes to pay and not nearly as much sex.

The girl, who had been a friend of Annette Mangan before she was strangled to death six months earlier, was not what Thorne had been expecting either.

She was rosy-cheeked, with small, bright eyes and a mop of curly hair. It did her credit, Thorne thought, that she had not tried to disguise the fact that she was every bit as middle-class as her voice revealed her to be, that she was happy with who she was. She was not quite a young Ann Widdecombe, but take away the diamond stud in her nose and she was nobody's idea of a third-year drama student.

'I didn't actually know Annette that well,' Zoe said. 'I told the police that at the time. I mean, as well as anyone else, probably . . .'

'Well enough to know if she was seeing someone?'

'I think so. I don't know.'

'There was no regular boyfriend?'

'No.' She sipped her fishy tea, and smiled. 'I mean, not unless she kept him hidden away somewhere.'

'You never saw her with anyone?'

Zoe shook her head. 'No . . . but she said something once that made me think there might have been a bloke. Just a throwaway comment or whatever, I can't remember exactly. Sorry.'

'It's fine,' Thorne said.

The girl put down her mug and looked at him. 'So, you don't think Annette was killed by a stranger?'

Unlike the murder in Bristol, there were no signs of forced entry at the small flat in which Annette Mangan had lived alone and the original SIO had speculated, quite reasonably, that she may well have known the man who had killed her. Like Leila Fadel and Patricia Somersby, she had not been dressed anywhere near as casually as one might have expected late in the evening. A black dress, stockings and heels. There had been no jewellery found on her body, but abrasions on several fingers had led the original investigation to believe that this was probably taken by her killer, along with her phone and laptop computer and the cash in her handbag.

Before Thorne could answer, a young man ambled into the kitchen and stood watching them. Now, this one was more like it. Bare feet and barely awake, in tracksuit bottoms and a faded Star Wars T-shirt; a beard that made him look as if someone had pasted glue on to his chin and then thrown pubic hair at it.

'This is Detective Inspector Thorne,' Zoe said. 'He's here to talk about Annette.'

The boy nodded and made a face, then turned and padded out again.

'What was all that about?' Thorne asked.

'What?'

'That look, just then.' Thorne knew the 'oh, *police*' look very well and it had not been what he'd seen on the boy's face. The expression had changed at the mention of Annette Mangan's name.

Zoe suddenly looked a little awkward. 'Well, if I'm honest, Annette was a little bit . . . strange.'

'I still think it was about drugs,' Barin Fadel said. 'They had break-ins at the surgery once or twice; you know, people looking for drugs.' His wife nodded, next to him. 'Perhaps whoever killed Leila thought she kept some at home. Got angry when they couldn't find any and our daughter simply got in the way.'

Kitson nodded as though she were considering it, but she knew such a possibility had been quickly dismissed first time round. Yes, if the man responsible for her murder had been a junkie he would certainly have stolen Leila's phone and any cash he could find, as the killer had done, but if he was looking for drugs, why wasn't the place ransacked and why leave without taking her laptop computer?

Why kill her at all?

'I know you said Leila had friends.' Chall looked at Mina. 'Could any of them have been men who were . . . more than just friends?'

Leila's father shook his head immediately. 'We would have known. She was always far too busy with her job, but if there had been anyone she would have told us.' He looked to his wife for confirmation, but her eyes dropped to her hands, now folded in her lap.

'What?' Kitson asked.

The woman seemed a little smaller suddenly, shrinking back into the sofa cushion. Her voice was smaller too, when she said, 'I did wonder sometimes.'

Her husband was staring at her. 'Wonder what?'

'If she was seeing someone, or at least trying to meet someone. At first I thought it was just wishful thinking, you know, because I wanted her to be happy, but then I got a feeling about it.'

'Why on earth didn't you say something four months ago?'

Kitson and Chall watched, and listened.

'Because it was just a feeling, but I think about Leila all the time, every minute of the day—'

'So do I—'

'And recently I've started to think that perhaps I was right. Some days she seemed ... brighter, you know?' She reached across and patted her husband's leg. 'Maybe only a mother would notice these things, but when she called me to talk or came round for a chat there was something in her voice ... a spring in her step.'

'We all have good days and bad days,' her husband said.

'No, it was more than that. She was buying new clothes, too, and sometimes she talked about eating at nice restaurants.'

'It could have been with one of the other doctors.' Barin turned to look at Chall. 'A colleague.'

'Perhaps,' Mina said.

'Did she ever mention a name?' Kitson asked. 'Just in passing, maybe?'

Mina shook her head, then turned as her husband stood up suddenly and walked across to the cupboard near the television. He picked up one of the photographs, wiped the frame with his sleeve and put it down again.

'Bloody photographs,' he said. 'We should have more than photographs.'

Several times, in similar situations, Kitson had trotted out something about happy memories, but, seeing the look on Barin Fadel's face, she knew how trite and meaningless it would have sounded. It *was* ...

'I keep a few things upstairs,' Mina said, leaning towards Kitson. 'Old baby things mostly, but there is nothing of her.'

'We had to clean out her flat afterwards.' Her husband had picked up another photograph. He placed his hand across his chest and looked at Kitson and Chall. 'God forbid you should

142

ever have to do such a thing. Clothes to a charity shop, all her books.'

'I kept her medical books.' It was almost as if Mina was speaking to herself, then she looked up at her husband. 'And we gave her computer to Hassan, remember.'

Barin nodded, put the photo back. 'Leila's younger brother was about to go to university, so that was ... something.' He walked back down and sat on the arm of the sofa. 'He was never quite as bright as his sister.'

'That's not fair—'

He raised a hand to indicate that he had not finished. 'But give him his due, he did very well in his exams and Leeds is a very good university.' He looked at Chall. 'Don't you think?'

While Chall was nodding and saying something about what a great city Leeds was, Kitson was thinking about everything Leila Fadel's parents had said about their daughter. Looking at the newly polished photographs on top of the cupboard and wondering why there didn't seem to be a single one in which the young woman was smiling.

The same three words in her head that had sprung to mind when she had first walked into the Fadels' front room and seen them.

Smart. Overweight. Lonely.

'Annette liked to keep herself to herself,' Zoe said. 'Obviously there's nothing wrong with that, but it just meant some people thought she was a bit stand-offish. Weird, even. Remember, she was a few years older than the rest of us, so it's not really a surprise that we didn't have that much in common. Annette just didn't really fit in, I suppose. She didn't want to smoke weed or watch bands.' Zoe rolled her eyes. 'She didn't go out and get hammered every night.'

Thorne watched the girl, happy enough for her to talk but finding it hard to imagine that these were her favourite leisure activities either.

'It wasn't like she was secretive, or deliberately trying to be all mysterious. She didn't give much away, that's all. I mean, she might have been sitting there on her own in her flat every night working, but nobody ever knew what she got up to, not really.'

'Up to her,' Thorne said.

'Yeah, right ... but if there was a group of us together and Annette wasn't there, which she never really was, people would talk about her and start to suggest things she might be doing. Just having a laugh, you know. I bet she's doing this or that ... just banter. Watching animal porn or hanging around in the local graveyard. Stupid stuff, and I know it sounds horrible, because of what happened to her, but nobody really meant it like that. It wasn't what anyone actually thought.'

'What did you think?'

'You want me to tell you?'

'I asked, didn't I?'

Zoe's grin was wicked. 'I think she had a whole other side to her. I think she was secretly a bit of a nympho.' She thrust herself back in the chair and shook her head. 'Bloody hell, listen to me. What a stupid word. I sound like I'm writing headlines in the *Sun* or something. No ... I think she just really liked sex, and why the hell shouldn't she?'

'Right,' Thorne said.

'If you want to know what I think happened, I reckon Annette used to go out to clubs and bars and try to pull strange men. I think she picked them up, took them home and shagged their brains out ... and I think, *that* night, she just picked the wrong man. Maybe she could tell there was something off about him, or maybe he couldn't get it up, but either way he lost it and ... you know. He killed her, nicked a bunch of her stuff for good measure and that was it.' She folded her arms and sat back, pleased with herself. 'I mean, it's possible, isn't it? It's as good a theory as any, right?'

Since it was the first real theory of any kind he'd heard,

144

Thorne couldn't argue. He said, 'You ever thought about becoming a detective?'

The girl laughed. 'Sorry. I want to be an actress.'

'No worries,' Thorne said. 'That's a very good skill for a detective to have.'

Thorne was walking back to his car, wondering how much NCP were going to sting him for, when Tanner called.

'How did it go with your mechanic?' he asked. 'Did he sort your big end out?'

'We might have another victim,' Tanner said. 'A new one.'

Thorne stopped, listened.

'I set up an alert on the system for sudden deaths matching our key criteria, and one came in late this morning from a Thames Valley team in Amersham. A bit closer to home, this time. Victim's name is Alice Matthews and it looks like she was killed some time on Friday night.'

'Friday? So how come—'

'She only worked part time and wasn't in on Friday, so nobody missed her and the body wasn't discovered until yesterday morning.'

Thorne started walking again. The phone felt hot against his ear.

'Tom . . . ?'

'Sorry . . . I should be back in about ninety minutes.'

'Looks like he's started another workout.'

Thorne said something that was just noise coming out of his mouth. He picked up his pace and swerved to avoid a pushchair; reaching hard into his inside pocket for his wallet, digging out change for the stupid *fucking* machine.

Thinking: Nobody missed her.

TWENTY-FOUR

Tanner stood in her kitchen and watched Thorne spooning out the food he'd picked up from a Thai place on his way over: red prawn curry and stir-fried lamb; salt and pepper chicken wings. The smell was fantastic.

'I could have cooked something, you know.'

'Really?' Thorne said.

'I could have ... knocked something up.'

Thorne leaned away from the worktop and opened the fridge. He looked inside then closed the door again. 'Yeah, thought so.'

'Thought what?' Tanner stepped across huffily and looked inside the fridge herself, as though a sumptuous array of fine foods might suddenly have materialised.

'I remember after Susan died, you said something about living on cheese on toast. I guessed she did most of the cooking.'

'I'm better than I was.' Tanner closed the fridge door.

'Anyway, I'm starving and those ready-meals are never big enough.' He handed her the plates on a tray and opened the two cans of Tiger he'd brought along. 'And who's got any energy left to cook? The day we've had.'

They took the food through to the sitting room and after Tanner had gone back to the kitchen to collect paper towels, they began to eat.

'I never told you about my conversation with Kyle Mason,' Tanner said. 'I meant to fill you in, but with everything else . . .'

Thorne nodded. Once he had returned from Canterbury, the rest of his and everyone else's day had been taken up with the murder of Alice Matthews: combing through the material rushed across by the team from Thames Valley, sending officers to reinterview the victim's two sons and ex-husband, then bringing all those involved in Operation Felix up to speed.

Pinning another photograph to the whiteboard in the incident room.

The interviews with Leila Fadel's parents and Zoe McCausland had been written up and filed. Someone had finally managed to contact Patricia Somersby's sister in Florida, but as she and Patricia had not been in regular contact, the woman had not been able to tell them anything they did not already know.

'Pat disturbed a burglar,' the woman had said on the phone. 'Right? That's what they told me.'

The officer had told her that they were simply making further inquiries and had promised to keep her fully informed of developments.

'Anyway, nothing earth-shattering,' Tanner said. 'Mason made a couple of interesting comments, but hopefully I'll get a bit more out of Graham French.'

Thorne spooned food into his mouth.

'The barber.' Tanner waited. 'The one who was also in Pentonville with Andrew Evans. See if he can give us a lead on the Duchess.'

'Right.' The truth was that for a second Thorne had not been able to place the name, and he knew Tanner had seen it. The latest in what was almost certainly a series of murders now seemed to be taking up all his available headspace.

147

'I'll write up my meeting with Mason and you can look at it tomorrow.'

Thorne knew that Tanner would probably do it as soon as he'd left, along with detailed reports on the rest of her day's actions. Thorne would usually put that side of the job off until the last possible moment, like homework. He was not beyond dictating reports on to his iPhone, then bunging some super-keen trainee detective twenty quid to sit at a computer and type them up for him.

'Four victims in six months.' Tanner clearly had less of a problem than Thorne when it came to holding the details of two investigations in her head simultaneously. She pushed food around her plate. 'We're a long way past killing cats.'

'Yeah, I reckon so.' Thorne had already finished eating and sat back, cradling his beer. 'Not that I've got any idea where we are.'

'If it was easy, somebody would have caught him already.' Tanner put down her fork. She took Thorne's empty plate, slid it beneath her own, then laid both on the tray which she placed out of harm's way on the low table in front of the sofa. He watched as she balled up the used pieces of kitchen towel then leaned across to drop them on to the tray, too.

Thorne shook his head and used his fingers to list the victims Tanner had mentioned. 'A widow in her late fifties, a mature student in her twenties, a doctor . . . '

'Leila Fadel was thirty-one—'

'Right . . . and now a semi-retired grandmother.'

'All single.' Tanner looked at him. 'All living alone. We need to remember what they've got in common.'

'In Norwich, Bristol, Kent—'

'One forced entry, which was probably done afterwards to make it look like a burglary; in all the other cases the victims let him in, or he was able to *get* in.'

'Or they knew him,' Thorne said.

Now Tanner sat back, too, though she looked rather less at

home with a can of beer in her hand than Thorne did. 'It's the same as when I do jigsaws.'

'What is?'

'You remember I like jigsaws?'

Thorne nodded. He had bought one and left it by Tanner's bed when she was in hospital the year before. '"Order out of chaos". Yeah, I remember you saying something like that, but you were off your tits on morphine at the time.'

'That's exactly what it is ... but, if you're only looking at the individual pieces, you're never going to get anywhere. It's just a mess. Yes, you might put some of them together, but all the time you're trying to do that you need to keep looking over at the picture on the box, reminding yourself what that is. That's the really important thing. Everyone always says there's nothing worse than a jigsaw with a single piece missing, but a jigsaw that's *really* useless is one that doesn't come in a box. One that hasn't got a picture.' She looked at him, as though the answer to the question she was about to ask was obvious. 'So, what's our picture?'

Thorne raised his can as though he were toasting something. 'Well, personally, I'm seeing a lovely picture of this bastard in the dock at the Old Bailey.'

'Now, I mean.'

'Or maybe getting shanked in prison, if we're really lucky.'

'It's a man who's trying very hard not to get caught,' Tanner said. 'Simple as that. I mean, some of them want to, don't they, deep down? That's probably what your Dr Perera would say.'

'Since when was she *my* Dr Perera?'

Tanner smiled and picked up a crumb of something from the settee. 'But we're looking for someone who does what he does because he's driven by ... well, who knows what ... but is still smart enough to take whatever steps necessary to ensure he can carry on doing it.'

'The geography,' Thorne said. 'The travelling around.'

'That's part of it.'

'And the things he takes.'

'Right.' Tanner turned to face him. 'These aren't . . . keepsakes for him to look at and stroke when he gets home. When a killer like this takes souvenirs, he takes locks of hair or items of clothing, small things that were precious to the victim. He doesn't take phones and laptop computers.'

Thorne nodded. 'He's trying to get rid of evidence. Texts or emails, whatever. He wants to destroy anything that would show us how he knew his victims.'

'That's certainly the picture I'm seeing,' Tanner said.

They sat in silence for a few minutes after that, and Thorne tried not to make it obvious that he was looking around the room; comparing it with the one he'd sat in once before. The furniture, though obviously new, looked much the same as that which had been destroyed in the fire, and Thorne was pleased to see that the arrangement of prints had been salvaged. There were only a few books on the shelves next to the fireplace, so it was too early to tell if they would end up colour-coded, as the previous ones had been.

Thorne smiled and shifted forward on the sofa. He said, 'Well then . . .'

Tanner got to her feet.

'I think I left my jacket in the kitchen.'

'I hung it up,' Tanner said.

'Course you did.'

TWENTY-FIVE

When Thorne got back to the flat, Helen was sitting in front of a TV show she didn't appear to be watching. Some men on an island, shouting at each other. Next to her, Alfie was stretched out on the sofa in his vest and pants, a flannel across his forehead.

'He's got a temperature,' Helen said. 'Not high enough for the doctor to get off her backside and come out, of course.'

'You want to take him to A and E?'

Helen shook her head. 'Calpol and a cold flannel should do it.' She leaned over and eased the thermometer into her son's ear. He moaned softly. 'All right, chicken . . .'

Thorne slipped off his jacket and moved across to perch on the arm of the sofa. 'How you feeling, Trouble?'

Alfie pushed out his bottom lip, clearly feeling sorry for himself, and turned away as soon as Helen had removed the thermometer.

'It's gone down a bit,' she said.

'Think he'll be all right for nursery tomorrow?'

'Well, if he isn't, I'll just have to call Jenny. I mean, I'd rather not.'

'Why?'

'I spoke to her on the phone earlier. We had words.'

Thorne got up and walked across to flick the kettle on. 'Not like you.'

'Yeah, well, she was getting on my tits, and I didn't know I might need her for this, did I?'

Thorne held up a mug, but Helen shook her head. 'About me, I suppose.'

'What?'

'The row with your sister.'

'Not everything's about you, you know.'

'Fair enough.' He moved to the fridge and opened the door. A last beer before bed was tempting, especially as it looked as though it might be a while before that happened. He took the milk out.

'Your name was mentioned, obviously.'

Thorne turned back towards the worktop, so that Helen wouldn't see him smile.

'I spoke to Phil as well.'

'How did that go?'

'We're friends again. I mean it wasn't like we *weren't* friends, but . . .'

Thorne mashed his teabag. 'So, which one of you said sorry first?'

'Does it matter?'

'I suppose not.' Thorne knew who his money would be on. Nobody knew better than he did how stubborn Hendricks could be when he felt like it, but Helen was in a different league. He carried his tea back to the sofa and squeezed in next to her.

'He more or less admitted I was right.' Helen was trying not to look too pleased with herself. 'Said that he was just being difficult.'

'I told you, didn't I?'

Alfie began to grizzle and Helen reached to stroke his arm

and straighten the flannel. 'He said the main reason he didn't think drugs should be legal was that taking them wouldn't be as much fun.'

'How can someone so smart be such an idiot?'

'I know.'

'I don't think Andrew Evans would think they were a lot of fun.' Thorne slurped his tea. Now, on television, some actor he vaguely recognised was steering a narrowboat through the countryside. 'Or Adnan Jandali's kids.'

'How's that going?'

'Yeah ... Tanner's working it, but she might need to do it on her own for a bit.' He told her about Alice Matthews; a case that had begun just over a week earlier with a few terrible jokes about cats and was now a full-on serial murder inquiry.

'You should get some sleep,' Helen said.

'No, I'll wait up with you.'

'Don't be stupid.'

'You go and I'll stay up with Alfie for a bit. There's probably some football on—'

'Go to bed.'

Thorne nodded, happy to have offered, but happier still that Helen was not to be argued with. 'Not sure I'll sleep much anyway.' He was still thinking about everything he and Tanner had talked about. A killer who was determined to stay one step ahead of them; the new picture and the briefing he would need to give the team first thing the next morning. He reached down for the bottle of Calpol on the floor and examined it. 'This stuff knock you out a bit, does it?'

'Not sure,' Helen said. 'It's just liquid paracetamol, I think.'

Thorne took the lid off and sniffed. 'I wonder what it's like in tea.'

TWENTY-SIX

There were a number of people moving at the edges of the incident room, going about their business, working different cases, while others – civilian staff for the most part – lingered and listened in, yet to become inured to this peculiar and perverse kind of excitement, because gatherings like this one were, thankfully, few and far between.

As was the kind of killer they were gathered to talk about.

Thorne stood, ready to address the dozen or so detectives assembled around the desks closest to him. The core members of the team. For many, this would be the biggest case they had worked, perhaps would ever work, and if Thorne could not quite taste the adrenalin or smell what was coming off those who lived in fear of dropping the ball, he could hear it.

In pencils tapped against the edges of desks. In cleared throats and in hands wiped against stubble.

'This operation is now focused on an individual who we strongly suspect has killed at least three times in the past seven months, and you all have details of those offences.' Thorne watched as pages were turned, waited for the rustle of paper to die down. 'But moving forward, we're going to focus all our attention on his latest victim. Alice Matthews, aged fifty-four, was murdered four days ago. She was strangled at her home in Amersham.' Though there was a picture of Alice Matthews contained in every officer's briefing notes, Thorne was aware that most of them had now looked up from their pages and were staring past him to the glossy ten by eight on the whiteboard behind him.

He turned to look at the picture himself.

A photograph taken by one of Alice Matthews's grown-up sons; a party to celebrate the christening of her first grandchild.

'Most investigations need a bit of luck.' Thorne stayed looking at the photograph, his back to his team. 'They need a break. We've been lucky . . . this is ours, because now we've got a fresh case to work, new leads, new evidence.' He turned round, saw all eyes on him. 'But Alice Matthews wasn't lucky, and neither were the people who care about her. Alice's eighty-three-year-old mother, all her friends and her two kids . . . shit out of luck. Her granddaughter certainly didn't get lucky, because now she doesn't get to grow up knowing her grandma.'

He stopped, nodded towards one of the newer members of the team who was scribbling in his notebook. 'Yeah, write that down,' he said. 'Tell yourselves first thing every morning. Tattoo it on your arses if you have to, but remember it. Because these are the people we're doing this for, and if we all do our jobs properly this is the moment when the man we're after runs out of luck too.' He let what he'd said sink in for a few seconds, then moved across to lean against a desk.

'Right.' Yvonne Kitson stood up. 'We're working on the assumption that our killer had made contact with Alice Matthews before the night she was killed, so we need to find out how.'

Had Nicola Tanner not been out chasing leads on the Evans/Jandali case, Thorne would have handed the briefing over to her, but he was happy enough to leave the nuts and bolts to someone

155

with whom most of the team were already familiar. In truth, Tanner's absence at this point had its advantages. She was more than capable of cracking the whip, but it was often more effective if those on the receiving end had an established rapport with the person dishing it out. Aside from Dipak Chall and a couple of officers who'd been drafted in from Kentish Town, Kitson had worked with everyone in the room for several years.

'Our suspect appears to have taken Alice's phone and computer,' Kitson said. 'Same as with his earlier victims, and we think he does that because they would make it very clear how the contact was made. He's not nicking those things on the spur of the moment, so what's he trying to cover up?'

A hand was raised. 'Emails? Texts?'

'That's what we're thinking. So we need to talk to Alice's mobile provider, see what we can access.' She nodded at the predictable groans from those who had trodden this tedious path before. Endless paperwork, a time-consuming and expensive set of protocols. 'I know, a nightmare, and by the time we get anything out of them we'll probably all be picking up our pensions, but let's get the process started.'

A female DS at the front said, 'What about social media?'

'That, too,' Kitson said. 'Alice's ex-husband told the local team that she had a Facebook account, so that's looking like a real possibility. Facebook and Google are going to be even harder nuts to crack, but we need to get on it.'

'All the victims were single,' Chall said. 'So maybe we should be checking dating apps. Tinder or whatever.'

The officer sitting behind Chall dropped a hand on his shoulder. 'Know all about that do you, Dipak?'

A voice from the back. 'Grindr, maybe.'

Kitson nodded through the laughter. 'Absolutely, but it's not going to be easy without any access to search history. We do have one possibility as far as that goes, though.'

Chall turned to face the others. 'Not all the victims' computers

156

were taken. Leila Fadel's parents told us that they passed hers on to her brother.'

'Took it with him to university,' Kitson said.

'Why didn't the killer take that one?' the woman at the front asked.

'No idea,' Thorne said. 'Let's hope he messed up. Maybe it was hidden somewhere and he was in a hurry, but in any case, we need to get hold of the brother and get that computer back as quickly as possible.'

There was more nodding and scribbling, an outbreak of chatter.

Kitson raised her voice above it. 'So, while some of you are working with all that, we need to trace Alice's movements on the night she was killed. We're presuming that she'd been out for the evening, that she may well have been meeting her killer, so where did she go? How did she get there? Obviously we need to be looking at CCTV; the Thames Valley team have made a start on that, so you'll need to liaise with them.'

'There was alcohol in Alice's blood,' Thorne said. 'So chances are she didn't drive, but check ANPR just in case, then talk to all the local cab firms.'

Kitson glanced down at her notes. 'The PM also identified what looked like semi-digested pasta in her stomach, so we need to get her picture to every restaurant in and around Amersham that serves Italian food. Again, you'll need to work with local uniform to get this done quickly, but we need to find out where she went and who she was meeting.'

'Got to have been a date.' The officer behind Chall sat back and nodded knowingly. 'Always Italian, isn't it? More romantic.'

The woman at the front turned to chip in. 'I can't stand Italian. Give me a Nando's any day.'

'That's what I call a cheap date,' someone said.

The woman laughed. 'Yeah, I'm anyone's for a bit of spicy chicken.'

Thorne turned to look at the photograph again. He wondered if the man Alice Matthews went to meet had seen that smile. If he had showed her a smile in return, the dark fantasies taking shape behind it.

Kitson said, 'Right, can you divvy that lot up, Sam?'

While DS Samir Karim stood up and began allocating actions, Thorne and Kitson moved across to join DCI Russell Brigstocke, who had been listening from the far corner. They followed him out into the corridor.

'Good stuff in there, Tom,' Brigstocke said. 'That business about being lucky. Got them nicely fired up.'

'Haven't seen *you* that fired up for a long time,' Kitson said.

Thorne grunted in thanks or acknowledgement, he wasn't sure which. The truth was, he was feeling somewhat grubby and useless suddenly; a little afraid of being found out. He knew he'd made a good job of rallying the troops but, though he'd meant everything he'd said in the incident room, they were just words. These days, he found it hard to distinguish genuine passion from that which was simply . . . appropriate. Expected. He had not known Alice Matthews, had not seen the pain on the faces of those who had loved her. He could not even come close to imagining it, not really. It was his job to catch the man who had caused that pain, so he would do whatever was necessary, but being fired up, making sure everyone else was fired up, did not stop him feeling a little like a fraud.

He said, 'We're going to need a lot more luck.'

TWENTY-SEVEN

Sandwiched between a bank and a bookmakers, French's Hair & Beauty was set back from the High Road in a row of shops and takeaways opposite Wembley Central station. Looking in through the plate-glass windows, Tanner could see that the place was busy, and she was a little surprised, having clocked the prices on a menu of available treatments on the door. She wondered how many of the customers had needed to visit one or other of the businesses on either side before venturing in.

A short-term loan to get your roots seen to. A fiver on something in the three o'clock at Kempton Park, which might pay for a bikini wax, if you were lucky and had decent odds.

Tanner was greeted warmly by a receptionist when she entered and shown to a seating area. There was a selection of newspapers available on a wicker table, but before she'd had a chance to take in the headlines a young woman wearing a branded polo shirt was standing in front of her brandishing a list of hot drinks.

Tanner said, 'I'm fine.'

'They're complimentary,' the girl said.

'I should hope so.' Tanner took out her warrant card and said, 'I'm here to have a word with Mr French.'

The girl nodded, as though this was the most exciting thing that had happened to her all day, which it quite probably was, then turned and hurried across the salon, headed for the man Tanner knew to be Graham French, because he was the only man in there.

He looked over at her, nodding as the girl leaned towards his ear.

She almost certainly needed to get close, Tanner thought, to make herself heard above the noise. The hubbub of chat between stylists and their clients and the soft whine of hairdryers might almost have been soporific, were it not all but drowned out by MTV, playing simultaneously on three wall-mounted screens. She watched a girl walking from her workstation to the reception desk, moving in time to the music. Tinchy Tempah or Teeny Rascal or Dizzee Lizzee, whoever it was.

Tanner remembered a joke she'd heard somewhere . . .

So, how would you like your hair cut?

In complete silence, please.

Graham French was tall and thin; fiftyish, with gleaming teeth which Tanner guessed were false and a predictably luxuriant head of hair. It was bouffant and bouncy, suspiciously dark brown, but then Tanner had yet to meet a hairdresser with hair she approved of. She thought that bald men were probably the most reliable, pouring all their skill and dedication into something they didn't have and could only remember fondly.

He sat down next to her and spoke quietly: a thin, Midlands accent. The arm thrown casually across the back of his chair and the attempt at a smile could not quite mask the nervousness at speaking to a police officer that was hard-wired into most ex-cons. 'What can I do for you?'

Equally quietly, Tanner told him.

'Would it be all right if we went into the office? Well, I say office . . .'

'That's fine,' Tanner said.

She stood and followed him behind the reception desk and along a corridor lined with boxes of conditioner and hair-wax into a small room where a desk, a computer and a pair of tatty chairs took up almost all the available space.

French sat down. 'Most of the people here know I was in prison,' he said. 'It's never been a problem, because people understand that you make mistakes. Didn't lose a single regular, matter of fact, and I'm perfectly happy to talk about it, you know, if anyone asks.' He leaned over and pushed the door shut. 'Still, no point broadcasting it, is there?'

'Might have been trickier if you worked in a bank,' Tanner said.

'Yeah . . . fair point.'

French had done the best part of two years in Maidstone and then Pentonville, for fraud. Tanner had not checked the details, but credit fraud was her best guess. Or perhaps he had tried to get one over on the Inland Revenue, though for a sentence that long, it needed to have been a serious amount of money.

Tanner took her notebook from her bag and nodded back towards the salon. 'Swanky place.'

'Cheers.' French looked genuinely pleased. 'We really try to create a nice atmosphere, you know? Somewhere you can come and be spoiled, but not poncy.'

'Poncy prices, though.'

He smiled. Definitely false teeth, Tanner decided.

'Well, you have to make the business work and the rent on the place is silly money. My sister's the brains behind it all, does most of the hard graft.' He spread his arms wide. 'I'm just a scissors merchant who tries to keep my ladies entertained.' He dropped his arms. 'No, seriously though, she was the one who kept the salon up and running while I was away. Gave me something to come out to.'

'You need that,' Tanner said.

'Bang on. Most of the blokes I knew in there had nothing once they'd done their stretch. Just a few months catching up on the beer and getting their ends away, then doing something daft and coming straight back.'

'Andrew Evans told me you used to cut hair inside.'

French nodded. 'Oh yeah, I kept my hand in. Not like that was usually anything fancy, mind you, because most of the boys just wanted a number one, but now and again one of the black lads wanted stuff cut into the sides, gang symbols or whatever. Good way to make a bit of money as well . . . a few quid extra to spend on Canteen, which is always a result. Phone credit, chocolate or whatever. I mean, my sister sent a bit of money in, but it was hard enough for her running this place on her own. So . . . '

'Chocolate and phone credit?'

'Yeah, or fruit, you know. Writing paper, sometimes.'

'Very good,' Tanner said. 'But I'm guessing some of the extra money came in handy for buying your Spice.'

He sat back and nodded, a wry smile acknowledging that the chit-chat was over. 'Well, yeah, obviously. It meant that most of the time I could pay for the stuff straight off and not have to get it on tick like some of the other lads. I mean I know how pear-shaped that can go when you get out.' He leaned forward. 'That what happened to Andy, is it?'

'I can't go into details,' Tanner said.

'Got in over his head, did he?'

'Like I said.'

French shrugged. 'These people are your best friends when you're banged up,' he said. 'Sending in whatever you need. But you really don't want to get on the wrong side of them. It's hard enough getting off that shit.'

'Tell me about the Duchess,' Tanner said.

'Her?' He laughed. 'Well, piece of work *she* was.'

Tanner waited.

'She was . . . I was going to say *pleasant*, you know? Very friendly, liked to natter. But the truth is we were always pleased to see her, and she had a part to play, so who knows what sort of person she actually was.' He ran a finger down one of his sideburns. 'I cut her hair once, just after I came out, and I remember her saying she was married to a prison guard once upon a time. Don't know if that helps. Probably how she found out the way everything worked inside, don't you reckon? Inside information, literally.'

'Don't suppose she mentioned her ex-husband's name?'

'Well, if she did I've forgotten it,' French said. 'Sorry.'

'No worries,' Tanner said. A nice solid lead had probably been too much to hope for.

'She was always businesslike, I can tell you that. Good at what she did.'

'I spoke to a man called Kyle Mason,' Tanner said.

French nodded. 'I cut *his* hair plenty of times.'

'He seemed to think she might have had a connection to somewhere by the sea. Something she said.'

'Yeah?' French stared up at the ceiling tiles and thought about it. 'That rings a bell, I think, but I can't remember her saying anything specific.'

'You're sure she never mentioned a place?'

He shook his head. 'She usually had a bit of a tan though, come to think of it, like she got a bit more sun than most people. Yeah, maybe she's got a place on the coast.'

'That's what I'm trying to find out,' Tanner said. 'I could do with narrowing it down a bit.'

'I mean it definitely wasn't spray-tan, because we do that here and I know what it looks like.' He lowered his voice. 'Like you've been dipped in gravy. I don't put that in the brochure, obviously.'

'Is there anything else you can think of? Anything she might have let slip about her family or friends?'

'She had a kid. She definitely mentioned that.'

'That's what Kyle Mason thought.'

'A daughter, I think.'

Tanner wrote that down. Aside from the tip about the ex-husband, it was the only thing she had written down.

'I can tell you this,' French said. 'She was always very ... smooth, you know? Nothing rattled her. The trick with getting gear off her was always to hide what she gave you straight away. She could get it to you easy as you like ... in a flash, you know, but you had to get rid of it just as fast. You couldn't just hang on to it, stick it up your sleeve or whatever, because you'd be searched on your way out of the visiting hall, so you needed to put it where they wouldn't find it. I don't have to tell you where, right?'

Tanner shook her head.

'Well, she always found some way to give you the time to do that. I mean it only takes a few seconds, because you get good at it ... your hand straight down the back of your sweatpants, like ... ' He reached behind him, mimed a well-practised move. 'But she'd know exactly when you needed to do it, could give you the signal. She had her eyes on the screws all the time and always knew what the cameras were doing. *If* they were working.' He shook his head. 'Yeah, the Duchess was a one-off.'

Tanner put her notebook away. She didn't know if anything French had told her would prove ultimately to be of any use, and was wondering if this had been worth missing Thorne's briefing on Operation Felix for. When she looked up again, French was studying her.

'You fancy popping back one day, I'll do something with your hair.'

Tanner looked at him.

'Don't get me wrong, it's nice. They did a decent job. But I can do a better one.'

'I don't think I could afford it.'

French smiled. 'Mates' rates.'

'Against the rules,' Tanner said.

'Well, have a think about it,' French said. 'I promise you won't be disappointed. The coffee's good, too.'

Tanner stood up. 'Do you provide earplugs?'

TWENTY-EIGHT

For the second time that day, Thorne outlined the ongoing investigation into the murder of Alice Matthews and the hunt for her killer's three previous victims, though it was done somewhat less theatrically than it had been in the incident room at Becke House a couple of hours before. It was certainly not his job to gee up Detective Superintendent Simon Fulton, but looking at him, Thorne decided that would probably have been no easy task anyway. He could have walked into the man's office with a posse of motivational speakers and a horse trough full of cocaine, and might still have struggled.

Fulton listened, tapped out a few notes on his iPad, then sat back.

'It's very impressive, the way DI Tanner put all this together.'

'Yeah, she did a great job,' Thorne said.

Fulton nodded, hummed. 'Or perhaps some of the officers working these cases originally did a poor one.'

'Not for me to say.'

'No?'

'Easy to be critical with hindsight, isn't it?'

'The fact is, if any one of them had put in the extra work Tanner did and seen what she did, we might have a couple less dead women on our hands. A lot fewer dead cats.'

There was perhaps a grain of truth in what Fulton was saying, Thorne knew that, but some people were simply better at their job than others and he had seen nothing to suggest negligence. He knew how easily mistakes got made, because he had made plenty himself, and it was always nice and easy to point the finger at the failure of others. It was why there were so many high-flyers, like Fulton, for whom finding someone to blame was a default position.

'I think the truth is, this individual's been very good at hiding the connections,' Thorne said. 'Up to now, at least.'

'Fair enough.' Fulton shrugged as though the matter was closed, but Thorne knew it wasn't. If the investigation was successful, he guessed that the DS would happily acknowledge his own part, marginal as it was, in putting a dangerous killer away, then try to earn a few brownie points by looking to expose and punish those who might have done so earlier.

Justice done, a career or two screwed, and one rung higher up the ladder.

A good day's work at the office.

'Sounds like you've got everything covered with Alice Matthews,' Fulton said. He swiped at the screen of his iPad. 'Thames Valley uniform fully on board?'

'Sir.'

'Good. I'll put in a word with the Deputy Commissioner. See if we can speed things up a bit with the mobile phone provider and the social media platforms.'

'That would be useful,' Thorne said.

Fulton closed the cover on his tablet. 'I'm grateful that you took the time to come down and fill me in.'

While a whiny voice inside Thorne's head was screaming *Brigstocke made me do it,* he said, 'We're all after the same individual, so why wouldn't I?'

166

'Absolutely,' Fulton said. 'It's professional courtesy.'

'Right.'

'But not everyone would have taken the trouble. It's appreciated.'

Fulton's very white teeth were briefly on display, but something on his face suggested he knew perfectly well that the man smiling back at him had had his arm twisted. One dip into the DI's voluminous file at the Directorate of Professional Standards would have made it perfectly clear where he stood on such matters.

Tom Thorne probably thought *courtesy* was something women did when they met the Queen.

On a staircase above the yard at the back of Kentish Town station, Thorne stood staring down at the lines of patrol cars and a few ordinary-looking saloons that could chase down a Porsche if need be, sucking in breaths like a man in need of fresh air, while happily taking in the smoke from Christine Treasure's cigarette.

'It's not compulsory,' Treasure said. 'You don't *have* to dislike anyone with more pips than you.' She took a drag. 'I mean you're senior to me and I only think you're a *bit* of a twat.'

'It's not about rank.'

'Course it is.'

'He's slimy,' Thorne said.

'Yeah, well, you get covered in it, don't you? Climbing up the greasy pole.'

'It suits some people better than others.'

A PC who'd been smoking below them came trudging back up the stairs. He stopped to speak briefly to Treasure who was all business suddenly, talking him through the fall-out from a domestic disturbance he'd been called out to the night before. As the PC walked away, she turned back to Thorne and said, 'I mean, I'm no fan of the greasy pole.' She waggled her eyebrows like a cut-price Groucho Marx. 'I'm talking sexually, of course, though I do have a few replicas in the bedside table.'

'Shame,' Thorne said. 'I was hoping there might be a dildo or two on the wedding list.'

'No, mate, that's all covered. What we really need is crockery.'

Thorne's mobile pinged and he took it out to see that there was a message from Tanner.

'Your bride-to-be does know you're not a virgin, right?'

Treasure coughed and spluttered out a laugh.

Thorne opened the text:

Spoke to Graham French. Will fill you in later.
How did briefing go?

'My other half's been around the block,' Treasure said, grinning. 'Put it this way, I think between us we've had more pussies than an animal shelter.' She nodded towards his phone. 'Anything important?'

Thorne shook his head and slipped the phone back into his pocket, smiling at what might happen were Christine Treasure and Nicola Tanner ever to come face to face. Yes, they had one thing in common, but aside from the fact that the people they chose to sleep with did not have penises, greasy or otherwise, he could not imagine two people less likely to hit it off. Treasure would surely dismiss Tanner as Job-pissed, while Tanner would think that the sergeant's ... up-front declarations about her sexual antics were distasteful. Tanner thought Phil Hendricks's attitude to his sexuality was a bit 'showy', so Thorne's mind boggled to think of what she'd make of Christine Treasure.

Treasure took a final drag and flicked her fag-end down into the yard. She said, 'Talking of pussies ...'

Thorne told her what he'd told Fulton: the headlines.

'Well, if you need a few more bodies,' Treasure said. 'I mean, the right sort, obviously, happy to pitch in.'

'Thanks.'

'I'm sure Uncle Fester would OK it.'

'I might take you up on that,' Thorne said. 'Could do with all the help I can get.'

'Nah.' Treasure punched him on the arm. 'You'll catch this one.'

Thorne nodded, closed his eyes for a few seconds.

'That's why you can't stand the likes of Fulton,' Treasure said. 'Because you think they don't give a toss. You're wrong a lot of the time, by the way, but you always think they don't care and you do.'

'I'm not sure I do,' Thorne said.

'What?'

'Give a toss.' He turned to look at her. 'You should have heard me this morning. Saying exactly what needed to be said . . . pain and loss and holes in people's lives, you know? They ate it up. But I'm not sure I could put my hand on my heart and tell you I meant it.'

'Bollocks,' Treasure said.

Thorne shook his head. 'I wonder why that career as a therapist never worked out?'

'It's a defence mechanism, that's all. You're worried you might not get this bloke, and that's fair enough. I mean, you might not, so telling yourself you don't actually care one way or the other is going to make that a bit easier. Maybe you won't lie awake half the night, afterwards.' She laughed, softly. 'Don't give a toss? I've worked with you, mate, remember.'

'How could I forget?'

She leaned into him. 'You can try and fool yourself, if you fancy it, but you don't fool me.'

'You're wasted in uniform,' Thorne said.

'Yeah, you might be right.' Treasure adjusted her utility belt, straightened her stab vest. 'I'd like to hang on to it, though.' She waggled her eyebrows again. 'You know, just for the bedroom.'

TWENTY-NINE

'Is Andy OK?' Paula Evans drew deeply on an e-cigarette that looked like something out of *Doctor Who*. She puffed out a huge cloud of smoke and sat forward on the leather armchair. 'I deserve to know that much, at least.'

'I wish I could tell you more,' Tanner said.

'You haven't told me anything.'

'Yeah. He's OK.'

The woman nodded and sat back. She was short and slight, with old-fashioned NHS-style glasses and brown hair gathered into a scrunchie. She said, 'Something, I suppose.'

There were toys littering the floor in the living room, which Tanner would have cleared away, and washing up waiting to be done in the kitchen she had glimpsed on the way in. But not everyone lived the same way she did, and more to the point, she was not a woman who had watched her husband bundled into the back of a police car almost a week before and was now coping single-handedly with a three-year-old.

'He thought I didn't know,' Paula said. 'About the drugs. I mean, I presume it's got something to do with the drugs . . . the reason you've got him and he hasn't been in touch since that first night.'

Tanner said nothing.

'I'm not stupid, mind you.' Another chug on her vape. 'I know you don't keep someone that long because they've got a Spice habit, so there's obviously something else going on.'

'I know you're not stupid,' Tanner said.

'Good ... and you know that the fact you're not telling me anything makes the whole thing a damn sight scarier?'

'I'm sorry.'

Smoke hissed through Paula's teeth. 'Just doing your job, right?'

Tanner managed a weak smile, then looked around. Having spent only three months as a free man between Pentonville prison and a very different sort of confinement at Long Barrow Manor, it was easy to understand just how much Andrew Evans would be missing this place. Yes, it was chaotic and, Tanner guessed, fraught at times, but sitting there, she could feel the warmth of home; recognised it as something she had not felt herself since Susan had died. The comforting warmth of familiar things and of the people desperate for a loved one to return to them. There was a wife waiting who loved Andrew Evans dearly, and there was his son.

'Where's Sean?' Tanner asked.

'Nursery.' Paula nodded. 'First day he's been since you lot took Andy away. He's upset, you know ... missing his dad. I'm upset too, tearing my bloody hair out, but I've been trying not to show it when Sean's around, because he picks up on all that stuff.'

'Course.'

'See, last time his dad disappeared he didn't come back for eighteen months. Sean was only two then, but I know he remembers.' She shook her head violently, as though trying to dislodge something, then looked at Tanner. 'You got kids?'

'No.'

'Right ...'

Tanner saw the woman glance across at her left hand, though she was unsure what information could usefully be gleaned these days from the absence of a wedding ring.

'You're better off,' Paula said.

Tanner managed the wry smile she guessed was expected, though she knew Paula Evans was not being honest. It was the kind of thing harassed parents often said, but it was rarely meant. Most of the time they actually felt sorry that you were missing out or, worse, that there must be something wrong with you, with your choice.

Whether you had made one or not.

The truth was that, a few years before, she and Susan *had* talked about having children, but it hadn't gone much further than that. A few leaflets on adoption, an hour online looking at sperm banks. One of Tanner's brothers had jokily suggested that he could be a donor, but Tanner hadn't much liked the idea of raising a son or daughter that would also be a nephew or niece. Susan said there was a fellow teacher who might be keen. Eventually, they had dropped it, the same way the idea of getting married had blossomed quickly then come to nothing. A few over-excited evenings; domestic fantasies, which grew more improbable as Susan got further into the wine.

In the end, they had decided they liked things as they were.

'Why fix it if it isn't broken?' Tanner said.

Paula looked at her.

'Not having kids.'

Why fix it ... ?

It was more or less exactly what she and Susan had said to each other and suddenly Tanner found herself imagining what things would be like if she and Susan had made the leap. She would be where Paula Evans was now, bringing up a child on her own. No, worse than that, because in her case the absent parent would never be coming home and doing her job would have been next to impossible.

'Yeah, well, it's a bit late for me.'

'Sorry?'

Paula reached down to pat what looked like an extremely flat stomach and let out a theatrical sigh. She held out her futuristic-looking vape. 'I should be coming off this, really.'

Tanner said, 'Oh.'

'Yeah.' Paula took another good-sized hit on the e-cig she was about to give up. 'Oh.'

'Your husband didn't mention it.'

'That's because he doesn't know.'

'OK ...' For a few seconds, Tanner toyed with saying 'congratulations', but decided it might be tactless, or even wholly unwelcome.

'I didn't want to tell him when he was still so messed up.' She closed her eyes for a few seconds. 'I wish I'd told him that first night when he called from the police station.'

Tanner leaned forward. 'Would you like me to ... ?'

Paula shook her head.

'I think he could do with some good news.'

'I'll tell him myself. When I get the chance.'

Tanner nodded and sat back again. 'When's it due?'

'Not until November. I'm only two months gone.' She swallowed. 'He'll be back by then, right? Andy?'

Tanner looked away, but only for a few seconds. 'Listen, I know I've not told you very much, and that's because I really can't, but if it's any help, I can tell you Andy's getting clean. He's coming off the Spice.'

'Really?'

'And I *will* tell you he's helping us. I can't say any more than that, but I promise you he's doing something important. OK?'

Paula nodded and puffed out a series of short breaths. 'I'm probably pushing my luck, but I don't suppose you can tell me where he is? You know, just roughly.'

'I can't do that.'

'Is he in London? The outer Hebrides?'

'I've told you as much as I'm allowed,' Tanner said. 'More than I'm allowed.'

Paula shrugged, as though Tanner's response was the one she'd been expecting. There was a low rumble as a train went past somewhere nearby, and when it had begun to fade, she said, 'I'm not surprised ... you saying he's doing something good, because that's actually the sort of bloke Andy is.' There was a small grunt of laughter and suddenly there were tears in her eyes. 'What happened to that kid just destroyed him, you know? He was never really the same afterwards, like it just kicked all the joy out of him. So he went inside and he did his time because he knew he had to, but I didn't get the same Andy back. It was partly that stupid drug, I know that, but sometimes ... even now, when he's looking at me, I know that he's seeing that little lad. That split second when he looks up from his phone and sees the bike and knows there's nothing he can do ...

'Whatever he's been up to since he came out, I know that's down to the drugs, but take those away and he's a decent bloke. Yeah, he's an idiot and he's a bloody big kid and sometimes I want to slap him silly, but at the end of the day, he's basically good. He's a good ... soul.'

'I know,' Tanner said. 'I know he's been through a lot.'

Paula sniffed and smiled, reached across for a box of tissues on the cabinet next to her chair. 'He's strong as well, mind you. Whatever's going on, I know he'll come out the other side.'

'Look ... there might be a way you can tell him yourself.' Tanner remembered what she said to Andrew Evans the last time she'd spoken to him. 'About the baby.'

Paula waited. Her eyes widened and she curled her fingers through a few loose strands of hair. She looked like a teenager.

'I can't make any promises, though.'

Five minutes later, Tanner walked to the end of the Evans's path then turned to look back at the house. Two storeys in a well-kept terrace in Bounds Green. Not Hampstead or Highgate, not by a long way, but nice enough; a park nearby and decent schools. Andrew Evans had told her that Paula did some part-time work as a book-keeper, but even so, Tanner wondered how she would manage to keep up the mortgage payments.

She lifted her bag a little higher on her shoulder.

Even if Tanner had been in a position to tell Paula Evans everything, to assure her that her husband would be back to see his second child born, it would not all necessarily have been good news. She would still have been unable to promise that, when all this was over, he would be spared a return to prison. Yes, his help with their investigation would certainly be taken into account and the crimes he had committed had clearly been done under duress, but Andrew Evans had threatened a man with a gun and, ultimately, there were no guarantees of immunity. The law would run its course, and, naïve or not, Tanner clung to the belief that it would do so fairly, but she also decided, there and then, that when the time came she would do whatever she could to help his case.

She turned and walked towards her car.

She would bring Andrew Evans back to his family.

As Tanner's car turned the corner, the man who had been watching from the other side of the road put on his helmet, fired up his bike and roared away in the opposite direction.

THIRTY

Thorne was rapidly losing the will to live.

The estate agent led them into the kitchen. He held his arms out wide, as though it might miraculously increase the size of the room, and said, 'This is the kitchen.'

Thorne leaned close to Tanner and whispered, 'Thank God he's keeping us informed. That fridge and the dirty big cooker were confusing the hell out of me.'

Tanner shushed him.

'Seriously . . . if he says "wow factor" or talks about anything "ticking all the boxes", I might have to hurt him.'

'It's a pretty good size,' the estate agent said, 'and as you can see there's a very nice breakfast area, too.' He pointed to a table covered in a multicoloured plastic tablecloth. Thorne was grateful that he didn't bother telling them it was a table. 'Plenty of room for the two of you to sit and eat your toast or cornflakes or whatever . . . '

Thorne whispered again. 'Does he think we're a *couple*?'

'I don't know what he thinks,' Tanner said. 'But it's probably a fair assumption.' She looked down at the laminated sheet of property details she had picked up the day before. 'Anyway, what's so horrific about that?'

Thorne said nothing, followed Tanner as she wandered across to the window.

The estate agent strolled over to join them. He had thick glasses and a shock of dark hair, and though he was probably in his mid-twenties he looked younger, in a suit which was too big for him. The shiny tie was almost exactly the same shade of pink as his shaving rash. 'Yeah, not a bad view, is it?'

'It's a patio,' Thorne said. 'And a fence.'

'They've done a nice job with the borders though.' The man nodded and thrust his hands into his trouser pockets. 'Tall trees, so you won't be overlooked, and there's even room for a little shed, if that's your thing. Every man needs a shed, am I right?'

'I do need somewhere to keep my model trains,' Thorne said.

'Right.' The estate agent looked at him, as though unable to decide if Thorne was being serious.

'It's nice,' Tanner said.

The estate agent moved away again, presumably leaving them alone to continue drinking in the view. Thorne turned to see him aimlessly opening cupboards and running his fingertips across the worktops.

'You think it's nice?'

Thorne shrugged. 'I don't know.'

'Cheers, that's very helpful.'

'I told you, I'm rubbish at this.'

The two-bedroom ground floor flat was on a quiet street off the High Road in East Finchley. Driving over, Tanner had told him again that, once she had sold the house in Hammersmith, she could pay cash for a place like this and still have a good-sized nest egg left over. 'Maybe even enough for a little place in the country,' she had said.

'The *country*?'

'Just for weekends, you know.'

177

Thorne had shuddered theatrically.

Now, they continued staring out of the kitchen window. A black and white cat moved cautiously along the edge of the fence. It turned and spotted them and quickly jumped off again. Thorne pointed out the cat flap he'd noticed in the back door. 'That's one thing you wouldn't need to do.'

'Don't need one,' Tanner said. 'No way my cat's going outside again until we make an arrest.'

Thorne nodded, took another look around. 'Yeah, it's all right, I suppose.' He took out his phone and checked for messages. 'I don't really know what you're looking for.'

'Me neither,' Tanner said.

It was the end of the day and a new shift had taken over back at Becke House. A team with considerably more manpower than would normally be the case; chasing every lead and inputting every scrap of information that arrived in connection with the Alice Matthews investigation and the hunt for a man of whom she was just the latest in a list of victims.

The victims they knew about . . .

Patricia Somersby.

Annette Mangan.

Leila Fadel.

Not that Thorne or Tanner would ever be off the clock, not with a case like this one, and if neither of them mentioned it, it was only because they didn't have to. Each knew exactly where the other's mind was, that terrible landscape; knew that, in truth, there was precious little headspace available for well-appointed kitchens or mature treelines.

'Feel free to have a wander around on your own.'

They both turned, unaware that the estate agent had come back over to join them.

'You get more of a feel for a place without some idiot burbling at you, so I'll just lurk around in here.'

Without saying a word, Thorne and Tanner walked out into

178

the hallway like automatons and drifted into the smaller of the two bedrooms. The decor was clearly the choice of a teenage girl, but the clutter that might have been expected had been cleared away for the viewing. Cushions had been carefully arranged on the bed and the room smelled of lavender.

Thorne held his arms out. 'This is the bedroom.'

Tanner grunted, and half-smiled.

There were photographs on the window ledge and Thorne moved across to have a look. He picked up one of the photos, felt a little nosy examining it. He had heard about people who viewed properties almost every day with no intention of ever buying, but purely because they were driven by some prurient compulsion. Because, for whatever reason, they enjoyed the sneaky snapshot it gave them into other people's lives. Their tastes and habits, their domestic quirks. There were others he had heard about who went even further and made a habit of stealing something from each place they visited. Easily pocketable personal items that were unlikely to be missed. Thorne could only presume they got an extra kick from the trove of knick-knacks they amassed; the fragments of lives assembled into a voyeur's bizarre mosaic.

Pens, perfume, hairbrushes.

He looked down at the photograph again: the smiling husband and wife; the daughter who couldn't quite manage it. He put the photograph back.

'How did it go with Andrew Evans's wife?'

'Could have been better,' Tanner said. 'She's not in a good way.'

'What did you expect?'

'And she's pregnant.'

'They timed that well.'

'I was thinking ... if we take someone into protective custody—'

'It's not quite that.'

'No, but he's helping us with an investigation, isn't he?' Tanner sat on the edge of the bed. 'If we remove someone from their home, so that they can't earn money, is there some sort of fund we can use to help out the rest of the family? For mortgage payments, utilities, whatever.'

'I seriously doubt it,' Thorne said.

'I didn't think so.' Tanner looked at him. 'One more reason we need to find this woman fast. The Duchess . . . and the people who are employing her.'

Thorne slid back a wardrobe door, every bit as aimlessly as the estate agent had opened the kitchen cupboards. The teenage clutter had not been very carefully hidden. 'I'm not convinced that Evans would be bringing a great deal of money home even if we didn't have him. He'd have pissed away anything he managed to scrounge up on gear. You ask me, we're doing him a favour.'

Tanner ignored him, or wasn't listening. She said, 'I know I need to downsize, so somewhere like this is probably ideal. But I'm going to miss having stairs.'

'Really?' Thorne closed the wardrobe door. 'Good move if you ask me. A few more years and you won't be able to get up them anyway.'

'Cheeky sod. I'm a damn sight younger than you are.' Tanner nodded towards the kitchen where the estate agent was presumably still lurking. 'You should be flattered that he thought—'

Thorne's phone rang.

By the time he had ended the call, Tanner was on her feet and waiting eagerly to be told. It was clear that her mind was no longer on this or any other flat.

'We know where Alice Matthews went the night she died,' Thorne said.

'How?'

'The manager of an Italian restaurant in Amersham recognised her picture. There's no CCTV, but we've got a good description of the man she was eating with *and* the surname that was used to book the table. They're working up an e-fit now.'

Tanner grinned and made a fist. She said, '*Get* in.'

Buzzing with it himself, Thorne was nevertheless surprised at the energy he could see, could feel coming off his partner. He grinned back at her, knowing that he'd almost certainly be dead and buried long before Nicola Tanner ever needed a stairlift.

THIRTY-ONE

He had always rather enjoyed shopping, even when, like today, it was just for necessities. Shopping for special things, though, that was a real treat, and he especially liked hunting out smart clothes and shoes, which he knew was not something common to a lot of men. He liked to look good; to look like a man *should* look. He relished the buzz that came with a compliment or an admiring glance, even better if it was from another bloke, and who in their right mind wouldn't? There were the types, he knew, who claimed that they weren't bothered by that stuff, that being too concerned about your outward appearance was somehow trivial or shallow and what really counted was what was inside. He thought they were idiots, or liars. He could never understand the mindset of anyone who didn't care about what they wore or take pride in the way they presented themselves.

Though, for obvious reasons, the way he appeared to others mattered rather more to him than it did to most people.

He preferred to keep what was inside to himself.

He pushed the enormous trolley down the wide aisle of the cash and carry, stopped to load in a few boxes. He smiled, humming along with the tune that was echoing round the place, and thinking that if one or two of those he spent so many hours searching for had taken a little more care about the way they looked, they might not have needed to advertise.

Too late by then, of course.

Like turning a manky piece of fruit over to hide the rotten patch.

Ahead of him, a young woman was bending to heave up pallets of tinned goods, beans and tomatoes. He stopped to help and they talked for a minute or two, but he had immediately clocked the absence of adornment on her ring finger and, as he smiled and nodded and listened to her sing the praises of bulk buying, he mentally composed the kind of advertising campaign a manky piece of fruit like her would need.

Billboards, that might do the trick. He smiled again. Whatever might draw the attention of a man with eyesight problems and low standards.

'Thanks,' she said. 'You can pull a bloody muscle lifting these things.'

Only thing you're likely to pull, he thought.

He watched her walk away and thought about how very much he loved women, how he adored them. It was ironic, he was well aware of that, considering what people would say about him if they knew what he'd been up to. That was the point, though. He loved women who looked and behaved as women were supposed to; proper women who made the necessary effort, the sacrifices, just as proper men like him did. It certainly wasn't easy being a woman in this world, but that was only because it took time and effort.

Wasn't it worth it, though, being wanted?

The unwanted ones, the discards, well … they were something else entirely. Silk purse, sow's arse, simple. You could tart it up all you liked, but nothing made the rot spread faster than desperation.

The man at the till had seen him here plenty of times before and was as friendly as always, but that was all right, because he was happy enough to chat while his boxes and bottles were being scanned.

'Busy?'

'As always.'

'Good to be busy.'

He nodded, thinking about Alice Matthews, eyes like dinner plates underneath him.

'Been away anywhere?'

'Nowhere exciting.'

How she'd probably looked her very best, right at the end.

'Doesn't matter where you go, does it? Just good to get away, sometimes.'

'Oh yeah, I love it.'

Once he'd loaded the last of the boxes back into his trolley and handed over his credit card, he reached for a *Standard*.

He stared at the front page. A Met police e-fit and the name of the man whose face it was supposed to be. He read the appeal for information.

'Just pop in your pin when you're ready.'

He leaned slowly across. His finger hovered above the keypad.

'You all right?'

He let out a breath and stabbed in the number. 'Never better.'

At the same time, an elderly woman was shopping elsewhere for very different items. A local grocer's, round the corner from the flat she was now living in full time. Just a basket, in and out.

She had work to be getting on with.

It would all get back to normal eventually, the woman knew that, but she was still a little discombobulated by the change in routine, at having had to up sticks and get away so quickly. In this line of work, people got nicked all the time, course they did, and it wasn't usually a problem. Just a question of everyone keeping their heads down for a day or two. Putting business on hold. This was a bit more serious, though; she could tell that, even if nobody was saying very much. Andrew Evans was someone she had delivered to inside and out, and he'd been working for her bosses directly after he'd been released. She didn't know exactly what kind of thing they'd asked him to do, but she could hazard a damn good guess. I mean, if you were just being nicked for possession, supplying even, there weren't usually detectives banging on your door.

It was hard not to feel sorry for him, but she had to take care of herself.

The word had come down straight away and it was more than a polite suggestion. Time to shut up shop and move on. A pain in the backside, but at least she'd had somewhere to go.

She counted off the items in her basket, wandered towards the till.

A bolt-hole, that's what this place had always been, somewhere to take a break, but now it looked like she might be here a while, so she'd need to make the best of it. It wasn't going to be too much of a problem. The people she worked for did business all over, more branches than Starbucks, so someone like her was always going to come in useful, wherever the hell she ended up.

Someone as good at the job as she was.

As a kid, she'd always liked dressing up, playing make-believe. Only way to get through things, the sort of shithole she'd grown up in. There were still bomb sites around back then, she could remember playing in them. They still had rationing when she was a toddler for God's sake, so it was easier to pretend she lived the life of a little princess than deal with what she actually was. What she'd been born into. Watery stew went down more easily if you told yourself it was oysters or caviar, whatever they were, and she could always kid herself those piss-stinking balconies were the battlements of her father's castle; that puddles were moats and that it was probably a handsome prince banging on the door in the middle of the night.

Not like she ever got rescued, mind you.

Same sort of game she was playing now, acting the part in all those visiting halls, though she'd managed to put a bit of real treasure away over the years. Nice and safe in the bank. Enough to look after herself when the time came and to take care of her own little princess.

Her stomach tightened as she laid down her basket and thought about her daughter. The state of her when they'd last spoken. A girl with plenty of her own problems to deal with, who'd never been quite as convincing as her mother when it came to playing make-believe.

Lies were not the same thing.

The young man on the till stared down at the contents of her basket, then at her. He took out one item and scanned it repeatedly.

'Someone likes Mars bars.'

She smiled and shook out the plastic bag she'd brought with her. 'Sweet tooth,' she said.

THIRTY-TWO

Thorne checked his watch again.

'That won't make him get here any quicker,' Tanner said.

'How much longer, do you think?'

'Depends on traffic.'

'They'll have blues and twos, surely?'

'I doubt it.' Tanner looked entirely calm and unruffled, seemingly immune to the excitement and apprehension that had been crackling around the building since he'd arrived. It was as though the energy Thorne had felt coming off her two nights earlier had been internalised somehow; stored to be drawn upon later.

It was a trick Thorne knew he would do well to master. He had been told often enough.

'Trouble with you, you're flat-out or fuck-all,' Hendricks had said once. 'That's your problem, mate. Well, that's *one* of your problems. You need to pace yourself ...'

'Cooper's coming in voluntarily,' Tanner said. 'Remember?'

'Jesus.' Thorne got up and walked quickly to the far end of the incident room. He stepped out into the corridor and pushed through the door into the Gents. A young DC who'd been seconded from Kentish Town was on his way out.

'All set?'

Thorne nodded and moved past, trying to look as though he had barely thought about it.

'Reckon it's him?'

'There's every chance,' Thorne said.

Though the call of nature had not been urgent, he made use of the facilities anyway, then stared at his reflection as he washed his hands. He leaned close to the grimy mirror and decided he'd looked better, then realised it was more or less what he thought whenever he caught sight of himself these days.

Better, younger, happier . . .

Perhaps there was something that would very soon be done about one of those things, anyway.

Reckon it's him?

Every chance of a quick result. Every chance he was about to come face to face with the man who'd murdered Alice Matthews and at least three other women. Or at least, as quickly as it took a squad car to get here from Luton. When Thorne glanced at his watch again, he saw that it was only three minutes later than it had been the last time he looked.

He got back to his office, where Tanner was poring over paperwork, a few seconds before Chall stepped in.

'I finally got hold of Leila Fadel's little brother,' the DS said. 'He confirmed that he'd inherited Leila's computer and taken it with him to university, but he says there's nothing on it.'

'OK, tell him not to touch it again,' Thorne said.

'It doesn't matter—'

'We'll send a car for it and let the geek squad have a look. Get into the email archives, whatever.'

Chall shook his head. 'No, there's literally nothing on it. He said the hard disk had been wiped clean by the time he got it. He thought his dad had done it before giving it to him.'

Tanner nodded, as though it made perfect sense. 'So, the killer steals them, or he erases everything and leaves them behind. He makes it look like a burglary or he doesn't. All part of trying to conceal a pattern.'

Thorne sighed and swore under his breath.

'And I'm still chasing the various mobile providers,' Chall said.

Thorne looked at him. Clearly, Fulton's offer to put pressure on had been forgotten or was simply proving useless.

'Honestly, it's easier to get information out of the Pentagon.'

'So, chase harder,' Thorne said.

Chall nodded and moved towards the door.

'Get somebody else on it with you. Last time I checked we had lots of people and lots of phones. And you need to talk to whoever's running that website Cooper mentioned at the station in Luton.'

'Sir,' Chall said.

'Nice bit of man-management,' Tanner said, when the DS had gone. 'He comes in here and makes it very clear how hard he's working and you send him out feeling like he's done bugger all.'

Thorne wasn't listening. He said, 'Means nothing, this bloke coming in off his own bat.' He sat back, thinking through some of the things Melita Perera had told him; some of the clever moves made by the killers he had come across before. 'Could all be part of it . . . '

Following the pictures that had appeared in the newspapers the previous day and been shown as part of a hastily assembled TV appeal, a man named Gavin Cooper had come forward and identified himself. With a solicitor in tow – because, he had said, it seemed like the 'sensible thing to do' – he had presented himself at his local police station first thing that morning. He had made a short statement and was currently being driven down to Becke House. He had told officers several times already that he was keen to help, if at all possible.

Thorne looked at Tanner. 'I mean, if this bloke's as smart as you reckon he is, isn't there every chance he's also just cocky enough

189

to show off a bit? To come marching in here like a good citizen, knowing that we've got nothing? Wouldn't he be "keen to help"?'

'It's possible,' Tanner said.

When the phone rang, Thorne sat forward as if a gun had gone off and watched Tanner reach across to answer, as though it might just be someone offering her a phone upgrade, or her mother calling to pass the time of day.

She said, 'Right,' and when she'd hung up she said, 'They're at the front desk.'

Thorne stood up.

'Go steady, Tom.' Tanner leaned down to pick up her bag. 'I only said it was possible.'

Thorne scowled, like a child being reminded to brush his teeth, and walked slowly to the door. He paused and, for all it was likely to be worth, took a breath.

Flat-out or fuck-all.

Looking very much like a man not troubled by nerves or thrown by the unusual surroundings in which he now found himself, Gavin Cooper stared expectantly across the table at Thorne. His solicitor – a young woman named Stacey Poole – was still very much in tow and appeared every bit as relaxed as her client. There was an ease between them. Had Thorne not known – for obvious reasons – that it was not the case, he might have mistaken them for a couple. He had certainly encountered a good many marrieds seemingly less content in one another's company.

Once the recording was underway, Thorne reminded Cooper that he was not under arrest; that he was being interviewed under caution and was free to leave at any time. Cooper said that he understood. He gave his full name and address when asked; then, after a barely perceptible nod from his solicitor, said, 'For the record, I've come to this station of my own volition, having seen my name and a crude photofit of me on various television appeals and splashed across the front page of several newspapers.' He had the kind of voice that would have sounded good on radio, Thorne thought. It went with the sports jacket and pale pink shirt, the smile that was trying too hard. He leaned back and folded his arms. 'I'm here to help. If I can.'

Deciding that the man was what his father would have called a 'spiv', Thorne glanced across at Stacey Poole. She seemed happy enough to say very little, but he knew that she was no shrinking violet. Ten minutes before, he had spoken briefly to her alone; outlining, as he was obliged to do, the reasons they were so keen to speak to her client.

She had raised a hand to cut him off. 'Mr Cooper is here because he wishes to be. Simple as that. He's here so that he can be eliminated from this inquiry as quickly as possible.'

Thorne had pointed her towards the interview room and said, 'Well, let's see what we can do about that . . .'

'We do understand that you've chosen to come forward,' he said to Cooper now. 'And we're very grateful.'

'Yes, thanks for doing this,' Tanner said. 'We'll try not to keep you.'

'I've advised you of your right to free and independent legal advice.' Thorne glanced at Poole again. 'But that obviously won't be necessary. Strictly speaking, it isn't really necessary at all . . . so I'm wondering why you felt the need.'

'I thought it was a good idea, that's all,' Cooper said. 'You hear stories, don't you?'

'What kind of stories?'

Cooper didn't seem keen to elaborate. Instead he looked at the woman sitting next to him. 'Mrs Poole is my sister-in-law. So . . .'

'That's handy.'

'Cheaper too, I should imagine,' Tanner said. She turned a page in her notebook. 'Could you tell us about your relationship with Alice Matthews?'

If Cooper was shocked by the abruptness of Tanner's question, he didn't show it. 'Hardly a relationship,' he said. 'I met her once.'

'Tell us about that,' Thorne said.

'We were matched on a dating website. I told your colleagues all this first thing this morning.'

Tanner glanced down. 'That would be . . . Made In Heaven?'

Cooper nodded.

'How does that work?' Thorne asked.

'Well, it's not exactly rocket science. I mean, plenty of people do it. You just register your details, answer a questionnaire that takes half an hour, pay them a monthly fee and they send you matches.'

'So, what exactly were you looking for, Gavin?'

For the first time, Cooper appeared uncomfortable. 'Come on, what's anybody who does this looking for?'

'I don't know,' Thorne said. 'True love? Companionship? Sex?'

Stacey Poole shifted in her seat.

'I was looking for a partner,' Cooper said. 'I still am. I got divorced six years ago and I'd like to be with someone.' He shrugged. 'I don't think there's anything strange or . . . shameful about that. I know that most relationships start at work statistically, but there's not a lot of romance in chemical engineering, and I'm way too old for clubbing or any of that nonsense. So, I just thought, why not?'

Tanner smiled. 'Maybe I should try it myself.' She turned a page. 'So, you were matched with Alice Matthews . . .'

'Yes. We exchanged a few messages on the site, then moved across to private emails.'

'How many emails did you send her?' Thorne asked.

'Half a dozen, maybe.'

'What were they about?'

'Just chat to begin with . . . families, hobbies, whatever. Then once we agreed to meet, it was just about making the arrangements. What kind of food did we both like, where we should go.'

'So, you met Alice Matthews for the first and only time eight nights ago on April the nineteenth, after you'd booked a table at the La Cucina restaurant in Amersham. Is that correct?'

Cooper said that it was.

'How did that go?'

'It was . . . nice. *She* was nice. I still can't believe anyone would want to hurt her. She was lovely.'

'Not lovely enough though.'

'Excuse me?'

'For you, I mean?'

'Not in that way . . . no. We didn't really click.'

'Did you think she was attractive?

'Yes, but—'

'Did you think she was sexy?'

'Well, she wasn't really my—'

'Were you hoping you might end up in bed together? Did you suggest it?'

Cooper was looking rattled suddenly and Poole reached over to lay a hand on his arm. 'You don't have to answer any of these questions, Gavin.'

'No, you don't have to,' Thorne said. 'But I thought you were keen to help.'

'Look, we got on really well, all right? We talked all the way through the meal, we had a laugh, but there wasn't . . . you know, there was no . . .'

'Spark?' Tanner suggested.

'Right, and it was obvious we both thought the same thing.'

Thorne nodded. 'So, what happened afterwards?'

Cooper shrugged. 'We went home. Well, I presume she went home . . . I read about what happened in the papers, obviously. I paid the bill and we walked out to the car park together and said goodnight. We said we'd keep in touch. I got in my car and drove home.'

'You went straight home? Is there anyone who can confirm that?'

'I live alone.'

'Do you have any neighbours who might be able to confirm what time you got in?'

'Possibly, you'd need to ask.' Cooper shook his head. 'But aren't there ways you can check all this?'

Poole sat forward. 'Of course there are. Automatic number plate recognition, mobile phone data.' She looked at Thorne. 'I presume all this is in hand.'

'Right,' Cooper said. 'You can check where my phone was, can't you?'

'Yes, and we will. Could you give us your mobile number?'

'If you want. I have two phones, actually.'

Tanner nodded, as if she was impressed. 'You're not dealing drugs on the side are you, Gavin?'

Cooper barked out a humourless laugh. 'I have one phone for work and another for private use. Same as a lot of people.'

'Could you let us have those numbers?'

Cooper reeled them off, then stared at Thorne, waiting.

'Have you had other dates through Made In Heaven?'

'A few.'

'None that worked out though?'

'Not yet,' Cooper said. 'It can take a while. Some people aren't always what they claim to be.'

'Are you?'

Poole opened her mouth, but Cooper got in first. 'Yes, I think so. I mean, everyone exaggerates a bit, I suppose, and nobody says that they're fat and ugly with bad breath, do they? But I certainly didn't claim to be George Clooney.'

'Have you ever gone on a date with any of these women?' Thorne looked at him as he quietly spoke the names of the three victims they believed had been killed by the man who had murdered Alice Matthews.

Patricia Somersby, Annette Mangan, Leila Fadel.

Cooper shook his head. 'No. I think I was matched with an Annette a month or so ago, but not with that surname.'

'We're going a bit further back than that,' Thorne said. 'Could you tell us what you were doing on October ninth and thirtieth, last year?'

'Not off the top of my head. Can you?'

'How about December twenty-eighth, last year?'

'Well, not specifically,' Cooper said. 'But I can check. I'd need to call the company, get them to look at my work diary.'

'That would be very helpful.'

Cooper looked at his watch.

'Are we keeping you?'

'I'm just trying to work out the time difference. It's probably still too early.'

Thorne looked at him.

'In Toronto. Still a few hours before anyone gets in.'

'Sorry?'

'That's where I was working,' Cooper said. 'I was on secondment to an arm of the company based over there.' He relaxed suddenly, seeing the look on Thorne's face, sensing immediately that he had inadvertently produced his get out of jail free card. 'I only came back from Canada three months ago.'

Cooper turned to Poole and shook his head as though he was dealing with incompetents. Muttered something, smiling. Thorne watched Tanner close her notebook, then reached across to turn off the recorder.

THIRTY-THREE

The matchmaking business conducted by the Made In Heaven agency appeared to take place exclusively online, so Dipak Chall spent fifteen minutes trawling through company databases before he was able to find a phone number. Even then, the woman who answered his call immediately attempted to direct him back to the agency's website.

Chall interrupted and informed her that he was a police officer.

'Oh, well, that's good,' she said. 'Bit of a cliché, I know, but plenty of our female clients have a thing for a man in uniform.'

'I don't wear a uniform,' Chall said, 'and I'm not calling because I'm interested in your services. I'm calling to enquire about two of your clients, Alice Matthews and Gavin Cooper.'

'Right . . . '

'Can I start by asking you to confirm that these people are registered with your agency?'

'Well, I don't recognise the names,' the woman said. 'But we have got rather a lot of clients, and anyway, I'm afraid—'

'So, can you check if—?'

'I was saying . . . we're members of the Dating Agency

196

Association, so we have to comply with the requirements of the Information Commissioner's Office and the Data Protection Act.'

'Yes, but, once again, my name is Detective Sergeant Dipak Chall and—'

'Thing is, I can't just give that kind of information out over the phone. I mean, you should know that.'

Chall looked across to see Yvonne Kitson watching him. He shook his head. 'I understand that, but I have to tell you that I'm part of a team investigating a homicide and it's our belief that the victim was registered with your agency.'

There were a few seconds of silence. 'One of the people you mentioned?'

'That's correct. Alice Matthews was murdered just over a week ago.'

He heard the woman sigh before she said, 'Bloody hell, not again.'

Chall sat forward immediately, raising his hand and waving Yvonne Kitson over. He picked up a pen and reached to drag a sheet of paper across his desk.

'Sorry . . . could you repeat that?'

THIRTY-FOUR

From a window in a first floor stairwell, Thorne and Tanner looked down and watched Gavin Cooper and his sister-in-law climb into the same car that had brought them. As the Volvo eased out of the car park, Thorne turned away and leaned back against the wall.

He said, 'I'd've been happy to let the smug wanker take the bus.'

'It was never going to be that easy,' Tanner said. 'You didn't really believe it was him, did you?'

'I hoped it would be.'

'Well, course you did.' She took a small make-up pouch from her bag and opened a compact. She frowned and ran fingers through her hair, which she had been fussing with all morning. 'I knew he wasn't our man the second he walked in.'

'No, you didn't.' Thorne looked at her. 'And since when did you think hunches mean anything?'

'I don't.' Tanner put her make-up away. 'He didn't really strike me as being very bright, that's all.'

'Bright?'

'OK, then ... *capable* of what this man's done.' She took a few steps up towards the Operations Room, then turned. 'Come on, we've got a lot of work to do. I know how much you wanted this sorted quickly, but it's not going to happen, so now's exactly when we need to get our nuts down.'

Thorne knew Tanner was right; how stupid he'd been even thinking that the man they were after was going to present himself to them, tied up in a nice neat bow. Yes, he'd been given a bloody nose in that interview room, but he'd had plenty of them before, because they were an occupational hazard and the damage was rarely permanent.

It was what happened when you ran straight into a brick wall.

'It can't just be a coincidence, though.' Thorne stepped up to follow Tanner. 'Alice Matthews meeting a stranger for dinner on the night she was killed.'

'It's unlikely,' Tanner said. 'But that still might be exactly what it is.'

Thorne shook his head. 'The other victims were all single women, who'd had some kind of communication, texts or emails, that the killer didn't want us to find, right?' Tanner nodded and they kept on climbing. 'Annette Mangan's friend had an idea she was meeting someone and so did Leila Fadel's mother. So, Gavin Cooper can have alibis coming out of his arse, but him meeting Alice that night still feels to me like it's part of this somehow.' They paused for a few moments at the door. 'The picture on that box of yours ... '

They walked into the Operations room to see Dipak Chall deep in conversation with Yvonne Kitson, before glancing up when they came in and instantly raising a hand. Tanner led the way over to them, recognising a look on her DS's face that Thorne was less familiar with.

News. Good or bad.

'I talked to a woman at that website,' Chall said. 'The one Cooper was registered with.'

Thorne leaned against the desk. 'Yeah, well, it's academic now. Cooper's in the clear.'

'I know.'

'And sorry for being a twat earlier, by the way. I know everyone's knocking their pipes out.'

'It doesn't matter,' Chall said.

'Why is it academic?' Tanner looked at Thorne. 'Not a coincidence, you said.'

'It isn't a coincidence.' Chall raised the papers he was clutching.

'Put it this way,' Kitson said. 'It would be amazing if it was.'

Thorne and Tanner looked at them.

'In June last year, a woman called Karen Butcher was murdered.' Chall stabbed at the papers in his hand. 'Strangled to death at home in Coventry. She was registered with Made In Heaven, and matched with a man named Terry Summers, who was eventually charged with killing her.'

'Charged?' Tanner looked at him. 'Was he convicted?'

'Oh yes,' Kitson said.

Thorne opened his mouth and closed it again, then pointed towards his office and walked away. Chall, Kitson and Tanner quickly followed and once Tanner had closed the door behind her, Thorne nodded, keen to hear the rest of it.

This new development would, of course, be passed on to everyone involved in the investigation, but as the core team, it was important they process the information first, and it was clear that Chall had not finished.

'Obviously, I've asked the woman at the website to check their records to see if Patricia Somersby and the other victims were also registered and she's promised to come back to me, but in the meantime me and Yvonne have been looking into the Karen Butcher case.'

'She had a date with Summers after the website matched them,' Kitson said, 'and was found dead the next morning. Summers had no alibi and they had DNA evidence of some kind—'

'We don't know the details,' Chall said. 'I've requested the file on the original investigation.'

'Summers claimed all along that he had nothing to do with it, said he went home after he and Karen Butcher had gone out, but the jury weren't having any of it and he was sent down for life.'

Tanner pulled a chair across and dropped into it. 'Shit.'

'What?' Thorne asked.

'I only looked at unsolved cases.'

'Well, course you did. That's what I asked you to do.'

'I should have been more thorough.'

Thorne looked away. He knew there was little he could say that would stop Tanner beating herself up about this perceived failure. She seemed almost as good at it as he was. He turned back to Kitson and Chall. 'Right. Sounds like we should go and have a word with Terry Summers. He can't have had anything to do with the more recent murders, but let's see if he still says he wasn't responsible for the first one.'

'Problem,' Chall said.

'Summers never stopped protesting his innocence,' Kitson said. 'Right up until he hanged himself in Wakefield six months ago.'

Now, Thorne dragged a chair across. Kitson and Chall leaned back against desks. Clearly deciding that if there was more self-flagellation to be done she would do it later, alone and in private, it was Tanner who broke the silence.

'OK, so now we've got a picture that's starting to make sense,' she said.

'Really?' Thorne sat back and stretched out his legs.

'Let's suppose that Terry Summers was innocent.'

'What about the DNA?' Chall asked.

'Well, we don't know what that is yet. Whether there was a mistake made in processing it. How easy it might have been to fake, or plant.'

Thorne, Chall and Kitson stared at her, while a wash of

something like inspiration passed quickly across her face, then a grimace of doubt and, finally, a flash of possibility.

'Now, *that's* how to hide a pattern,' she said. 'He kills his first victim, and provides the police ... somehow ... with the most obvious suspect on a plate. Then, when he does it again, there's no way they're ever going to connect the two murders, because the first one is nicely done and dusted with the culprit safely locked up. Then he disguises another one as a burglary, he moves around the country, uses various means to hide the electronic evidence ... he's not made it easy, I'll give him that much.' Her eyes widened, as another crucial piece of the puzzle slotted into place. 'And if anyone does make a connection, even with *one* of the other murders, because of the way he does it there's always going to be a perfect suspect front and centre.'

'The likes of Gavin Cooper, you mean?' Thorne said.

Tanner nodded. 'Whichever poor sod the victim happens to go on her date with.' She sat back, clearly as happy as she could be with the picture. 'He's not just looking for the women he's going to kill, he's looking for the men they get matched up with. They need to fit the bill as well, because he needs ideal candidates to pin the murders on if he has to.'

'So, how does he find them?' Thorne asked. 'He obviously knows when these people have been matched and somehow he finds out when and where they arrange to meet. I think it's safe to say our dating site's right in the middle of this ...'

'Maybe it's someone who works for the website,' Chall said.

Thorne nodded, thinking.

'Or he's a hacker of some sort,' Kitson said. 'Hacks into the Made In Heaven website, sees who's getting matched with who, then when he finds a couple he likes the look of he hacks their private emails so he knows the time and place they're meeting up.'

'Easier if it's your own computer system,' Thorne said.

'Yvonne's got a point though,' Chall said. 'We already know he's computer-savvy, because he wiped the hard disk on

Leila Fadel's laptop. I mean, I wouldn't know how to do that, would you?'

'I'm not discounting anything,' Thorne said. 'But for now, get back on to that website and tell them we need to know if the other victims were on their books. Make some noises about shutting them down if you need to.'

'Yeah, put the wind up them a bit,' Kitson said. 'And tell them we'll be paying them a visit.'

'No.' Thorne and Tanner said it virtually simultaneously.

Thorne stood up; buzzing again, that brick wall crumbling as suddenly as it had appeared. 'Don't tell them.'

THIRTY-FIVE

The counsellor – 'call me Rob' – told him their time was about up for the day, so Evans got up and walked to the door.

'We're well on the way,' Rob said. 'The physical withdrawal's almost run its course. That's only half the job, obviously, but you've got every reason to be proud of yourself.'

Evans closed the door behind him and nodded to the copper who was sitting on the landing with a newspaper.

'All good?'

'Getting there,' Evans said.

He walked down the wide staircase, through the main living room and pushed open the French doors into the garden. It was bright, but cold, and he shivered a little as he stepped outside. Walking across the main lawn and down the slope towards the trees, Evans spotted another copper, fifty yards or so away by the empty swimming pool. The copper, lanky and rail-thin, raised a hand and Evans waved back.

They all seemed pleasant enough.

It still felt strange being the sole resident; the only one who couldn't toddle off home at the end of the day. There *had* actually been some company for the last few days, but the boy called Cristian had gone this morning, taken away before Evans was up. He'd known it was coming. The two of them had been allowed to hang out, left alone to watch TV together for an hour or two in the evenings, and, in broken English and in strict contravention of the rules, the boy had told him he thought his mother was being threatened. Clearly a recovering smack-head, he had told Evans he was supposed to give evidence against a gang of people-smugglers who sounded every bit as dangerous as the drug gang Evans now found himself on the wrong side of. 'I tell the police I've changed my mind,' the boy had said. 'Simple as that. Even if I go to prison, I won't risk my mother getting hurt.'

Now Evans understood what Tanner had meant when they'd been talking about Paula. It didn't make him feel any better, though. Just because his wife hadn't a clue where he was, didn't even know why he had been spirited away, it didn't mean that the people he'd been working for wouldn't ask the question, and he knew better than most that they didn't waste time making polite enquiries.

He remembered the look on that junkie's face when he'd lifted the gun up.

He tried not to think about it, to tell himself that whatever drugs had yet to be flushed out of him were making him paranoid. That everything would be done to keep Paula and Sean safe.

He jogged down the hill to the perimeter, pushed his fingers through the holes in the fence and wrapped his fists around the thin metal strips. He looked right and left, but couldn't see anybody. He knew there were patrol cars making regular passes, cameras dotted throughout the grounds, but still, he didn't reckon the place was quite as secure as everyone made out. What was to stop him stealing something from the kitchen and cutting his way through the fence?

It didn't look like it would be that hard.

He had never seen it, but he presumed there *was* a kitchen, somewhere. One of the cops had told him that when there were a few more residents someone would be brought in to cook for everyone, staff and inmates. But they'd decided it wasn't worth the effort when the place was so empty, so he and the members of staff who stayed overnight had been sending out for takeaways. Curries and Chinese, pizza and KFC. It was a damn sight better than he'd been used to inside, but he still wasn't keeping everything down so it didn't make a lot of difference anyway. As it was, he liked fast food as much as anyone else, but more than anything he wanted to be at home, sitting at the table next to Sean and eating something that he'd cooked with Paula. Pasta maybe, or a nice roast. Beans on toast . . . biscuits. Anything.

He turned and trudged back towards the house and climbed up the stone steps that ran to the paved balcony outside the sitting room. He stopped at the top of the steps, spun slowly around and sat down.

He closed his eyes, took deep breaths, tried to concentrate on the sound of the water running from the fountain away to his right.

Only half the job...

Call Me Rob had no idea, though it wasn't for want of trying. Evans just wasn't ready to talk about any of it, not yet. Hard enough getting himself straight without spewing any of that up.

The walls of the cell he still spent a few terrible seconds every morning thinking he'd woken up in. The stink and the noise and the wish that one of the nut-jobs on his landing might snap and kick the shit out of him because he needed to *feel* something . . . and the look on the woman's face; the mother of the boy he'd killed. Screaming down at him from the visitors' gallery when the sentence was read out. Arms reaching out to hold her back and bubbles of spit at the corners of her mouth.

And now another image, clear as day, of his wife; a gun to her head, a knife pressed across her throat.

Evans looked up to see the cop who had waved walking towards him and he watched him come.

'Got the place to yourself again, then, Andy?'

'Anything from DI Tanner?'

The cop sniffed and stared out across the gardens. 'Not a dicky bird, mate. Want me to get a message to her?'

Evans said it was fine, nothing urgent, and lowered his head until the copper strolled away again.

He looked down at his feet; the trainers tapping against the stone.

His stomach churned and acid rose up into his throat.

He hoped more than anything that Tanner got her act together and caught the Duchess soon, but right that minute he would have given almost anything to have the old woman pay him a visit.

THIRTY-SIX

There had been no recurrence of the raised temperature of a few nights before, but Helen was still keeping an ear out for Alfie, and, sprawled on sofa and floor after dinner, the three of them were taking care to keep the volume down. Hendricks had brought Chinese food over; something of a peace offering as it was the first time he and Helen had seen one another since their disagreement almost a week before.

They were certainly not going to talk about drugs again, though Helen's mood was already good enough for her to raise no objection when Thorne had slipped a Johnny Cash CD on.

American II: Unchained.

The perfect soundtrack to a nice, cosy chat about murder.

'It's just a glass,' Hendricks said.

'Yeah, just a glass, but it's what swung the jury,' Thorne said. 'What put Terry Summers away.'

'Easy enough, you ask me.'

'A glass found in Karen Butcher's living room, with Terry Summer's prints and saliva on it. Next to one with Karen

Butcher's DNA on it, like the two of them had gone back to her place for a drink after their dinner.'

'Yeah, but even I can figure out how the killer might have set that up. And I'm just an ignorant northerner.'

'Nobody's arguing.'

'Go on then,' Helen said.

Hendricks leaned back against the sofa. 'He waits until they've left the restaurant, then swipes their glasses before the waiter's had a chance to clear the table. Piece of piss.'

Helen looked at Thorne. 'He's not wrong. We both know how easy it is to do if you've planned it.'

She did not need to elaborate. In the case they'd all worked in Helen's home town of Polesford a year or so before, a suspect had been wrongly arrested on the strength of a discarded cigarette butt, picked up then planted by the real killer. Forensic evidence like that, or the glass found at the Karen Butcher crime scene, rightly carried substantial weight with coppers and members of the public alike, but all three of them knew that once malicious intent or simple human error was thrown into the mix the Gospel according to DNA was rather more flawed than viewers of *CSI* liked to believe.

'It means he's watching them,' Thorne said. 'In the restaurant or the bar or whatever. When they meet.'

Helen grunted her distaste. 'Like he's not creepy enough.'

'Well, he's got to, hasn't he?' Hendricks said. 'He needs to see the man leave, so he knows it's safe to follow the woman home.'

'I'm betting he knows where she lives already,' Thorne said.

'Every chance, if he's got access to their account on that website.'

'So, what happens if the man *doesn't* leave?' Thorne looked from one to the other. 'I mean, what does the killer do if our singletons decide they fancy the pants off each other on that first date and go home together?'

Hendricks shrugged. 'He moves on. Goes back to his sad little bedroom and finds himself another couple.'

'Our singletons get lucky in every sense,' Helen said.

Hendricks reached across for the wine bottle on the TV stand; poured himself a top-up, while the Man in Black sang 'Sea of Heartbreak', like that deep dark body of water was one he was all too familiar with.

'Makes me glad I'm not single any more,' he said. 'I reckon I'd rather go back to cottaging than risk any of this internet dating stuff.'

'You sure about that?' Helen said.

Hendricks sat back again and grinned. 'Happy days.'

'Really?' Thorne asked. 'Everything OK with you and Liam?'

'Yeah.'

They looked at him.

'Yeah ... but ... just because you've gone vegetarian doesn't mean you don't occasionally miss a big, fuck-off bacon sandwich.'

'Or a big, fuck-off something else,' Helen said.

Hendricks looked pleased with himself in a way that reminded Thorne of Christine Treasure. 'No worries on that score. Liam's got *plenty* to offer.'

'Too much information,' Thorne said.

'I just mean that sometimes you miss a bit of adventure, that's all. You miss ... ' He stopped. 'Christ, I nearly said "the danger".'

Helen turned to look at Thorne. 'There's probably men and women registering on that website right now.'

'I know.' Thorne said it rather more sharply than he had intended. 'We close it down, though ... he's going to know we're on to him.'

'Uploading pictures which may or may not be genuine.' Hendricks swirled his red wine around and spoke quietly, as if he was talking to himself. 'Answering all those endless questions about their personalities and hobbies. Likes and dislikes.' He stared down into his glass. 'Can't imagine too many of them would be happy to be meeting a serial killer.'

*

210

Driving east through drizzle on the North Circular, Tanner listened to people arguing about globalisation on Radio 5 Live and decided that, when she retired, she wanted a dog.

When . . .

That time was still a good way off, besides which she wasn't certain that once she'd done her thirty years she would take the option to walk away. It was no longer compulsory and, after all, she would still be in her early fifties. There were plenty, and she knew several, who were burned out well before then, couldn't wait to take the pension and run, but she didn't think she'd be one of them.

She hoped she wouldn't be.

A few years before Susan had died, there had been an ongoing discussion about getting a dog that had lasted rather longer than the one about having children, though the end result had been much the same. Tanner had grown up with dogs, but Susan had been a good deal less keen. She had said, quite rightly, that Tanner's uncertain work timetable would result in her having to take on the majority of the dog-duties, besides which she was worried about how the cat would react.

Tanner had found it hard to argue, and in the end, had given up.

Now, though, as a single woman, there would be nothing to stop her. She was sure that the cat could cope, would still be the boss, especially if she got a puppy, though she also thought a rescue dog was a good idea and knew that the majority of those were fully grown. It was certainly something she would need to bear in mind if she was going to carry on looking at flats. A garden would be important, and a decent park nearby.

Presuming that, when the time came, she was still a single woman.

She drifted into the inside lane and slowed a little.

As things stood, it was almost impossible to see any sort of future that involved any kind of significant other, but equally hard to picture herself growing older with nothing but the Job to talk about and only a dog for company. Right then, that seemed the more likely outcome. She knew, of course, that there were dating sites and apps catering specifically for gay women, and she found herself wondering how terrible she would feel, taking a step like that; how long it would be before she could even consider looking without feeling guilty.

Perhaps it was just because of developments in the Alice Matthews case that she was even thinking about such things. Lonely women: separated, divorced, widowed.

Perhaps that was why she indicated and pulled across on to the hard shoulder. Why she put the hazard lights on and turned off the radio, and sat there until she'd stopped crying.

Half an hour later, she had found a parking space at the end of the road in Bounds Green and walked slowly up to the unmarked car. The passenger side window slid down and Tanner showed her warrant card.

'All quiet?' She looked across at Paula Evans's house. There were no lights on.

The officer in the passenger seat nodded towards his colleague. 'All except his rear end. I should step back a bit if I were you.'

'A few cars,' the driver said. 'But none that looked out of place; nobody slowing down.'

'We took the numbers anyway.'

'A couple of lads smoking weed on the corner . . . a fox helping himself to a bird that had been run over. Sod all else.'

Tanner nodded and took her bag from her shoulder. 'Why don't you two take a break for half an hour? Go and get a coffee or something.'

The two officers looked at each other, nodded.

'Go on . . . there's a petrol station round the corner.'

Tanner watched them walk away and climbed into the driver's seat. She left the window open and leaned towards it. She tuned the radio in to 5 Live and stared at the dark house and wondered how long Paula Evans would have to spend alone.

She decided that, if and when the time came, she'd get a Labrador or a golden retriever. Something solid and dependable. Susan hadn't much cared for dogs at all, but those had been her favourites.

THIRTY-SEVEN

A junior stylist had done the washing, massaged Tanner's head briefly – checking to make sure the pressure was OK – then towel-dried her hair. She'd led Tanner across to the mirror and given her a newspaper to read, but before there was time to open it Graham French had arrived to take over.

He said, 'Thank you, Keisha.' Then, 'Right, so what are we doing?'

Tanner hesitated, then did her best to explain what she was after, why she had decided to take French up on his offer, though in the end it sounded as though she wanted exactly the same cut that she already had. 'Just a bit tidier,' she said. 'Smarter, you know?' She briefly caught French's eye in the mirror. 'Whatever you think, really . . . '

The hairdresser placed a hand on either side of her head, lifted the still damp hair and examined it. He let it run through his fingers. 'There's a *bit* of grey, but not a lot.' He cocked his head. 'Shall we get rid of it?'

'It's fine.'

'You sure?'

'Like you said, there's not a lot. I'll probably go full-on Granny-chic when the time comes.'

'You're lucky.' He lifted the hairdryer from its metal holster. 'You'll be one of those women who look *amazing* with grey hair. Like Helen Mirren.'

'I'll settle for that,' Tanner said.

French gave Tanner's hair a thirty-second blast with the dryer then reached for his scissors and went to work.

Tanner had always disliked this bit, unsure as to where she should look. It somehow seemed wrong to stare at herself in the mirror for that long, and if she closed her eyes there was always the worry it would be mistaken for relaxation or, even worse, ecstasy. She certainly couldn't look at whoever was doing the cutting, in case their eyes met. In a mirror, that moment always seemed oddly more intimate than it might otherwise. In the end, she settled for keeping her head still, lowering her eyes to the newspaper and trying to read. It was difficult, and not helped by the strands of hair that slid down the nylon cape on to the pages, so she gave up, fixed her gaze on a space six inches above her head and listened to the music. It was rather more ... ambient than it had been the last time she was here, which was a huge relief. Perhaps, she thought, the beats were cranked up when the place was busier. She had come in deliberately early, asking for the first appointment when she had called, and she was pleased to be the only customer they had.

In and out, with as little fuss as possible.

'Must be hard trying to look stylish all the time,' French said. 'Doing your job.'

'Why's that?'

'You know, all that chasing around.'

'It's not *The Sweeney*.'

French laughed. 'I bet you'd give them a run for their money.'

'Back when I was in uniform, maybe. You have to wear those stupid hats all the time, so your hair always looks rubbish.'

'You prefer being a detective then? Plain-clothes, I mean.' He straightened up and smiled, looked at Tanner in the mirror. 'Not that they *are* plain, obviously.'

Her eyes flicked briefly across to the thick gold bracelet that swung at French's wrist as he worked. 'The best M&S has to offer.'

French hummed as he worked, occasionally breaking off for a few seconds to deal with a query from the receptionist or give instructions to one of the junior girls. Tanner turned a couple of pages in the newspaper.

'Any luck finding the Duchess?' French asked.

'Not as yet.'

'Yeah, well, she's not daft. Does she know you're looking for her?'

'Possibly.'

He nodded. 'She can certainly take care of herself, that one. I always thought she was very ... self-contained, you know what I mean?'

Tanner said she wasn't sure.

French stopped cutting, though he still worked the scissors in his hand. He lowered his voice. 'I always got the impression that apart from the actual drugs, she organised the rest of it herself. Like a ... cottage industry or whatever. I think she wanted to be in control of all that stuff, took pride in doing it properly. Hollowing out the Mars bars, spraying those kiddies' pictures. I'm guessing she was given the Spice by the people paying her wages, but then she did everything else.' He went back to Tanner's hair, slowly using the comb to assess the length.

'You saying she bought the phones in bulk?'

'I would have thought so. She certainly got through her stock quick enough.'

'Like you buying in boxes of shampoo and volumiser?'

'Makes sense, doesn't it? If you're a grocer you buy several cases of baked beans at a time, don't you? Saves messing about, and it's a damn sight cheaper.'

Tanner nodded, thinking.

When he was almost done, French excused himself and stepped across to take a call at the reception desk. Tanner quickly took her phone from her bag and made a call of her own.

'Listen, Dipak ... how do you feel about taking on a *really* tedious job?'

Chall laughed.

'I'm serious. You're not going to enjoy it, but it needs doing.' She told Chall what she was after and he stopped laughing. Without leaving him any time to ask questions, she apologised for dumping it on him.

'I'll live,' Chall said. 'Just.'

When she'd hung up, Tanner picked up the newspaper and began to flick through it, still thinking about what French had told her about the Duchess and wondering if she was now wasting Chall's time as well as her own. She stopped when she saw a story tucked away at the bottom of a page. French came back, saying something about bolshie clients, then looked down and spotted the story that had caught Tanner's eye.

'Bloody hell,' he said. 'Have they still not caught that nutcase yet?'

Tanner had not finished reading. Three paragraphs about the dismembered body of another cat, laid out ritualistically in a front garden in St Albans. Quotes from those earlier victims Thorne had interviewed a week and a half earlier and a statement from an unnamed officer assuring the public that the hunt for the perpetrator had been stepped up.

'I swear to God,' French said. 'Anyone who can do that to a defenceless animal ... '

The junior who had washed Tanner's hair moved across and looked at the paper. She shook her head. 'That's so gross.'

Tanner moved a finger across the newspaper. 'Trust me, we're doing everything we can.'

The girl nudged French. 'You should tell her what you told me.'

'What?'

'That horrible story, you know? The bloke you were inside with.'

'Oh. Well . . .'

When the girl had walked away, Tanner said, 'What story?'

French stepped slowly round Tanner's chair and spun it a little until he was facing her. 'Listen, I'm probably talking rubbish here, only I've been thinking about this ever since I started reading about what was happening to all those cats. It's why I told Keisha, and . . . well, you never know, it might be something to pass on to whoever's in charge of it.'

Tanner waited.

'There was this bloke I was in Maidstone with. Before I went to Pentonville. I mean, I steered well clear of him, same as most people did, because he was . . . not right, you know?'

'What do you mean, "not right"?'

French lowered his voice again. 'So, they brought a couple of cats in one time . . . not for the prisoners, though they do all that kind of thing in America, use animals for therapy or whatever. No, they just brought these ones in because the place was crawling with rats. Huge things running around on the landings and in the kitchens. Anyway, two days after these cats came in, they were found all cut up in the exercise yard. In pieces, literally . . . and everyone knew it was him, this bloke I'm on about, because he was bragging about it. Said he couldn't stand them. You can check all this with the prison if you like . . . I mean, he was never done for it or anything, and he was released pretty soon after that anyway.'

'What was he in for?' Tanner asked.

French said, 'Rape,' like he might have said, 'overdue library books' and grimaced. 'We were all a damn sight happier when he'd gone, I can tell you that much. Like getting rid of a bad smell. Still had the rats, mind you . . .'

Tanner closed the newspaper. 'What was he called?'

218

French leaned closer and told her the man's name, then repositioned the chair and moved back behind it. He gave Tanner's hair a final once-over with the dryer, applied a little spray then made a few last-minute adjustments with his fingers.

He stepped back and grinned at her in the mirror.

'Gorgeous.'

THIRTY-EIGHT

This was how things were now, Thorne supposed, as he got his first look at the place, when you ran what for all he knew was a multi-million-pound business that took place exclusively online. The hub of your empire was actually no more than two rooms at the top of a nondescript terraced house in Rugby. A middle-aged woman called Caroline Marchant, who had taken Chall's first call and subsequently several others, had opened a front door to reveal two more beyond a small hallway. Surprise had quickly given way to nervous enthusiasm and she had barely paused for breath as she led Thorne and Kitson through one of the doors and up a narrow flight of stairs.

A telephone voice that couldn't quite disguise the Midlands accent.

'Well, I suppose it's as convenient a time as any. Or as *inconvenient*, I should say. I mean yes, it would have been a bit easier if we'd known you were coming, but I'm sure we can sort something out, do our best to help, now you're here . . . as you've obviously driven all the way up from London. How was the drive? The M1 can be a pig first thing. Or did you come on the train?'

The stairs led straight into a medium-sized room containing

two desks, on each of which sat a pair of large computer screens. A younger woman turned from one of the desks and smiled.

'This is Sandra,' Marchant said. 'She does all the financial stuff, keeps on top of subscriptions, handles the accounts and so on.' She nodded towards their visitors, then moved quickly to turn off the radio on the younger woman's desk. 'These are police officers.'

Thorne introduced himself and Kitson as the woman stood up and stepped across to shake hands. She was tall and skinny with long dark hair; almost the exact physical opposite of the woman Thorne presumed was, at least nominally, the boss. 'Sandra Cook. I do the boring bits.'

'Rubbish.' Marchant smiled. 'I can barely add up, so without you we'd all be in big trouble.'

Thorne looked around. There was a wall calendar, a few posters – sunsets, kittens, WORK HARD AND BE NICE TO PEOPLE – and an old-fashioned metal filing cabinet with a kettle on top; a tray and three upturned mugs.

'So, how many of you are there?' he asked. Through the door he could see another room at the end of a short corridor, a sofa and armchairs.

'Well, I suppose I'm what you'd call the creative powerhouse of Made In Heaven,' Marchant said. 'I write everything on the site, arrange the advertising, what have you. Sandra comes in three days a week to do the books and then there's Ken, who's our technical wizard and handles all the computer and database side of things.' She nodded towards an empty chair. 'Kenneth Ablett.'

'Where's the wizard today?' Kitson asked.

'He's only part time, too. Today's not one of his days, I'm afraid.'

'Could you give us his address?'

'I could call him, if you want. He only lives five minutes away and I'm sure he wouldn't mind popping in.'

'That's perfect.'

221

'Why don't you go through and sit down?' She pointed to the second room. 'I'll give Ken a quick ring.'

Thorne and Kitson did as Marchant had suggested, the woman shouting after them, to let them know the door on their left was a toilet, should either of them need it. Kitson took swift advantage. Thorne carried on and dropped on to a large leather sofa, not quite able to make out the short conversation between the two women in the office, or whatever Marchant proceeded to say on the phone.

The room was stuffy and the windows needed cleaning and they had clearly bought a job lot of cheesy or inspirational posters. There were two more filing cabinets against one wall, a small TV in the corner and, somewhat incongruously, an exercise bike.

Thorne took out his phone to check messages. He was immediately offered access to a Wi-Fi network called MadeInHeavenGuest, which was password protected.

Some security, at least.

He tried *amatch*, then *marchant*, then gave up.

Kitson walked in, quickly followed by Marchant. They both sat down.

'Ken's on his way.'

Thorne thanked her, wondering why she hadn't offered them a drink. It was usually a go-to tactic when people were nervous and the truth was he could have murdered a coffee.

'And Sandra's bringing some tea through.'

Tea would do. 'You must be psychic,' Thorne said.

Marchant smiled. 'Well, you have to be able to read people,' she said. 'If you're in this game. Bringing strangers together.'

'Well, that's what we're here to talk about, but I have to say I'm wondering why you were so surprised to see us?'

'I don't know . . . not *surprised*, exactly.'

'Five women registered with your agency have been murdered in little under a year. Four in the last six months. So it's hardly a bolt from the blue is it, us turning up?'

The woman folded her hands in her lap. 'I suppose not.'

'Thank you for getting us that information so quickly,' Kitson said.

That first phone call had confirmed what they already knew about Alice Matthews and provided the game-changing information about the murder of Karen Butcher. Then, after some pushing from Dipak Chall, Marchant had finally come back to confirm, with 'shock and sadness', that Patricia Somersby, Annette Mangan and Leila Fadel had also been registered with her dating site.

Single and looking for matches, which Made In Heaven had provided.

'Well, it wasn't easy. We have hundreds of clients, and it's not like we know any of them personally. Even when we looked . . . well, obviously it was Ken who did all that . . . several of the women had registered under different names. That isn't unusual, because sometimes people are embarrassed about using an agency like mine, but it meant we had to go back through their financial information. Direct debits and what have you. It was a hell of a shock, I can tell you. Horrible, just . . . horrible.'

Thorne sat back. 'Tell me how this business works.'

Marchant seemed more than happy to talk; on safe ground. She paused only briefly when Sandra Cook arrived with the drinks, and continued as Thorne and Kitson mumbled thanks, said yes to milk and no to sugar. 'Well, it's like any other business. I mean, retail is retail, but you'd get different answers if you were talking to the man who runs the local corner shop or the CEO of Marks and Spencer. For a start, there's a subtle difference between a dating agency and a matchmaker. There are some companies who offer a more bespoke service, who meet their clients personally, tailor their profiles and so on. Of course, you pay through the nose for that, thousands of pounds a year in some cases, and it's all a bit over the top if you ask me, but those businesses have no shortage of clients. The ones who deliberately target single people with money to burn.'

Thorne had taken two slugs of tea before he ran out of patience. 'I mean *your* business.'

'Well, obviously we're a somewhat smaller operation.'

'Boutique,' Kitson suggested.

Marchant flashed her a thin smile. 'Well, we still have a lot of clients, but we don't offer quite that degree of ... personalised service. To be honest, a lot of that is nonsense anyway. These bigger agencies that claim to have in-house psychologists and lifestyle coaching. Grooming tips and fashion advice and so on. They're just charging people a fortune for what amounts to much the same as we offer.'

'You're the bargain basement end of things,' Thorne said.

'No, I wouldn't say that.'

'A more basic service, then?'

'A more streamlined service.'

'So, how much does it cost?' Kitson asked.

Marchant looked at Sandra Cook.

'Well ... there are a few different packages.' Cook looked a little uncomfortable at being put on the spot. 'It depends how long you sign up for, but a basic membership at twenty-nine ninety-five per month for a minimum of six months, offers online registration and a guaranteed number of matches per week.'

'I can promise you we offer a very thorough service,' Marchant said. 'Matches are made scientifically following a rigorous registration process.'

'Scientifically?' Thorne looked at her. 'Really?'

'Oh yes, we use all sorts of complicated algorithms ... but I think Ken had better explain how all that works.' She smiled and shook her head and Sandra Cook did the same. 'I can just about manage to send an email, and that's on a good day.'

'See, I registered with your agency yesterday afternoon,' Thorne said.

Marchant cocked her head. 'Oh.'

'I'm not actually looking to meet anyone, I just thought it

224

might be an interesting exercise, you know? To hand over my twenty-nine ninety-five and take the same steps each one of those five murder victims had taken. To go through your rigorous registration process.' He looked at Kitson, who nodded, as though this was the first she had heard about it. 'It certainly takes a while to answer all the questions, I'll give you that much, but I'm not absolutely convinced it was time well spent.'

Marchant blinked and swallowed.

'No luck then?' Kitson asked.

Thorne shook his head sadly. 'I said I was a heavy smoker who was also a staunch atheist and by the end of the day I'd been matched up with several committed Christians and at least a couple of prospective partners whose pet hate was smoking.'

'Well, nothing's one hundred per cent,' Marchant said.

'You get what you pay for.'

'But if you'd taken the time to read the testimonials from hundreds of satisfied clients—'

Kitson cut the woman off. 'None of whom you've ever met, correct? The same would go for Alice Matthews and the other women who were killed.'

'As I've already explained,' Marchant said, 'that's not how the agency operates.'

'Makes sense.' Kitson turned to Thorne. 'So none of them would be known personally to anyone at the agency or be recognised later on. No pictures on the front of newspapers that were likely to catch anyone's eye.'

Thorne nodded, stared across at Marchant and Cook. 'Yes, we were wondering why you hadn't made the connection. Five murdered women, all of them on your books. That might explain it, I suppose.'

'Like I said, we've got a great many clients.'

'Even so—'

'Well, you didn't make the connection either.' Marchant looked from Thorne to Kitson. 'Until now.' She sat back and folded her arms. 'I mean, whatever you think about how this agency works, surely you can't believe we're supposed to do the police's job for them.'

A few seconds of awkward silence were broken by the sound of a key rattling in a lock one floor below them and it was another half a minute before the man Thorne presumed to be Kenneth Ablett entered and stood in the doorway taking the visitors in.

He sat down on the arm of Sandra Cook's chair and said, 'Looks like I missed out on the tea.'

He was a shortish thirty-something, with a neatly groomed goatee and dark hair tied back into a man-bun, but was otherwise far from being the stereotypical geek Thorne had been expecting. He looked as though he took care of himself, and was smartly dressed in chinos, a soft leather jacket and highly polished brogues. Thorne found himself wondering exactly how the man had been planning to spend his day off.

Marchant made the introductions.

'Caroline was just telling us about your computer system,' Thorne said. 'How you're in charge of maintenance and so on.'

'That's right.' A low, accentless voice. Colourless.

'Did you set it up?'

'Yeah.' He glanced down at Sandra Cook. 'It's fairly straightforward if you know what you're doing.'

'How secure is it?'

'As secure as any.' He shrugged. 'Or as insecure.'

'Would you know if it had been hacked?'

'Yeah, course. It's been hacked a couple of times.'

Thorne and Kitson exchanged a look. 'What happened?' Kitson asked.

Another shrug. 'Just the kind of thing you'd expect. Porn stuff. People log into their account to check their matches and instead of the partner of their dreams they get hard-core porn images.'

'It was disgusting,' Marchant said. 'It really upset some of our clients.'

'I bet,' Thorne said.

'Probably only *some* of them.' Ablett glanced down at Sandra Cook again, grinning. She giggled and reddened. Marchant did not look impressed.

'Just smart-arse kids, probably,' Ablett said. 'Easy enough to put right, change a few passwords, whatever.'

'I thought you said it had happened twice,' Thorne said.

'Yeah, well, if they're clever enough to get round it once, they're clever enough to figure out how to do it again. It's just a game, really.'

'Why would anyone do something like that?'

He looked at Thorne as though it were a very stupid question. 'Because they can. Because they want to find out *if* they can. Because they're bored.' He looked at Sandra Cook again, who nodded in agreement. 'That's what most hacking is. Just dicking about, really.'

'We'll need to get our forensic computer team in to take a look.'

'Fine with me,' Ablett said.

Marchant sat forward. 'Does that mean all our systems will be shut down?'

'Hopefully not for very long,' Thorne said.

'What about . . . longer term? I've sunk every penny I've got into this business.'

'Well, bearing in mind what's happened, I can't make any promises at this stage.'

'Why us, though?' Marchant looked to her computer wizard for an answer, but Ablett shook his head. 'After that man Summers, I mean. Why would someone else target us?'

'Nobody's targeting you,' Thorne said. 'They're using you to target your clients. And we're not convinced it's a different individual.'

Marchant looked confused. 'But Summers can't have been responsible for these other victims. He's in prison.'

'Terry Summers is dead,' Kitson said.

Marchant stared at her, trying and failing to process the information.

Watching her face fall, her struggle in the few seconds that followed to summon a little strength and dignity, Thorne came as close as he was ever likely to get to feeling sorry for the woman. It wasn't very close.

'So what's likely to happen?' she asked.

'Well, I'm hoping we catch the individual responsible for the deaths of five women.'

'Yes, that goes without saying, but, I mean . . . are we going to have to shut the agency down?'

Thorne thought it was more than likely and that it would be doing a lot of gullible individuals a big favour. He wondered what he should say, what the correct response should be, as a police officer with no agenda beyond seeing justice done. In the end, he decided that honesty was the best policy, but tried not to show just how much he was enjoying it. He said, 'I can't see you getting round this sort of publicity, however creative you are.'

'Sorry, but it *is* likely to come out at some point.' Kitson reached across to place her mug back on the tray, and stood up. 'It would certainly be worth looking at a back-up plan.'

'What if I don't have a back-up plan?'

'Well, I can work anywhere,' Ablett said. 'No shortage of jobs in IT.'

Sandra Cook stared down at her feet. When Caroline Marchant turned to stare at Ablett, she looked as if she'd been slapped.

Ablett sniffed and picked at a loose thread on the seam of his chinos. 'Just saying . . . '

Driving back towards the motorway, Thorne said, 'We should probably talk to all the men Patricia Somersby, Annette Mangan and Leila Fadel were matched with.'

Kitson looked at him. 'Really?'

228

'I know, it's a waste of time and it's exactly what the killer wants us to do, but it needs to be done. If we get to trial … *when* we get to trial, we don't want some smart defence lawyer pointing out that we hadn't properly considered other suspects.'

Kitson stared out at the shops and houses, hunched pedestrians hurrying through rain that was getting heavier. 'Marchant's question was fair enough.'

'What, were we going to shut them down?'

'Why them?'

'Well … because it's a tinpot operation,' Thorne said. 'Anonymous. No personal contact, nothing other than a list of gullible clients handing over money and getting matched up. If it wasn't that site it would just have been a similar one. I'm guessing there's loads of them.'

'You don't think our man might have a personal connection with this particular site?'

'We'll find out.' Thorne swore and stepped on the brakes, having just missed a green light. 'Let's get everything we can on our unassuming computer wizard. We should probably have a good look at Sandra Cook as well … I got the impression they might be more than just workmates.'

'Yeah.' Kitson shook her head. 'She certainly found him a lot more entertaining than I did.'

'And we need to get forensics in to take that computer system apart as soon as we can. See just how clever Kenneth Ablett is.'

'You fancy him for it?'

Thorne stared at the red light and drummed his fingers against the steering wheel, remembering how wrong he'd been about Gavin Cooper. 'Not sure I'd go that far,' he said. 'But as of now, there isn't anybody else.'

Then Nicola Tanner called and gave him a name.

PART THREE

THIS BLOODY JOB

THIRTY-NINE

They sat close together, drinking coffee on one of the many sofas in the main sitting room. It was cold and Tanner hadn't bothered to take her coat off. 'I still can't get over the size of this place.' It seemed even bigger and less welcoming than the last time she had been here; the austere fireplace remained annoyingly empty. 'I've been to see flats you could fit in this room twice over.'

'You moving?'

'Well, I'm looking.' She glanced at Andrew Evans and saw that he was waiting for her to say more; eager for conversation. 'Somewhere handier for work, you know.'

'Right.'

The door was open and Tanner saw one of the officers slow and glance in as he passed the doorway. 'You must be feeling lonely, Andrew.'

'Yeah, a bit.' Evans shrugged and stretched out his legs. 'There's a couple of other people here now, but we don't interact much. It's not exactly a holiday camp.'

Tanner nodded. She'd been informed on each occasion Long

Barrow Manor was expecting a new arrival; a written reminder of the protocol, as patronising as it was unnecessary.

'We're not really supposed to talk to each other. I mean, sometimes we do, but they try not to give us the chance.'

'That's how it works,' Tanner said. 'Somebody lets something slip and it puts the other person at risk.'

'At more risk.'

Tanner said nothing.

'I mean just "hello" or whatever, maybe a word or two when we're all eating, but there's usually plenty of officers around. There's more of them than there are of us.' Evans shook his head and smiled, visibly more relaxed than the last time Tanner had seen him. The most recent report sent by the facility's on-site counsellor had been positive. The physical withdrawal from the drug was almost complete, she had been told, though that was only the first part of the process.

Evans leaned closer to her and lowered his voice, even though there was nobody there to eavesdrop. 'One of the new blokes is like something out of a Guy Ritchie movie, I swear. Messed up teeth, looks like he'd happily rip your head off . . . must be part of an organised crime thing. The other one's younger. I don't know . . . maybe he's giving evidence in a drugs-related case, same as me?' He looked at Tanner, enjoying the cloak and dagger. 'Am I close?'

'I can't say.'

'I mean, they're both spending plenty of time with Call Me Rob, so they've obviously both got . . . issues. The gangster bloke looks like a major boozer. Got one of those noses, you know? Like a chewed tomato.'

'I can't say, because I don't know.'

'Really?'

'They're working with different forces,' Tanner said. 'So honestly, your guess is as good as mine. All I can tell you is that anybody who gets brought here is helping the police investigate

234

some seriously dangerous people.' She saw his face change. 'But you knew that anyway.'

'Hard to forget.'

'Anyway, *you* certainly seem to be making progress with ... what did you call him? The counsellor ... '

Evans inched away from her. 'Yeah well, problem with that is, the clearer my head gets, the more time I can spend thinking about just how much shit I've dropped myself in.'

There was no longer any sign of a tremor, no tapping of his trainer against the grey carpet, but Tanner could see that Evans was still tense, still terrified; as eaten up by guilt as he had ever been.

She said, 'We're going to get you out of it.'

'Yeah?'

Tanner reached for her bag, opened up the file she'd brought with her and carefully laid out the sheets on the low table in front of them. Printouts, photographs. Evans sat forward and stabbed at one of the pictures: an old woman with big glasses and candyfloss hair.

'There she is.' He spoke quietly, but his voice was thick with distaste. For the woman in the photograph or for himself. 'The Duchess.'

'They're *all* her,' Tanner said. 'These are a few of the IDs she used to visit various prisons. All in different names. Fake driving licences, passports, whatever. The prisons took copies every time she visited, so we had them sent across.' She pointed. 'See how good she is at changing her appearance?' They stared at the pictures of what appeared, at first glance, to be several women of anywhere between fifty and sixty-five. 'Different glasses or no glasses, different wigs, make-up, whatever. We know that most of the time these things aren't exactly scrutinised anyway, so she didn't have any problem.'

Evans sat back slowly. 'So, is any of this going to help you find her?'

'I've circulated these to all forces in the country, with regular follow-ups to those in coastal locations, because more than one witness thought there was a link to somewhere by the sea. So, Devon and Cornwall, Kent, Dorset, Norfolk. They've obviously gone to every prison in the country as well, in case she decides to go back to work. So yes, I'm hopeful.' She looked at him, well aware that nothing she had said would raise his or anyone else's spirits, and that she hadn't really answered his question. 'We are pursuing several other lines of inquiry, Andrew.' 'Several' was an exaggeration, as, quite probably, was 'inquiry'. The last time she'd seen Dipak Chall, he looked like a man who had been asked to punch himself in the face eight hours a day. 'I'm every bit as keen to find this woman as you are, and she can lead us to the people she's working for. The ones responsible for all this.'

'How long?'

Andrew Evans sounded tired. He was intelligent enough to know this was a question that didn't have an answer, but desperate enough to ask it anyway.

How long will I be here?

How long will my wife be in danger?

How long until we can see each other again?

Tanner felt something twist and settle in her stomach. She reached for her bag again, took out her mobile and began scrolling through her contacts. She said, 'I'm moving because my partner died. The house we lived in is just too big now, that's all.'

Evans blinked. Said, 'Sorry.'

'It's fine. It's just a house.'

'Is it?' He looked about as convinced as he had been by Tanner's progress report.

Tanner straightened up and dialled a number. When the call was answered she listened for a few seconds, then said, 'Yes, he's with me.'

Evans sat forward fast.

She handed the phone across and said, 'Someone who wants to talk to you.' She picked up her bag and waited until he was looking at her. 'You know the rules, Andrew. I'm trusting you.'

Tanner stood and walked quickly towards the doorway. She turned, just in time to see Evans's eyes close, and watched his face soften before she shut the door behind her.

Paula sounded happy enough, but he could hear the effort in her voice; the brightness a little forced. She did not ask him where he was, or what he was doing, and he guessed she had received much the same pep talk from Tanner as he had.

She said, 'Things are fine here, really.'

'That's great.'

'Quieter, obviously.' A laugh, again a little strained.

'How's Sean doing? Is he there?'

'He's at nursery.'

'Yeah, right. Stupid.'

'He's good though, into everything.'

'What have you told him? Why I'm not there, I mean.'

There was a pause. He heard her suck in a fast breath. 'I said you were having a holiday.'

Evans turned and saw an officer staring in at him through the French windows. He stared back. 'Tell him I'll bring him something home, OK?'

'Don't worry, he already mentioned it.'

Now, Evans laughed, and he bit it back before it became a sob.

'Andy—'

'Yeah, I'm—'

'There are police outside,' she said.

Evans went cold. 'Yeah?'

'Sitting in a car on the other side of the road. I mean . . . I was scared until I found out they were police, you know? Now I take them tea every so often, chat for a bit, but they're always look-ing around, like they're keeping an eye out. Actually, I should probably be *more* scared, shouldn't I? That someone thinks they need to be there. Andy . . . ?'

'It's just a routine thing, OK? I promise, everything's going to be fine.'

'You swear?'

'I'll be home soon and I'm going to be different.'

Another pause. 'Everything's going to be different,' she said.

He could hear the tremble in her voice. 'What's happened?'

She told him about the baby that was on the way, the second child they'd been talking about before he'd been taken. She said that she was just beginning to show, and he shouted and grinned, and he started to cry when she told him that it was going to be fine.

'Don't.'

'I should be there . . . '

'Just remember how much you've got to come home to, all right?'

He couldn't speak.

'I love you,' she said.

The door opened, and Tanner's head appeared briefly around it. The look on her face made it clear that his time was almost up.

'You too,' he said.

He told her to tell Sean how much he missed him, to take care of herself and the baby, and there were only a few seconds left to talk after that. How much better he was feeling in himself, the jobs he'd been thinking about going after when he got back. A selection of small lies.

He ended the call and dropped back on to the sofa.

The elation he'd felt at hearing his wife's voice – her shocking, wonderful news – had gone before he was still and settled. Like the blood draining from that junkie's face. Quick as that kid coming across his bonnet; saucer-eyed in the fraction of a second before the gunshot-crack and the bloodied spider-web.

He felt agitated and afraid.

He wanted to get high.

FORTY

'Unfortunately, I remember Aiden Goode only too well.' The deputy governor of Maidstone prison sat back and sighed. 'He's not one of those you tend to forget.' Jeremy Powell had a thin face and a beard that he tugged at almost constantly, as though actually trying to tear out chunks of hair. He looked a good deal older than his forty-two years. 'So, what's he been up to?'

'I'm sure you understand that we can't go into details,' Thorne said.

'We need to find him,' Kitson said. 'That's as much as we can tell you, I'm afraid. We want to talk to him urgently in connection with an ongoing investigation.'

Powell nodded and pulled a thick manila folder towards him across his desk. 'Of course, and I also understand that seeing as you're both detectives with the Homicide unit, it must be a fairly serious investigation. You're not likely to be after a man like him because he hasn't taken his library books back.' He opened the folder. 'Not that he was a prisoner who spent much time in the library . . .'

Since Nicola Tanner had passed on the name given her by

Graham French the day before, and the reason it might be significant, the team had been working flat out to track down Aiden Goode, a forty-three-year-old released from prison in February the previous year, having served eight years of a fifteen-year sentence for multiple offences.

Violent sexual assault.

Attempted kidnap.

Rape.

The man they were looking for had been found almost immediately, but then, just as quickly, lost again.

After being released, Goode had returned home to live with his wife in south London. They had regularly attended relationship counselling sessions together. He had seen his probation officer once a week, taken a series of short-term jobs when not registered for Jobseeker's Allowance and, while hardly qualifying as upstanding citizen of the year, appeared to have been gradually reintegrating himself into society.

Then, five months after his release, Goode had vanished.

'Just before Karen Butcher was killed,' Tanner had pointed out to Thorne, late the night before. 'He cons everyone into thinking he's a changed man, then starts offending again. Only now it's a damn sight worse . . .'

This positive development, at least in terms of identifying a suspect, was about as good as the news got. A bubble of hope that burst almost instantly. The whip was duly cracked and the overtime payments authorised, but however hard and deep the team had dug, it quickly became apparent that, having taken the decision to disappear, Aiden Goode had become an expert at staying invisible.

Traceless . . .

In the previous nine months there was no active record of him with the DVLA or HMRC. He had not used the mobile phone, credit cards or email accounts registered to him and had not interacted in any way with social media. There had been no

240

communication with family members or known associates. He had not seen a doctor, claimed benefit or come into contact with the police, and his name did not appear on any death certificate.

'Dropped off the grid,' Tanner had said.

Just the two of them left by then, hunched over screens in a semi-dark office. The discordant hum of sleeping computers and distant traffic. Empty coffee cups and grease-stained pizza boxes on the desk behind them.

Thorne had stared down, scratchy-eyed, at the face on his monitor; the last known photograph of Aiden Patrick Goode, taken just before his release from prison. 'Or become someone else . . .'

'So, what was he like?' Thorne asked now.

'Well, officially, it's all in there.' Powell nodded towards the file he had handed over, the six-inch thick sheaf of papers that Thorne and Kitson had divided up and were now flicking through.

Aiden Goode's IIS file.

'But it doesn't really tell the whole story.'

The Inmate Information System provided what amounted to a complete history of a prisoner's time at Her Majesty's pleasure: case notes; visitor lists; work details; rehab programmes and educational courses taken; disciplinary action; letters and statements.

'Yes, you can see that this particular prisoner went to all the right groups and classes, ticked the boxes he needed to, but it's just a record. Files that have to be filled in to keep the likes of me and my superiors happy. The prison authorities. You won't get a real sense of the man from anything that's in there.' The beard-tugging became a little more frenetic and Powell swallowed hard, as though something bitter had risen into his throat. 'In theory, Goode was the kind of prisoner you dream of. While he was here, he didn't do a single thing that would put so much as an extra day on his sentence . . . well, not anything that was ever seen or reported. But I'd rather be locked in a cell with any one of the habitual troublemakers we've got in here, the ones my officers get out the body armour for, than spend five minutes with Aiden Goode. He wasn't someone I was pleased to see paroled, and I made my feelings about that very clear at the time, but I wasn't sorry to see the back of him.'

'We spoke to a former prisoner who'd been here at the same time,' Kitson said. 'He said it was like getting rid of a bad smell.'

'A stench,' Powell said.

Thorne leafed through pages – details of Goode's movements between wings, a trip to a local hospital for dental work – until something caught his eye. He took a sheet of paper from the file and showed the entry he was interested in to Kitson. He turned back to Powell. 'Advanced computer classes?'

'Yes, he had an aptitude for it. I think it was something he'd started when he served some time elsewhere and he was very keen to carry on when he was with us.'

'How advanced is advanced?' Thorne asked.

'I'm not sure. I could try to dig out a syllabus if you like.'

'Advanced enough to hack someone else's system?'

'Well, that's certainly not something they teach.'

'He was good though, you said?'

Powell nodded. 'He could easily have carried on when he got out.'

Thorne said he would need a copy of Goode's course work, any exams he had taken. Powell told him he would get them anything they needed.

'So, tell us about this business with the cats.'

The deputy governor pointed to the papers in Thorne's and Kitson's laps, before his fingers went back to work at his beard. 'That's all there in the file, too. We'd been having a major problem with rats and the traps were useless, so we brought a couple of cats in. Two days later the poor things were found mutilated.' He shook his head. 'Dismembered. Laid out.' He watched as

Thorne and Kitson pored over the relevant pages. 'You'll see from the statements that none of my officers had anything other than a strong suspicion Goode was responsible.'

Thorne read through a statement made by Aiden Goode himself when he was questioned about the incident.

Why would anyone do something like that? To an innocent creature, I mean. Sick, that's what it is. Whoever did it needs to watch their back, all I'm saying, because if people in here find out who it was, things could turn seriously nasty.

'He was almost certainly responsible,' Powell said. 'But without proof, it doesn't go on a prisoner's record. We have the same need for evidence that you do.'

'Why do you think he did it?' Thorne asked.

Powell turned his palms up. 'Perhaps he hated cats as much as he hated women. There's certainly no doubt about *that*. If he'd shown the slightest hint of remorse for what he'd done to his victims, he might have been released even sooner than he was. He may have said he was sorry to the parole board when it was necessary, but I saw no sign of it.'

Thorne thought about what he'd seen on that face he'd spent so long staring at the night before. Nothing that had struck him as shame or regret. It wasn't what anyone would call a smile, certainly not that, but there had been . . . something around the eyes.

An invitation of some sort. A challenge.

It had been late, Thorne told himself. He'd been tired. Perhaps he had just seen what he had needed to see.

Kitson pulled out another sheet. 'Not much in the way of Authorised Visitors.'

'No, just the wife.' Powell grunted. 'She came every week, if she could. Stuck by him for some reason.'

'She needs her head examined.'

'I'm guessing she was scared of him,' Powell said. 'Plenty of people were.'

Perhaps it had been plain and simple confidence, Thorne

thought, that he had seen on Aiden Goode's face. Knowing how easily you frightened people could give you that. He looked at Powell and said, 'The truth is, we can't find him. He's dropped out of sight completely.'

Powell nodded, as though this wasn't much of a shock. 'There's actually a statement about that in the IIS, too. One of my officers overheard him talking to another prisoner, telling him how easy it would be to go off radar . . . something like that. Another thing the parole board chose to ignore.'

'I don't suppose he gave any helpful details?'

'Like I said, it was just something somebody overheard.' Powell flashed a thin smile, there and gone. 'I certainly haven't had any postcards.'

'Worth a shot,' Kitson said.

'They don't always get it right, you know?' Powell watched as Thorne and Kitson put the paperwork back together. 'The Ministry of Justice and the people they appoint to decide who's safe to put back out on the streets. Well, you know that better than anyone, because you're usually the ones who have to pick up the pieces.' He took the file back when it was offered, pushed it to one side of his desk. 'I know you can't tell me what it is that Aiden Goode's done, but if it's what I think it might be, I can't really say I'm remotely surprised.'

FORTY-ONE

It was the same bar as last time, the tables starting to fill up with those settling in good and early for a session or grabbing a quick one before heading home. Looking around, Thorne guessed there were a few bankers getting stuck in and others for whom the word would apply as rhyming slang; certainly a smattering of lawyers from the chambers dotted around Lincoln's Inn. Right or wrong, he could not imagine that too many of the customers had quite the same need of a drink at the end of their day as he or the woman sitting opposite him did.

Thorne raised his glass. Said, 'Thanks for this.'

'Not a problem,' Melita Perera said.

'A bit last minute, I know. Sorry.'

He had got back from Maidstone after lunch and spent a couple of frustrating hours in the afternoon trying and failing – along with everybody else on the team – to make any headway in the search for their major suspect. After a terse discussion with Helen about arrangements for the evening and with the story Jeremy Powell had told him and Kitson still rattling around in his brain – that stench he was starting to get a good whiff of – Thorne had decided he needed to fit in a quick chat with someone who knew more about the likes of Aiden Goode than anyone.

'As long as it's not another game show.' The psychiatrist reached for her own glass.

Thorne looked at her.

'On the hotspot, like last time.' Perera smiled. 'Stab or strangle?'

'You picked the right one,' Thorne said.

'Lucky guess.'

Thorne took another drink, swallowed. 'I don't think so.' The skirt and jacket were lighter, he thought, than those she had worn last time, and something about her hair was different. 'Did you ... get a chance to look at the material I sent?'

'I read it through once, yes.' She reached down for a thin leather satchel and removed a sheaf of notes. She laid them on the table. 'As you said though, it was a bit last minute.'

'It's fine,' Thorne said. 'I don't need a written report or anything. I just wanted to know what you made of it, that's all.' His turn to smile. 'Wondered if you could take a few guesses.'

Rolling her eyes, she put down her wine, leaned forward and began to turn the pages.

A little more of it was down, Thorne decided. Her hair. Last time she had tied it up with a band. 'So, what about the cat killings, then? The fact they haven't stopped, I mean.'

Perera glanced up. 'Well, of course, it might mean that the homicides *have* stopped. For a while, at least. If your cool-down theory is correct.'

'Yeah, well, I'm starting to doubt that.'

'Nothing's ever going to be cut and dried,' she said. 'Not with this sort of offender. Maybe they're just keeping their hand in with the cats while they look for another victim, or they could be doing both at the same time. Maybe there's no rhyme or reason to it at all.'

'No ... he's organised. He knows exactly what he's doing—'

Thorne stopped and looked at her, remembering what she had said a fortnight earlier.

Perera shook her head, reading. 'Don't worry. I know I hedged my bets a little last time we met, but I'm as certain as I can be that it's a man who's responsible for these murders. A man who hates women.'

Thorne didn't think a degree in psychiatry was necessary to work that much out. 'Well, Aiden Goode is definitely one of them.'

Perera raised a hand. 'I should say, certain kinds of women.'

Thorne waited.

'I was just wondering if there was rather more to the whole dating agency thing than just being a nice easy way to select his victims.'

'Well ... they're single women and those are the ones he's after. Easy to load suspicion on to the men they go on dates with. Easy to find out everything about them.'

'Yes, but that's exactly what I'm talking about. What if it's *because* they're women who are ... looking for someone? Who are advertising, if you like.'

They stared at one another for a few seconds. Perera looked briefly across at the two young men who were taking seats at an adjacent table.

She leaned forward and lowered her voice.

'Perhaps that's *why* he targets them. Perhaps he's a man who is repulsed for some reason by women who ... put themselves on display like that. Women who are older or maybe a little overweight or not what he's decided is conventionally attractive, yet still have the audacity to say "here I am".' She held her arms wide and looked at him. 'If that's how he sees them, if "flaunting" themselves in that way doesn't conform with his twisted idea of how a woman should behave, he would regard the women on that website as needy and pathetic. As worthless.' She sat back slowly, taking her glass with her. 'Look, you said you wanted me to make a guess. So ...'

'Yeah ... that all makes sense,' Thorne said. 'Well, not *sense*, but you know what I mean.' He saw that one of the men who had just sat down was looking at them; looking at Perera. The man caught Thorne's eye and turned away. 'So, what about Aiden Goode, then? You think that sounds like him?'

'I'd need to see the details of his offences,' Perera said.

Thorne had guessed, even as he was asking the question, that she would not commit herself to quite that extent. A piece of educated guesswork was one thing, but an unprofessional stab in the dark was rather too much to hope for. 'It's more or less the only name we've got,' he said.

'What do you think?'

Thorne *had* seen the details of the offences for which Aiden Goode had been convicted. The MOs were certainly rather less convoluted, but there was no question that his crimes had been about power and hate; that he had seen his victims as insignificant.

He could still picture the look of revulsion on Jeremy Powell's face.

'He fits the bill,' Thorne said.

Perera finished her drink and watched as Thorne downed the last of his. Every table in the place was now taken and customers were queuing at the bar. She slid the papers back into her satchel and said, 'Shall we have another one?'

Thorne looked at his watch.

'Oh. If you need to be somewhere ... '

He did, but, inexplicably dry-mouthed, Thorne sat there humming and hawing, desperately trying to work out how long he would need to get where he was going. If there was time for at least one more quick drink. If he could make a call and cancel, because there was nothing that couldn't be talked about the following morning. Not really.

Perera raised a pair of perfectly shaped brows. 'Meeting someone? I'm guessing it's a woman, judging by how worried you are about being late.'

'Yeah ... but not like that.' Thorne hoped his smile would make it clear what *that* meant, but the smile he got in return only made things more difficult. Another few seconds ticked past, before common sense made its unwelcome presence felt.

'I'd really love to stay for a bit. Honestly.' The sigh Thorne let out was heartfelt and tasted of Guinness. 'But the woman I'm meeting is a bit of a stickler.'

FORTY-TWO

This time it was Thorne's place – *Helen's* place – and Tanner chose to bring fish and chips. Thorne, who was very happy to eat from the paper, fetched beers from the fridge and smiled as Tanner helped herself to a plate and a roll of kitchen towel.

'Helen's got a late one,' Thorne had told her when they'd been deciding where and when to get together. 'And Alfie's staying with her sister, so we'll have the place to ourselves.' He wasn't sure then, or now, why he'd felt the need to go into detail. It was as much about reassuring himself as explaining the situation to Tanner, after the tetchy exchange of texts earlier in the day.

Nicola T might come over later. ok?

I won't be there.

Just a catch-up, not for long.

Doesn't matter.

Helen's mood had clearly not softened a great deal since their argument that morning. She'd snapped at him, irritable in the wake of another difficult conversation with her sister, and Thorne had snapped right back.

'I prefer haddock, actually.' Tanner delicately squeezed a blob of ketchup on to the corner of her plate. 'But for some reason, your local place only does cod.' Thorne took the bottle from her and squirted ketchup over everything.

They ate.

'How was Evans?' Thorne asked.

'He was OK when I got there.' Tanner scraped batter from her fish. 'A bit of a mess after he'd spoken to his wife. Once she'd told him about the baby.'

'Worried he's not going to be there when it's born.'

'With good reason,' Tanner said. She told Thorne about the job she'd given Dipak Chall; the only solid line of inquiry she was pursuing on the Adnan Jandali murder. The hunt for the woman called the Duchess.

'You never know,' Thorne said.

'I know we should be doing more, but I'm out of ideas. Whoever killed Jandali went to ground every bit as fast as the Duchess. No trace of that motorbike, no evidence other than the stuff we've got on Evans and we know that was all planted. Every time there's so much as a sniff of someone who might have information, they've mysteriously become deaf and dumb by the time we get to them.'

'You're after some scary fuckers,' Thorne said. 'Always the same way.'

'Doesn't help Andrew Evans though, does it?'

Thorne grunted and chewed. He was finding it hard to have too much more sympathy for the man being held at Long Barrow Manor than he did when they'd first brought him in. Evans must have had some idea of the kind of people he was dealing with; at least by the time he was waving a gun about and demanding money with menaces.

251

'Sitting there going mental,' Tanner said, 'while his wife's up the duff and he doesn't know what's going on, and the best I can do is send somebody online shopping.'

'You said yourself, what else can you do?'

'I can get him home to his family.'

Thorne looked up and saw the concern on Tanner's face. Now he felt it too; a flutter of something close to it, at any rate. Perhaps it was simply because he had too much else on his mind to spend a lot of time worrying about what Andrew Evans was going through.

'Sorry I haven't exactly been pulling my weight,' he said. 'On the Jandali murder. Evans . . .'

Tanner looked at him.

'You pitched in on my case and I promised I'd do the same with yours. I know I haven't exactly been keeping my end up.'

Tanner smirked.

'Seriously.'

Tanner shook her head and speared a fat chip. 'First off, your case has got way bigger than anyone thought it would, so it's obviously your prime concern. And secondly, don't worry.' She smiled and popped the chip into her mouth. 'Because you *will* pay.'

Thorne didn't doubt it.

They carried on eating half-heartedly for a few minutes, but neither could finish. Tanner was on her feet and clearing the table before Thorne could stop her. She scraped leftovers into the bin then dropped papers and empty cans into the recycling. As she was rinsing her plate under the hot tap, she said, 'So, what about this cat business?'

'What about it?'

'If he's still doing it, or if he's started again, what does that do to your theory? Is he cooling down?'

'I talked to Perera again,' Thorne said. 'Came straight here from seeing her, actually.'

252

Tanner put the plate into the dishwasher and closed the door. 'Oh, you did.'

'She still thinks it's a perfectly reasonable theory, but she reckons it's never going to be that straightforward. Maybe he's been killing cats all the time. Or maybe he's killing them again now because he can't find human victims quickly enough.'

'That doesn't sound good.'

'None of it sounds good.'

As Tanner moved across to sit down again, Thorne fetched her a bottle of water from the fridge and grabbed another beer for himself.

'So, everything's pointing towards Aiden Goode.'

'Seems to be.' Thorne opened his beer. 'Everything the deputy governor at Maidstone told us puts him in the frame and nothing Melita said takes him out of it.'

'Melita?'

'Perera. It's her name.' Thorne turned away, but sensed a smirk.

'Fine ... but I think we should still find out a bit more about that computer bloke at the dating agency.'

Thorne hummed, non-committal. Ablett ...

'He's got to be worth looking at.'

Thorne stared at the can in his hand, flicked at the ring pull. 'Bloke didn't set off any alarm bells with me, but I'm starting to wonder if I'm any good at reading people these days. If I was ever any good.'

'Don't be soft,' Tanner said.

Thorne was not in the mood to be easily reassured. 'Maybe it's something that just starts to go a bit when you get older.'

'Oh, come on, it's the exact opposite. I mean ... it's not a *knack*, is it? It's about experience.'

'Like having less energy. Less everything. Like your eyesight and your hearing going, like having to sit down when you put your bloody socks on.'

Tanner laughed. 'It's when you have to put your trousers on sitting down that you need to start worrying, mate.'

Thorne remembered his conversation with Christine Treasure. Her suggestion that these waves of self-doubt were really a form of self-protection. Insulating himself in advance against the chill of a bad result, or no result at all. He took a swig of beer. He sighed and said, 'You're probably right. As usual.'

'Be handy if it *was* him,' Tanner said. 'Ablett.'

'Yeah, at least we know where he is.'

'Might close one of our cases, at least.'

'How does that fit with your picture, though? A killer who's doing his best not to be found and then he's right there in the first place we go looking.'

'Why not? Plain sight and all that. Ah . . . ' She held up a finger as though she'd suddenly remembered something and began fishing in her bag for her phone. 'So, what are you going to do about the website?'

'What d'you mean?'

'Once the forensic team have finished with it. I think Russell's getting jumpy. Public safety and all that.'

'I'll talk to him,' Thorne said.

With her phone in her hand, Tanner stabbed and swiped, then moved her chair so that Thorne could see the screen as she scrolled through the pictures. 'Another couple of flats I quite fancy.'

'So you weren't persuaded by that view of a fence and the ample shed room, then?'

'I'm seeing one tomorrow night. You know, if . . . ?'

Thorne held up his hands. 'Sorry, I can't tomorrow. I haven't really seen much of Helen the last few days.' He was thinking on his feet, guilty suddenly. 'So . . . '

'Not a problem.' Tanner moved her chair away again and dropped her phone back into her bag. 'It's not like you were a lot of help last time.'

'We should probably just have a quiet night in.'

'It's fine, Tom, honestly.'

'Quality time, you know?'

Tanner nodded and, as though taking Thorne's words as some kind of cue to leave, ducked down again to pick up her handbag.

'The next one, I promise.' He caught a glimpse of a tired smile as Tanner straightened up, and watching her reach for the coat on the back of her chair, Thorne wondered just how long it had been since she had enjoyed quality time with anyone.

FORTY-THREE

There were more pictures now, more names scribbled on the whiteboard that had been wheeled into the Incident Room. More chairs that had been dragged from corners or behind desks and more people than last time waiting: nursing takeaway coffees and pretending to be rather more alert than they were; flicking through the briefing notes that had been handed out ten minutes earlier.

Then, more faces turned his way.

'I know it's early,' Thorne said. He smiled, acknowledging the expansive yawn from a female officer sitting near the front. 'But hopefully, you've had a chance to look at the forensic report on the Made In Heaven computer system. I don't understand most of it myself, but you can just skip to the end.' He waited while pages were turned. 'The site was hacked on two separate occasions and it was made to look like someone was just pissing about. A few hard-core porn shots.'

A hand was raised. 'Shouldn't we get a chance to see those?' The officer turned the pages of his notes, as if he was looking for something. 'You know, so we've got all the information?'

There were a few more comments after that, pockets of laughter. Waiting for it to die down, Thorne remembered waking in the early hours and kicking off the duvet; staring up at the outline of the light fitting in the warm dark and rehearsing his performance. Putting the words together, the right mix of urgency and confidence. Helen had been lying with her back to him and he wasn't certain how long she'd been there. He'd called it a night before she'd got back and couldn't remember her coming in. Perhaps it had been her getting into bed that had woken him, but he was confused, disoriented. He didn't know if she was awake or asleep, and, when he'd reached across to touch her shoulder, there was no reaction. He hadn't said anything.

Now, he looked down at Tanner, who was sitting closest to him. She and everyone else was waiting for him to carry on. 'The first time the site was hacked, the system was actually compromised at a much deeper level. The hacker was able to gain admin privileges and get into the database. From there he was able to get individual email addresses and, if he's as good as this report suggests he is, he could easily have accessed their online information, social media messages, the lot.'

Thorne waited a few seconds.

Helen had still been asleep when he'd left for work . . .

'So . . . that's how he's doing it, but as far as his identity goes, we're now looking at two major suspects.' Many eyes followed his to the two new photographs on the whiteboard, while others dropped to the black and white copies in the briefing notes. 'We've had a good look at the Made In Heaven team and there's nothing about Caroline Marchant or Sandra Cook to get very excited about. But Kenneth Ablett, our computer expert, isn't exactly squeaky clean . . .'

'He's never actually been arrested,' Chall said.

'No, but he's certainly known to police.'

'He was lucky.' Kitson turned to Chall. 'The woman concerned decided not to press charges.'

'Let's have Kenny in for a chat,' Thorne said. 'See how he behaves when we've got *his* admin privileges.'

The female officer who had yawned so theatrically, but was now looking wide awake, raised a hand. She said, 'If it *is* Ablett, why would he bother to hack his own computer system? I mean, if he had access to all that information anyway.'

'Because he's clever,' Tanner says. 'Thinks he is.'

'Oh, Ablett definitely fancies himself,' Kitson said.

Chall nodded. 'He makes it look like someone else got into the system just in case anybody ever traces things back to the agency. He's protecting himself, basically.'

'We'll find out soon enough,' Thorne said. 'But in the meantime, we've still got Aiden Goode.' This time he walked across to the whiteboard and jabbed at the face in the photograph.

That trace of a smile, like he was daring someone.

'Only we haven't got him, have we?'

Thorne looked across at the young officer who had spoken up. One of those assigned to the team from Kentish Town.

'And it's not like we haven't been looking.'

The young man had a point, of course.

'Goode's prison record makes it very clear that he'd talked about disappearing,' Thorne said. 'Going off the grid. Everything we've been told about this individual puts him very much front and centre of this.' He looked back at the officer and thought about those conversations with Tanner and with Treasure. The self-doubt, real or otherwise. Whether or not he'd lost the ability to read people, he knew a man in need of a bollocking when he saw one. 'And no, you're bang on, we haven't got him yet, and I'm really sorry if that makes things a bit tricky for you, if it means you need to get your head down and do a bit more graft than you're used to ... but if you're unhappy, you're more than welcome to request a transfer and fuck off back to Kentish Town. Fair enough?' He looked away as the officer began to redden, as heads began to turn. 'We work harder, OK? We work harder and

258

longer, and we find him. Aiden Goode is not Lord Lucan . . . he's not an international man of mystery. He's just a pissy little rapist who cuts up animals for a laugh. A loser, who thinks it's his God-given right to brutalise women and may well have killed five of them already. We all go back to work and we find him.' He looked from face to face – Tanner, Kitson, Chall – then finally turned his attention back to the young officer from Kentish Town. He waited for him to nod, and nodded back, then pointed to DS Samir Karim. 'Right then, Sam will be doling out the actions . . .'

As everyone began to drift back to their desks, Thorne watched DCI Russell Brigstocke move towards him from the back of the room. Thorne smiled, but he could guess what was coming. His boss looked every bit as jumpy as Tanner had told him he was.

'A word,' Brigstocke said.

Tanner caught Chall before he sat down again. He didn't appear thrilled to have been intercepted.

'How's it going, Dipak?'

The heavy sigh made it clear he knew she wasn't talking about the dating agency case. 'Well, you weren't wrong,' he said. 'About how tedious it would be.'

She followed him to his desk, stood behind his chair when he sat down. 'I never meant for you to do it on your own.'

He turned to look at her. 'Are you kidding? I've got a couple of nice keen trainees working on it with me.' He nodded towards two officers, phones pressed to their ears at the far end of the room, then moved the mouse and clicked to open up a folder on his desktop. 'I reckon they'll probably quit altogether after this.'

'Well then, everyone's happy,' Tanner said. 'You're making all the necessary job cuts single-handed.'

Chall said, 'With respect, boss,' and stuck up his middle finger. 'So, what have we got?'

The DS quickly opened half a dozen different documents,

then shrunk them so that Tanner could see them all at once. 'You any idea how many of these things there are for sale?'

'It's a growth industry,' Tanner said.

She peered at the first one; an image of a minuscule mobile handset pinched between two fingers. Another was dwarfed by a Coke can, while others had been pictured alongside standard-sized mobiles or matchboxes. All had much the same advertising copy.

World's Smallest Phone!!!

Mini Phone 100% Plastic.

Best-selling Spy-Phone.

'Spy-phone, my arse,' she said.

'Arse is exactly right,' Chall said. 'Look at this crap.' He pointed to all the buzzwords that were highlighted; the key search terms that were being used to market the phones. Micro, Cell, Jail, Discreet, Fool the Boss. 'How is having a small phone supposed to fool your boss, anyway?' Both already knew that the answer to the question was irrelevant. That, in the context of these knowing adverts, BOSS actually stood for Body Orifice Security Scanner. 'Like they're small enough to slip in your top pocket or something, when we all know exactly where they're supposed to go. Seen this?' He pointed to the list of additional features on one item. LOW RING TO AVOID UNWANTED ATTEN-TION. 'Right, because you don't want the *Star Wars* theme tune going off when one of these is rammed up your jacksy, do you?'

'No, I suppose not,' Tanner said.

Chall turned to look at Tanner. 'Most of them are on eBay, but there's plenty of other sites selling them. Hundreds of them.'

'You'll get there,' Tanner said.

'So, we're tracking down the sellers one by one—'

'Good.'

' . . . *and* having to deal with sodding eBay.'

Tanner reached across him to move the mouse and leaned in to look at several more of the items for sale. 'Got to be done.'

'And I mean it's not like we haven't got plenty to do on the dating agency case. Well, you heard.'

'Sorry, but the Duchess is the only person who can give us so much as a chance of clearing the Jandali murder up, and until someone has a better idea, this is our best chance of finding her.'

Chall shrugged, rolled his head around. 'Yeah, well. I could do with the overtime, tell you the truth.'

'So, there you go then.' Tanner rested a hand on the DS's shoulder for a second, before turning away. 'Don't say I never do anything for you.'

FORTY-FOUR

Brigstocke closed his office door and said, 'So, what's happening, Tom?'

'You heard,' Thorne said. 'We're bringing Ablett in and we're going after Goode. Specifically, we'll be targeting his family and known associates, significant anniversaries. Going back to double check with the Border Force and all the other major databases . . .'

The DCI waved for him to stop then sat down and watched Thorne run out of steam.

'I'm talking about the dating site.'

Thorne took a seat. 'Well, once this is put to bed I'll be very happy to see the whole poxy business closed down. Probably be a few lawsuits flying about, once everything gets out.'

'You're not daft, Tom, so don't make out like I am. You know very well I'm talking about now. What are you going to do about that website, right now?'

Thorne closed his eyes for a few seconds. He had known this was coming but had been trying not to think about it. It was going to be a fight he had not trained for and he would need to rely on ringcraft, knowing very well that Russell Brigstocke had plenty of his own.

He said, 'If we shut it down now, we'll lose him.'

'You can't be sure of that.'

'He'll know we've sussed it.'

'Sorry, but we might have to take that chance.'

'So he'll stop, for a while and find some new way to work.'

'You said it yourself, out there.' Brigstocke pointed towards the Incident Room. 'He uses that website to find his victims, to select them. Even a three-year-old could figure out that while it's still up and running, while people are still signing up to Made In Heaven and going on dates, there is a significant threat to life.'

'Well—'

'A three-year-old, Tom.'

'Shutting it down doesn't eliminate that threat, though, does it?'

'As far as I can see.'

'It moves it somewhere else, that's all. He's not just going to think, *Oh, well, I've had a good run,* and knock it all on the head, is he?'

Brigstocke looked at him. 'Have you any idea how much shit we'd be in if we didn't do anything? If another woman was killed and it came out later on that we *knew*?'

'Oh, a fair amount, I reckon.'

'Well, I'm glad you agree with that, at least.'

'Thing is, are we really going to be in any less trouble if we shut it all down here and he turns up six months from now and kills a woman somewhere else? Kills several more women? I mean, even a three-year-old can work out that shit is always shit.'

'Don't push your luck, Tom—'

'Someone else's, maybe, but those shitty footprints are still going to lead back here.'

They had been here before, plenty of times. Any number of hard-fought arguments. For Thorne, whenever Brigstocke was passing on pressure from above or trotting out procedure, the outcome was usually about the degree to which the simple thief-taker his boss had once been was subsumed by the demands of management. Could Thorne work his way into the cracks between those two very different roles? How shamelessly could he appeal to the copper that he knew was still lurking in there somewhere?

Sometimes, it just came down to the mood the DCI was in.

'Public safety has to be our primary concern.'

'I get that,' Thorne said.

Brigstocke picked up a piece of paper and waved it; reached for a mug and held it up. 'It's on the bloody *logo*, for heaven's sake.'

THE MET: WORKING TOGETHER FOR A SAFER LONDON.

'*He's* the threat to life,' Thorne said. 'The man that's doing this. Which is why I want to catch him—' He flinched when the mug was banged back down on the desk.

'*I* want to catch him, too.' Brigstocke shook his head. 'Jesus . . . look, you need to give me a *contingency*, all right? You want to carry on with this, we have to find a way forward that eliminates risk.'

'OK.' Thorne waited. It was usually a good idea to see what Brigstocke came up with and negotiate from there. It was all he could do on this occasion, when he had no suggestions of his own.

'We need to take complete control of this website,' Brigstocke said. 'Set our own parameters.'

'Right . . .'

'You'll need to contact all the agency's clients. If he's hacked into their emails, it'll need to be done by phone, obviously.'

'Are you kidding?'

'Do I look like I'm kidding?'

'What if the killer's registered himself?'

'Again, we'd have to take that risk.'

'We'd actually be warning him off personally.'

'Have you got a better idea, mate? Have you got any ideas?'

Thorne began scrabbling for some. 'We'd only need to make

contact with anyone who's been matched since Alice Matthews was killed. That's how it's been working so far. Each victim has been selected from the matches made since the last one.'

Brigstocke considered this for a few seconds. 'OK, I'll buy that.'

'And just the women, right? No reason to think any of the men are actually in any danger.'

'Fair enough. Still has to be done, though.'

Thorne turned to look out of the window. A fat pigeon was hunkered down on the ledge. 'What exactly are we supposed to tell them?'

'Whatever's necessary.'

'"Listen, there's this killer running about, and he's probably got all your details, so you might want to rethink that date you're planning on Friday night"? We'll just be scaring people.'

'You tell them that the website has been hacked and some of their personal information may have been compromised. Actually, probably best if *you* don't tell them anything, because we don't really want any of this coming from a Homicide unit.' The DCI sat back, thinking. 'Safety's the most important thing here, but we don't want to create panic either. Contact each woman's local force, make sure they're fully briefed and get them to make the call.'

'What if one of these women goes to the press?'

'Christ's sake, Tom, do you want this on a plate?'

'I'm just thinking it through—'

'They're told that their co-operation is much appreciated, that they'll be assisting police with an important investigation and that under no circumstances are they to mention this to anyone, because they'll be compromising a major operation.' Brigstocke held his arms out wide. 'I can write all this down for you, if you like.'

'It all helps,' Thorne said.

Brigstocke did not smile. 'Obviously, *if* any dates are made, there'll need to be appropriate surveillance and protection put in place, which is going to mean liaison with the relevant force. I'll leave that particular nightmare in your hands, because you deserve it, and because I'm not going to do your job for you any more than I already have.'

Thorne nodded, stood up.

'Put a dedicated computer forensics team together, a logistics team ... get it done, OK? And there's really no point walking out of here with a face like a smacked arse, because it's the best you're going to get. If you can't make this work, I don't give a toss if it's compromising your operation ... I'll pull the plug.'

Thorne walked quickly from Brigstocke's office back into the Incident Room. Yvonne Kitson looked keen to talk to him about something, but instead he marched straight over to the desk where the officer he'd shouted at fifteen minutes earlier was working at his computer.

'Sorry,' he said.

The officer looked up and smiled. 'It's fine, sir.'

'Sorry ... because what I meant to say before was, you can fuck off back to Kentish Town any time you like.'

FORTY-FIVE

It was comfortingly basic and a lot cheaper than places in the centre of town. There was no TV or piped techno music to drown out conversation, but more important it was the closest pub to Hornsey mortuary; no more than a five-minute walk for Hendricks and on Thorne's route home.

More or less.

'Funny how we always seem to get a table,' Thorne said. 'You noticed that? How nobody's ever that keen to sit near us.'

Hendricks shrugged. 'Who's complaining?'

His friend's appearance might have had something to do with it, of course, the piercings and the elaborate tats, but Thorne sometimes wondered if there was perhaps a lingering whiff of formaldehyde that they no longer noticed, but which was enough to put other drinkers off their beer. Or maybe the pair of them just didn't usually look as though they would welcome company, which was probably because they usually didn't.

Either way, he was relieved to see that Hendricks looked every bit as ready for the beer in front of him as Thorne was.

'Tough day?'

'About average,' Hendricks said. 'Two strokes and a stabbing, and a partridge in a pear tree. You?'

Thorne put away half his beer while he told his friend about the accommodation he had come to with Russell Brigstocke; an operation that had just become seriously delicate. 'Could have been worse, I suppose. At least we don't have to shut the site down, but now we've got to make direct approaches to a lot of the women who've registered. Which means they're involved, like it or not.'

'Don't forget, one of them might already be getting eyed up by you know who.'

'I wish I did know who.' Thorne took another drink. 'If it *is* Aiden Goode, I need to be going after him, instead of fannying about so that Russell gets his "contingency".'

'Can't you narrow it down a bit further, make things slightly easier? The list of possible victims.'

'Well, it's only the women who've been matched in the last couple of weeks or so, since Alice Matthews was killed, and we're only concerned about potential dates being made on Fridays or Saturdays. All the murders have been on one of those two nights.'

'Most obvious night for a date, I suppose.'

'Yeah,' Thorne said. 'Narrows things down a bit, but that's about all we've got to work with. It's not like he's targeting any particular age group or physical type. Just ... women.'

'Single women.'

'Desperate women.'

Hendricks looked at him. 'Harsh.'

'I talked to the psychiatrist again,' Thorne said, shaking his head. 'She thinks that's exactly how the killer sees them. Too needy, too pushy. He's disgusted by the way these women are advertising themselves, because that's not how he thinks proper women should behave. Women are there to be pursued ... the thrill of the hunt, all that.'

'Well, he's certainly doing plenty of hunting,' Hendricks said.

Thorne picked up his glass again and glanced across at the bar. Two handy-looking sorts in work boots and dusty sweatshirts who had been looking in their direction quickly turned away and spoke in whispers. It was not quite a traditional old man's boozer – there were no beer mats stuck to the wall or farting dogs asleep underneath tables – but clearly the sight of someone who looked as if he'd walked off the set of *Hellraiser* was causing something of a stir. It was certainly a very different establishment from the one in which Thorne had met Melita Perera the night before, and he guessed there weren't too many regulars troubling the mute barman for a mojito or a cheeky glass of house red.

'You really reckon he's clever enough?' Hendricks asked. 'To know you've rumbled him if you close the website down?'

'I don't think he's stupid.'

'Good job too. It's the stupid ones you need to be worried about.'

Thorne saw his friend lean forward, keen to share something. 'Go on, then.'

'The Dunning–Kruger effect.'

'Right . . .'

'It's a cognitive bias.'

'Stop showing off.'

Hendricks grinned. 'Basically, back in the nineties, some idiot in America hears that lemon juice can be used as invisible ink. So, he proceeds to rub it all over his face and rob a bank, convinced he'll be invisible to the security cameras.'

'Sounds reasonable enough to me,' Thorne said.

'Apparently this moron was gobsmacked when he was caught . . . couldn't believe it. Anyway, these two psychologists heard about it, so they ran some tests and discovered that very stupid people tend to dramatically over-estimate their own capabilities. Too stupid to know they're stupid, if you see what I mean, because the skills they lack are exactly the same ones they need to recognise their own incompetence. Essentially, it means that a lot of people who are thick as mince can have ridiculous amounts of confidence that's ... misplaced at best.'

Thorne nodded. 'And dangerous at worst.'

'Right.' Hendricks lifted his glass. 'Just look at who some of these morons vote for.'

'I don't think it matters much in the end,' Thorne said. 'I've had murderers who probably qualified for Mensa and I've had some who could barely string a sentence together. Doesn't make much odds to the people they killed.'

'Which ones are easier to catch, though?'

'Sometimes the clever ones get a bit too clever,' Thorne said. 'Let's hope this one does. As of now, he's making a very good job of staying invisible and it's not because he's covered himself in lemon juice.' He glanced over at the bar again as he drained his glass. The two men who had been looking over were now chuckling and talking in hushed tones to the barman and Thorne suspected that he and Hendricks were the topic of conversation. Right then, part of him would have been only too happy if that proved to be the case, if a remark were to be made a bit too loudly.

He wanted something to kick off.

He reached into his pocket when he heard an alert sound on his phone. A text from Tanner.

This flat's even worse than last one. Avocado bathroom FFS! Hope you and Helen are enjoying your quiet night in. x

Thorne put the phone away. 'Nicola.'

'How's her case going?' Hendricks asked. 'The Spice gang?'

Thorne turned back to his friend. 'Not really going anywhere. I haven't exactly been a big help.'

'Yeah, because you've had sod all else to worry about, obviously.'

'I suppose.' He held up his glass. 'Same again?'

Hendricks looked at his watch. 'Thing is, Liam's cooking, so ...'

'No worries.'

'Anyway, aren't you driving?' Hendricks looked and began to nod slowly, clearly able to see that Thorne was in no great hurry to get home. He said, 'Oh ...'

'Helen's sister,' Thorne said.

'Right.' Hendricks had heard this before.

'Helen's been fighting with her and then she takes it out on me.'

'Well, you're there, aren't you?'

Thorne nodded.

'Punchbag's part of the job description, mate.'

'Yeah, well I'm fed up with it. And the hours I'm working – *both* of us are working – there's not a lot of time to sit around and talk about it.' Thorne closed his eyes, and, when he opened them again, he was staring hard at the two men at the bar. 'I don't know ... that, and this case. Took it all out on some gobby DC this morning ... some newbie, barely started shaving. Getting it in the neck just because I am.'

'What about a hit man?'

Thorne looked at him.

'For the sister.'

'Not sure I can afford it.' Thorne sat back and managed the closest thing to a smile since they'd sat down. 'Mind you, I could always do it myself, I suppose.' He reached across to pick up Hendricks's empty glass. 'You could fake the post-mortem results for me.'

Hendricks grinned. 'What are friends for?'

FORTY-SIX

Her real name was Frances Coombs and she'd never been awfully fond of it, so it had been fun dreaming up new ones and creating all those fake identities she'd needed. More often than not she'd gone for old film stars; the ingénues and femmes fatales she'd watched growing up. Those impossibly glamorous women, whose lives she pretended she had, once she'd got too old for all that princess-in-the-castle stuff and moved away from the dump she'd grown up in.

She'd just mixed the names up a bit.

Joan Rogers, Audrey Davis, Grace Taylor . . .

She knew the nickname they'd given her too, some of the boys she visited in prison, and she wasn't unhappy about that either. Why on earth would she be? Plenty of worse things they could have called her, and wasn't it more or less exactly what she'd fantasised about, all those years ago, trying to keep her head above water on that terrible estate?

She'd earned that nickname, she reckoned.

She'd had to come up with a couple more names, now that she was back at work – Sophia Crawford, Barbara Leigh – and she was happy to be earning again, having something to get out of bed for, adding to that nest egg. She'd known it wouldn't be long before she was given the nod. Buying more of those stupid little phones and collecting packages, and the people she was dealing with down here were actually a bit nicer than they'd been up in London. Well, not quite so unpleasant, anyway. The bloke she'd talked to on the phone back then, when she was still working Wandsworth, Brixton, Pentonville, was decent enough, but she'd never really taken to that one who'd made the deliveries. Creepy so-and-so never took his motorbike helmet off for a start, barely said a dicky bird, and when he did she couldn't understand him.

Polish, she reckoned, or Romanian. One of the two . . .

She turned off the TV and wandered across to shoo a seagull off the window ledge. Size of the bloody things never ceased to amaze her and she couldn't get over the cheek of them; bold as brass the evil bastards were, like the foxes back up in London. Swooping down to nick chips off her plate or sitting there on the roof of her car, like they didn't give a monkey's.

Seagulls aside, she was already starting to think that she'd be happy staying here, as long as the work carried on. Asking herself what she'd say to them if they ever told her to come back. In the end, she probably wouldn't have any choice, because she wanted to stay close to her daughter and she couldn't see *her* settling for a life down here, with the grass and the sand and the silly little shops.

It was probably all a bit old and all a bit *white*.

Her girl had always preferred things a trifle more outlandish, more was the pity.

She thought about her daughter while she was making tea to take to bed, and it wasn't a big jump from there to thinking about some of those poor buggers she'd seen on the news. The Spice casualties in Manchester and other places, staggering around like they were half dead, or flat out and trembling on the pavement. The stuff was obviously getting way stronger than it used to be,

273

killing people now, for heaven's sake. She'd no idea how powerful the stuff she delivered was because she never asked. She'd seen a documentary a year or so back, a prison officer on the floor of the staffroom, writhing and shouting after he'd taken in a lungful, so she'd always known it was a lot stronger than the weed she'd occasionally smoked back in the day, but now things were getting daft.

That's why there was so much money in it, she supposed. So many nasty pieces of work. Why people got shot and stabbed, or fitted up like that poor sod Andrew Evans.

Not her fault though, none of it; she could always tell herself that. Aside from the trips to the toilet and the acid reflux, she didn't have any trouble sleeping. I mean, if somebody drank eight cans of White Lightning then got in his car and smashed into a bus stop, you wouldn't arrest the bloke in the off-licence, would you? Whose fault was it her husband had got cancer? His or the newsagent who sold him the fags?

She took her tea and carried it through to the bedroom.

If they wanted her to visit anywhere else, she'd go brunette next time, she decided. Get it done properly; somewhere decent instead of using that cheap dye from the supermarket.

She climbed into bed and listened to the sea and lay there thinking about nice new pictures and nice new names. Rhonda Hayworth or Maureen Sheridan. They sounded all right.

Rita Fleming, maybe . . .

FORTY-SEVEN

He'd looked at pictures the day after Alice Matthews, maybe even the same day now he thought about it, but it hadn't meant anything. He logged on and looked through a few pictures almost every day. Every night. It wasn't even about planning for the next one, not really. It was just a case of seeing what was out there, who had recently registered or been matched, eyeing up a couple of possibilities. That was all.

It certainly wasn't any kind of hunger starting to build. There was no uncontrollable craving that would inevitably grow stronger and demand to be satisfied, none of that claptrap. He'd read his fair share of that cut-price psycho-bollocks; no shortage of it on the internet or those cheap and cheerful true-crime channels way down at the bottom of his TV menu. All entertaining enough if there was nothing else to look at, but you couldn't take any of it seriously.

Bloodlust.

A killer's *perverted* drives and *twisted* mind.

Drivel, all of it . . .

I mean, this was a service he was providing, or as good as. Like those people … customs officers or whatever, whose job it was to weed out fake perfume or moody designer gear, to get cheap copies off the streets. The real thing was the real thing. How hard was that to understand? Nobody in their right mind would argue with that. Whatever something looked like, even if it had all the right labels and accessories, only something authentic was ever going to have the proper quality.

You bought cheap, you bought twice. You bought umpteen times.

He smiled.

OK, so maybe he was stretching the analogy a little, but, as far as he was concerned there were real women, who behaved the way a real woman should, and there were replicas. All the right bits in all the right places and maybe you'd make do with one in an emergency or if there was really no other option, but nothing you'd choose. Not worth having once you'd measured it against the genuine article.

A real woman had grace and strength and she always had confidence. She knew what she wanted and what a real man expected in return, because it was only real men she was interested in. She would never settle for anything but the best, because she knew what she deserved. She would never stop making the effort or paying attention, or taking the time to be that little bit sexier or more beautiful.

And she would *never* beg.

A replica couldn't even come close. A third-rate copy on the lookout for a man every bit as inept and desperate as she was. The way he saw it, some of them were no more than a notch above those sex robots he'd seen on TV. They even *felt* like women, at least the really expensive ones did. All the holes anyone would need, tits designed to order, but seriously, what kind of man would shell out for something like that? The kind of man who couldn't do any better for himself, simple as that, who made do with replicas.

The things some of the women put in their profiles, for God's sake! The things these no-hopers thought were *selling* points.

I want to bring creativity into a relationship.

I enjoy playing rugby and watching drag racing.

Likes: Politics/current affairs. Real ale.

He logged into the site, began to poke around. A few new names and photographs; a few more piss-poor little lives to marvel at or be disgusted by for half an hour before he turned in.

Ava. 36. Designer.

Christine. 55. Company Director.

Julie. 29. Retail Executive.

Oddest thing of all, and this always amazed him, some of them weren't even particularly awful to look at. He guessed that several of the pictures were every bit as fake as the women themselves, but even so, one or two of them were actually ... all right. The way they presented themselves was borderline acceptable, but the very fact that they *had* to, that there was this need to exhibit themselves in a shop window ...

Above all, what saddened him the most, was the fatal lack of dignity.

And *he* was the one that was supposed to have some sort of twisted hunger.

He scrolled and selected, he downloaded and printed out. It was as much about killing time as anything, because he wasn't actually on the lookout, not just yet. Of course, there was always the possibility that he would see something that was simply too perfect to pass by, like an immaculately tailored jacket or a beautiful watch or whatever, that he'd spot somewhere and be unable to resist.

But that wasn't the reason he was there.

He opened up Ava's profile and began to read.

Just browsing.

277

FORTY-EIGHT

The minute the man was on the ground, his legs kicking slowly like some kind of dying bluebottle, Kieran Sykes took out his phone and began filming. It was hilarious. It was better than the telly. He was pretty sure that if some of those daft home-video shows on the box were a bit edgier, he might have made himself a few quid.

The man had stumbled for a few yards before hitting the deck, leaned against a wall like he might be having a piss, and gone down like a sack of spuds.

Smacked his head good and hard as well, which hadn't done him any favours.

Kieran stepped into the road, dodged a van and kept on filming; zoomed in, even though the bloke wasn't thrashing around any more, providing his own over-the-top commentary to amuse his mates later on.

'*This* is what drugs can do. Drugs are evil! Behold . . . *this* man is a respectable politician, but one spliff laced with just a drop or two of the deadly "zombie juice" has reduced him to this. How can we protect our children? How can we stop this terrible drug from creating a plague of mashed-up undead who will surely destroy our inner cities ...'

Kieran was still laughing as he turned the phone off and ambled away towards his flat. Now there was no question that it was good gear he was selling. One spliff, that was all. Ready-rolled as well, for the buyer's convenience. To be fair, he preferred doing it, because aside from the fact that most of his customers were in too much of a hurry to be arsed doing it for themselves, it meant he could control the amount of the stuff he was shifting. He'd actually thought he was skimping, because that's what he'd always done, but this batch must have been considerably pokier than he'd been told. It was good news, because it meant he could put even less of it in next time.

Ker-ching!

Not such good news for that soppy sod he'd left spark out on the pavement, mind you. *Politician*, he thought, laughing out loud again. That was a nice touch ...

He crossed the Seven Sisters Road, thinking he might pick up something to eat, then deciding he couldn't be bothered when he saw the queue in the kebab shop. Ten minutes later, he turned into his street and was just thinking that cheese on toast would hit the spot when he saw the bike parked outside the house and the man sitting on his garden wall.

Kieran walked past him, and the man stood up. He was dressed from head to foot in black leather, like something out of a gay porn film, his crash helmet dangling from one hand.

'Sir ...'

Kieran turned round. Said, 'Unless you've got a pizza on the back of that bike, you can piss off.'

'I have a message for you, that's all.'

Kieran stepped towards him. What kind of accent was that, anyway? Eastern European, some shit. Like a vampire or a hooker.

'You cannot work here any more,' the biker said. 'OK? Not in Tottenham, not in Hackney. Not in ... north.'

279

'Say again, boss?'

'That's it. You don't sell any more because there isn't room. You understand?'

'Oh, come on, mate. You saying there isn't room in north London for an independent trader to make a living for himself?' Kieran smiled, waited, but the man looked straight through him. Kieran held out his arms. 'I'm only punting a few joints, for Christ's sake. It's beer money, basically.' When this got no reaction, Kieran dropped his arms and moved a step closer. 'Is it you saying this or some pussy who sent you because he can't be bothered to tell me himself? Making out like he's Pablo Escobar or whoever?'

The biker shook his head.

'Well, whoever it is, tell them that a bit of healthy competition is good for everyone, all right? It's the free market or whatever. It's what made this country great. No offence.'

The biker nodded. 'I was just told to give you the message. I gave you the message.'

Kieran turned away and walked towards the house, shouting as he stepped over the wall and trudged across the front garden. 'Well, message received, thanks very much.' Now he was laughing again. 'Received and filed under "couldn't give a flying fuck".' He used his left hand to dig for keys and his right to raise a finger.

The biker shrugged and put his helmet and gloves back on, then took the gun from his jacket pocket. He marched smartly up the path as Kieran pushed his key into the front door and shot him in the back of the head.

FORTY-NINE

Kenneth Ablett was one of those unfortunate people whose face made it seem as if he was constantly amused about something; whose expression fell naturally into what could best be described as a smirk. Kitson had noticed it when she'd met him at the Made In Heaven offices. It was fine, she thought, if you were one half of a comedy double act, but it played rather less well in an interview room. He had at least dispensed with the man-bun this morning, having decided quite sensibly that it was best not to antagonise the officers interviewing him any more than was absolutely necessary.

He had a fair amount of ground to make up.

He had been pleasant enough since arriving. He had declined the offer of legal representation and smirked his way through the caution while Dipak Chall had delivered it. He folded his arms and smirked some more while they waited for the long tone on the recorder to finish, for Kitson to take him through the formalities.

When she had finished, she said, 'I just want to talk to you about some of the things our computer forensics team discovered. What's been going on with your system.'

Ablett nodded. 'OK.'

'You were aware that the system had been hacked, you told us that a few days ago, but did you know that the hackers gained access that went way beyond a few hard-core porn shots?'

'You mean a dummy hack?'

'If you're talking about a hack that looks like one thing but is actually something rather more insidious, that's exactly what I mean.' Kitson looked at him. 'You still think it was kids, Mr Ablett?'

'Maybe.'

'Doing it because they can?'

'Or to see *if* they can.'

'Whoever hacked into the Made In Heaven system gained access to pretty much everything. All the databases, all the privileges, left no trace of his IP address.'

'Well . . . so, maybe not fourteen-year-olds, but people who are younger than we are, probably. Like that lad who sussed out the ransom-ware attack last year. WannaCry? The one on the NHS?' The smirk grew a little more pronounced. 'They gave *him* a job in cyber security.'

'Right, because he *stopped* a hack. I'm talking about someone who gained confidential information on all your agency's clients, then targeted them individually.'

'Spear phishing.' He nodded. 'When you tailor a hack to someone specific.'

'You certainly seem to know all about it,' Chall said.

'I work with computers,' Ablett said. 'You pick this stuff up.'

'Picked up enough so that you could do it yourself?'

'Just because I know what things are called—'

'So, you've never done it?'

'What, like *this*?'

'Have you ever hacked into anyone's computer, Mr Ablett? Have you ever gone "spear phishing"?'

'No.'

'Really?'

Kitson glanced down at a sheet of paper on the table. 'That's not what Judith Holloway thinks ...'

Ablett sat back and sighed. 'What the hell are you talking to her for? She's completely ...' He rolled his eyes and tapped a finger against the side of his head.

'When Miss Holloway went to the police eight months ago, when she *first* went to the police, she alleged that you had somehow accessed her private emails and text messages.'

Ablett shook his head.

'She claimed that, by doing that, you were able to find out where she was going and who she was seeing. That you kept turning up out of the blue, that on a number of occasions she saw you watching her. Enough times to convince her that you must have been spying on her remotely.'

'Yeah, well whatever she claimed, there obviously wasn't any evidence, was there? Else the police would have arrested me. And they didn't.'

Chall turned some pages. 'Actually, Miss Holloway's allegations alone would have been grounds to arrest you, but for some reason she declined to press charges.'

'There you go, then.'

'An officer who spoke to her back then thought that might have been because she was scared. What do you think about that?'

'Look, I told you, she's mental. She gets an idea in her head and then the next day she's off on something else. Bipolar, I reckon.'

Kitson nodded, as if that was a perfectly reasonable diagnosis. 'Are you a stalker, Mr Ablett?'

'No, I'm not.'

'So, you weren't stalking Judith Holloway?'

'I just said, didn't I?'

'So, what was the nature of your relationship?'

'There wasn't one. Yeah, I fancied her, so I asked her out. We went for a drink a couple of times and that was it.'

'She wasn't interested?'

'Well, it was ... mutual, actually. It wasn't really going anywhere, so ...'

'Yet for weeks afterwards you somehow managed to be at the
same places she was at the same times. In shops and bars and
restaurants. On several occasions she saw you on the other side
of the road when she left work.'

'She's paranoid.'

'She took pictures on her phone.'

Ablett shrugged. 'Yeah, maybe I bumped into her a couple of
times. Rugby's not a very big place, not the centre, anyway. I'm
always running into friends or whatever.'

'Have you run into Miss Holloway lately?'

'No.'

'That's probably a good thing,' Chall said. 'Because according
to the report written at the time, you were told in no uncertain
terms that if she made another complaint, you'd be arrested
anyway. Whether she wanted to bring charges or not.'

Ablett said nothing. He tossed his hair back, ran stubby fingers
through it.

'Tell me about Sandra Cook,' Kitson said.

'What about her?'

They were doing a little fishing of their own now, but a few
days before Thorne had sensed something between Ablett and
the woman who looked after Made In Heaven's financial affairs,
so Kitson decided it was well worth a try.

'How would you describe the nature of your relationship
with *her*?'

'I work with her.'

'Nothing else?' The way Ablett shifted in his seat told Kitson
that Thorne's instinct had been spot on.

'We've been out once or twice, that's all.'

'Been out?'

'Yeah. The pub, the pictures.'

'Are you and Miss Cook having a sexual relationship?'

Ablett returned Kitson's stare. 'That's the plan.'

'And have you ever run into her, accidentally? What with Rugby being such a small place? Ever bumped into her at the shops or when she's been out with friends?'

'No.'

'Does she know about your ... history with Judith Holloway?'

'No.'

'The stalking, the spying.'

'I told you—'

'Because she probably wouldn't be too impressed, would she? I reckon that might scupper your plan a bit.'

Ablett shifted again, pushed his chair away from the table. 'You said I was free to go at any time, right?'

'Absolutely,' Chall said. 'Before you shoot off, though, could you tell us what you were doing on Friday, April the nineteenth?'

'What?' Ablett puffed out his cheeks, shook his head slowly, like he was trying to remember. 'I'd need to check my diary.'

Kitson looked down at her notes. 'And on June the twenty-second, October the ninth and thirtieth, and ... December the twenty-eighth last year?'

'How am I supposed to remember that far back?'

Kitson smiled. 'I bet you're one of those really organised people who has a diary on your phone. Syncs up with your computer, all that.'

Ablett blinked.

'Easier to get it out of the way now,' Chall said. 'Just have a quick look, so we can tick all our boxes, and off you go.'

Ablett was breathing noisily through his mouth as he reached into the pocket of his soft leather jacket.

Finally, that smirk had disappeared.

FIFTY

The woman shrugged. She'd been doing a lot of shrugging.

'Really?' Thorne looked at her. 'You make it sound like your husband just nipped out to pick up a pint of milk one day and never came back.'

Tracey Goode shrugged again. 'What it felt like.'

It was a ground floor flat behind Walthamstow station. 'Cosy' is how an estate agent might have described it, though 'poky' was the word that had sprung to Thorne's mind when he and Tanner had walked in. They had glimpsed a postage-stamp patio from the narrow hallway and the front room was furnished with a leather three-piece and widescreen TV that barely left space to move.

Tracey Goode was barefoot, her legs folded beneath her on one of the huge armchairs. She had short, peroxide-blonde hair and piercings that Phil Hendricks would have been proud of. She swigged an energy drink from a plastic bottle and pulled at the neck of a sweatshirt that was far too big for her.

'So, he just went to work,' Tanner said.

'Well, that's what I thought.' Tracey unfolded one leg and

stretched it to rub her foot against the large dog that was lying next to her chair. 'Never got there, though. At the time, I thought he'd just gone on a bender for a day or two, something like that. I mean, it's not like he was loving going to work or anything. His probation officer encouraged him to take the job, but Aiden couldn't stand it. A cleaner, I mean, really? He was better than that.'

'Better how?' Thorne asked.

'He had qualifications.'

'You mean the ones he picked up in prison? The computer stuff?'

Tracey nodded. 'He had a couple of O-levels, too. Geography and something else. Too qualified to be pushing a mop around, anyway.'

'He'd done that before, had he?' Tanner smiled at her. 'Gone on a bender?'

'A couple of times, yeah. I mean, you can go a bit funny inside, can't you? You need to let your hair down now and again.'

Thorne wanted to point out that Aiden Goode had been a bit 'funny' before he'd gone to prison. Instead he just nodded and said, 'So ... when he didn't come back, when you realised he wasn't just away somewhere letting off steam, what did you do?'

'I called the police.' Another shrug. 'What you do, isn't it?'

Thorne said that it was.

'Didn't take it seriously, mind you.'

Thorne nodded, as if he was sorry, but he didn't feel very much like apologising on behalf of his colleagues, for whom a forty-two-year-old ex-con walking out on his wife had not been a priority. 'Where did you think he'd gone? When he didn't come back?'

'Not a clue,' Tracey said. 'But that was when I started to wonder if there was something else going on. Because he'd taken things.'

'What sort of things?'

'Well, not like his passport, nothing like that. But a bag of clothes, a few bits and pieces. It took me a few days to even realise they were missing. I didn't know he'd taken anything with him, because I was still in bed when he left that morning.'

'And this was what . . . a year or so ago?'

'Yeah, almost exactly.'

'And you've not heard from your husband since then?'

'Not a word.'

'No phone calls, letters, nothing?'

'I said, didn't I?' She didn't raise her voice, but the icy smile spoke volumes. She swigged from her bottle. 'He just buggered off.'

'Have you spoken to any of his friends?' Tanner asked. 'See if they've heard anything?'

'Well, Aiden's friends weren't really my friends.' The smile was slightly less glacial. 'He liked to spend time with his mates on his own. I think most blokes do, don't they?'

'Depends on the bloke,' Thorne said.

Tanner glanced down at the notebook that was open on her knees. She read out three names.

'Yeah, them,' Tracey said. 'You should talk to them.'

'We have,' Thorne said. The men Aiden Goode was known to have associated with in the months between his release from prison and the time he disappeared. Pubs, clubs, football matches, a boys' trip to Thailand. All three claimed that they had not spoken to Aiden Goode for over a year and denied any knowledge of his whereabouts.

'Done a runner, hasn't he?' one of them had said. 'Started again somewhere else. Jammy bastard.'

'They tell you anything?' Tracey shook her head without waiting for an answer. 'No, well they wouldn't. Especially if he was shacked up with someone else. Stick together, that lot.'

When the dog got slowly to its feet and waddled out into the hallway, Thorne stood up and asked if he could use the toilet. Tracey Goode shrugged again.

For a minute or so after Thorne had gone, Tanner said nothing. She watched Aiden Goode's wife finish her energy drink, waited until she'd finished shouting at the dog which had begun barking to be let out from the kitchen.

'Why did you stay with him, Tracey? After what he did?'

The woman drew her legs beneath her again. 'I'm not convinced he did anything.'

'Not convinced?'

'He's never been like that with me. Never been rough.'

'That doesn't mean anything,' Tanner said.

'Well, it does to me. Yeah, so he was probably messing about with those girls ... flirting or whatever. That doesn't mean the little slags weren't lying about all the rest of it.'

'The jury believed them.'

Tracey shook her head. 'Yeah, well, I gave him the benefit of the doubt, didn't I?'

Tanner just stared.

'I mean I wouldn't take him back now. Not after he just walked out on me without a word. You don't treat people like that, do you?'

When Thorne came back in, he didn't bother sitting down.

'That's *my* razor in the bathroom,' Tracey said. 'For my legs.'

'Sorry?'

'I know exactly what you were doing up there ... what you were looking for. I'm not stupid, you know.'

'I was having a piss,' Thorne said. 'And I put the seat back down afterwards.'

She pointed at Tanner. 'I was just telling her ... I wouldn't have Aiden back in this house even if he did show up again. Anyway, I'm done with blokes right now. I've got my dog for company, and I've got my Rabbit upstairs, if you know what I'm saying.' A nod at Tanner. 'She knows what I'm talking about.'

Tanner stood up. 'I'm afraid not.'

Tracey turned to Thorne, conspiratorial. 'Trust me, she's a liar.'

'How about giving me the benefit of the doubt?' Tanner said.

FIFTY-ONE

They were walking towards the tube station when Tanner's phone rang, and after a five-minute conversation, during which there was a good deal of sighing and some very choice language, she spent the rest of the journey filling Thorne in.

'A fatal shooting in Tottenham, night before last,' she said. 'Some low-rent drug dealer named Kieran Sykes. Plenty of people heard the shot and they've got several witnesses who saw the shooter, who was dressed in bike leathers, get on his motorbike and ride away.'

'Ah,' Thorne said.

'Sounds a lot like the people who had Adnan Jandali killed and fitted Evans up for it. Same hitman. Territory this time, the sound of it.'

'And we're only hearing about this now why?'

'Got picked up by a team in Edmonton and it's taken them this long to figure out that we might be interested. For pity's sake . . .'

'They getting anywhere?'

'What do you think? People heard the shot, someone called it in, but as soon as a copper knocks on the door they've got bugger all

291

to say. So far, nobody's even been willing to admit they knew what Sykes did for a living. Making out he was a choirboy or something.'

'Yeah, no surprise,' Thorne said. 'Easier to pretend that stuff's not happening on their doorstep, and they're scared about what might come back to bite them if they say anything. Hard to blame anyone.'

Tanner grunted in agreement, but looked very much as though she needed *someone* to blame.

'They get CCTV, ANPR?'

'They caught the bike on camera a couple of times going north on the Seven Sisters Road, but it's a stolen plate. No forensics at the scene. What they've got is bugger all.'

They walked on, past something that called itself a casino but was no more than a glorified gaming arcade. It seemed to be doing very good business. They passed a pawnbroker and the somewhat less glamorous façade of a Travelodge.

'Glad to see it's not just us then,' Thorne said.

Tanner looked at him. 'I can only work with what I've got, you know.'

'I know. *Us*, I said.'

'Well, nice to hear you're still on board.'

'All right, so I know you've done most of the work on this one, but to be fair there hasn't been a fat lot to do.'

'Yeah, well there might be after this.' Tanner fished in her handbag for her Oyster. 'Double murder inquiry, now.'

'I'm like a coiled spring,' Thorne said.

On the train from Walthamstow Central, heading towards King's Cross, Thorne sat and watched the young woman opposite. She looked tearful, yet oddly determined as she typed something into her phone. Was she breaking up with someone or had she just been fired? Had her favourite boy band announced that they were splitting up or was she responding to news of a genuine tragedy? A few seats away a middle-aged man smiled

292

at something on the screen of *his* phone. It might have been an amusing cat video or pictures of his first grandchild, or it might have been the news that his company had just completed an aggressive takeover and put several hundred people out of work.

It was hard to read people at the best of times.

'I want surveillance on Tracey Goode,' Thorne said, as the train pulled out of Finsbury Park. 'Overt and covert. Let's clock her movements for a day or two, then get some recording equipment set up in her house. God knows if we'll find room to hide it, mind you.'

Next to him, Tanner lowered the copy of *Metro* she had picked up when they'd got on the train. Thorne was not convinced that she'd actually been reading it, guessing that she was still thinking about this latest drugs murder. The gang they were putting Andrew Evans up against that was proving even more ruthless than they had first thought.

'Did you find something in her bathroom?'

'Bedrooms are always better,' Thorne said.

He was expecting a lecture about procedure, about flouting important regulations relating to illegal searches, but it never came. The stern look was still enough to make him uncomfortable.

'Far side of the bed ... there was a motor racing mag on the floor. *F1 Monthly* or something.'

'So?' Tanner turned to him. 'Doesn't mean there's been a bloke around. Actually, Susan was really into Formula One, so I don't see how one magazine proves anything.'

'I don't understand why *anyone's* into it.'

'Hardly grounds for an arrest, is it?'

'I still don't think she's being upfront with us.'

Tanner went back to her paper. 'OK. Well, it can't hurt.'

'We should get eyes on Aiden Goode's so-called friends as well, see if we can push their buttons. And I think we should press for a mobile phone intercept on the formerly faithful wife.'

'Right.' Tanner rolled her eyes. 'And I can guess which one of us is going to be spending hours filling in the forms.'

They both knew only too well that clearance for a phone intercept was subject to the Regulation of Investigatory Powers Act, and that, under RIPA, a warrant would have to be issued by the Home Secretary. It would not be straightforward and any evidence obtained via an intercept would be inadmissible in court, but Thorne felt it would be worth Tanner's trouble. Besides which, he had better things to worry about.

Worse things.

Today was Friday.

Date night . . .

FIFTY-TWO

At the door, Call Me Rob stopped and said, 'You've done amazingly well, Andy. The drug's near enough out of your system completely.' He shook Evans's hand then pointed to his head. 'Now, it's all about what's in here.'

Every bit as irritated by the counsellor's patronising tone as always, Evans smiled and nodded, feeling rather like he had as a child on his way out of the dentist's surgery. A pat on the back and a nudge towards the room where his mother sat waiting with a copy of *Puzzler*. All that was missing was the oversized badge pinned to his jacket saying *Brave Boy!*.

'You've done the hard work.' The handshake had already been going on a little too long for comfort when Rob added his other hand into the mix; wrapped and squeezed. 'Now, you just need to stay strong.'

'Don't worry about that,' Evans said.

The hard work . . .

In retrospect, a few fillings seemed like a doddle by comparison.

Walking back towards his room, Evans passed one of the friendlier officers; the tall, skinny one, whose name was Barrett.

Evans stopped to exchange a word or two and agreed to join him for the football being shown on Sky later on. They talked about the two new guests who had arrived a couple of days before; a pair of Asian lads Evans thought might be brothers. Evans had yet to exchange a word with either of them, but Barrett told him they were nice enough, considering.

Evans walked away, wondering what habits the newcomers were trying to kick and what sorts of crimes they might have committed. Major players or small fry, masterminds or idiots? He wondered what they guessed at when they asked themselves the same questions about him.

He decided that he probably looked exactly like what he was.

A man who appeared strong enough, but was actually too weak to hold on to anything that mattered; who had known the choices he made would hurt those closest to him, but had made them anyway. A waster, who had wrecked his own life more than once and was now doing the same to others.

A thug, who was good for nothing. Human flotsam.

Back in his room, Evans lay on a bed that was too soft and thought about what the counsellor had said. Call Me Rob might have talked to him like he was a simpleton, but in terms of where the problems lay, he'd been bang on.

It's all about what's in here . . .

So much stuff slopping about in his head, so hard to get things straight.

The drug was what had got him into this mess, the drug was the cause of everything, the drug was the devil. True enough, he no longer craved it as he once had, didn't lie awake in pain any more.

And yet . . .

He could still remember that hit and that smoky release. Time like a dribble and then a rush. Not knowing where the floor was, or the ceiling, and not caring either way because nothing mattered any more.

So, how long until that stopped being a happy memory, until

he stopped dreaming about it? How long before he really earned his big, stupid badge?

Brave Boy?

Messed-Up Boy! Arse-About-Face Boy . . .

How else could you explain the way he felt about Nicola Tanner?

She was the only reason he wasn't rotting on remand somewhere, waiting to go on trial for murder. That's what the people who had set him up were banking on; all the lovely evidence they'd so helpfully supplied being more than enough to put him away. They knew very well that nine out of ten coppers would simply not have bothered listening to his sob story, because they didn't need to. Even if your average copper had believed him, they'd just have spent five seconds thinking about that open and shut case they'd been handed on a plate – the prints, the DNA, all that – then trotted off to the CPS like pigs in shit and settled for the result. Of course they would.

The pond-life who had set him up hadn't banked on Nicola Tanner, though.

And yet . . .

He hated her . . . resented her at least, even though he knew it didn't make sense, because she was also the reason he was here. The reason he wasn't with Paula.

Friday night and he should have been at home with his wife. A takeaway, maybe, and settling down after they'd put Sean to bed. Talking and TV. He should have been lying beside her, listening to her breathe; sliding in close as she drifted off to sleep, then reaching across to cradle her belly, feeling for the kick.

His new son. His daughter . . .

Evans sat up, stared at the pale yellow wall for a while, then watched himself reach for one of the paperbacks piled on his bedside table. Second-hand thrillers that one of the cops had brought in after Evans had said he enjoyed them. He turned to the last page he'd been reading and tried to focus, but the words wouldn't register in any way that made sense.

He needed to sleep, had asked for something that might help but had been told it wasn't allowed.

He sat back and closed his eyes. A cop's phone rang downstairs and he heard a door close somewhere as he lowered the book slowly into his lap and clutched at the duvet. He knew that in stories like the ones in his tattered paperbacks, the good guys usually came through in the end and the bastards got what they deserved. It was probably why he liked them. Only trouble, Andrew Evans couldn't say which of those he was any more, wasn't sure he'd ever known.

In truth, there wasn't a lot he did know, stuck here in this five-star hospital that was really a prison; protected and prodded at for weeks or months or who knew how long. If he was going to end up in prison, if his wife and son were really safe. How long it would be before he stopped feeling like there was a cement block sitting on his chest. If he would get to see his baby born.

He knew that this was all they were, though. He was certain of that much, at least.

Happy endings and getting what you deserved.

Just stories.

FIFTY-THREE

'What's so important?'

Thorne laid the phone back on the arm of the sofa.

Both he and Helen were well used to fielding Job-related calls at unsociable hours; receiving messages of one sort or another, but rarely cause for celebration. Helen could clearly see that Thorne was more preoccupied by this possibility than he might normally be. Waiting for news, though his expression made it hard to tell if it was good or bad.

Thorne knew he had that kind of face.

He reminded her what was happening. The dates arranged for tonight through the Made In Heaven agency; in Northampton, Bournemouth and Hull. Three meetings that were being carefully monitored by dozens of plain-clothes officers across separate forces, at locations that had been scouted in advance. The man they were all looking out for, who would have known every bit as much about the men and women involved as the police did, and might well be doing some monitoring of his own.

Watching two people eat or chat; nervous and excited. Disgusted by it, waiting for his chance to act.

When Helen looked at him, Thorne immediately realised that he wasn't reminding her of anything, that he hadn't actually told her any of this before. They had both been working long hours, but that wasn't unusual and he knew it was more than just a lack of opportunity. Unspoken, but obvious enough. The tension had been growing for a while; the sulks and the snapping he'd been moaning to Phil about. Something cracked that was threatening to fracture and left little room for conversation that went beyond the merely practical.

Arrangements for Alfie. Washing, shopping, bins.

'So, go on then, what would you do?' Thorne smiled, trying. 'If I wasn't around. Reckon you'd ever use one of these dating agencies?'

'What, because that's the only way I'd be able to find anyone else?'

'No, course you would ... you'd be beating them off with a shitty stick.'

'Yeah, right.'

'Just wondered if you'd ever do the online thing, that's all.'

Helen inched away from him. She reached for the remote and muted the sound on the TV. 'Seriously?'

'A lot of people do.'

'You planning on going anywhere?'

'No, but ... I might get hit by a bus.' Thorne winced, inwardly. Helen's partner Paul had been killed at a bus stop; mown down by a car, just before Alfie was born. He watched her blink and glance away. 'Just saying.'

'Well, let's hope not.'

'Or you might decide to kick me out.'

'Much more likely.'

'There we are then.'

'It's definitely a possibility.'

'Make your sister happy.' Before he could stop himself.

Helen's face darkened as quickly as the mood, which, just

for a minute or two, Thorne's stupid turn of phrase aside, had seemed to be changing for the better. She moved further away, to the far end of the sofa. Said, 'Why do we always end up talking about Jenny?'

'We don't,' Thorne said.

'Often enough.'

'Yeah, all right, but only ever when things aren't great . . . when she's been pouring poison in your ear. Winding you up.'

Helen looked away. 'Christ, this again.'

'Because we need to get it sorted,' Thorne said. 'Look, I don't know if she really has a problem with me, or if it's all just about you and her and I'm getting caught in the middle.' He waited; a necessary pause before stepping on to dangerous ground. 'Is it about Polesford?'

Helen's head whipped around.

'What happened back then . . . '

The secrets about Helen's abusive childhood, which had emerged during the case they'd both worked in her home town the year before, had been understandably painful for her to confront. She would be dealing with them for the rest of her life, Thorne understood that. He had not been privy to the difficult conversations that had followed between Helen and her younger sister, but knew that a relationship which had been tricky enough to begin with, had now been redefined by something far darker than sibling rivalry.

'Maybe she feels guilty,' Thorne said.

Helen shook her head.

'She knows you were trying to protect her. So, now she's—'

'It's not that.' The muscles worked in her jaw as she rubbed at the arm of the sofa. 'It's complicated.'

'Well, it's simple enough from where I'm standing. You go and see your sister, or you talk to her on the phone. She can't stop herself needling you by saying something bitchy about me and you leap to my defence.' He tried to smile, but it wasn't altogether successful. 'At least I *hope* you do . . . but then you come back and, for whatever reason, I get it in the neck.'

'That's not true.'

'It's what happens. You talk to Jenny and I know there's a row coming. I mean, to be fair, you probably don't even know you're doing it.'

'Why would I be pissed off at you?'

'I don't know . . . maybe because a bit of you thinks she's right. I mean, I'm older, we don't agree about music or football, I'm a miserable sod.'

Helen smiled, wobbly. 'I don't need my sister to tell me any of that.'

'Maybe because I'm not Paul.'

Helen looked away again, the smile slipping.

'Sorry. I didn't mean that.' He reached across and lifted her hand. 'Look, I've got no idea why it happens, why your sister keeps making things difficult, if she's doing it deliberately. But you know . . . things aren't great, are they?'

They said nothing for a minute or so after that; stock-still watching the muted TV, until Helen stood up and moved across to the kitchen. She made herself tea, wiping surfaces that were already clean as she waited for the kettle to boil. Then she said, 'I'm going to bed.'

'OK.'

'I'm knackered.'

'OK.'

She stopped at the door and turned, cradling her mug. She said, 'I do know I'm doing it. What you said.'

Thorne was already looking at his phone again.

Tanner rarely dreamed of her murdered partner.

She was grateful for that small mercy, because afterwards, she remembered each image and word spoken; the details pin-sharp, as though from a movie she had just watched. She remembered every feeling too, the fierce stabs and deadening punches of them. Waves sweeping in suddenly to crash over her again whenever the memory was recalled, unbidden. In a meeting, in a car, during some trivial conversation at work; a familiar phrase or a song on the radio. Sadness, most often – wet and heavy, until she was sodden with it – a hot rush of elation once or twice, but always anger.

Perhaps it was no kind of mercy at all.

She had got home just after nine o'clock, read through the report she had made on the interview with Tracey Goode, then double-checked the applications for various forms of surveillance which would hopefully get signed off the following day. She had talked to the SIO on the Murder Investigation team at Edmonton and been told they were wading through treacle and that no more useful evidence on the Kieran Sykes shooting had come in. Not even any that *wasn't* useful. She had conferred by phone with the duty officer at Long Barrow Manor and received an update on Andrew Evans's progress, then immediately put an Airwave call through and spoken directly to the officers on the overnight shift outside Evans's house, to check that all was well.

She had fed the cat, thrown away the junk mail and microwaved a baked potato for herself.

She had taken off her make-up while glancing through the evening paper.

After making sure that front and back doors were locked, she had showered and got into bed, then she had fallen asleep within minutes and stepped out into the garden to meet Susan.

Her partner was waiting on the patio in the late afternoon sunshine, relaxing on a chair. One of a set she'd spent a weekend putting together after they'd carted them home from the garden centre. Swearing and sweating, while Tanner had chipped in with unhelpful suggestions and stared at a page of barely legible instructions that might just as well have been written in Chinese. Susan sat there now and swigged from a bottle, the top half of her face in shadow, her hands shielding her eyes from the glare.

Susan swallowed and smiled. She said, 'Come on, love, it's just a couple of beers, don't make a fuss.' The smile became a chuckle. 'Why don't you have one ... stop being so proper and relax for a bloody change? It can't hurt, can it?'

The cat had been asleep on her side at Susan's feet, but now she opened her eyes and rose up slowly to arch her back before hissing her agreement. Just a hiss, but Tanner knew exactly what the cat was saying.

Life's too short.

Let yourself go.

You'll wish you had ...

Tanner wanted to, would have loved to take the ice-cold bottle that Susan was proffering, but then she looked at all the other bottles; hundreds of them, emptied and scattered around in carefully laid out arrangements or swinging gently from the branches of a tree. The soft clink as one bottle kissed another.

The brightly coloured flower placed in each one.

Their garden of petals and glass.

Then Susan shook her head and Tanner raised her face up to see the sky bruise, then blacken, and the rain hissed louder than any number of angry cats as it fell. When Tanner looked back, the cat was splayed out among the broken bottles and crushed blooms. Its head and tail were missing, its fur matted and sodden, the blood pooling on one side, running slowly away on the other, tracing the cracks between the concrete slabs. Susan's hair was plastered to her scalp, and when she removed her hands from her eyes, Tanner saw the ragged holes where her eyes had been before they were burned out. Bleached black ...

She said, 'Just a beer. For Christ's sake, Nic.'

She leaned down blindly, making noises with her mouth and calling the cat—

Tanner lifted her head fast from the sopping pillow and

reached for the phone on her bedside table. It was in her hand as the alert sounded again, a repeat of the tone that had woken her, that told her she'd been sent a text message.

It was from Thorne.

> All three targets, Hull, Bournemouth, Northampton, safely back at home addresses. Properties being monitored, no sign of suspect. Hate the fact that I'm more disappointed than relieved.
> Hate this bloody job.
> TT

FIFTY-FOUR

It was Thorne's worst nightmare.

An overly air-freshened conference room at New Scotland Yard; PowerPoint and power games and several people he did not know sitting around the table, quietly sipping their mineral water and making notes with their nice, sharp, Met Police pencils. Some he knew by reputation, but in most cases that was more than enough. A deputy assistant commissioner whose ascent through the ranks had been as quick as the temper she struggled to hold in check. An assistant chief constable who liked to pretend he was one of the lads when he was not cutting their overtime or making them redundant. A media liaison officer who nodded a lot and seemed welded to her iPad, studying Thorne as though trying to work out how much weight he would need to lose before he would look good on camera.

Whether Botox might be a good idea.

Fulton was there too, of course, his head as highly polished as the furniture, and at the far end of the table, perched nice and close to the DAC and looking as if he'd eaten several raw lemons for breakfast, Chief Superintendent Trevor Jesmond seemed as keen as usual to piss on Thorne's chips. On anyone's chips. He was someone Thorne had found himself pitted against several times in the past, who had probably left the greasy pole a damn sight greasier by the time he'd scrambled to the top of it.

Looking at them, Thorne found it hard to believe that any of these people had ever been coppers in the true sense of the word; that any of them had ever been like him.

Felt the same things.

Hurt the same way.

'You're asking a great deal.' The PowerPoint presentation at an end, Jesmond watched as the media liaison officer stood and raised the blinds to let in the tepid, mid-morning light. He smiled, but the eyes stayed as dead as always. Like a stuffed fish.

Thorne smiled back, because he had to. It made him want to brush his teeth or at the very least gargle with something.

'What we're suggesting will certainly require a good deal of effort, yes,' Brigstocke said. 'Money and resources. But I trust my team when they tell me it's necessary and I agree with everything DI Thorne laid out in the presentation.'

'That's good to know,' Jesmond said.

Thorne was pleased to have Brigstocke in there with him banging the drum and having Nicola Tanner sitting alongside him could only strengthen his pitch. The support of a good copper with a spotless reputation would surely count for something.

Jesmond lifted the folder in front of him as though the weight of it might somehow be significant; the visual presentation printed out as a set of operational notes for each attendee. A clutch of laminated pages, meticulously classified and fully indexed.

Operational aims

Human resources

Technical support requirements

Health and safety concerns ...

'It's very impressive.' Jesmond nodded towards Thorne, but could not resist a knowing glance at Tanner, clearly well aware which one of them had put everything together. 'But bearing in mind what you're asking, it needs to be. The question remains, though, is it impressive enough?'

'I'm not trying to *impress* anyone,' Thorne said.

Brigstocke shot Thorne a look before he could continue; a reminder of what he'd told him on their way in. A simple piece of advice he must surely have known was falling on deaf ears.

Let me do the talking.

Jesmond laid the folder down and turned to Fulton. 'Where are you on this, Simon?'

Fulton looked like a rabbit trapped in headlights. 'Sir?'

'Well, seeing as this started off as your investigation, we'd be interested to get your take on these suggestions. On moving the operation forward in this ... new direction. I mean, we do appreciate we're a long way past a few dead cats.'

Thorne could only marvel at a capacity for callous understatement as unlimited as the man's ineptitude. He sat back hard and waited, guessing that he'd get pretty decent odds on Uncle Fester taking any position beyond playing it safe, that the man from Kentish Town stepped out of his comfort zone about as often as he had a haircut.

'Well, I can certainly see some merit in what's being proposed,' Fulton said. 'And obviously I applaud the initiative.' He glanced towards Thorne and Tanner. 'The ambition. That said, we should also consider the ramifications were this not to prove a fruitful course of action.' He nodded towards the media liaison officer opposite him. 'If a failure like that were to come out ... well, I'm not sure it would play awfully well in the press.'

Jesmond hummed his approval as the media liaison officer scribbled something.

Thorne mentally collected his meagre winnings, fists clenching in his lap as he wondered just how strong this fence that everybody seemed content to sit on could possibly be. When he raised his head and saw the DAC staring at him, he did his best to summon an expression of confidence and readiness, though he knew very well – because he had been told it often enough – that it almost certainly appeared more cocky than confident; as if the only thing he was ready for was a scrap.

Deputy Assistant Commissioner Lucinda Abbott said, 'DI Thorne . . . I'm keen to hear why you're unhappy with the investigation as it stands.'

'Not *unhappy*—'

'As I understand it, the monitoring of couples meeting through this dating website was done at your instigation. There had been a suggestion from DCI Brigstocke to shut the website down altogether.'

'That's true.'

'I was eventually persuaded that to do so would have been a mistake,' Brigstocke said. 'That provided all necessary steps were taken to ensure public protection, this was the right course of action.'

'OK,' Abbott said.

Thorne nodded, aware that the pints owed to his boss were racking up. 'I still believe we did the right thing, but the simple fact is, we're not seeing any results. Yes, we're keeping people safe, but it's not getting us any closer to an arrest. We've now had two full weeks . . . two Fridays, two Saturdays and all that's happened is that a few couples have had some nice dinners and a few coppers have clocked up some decent overtime. Meanwhile there's still no trace of our main suspect. The only thing we've discovered through covert surveillance on Aiden Goode's wife is that she's shagging somebody else and the media stories we've planted haven't got us anywhere.'

Jesmond cleared his throat. 'Unless I've missed something, there's still no concrete evidence to suggest that Aiden Goode is the man responsible for these murders.'

'As I said, he's our main suspect.'

'Your only suspect.'

'That's why he's the main one.'

Jesmond ignored the sarcasm. 'Has it occurred to you that Aiden Goode might be dead?'

'It's occurred to me that he might want us to *think* he's dead.'

Assistant Chief Constable Allan Shand finally spoke up. 'That has to be a possibility, Trevor.'

Thorne reckoned he now owed the ACC a drink, too. 'We need to make things a bit easier for him,' he said. 'For Goode. We've got a computer forensics team monitoring the Made In Heaven website twenty-four hours a day, and intelligence from them makes it very clear that it's still being accessed illegally on a regular basis. Obviously, whoever's doing it is way too smart to leave any usable trace, any online fingerprint or whatever, but we've got concrete evidence that he's looking.' He paused, to let that sink in. 'Now we need to put a victim in his lap, instead of wasting our time while he finds one for himself that we can't protect. That's why we need to change things up, and why we're basing this proposal on solid information from the geographical profiler that Detective Superintendent Fulton brought in.'

Seeing only blank faces, Thorne decided on an approach that might hit closer to home.

'Aside from anything else, just doing what we're doing now . . . if you'll excuse the language, ma'am . . . we're just spunking away money and not seeing any return.' He looked at Abbott, well aware that, if the stories he'd heard were true, she routinely used language that would upset a docker with Tourette's. Aware, too, that if he got what he wanted and his plan proved to be less than 'fruitful', he would almost certainly find himself on the receiving end of it.

'I appreciate your concern for our budget,' Abbott said. 'Or rather I would, if what you were proposing wasn't going to cost three times as much.'

'At least,' Jesmond said. 'It's a hell of a lot to put together.'

'We're trying to be proactive,' Tanner said.

Thorne turned to look at Nicola, relieved and grateful that she'd finally stepped into the fray. 'That's right.'

'Isn't that what we're supposed to do?' Tanner looked from Abbott to Jesmond to Shand. 'I get memos about it every other week. I've been to the seminars.'

Thorne nodded enthusiastically, though he'd rather have stuck needles in his eyes than read official memos or ponce around on beanbags, and watched Russell Brigstocke make a Herculean effort to keep the smile from his face.

'Proactive is good.' The MLO smiled and looked towards the three senior officers. 'All our data suggests that the public responds very positively to proactive operations.'

Shand nodded. 'Modern policing always plays well.'

'That's exactly what we're trying to do,' Tanner said.

Thorne was pleased to see that, Jesmond aside, reactions around the table were suddenly looking rather more positive, even if the very concept of 'modern policing' was one that made him want to punch something. It was a phrase that tripped easily off the tongues of top brass or media types, but he knew that, in terms of the Job, day to day, it meant less than nothing. Yes, there were new approaches to investigation that harnessed cutting edge scientific or psychological techniques. Things had advanced in terms of the force's approach to civil liberties and tackling some of the more unpleasant crimes that reflected unwelcome changes in society.

But Thorne also knew that buried at the back of a drawer in his office was a list of rules dating back over a century regarding proper conduct at formal detectives' 'luncheons' that were still enforced today. What to wear, how to address senior officers, the correct implementation of 'fagging'. He had a similar list regarding the schoolyard punishments to be meted out to newbies in uniform, should they use the Q-word if a shift was less busy than expected or fail to make the sergeant his tea when required. All the forensics in the world and any number of progressive amendments

311

to the Police and Criminal Evidence Act could not disguise the fact that plenty of coppers carried on as though they still had wooden truncheons while blue lamps burned outside police stations.

'I think we probably have enough information to be going on with,' Abbott said.

'More than enough,' Jesmond added.

'I want to thank everyone for coming this morning.' She laid a hand flat on top of her folder, patted it gently. 'I can promise you we'll weigh everything up very carefully before we make our decision.'

'Fair enough,' Thorne said. 'But can you try to do that as quickly as you can?'

There was just a flash of the temper Thorne had heard so much about, but it was quickly extinguished by an icy smile. 'We'll try not to keep you waiting, DI Thorne.'

After a few seconds of awkward silence, Thorne, Tanner and Brigstocke pushed their chairs away from the table and stood up.

'Actually, Russell,' Abbott said, 'would you mind staying on for a few minutes?'

The DCI dropped somewhat reluctantly back into his chair as Tanner and Thorne gathered up their belongings.

'Just a couple more things to talk through.'

Turning at the door to see Jesmond smiling at him, those stuffed fish eyes, Thorne felt his stomach turn over. He smiled back, and wondered just how much air freshener would be needed if he were to chuck up his chips on the spot.

While Tanner used the Ladies, Thorne pushed out through the revolving doors and was surprised to see Christine Treasure leaning against a wall, smoking. She smiled as Thorne approached, then saw the question on his face, right before she gleefully blew smoke into it.

'I volunteered to drive Uncle Fester,' she said.

'Since when do you volunteer for anything?'

'When I want to find out what's going on and the boss won't tell me.' She grinned and punched Thorne on the arm. 'You will, though.'

His arm had almost stopped hurting by the time he'd told her.

'Fuck,' she said. 'Bold.'

'You know me.'

'Yeah well, there's a thin line between bold and mental.' She flicked her butt away. 'Think they'll go for it?'

'God knows. The only thing with my name on that Jesmond would approve is a resignation letter, but I couldn't tell you which way the others are likely to jump.'

'Well, if they do, I'd be happy to get involved.'

Thorne laughed. 'Seriously?'

'Why not?'

'Reckon you could pull it off?'

Treasure's eyebrows went into full-on Groucho mode. 'Oh, I'm not sure I'd want to go *that* far. Certainly not on a first date. To be honest, pulling anything isn't really my area of expertise.'

'Really?'

'Pushing, on the other hand. Thrusting ... '

'Well, thanks for the offer, anyway.' Thorne was moving back towards the entrance. 'I'll bear it in mind.'

'Got my present, yet?'

'What?'

She shouted after him. 'Nuptials, mate. I want something decent.'

'I'm saving up.'

Walking into the Gents, Thorne discovered Brigstocke washing his hands.

'What was all that about, then?'

Brigstocke shook water from his hands then stepped across and spoke above the roar of the dryer. 'Nothing much. They just wanted to know what I thought.'

'You already told them what you thought.'

313

'Yeah.' Brigstocke turned to look at him. 'You're welcome, by the way.'

Thorne was staring at himself in the mirror. Hendricks, Helen and the rest were right: confident *did* look like cocky. 'I owe you one.'

'One?'

'You know what I mean.'

'I want to see that credit card behind the bar next time we're in the Oak.'

'That might get you half a lager, if you're lucky,' Thorne said.

'They wanted to be sure I was completely on board with it,' Brigstocke said. 'That's all. That I wasn't just saying I thought it was a good idea because I was being loyal to my team.'

'What did you tell them?'

'I lied.' The dryer stopped. 'I told them I really thought it was a good idea.'

'Come on, Russell—'

'Look, it's not a shit idea.'

'Praise indeed,' Thorne said.

Brigstocke opened the door and took one step out. 'Probably what your friend Dr Perera would call counter-intuitive.'

'I think "desperate" is closer to it.'

A few minutes later, Thorne followed his boss out and saw Tanner waiting in the lobby. The lift doors opened as he reached her and they watched Jesmond and Shand step out together. Deep in conversation, the two senior officers did not look at them as they passed.

'Nice to see the Chuckle Brothers are still working,' Thorne said. He watched as they pushed through the revolving doors, to where cars were doubtless waiting to ferry them back to their offices. Or crypts.

'I just met your mate Treasure,' Tanner said.

Thorne stared at her, eager to hear and gutted to have missed the inevitable fireworks. 'And . . . ?'

'She's certainly full-on.'

'One way of putting it.'

'She's great, though, isn't she?'

'*What?*'

'She invited me to her wedding. Ashamed to say it'll be my first lesbian one. You had any thoughts about presents?'

Thorne was stunned. He shook his head, spluttering his disbelief, his annoyance at having been so wrong about what would happen when these two very different women confronted one another. 'But that's like . . . matter and anti-matter, or something. How the hell can you . . . *like* her? I mean, yeah she's great . . . you know, in small doses, but I'd never have thought you and her would . . .' He gave up, continuing to shake his head as the two of them drifted towards the exit.

'So, how d'you think it went up there?' Tanner asked.

Thorne grunted.

'I thought we made a pretty decent job of it. Yes, Jesmond's obviously a twat and he doesn't like you much, but I think we're in with a shout.' She stopped at the doors. 'Tom?'

Tanner and Treasure. Jesmond and Shand.

Aiden Goode . . .

He'd always thought he was good at this stuff, that it was what made him a decent copper. Half-decent. Not instinct, none of that feel-it-in-your-water rubbish, just . . . experience. But as far as reading people went, reading situations, Thorne was beginning to feel positively illiterate.

'You're asking the wrong person,' he said. 'Right now, it feels like I couldn't pick the winner in a one horse race.

FIFTY-FIVE

Four days after the meeting at Scotland Yard, and three since Thorne's plan had been given operational clearance, Dipak Chall waved Tanner across to his desk. It was the first time she'd seen the DS smiling since she'd tasked him with looking into sales of miniature mobiles over a fortnight earlier. The job satisfaction was clearly every bit as diminutive as the phones themselves.

'Got something?'

'Something,' he said. 'Maybe ...'

Chall began scrolling through screenshots as Tanner moved a chair from an adjacent desk and sat down next to him. 'So, I've been talking to people selling these bloody things. Trying to, anyway, because a lot of them are in China or the Middle East and it's a nightmare just trying to get contact numbers.'

Tanner looked at the photos: phones even smaller than the ones Chall had first shown her. Handsets pictured alongside coins or paperclips. Chall stopped at one that was shown perched on top of someone's finger, to illustrate that the finger was bigger than the phone.

'Smaller than a disposable lighter,' Chall said.

'How would you even press the buttons?' Tanner asked.

Chall shrugged. 'Use a matchstick or something? Anyway, I finally tracked down a seller who sold twenty-five of these last week.' He called up another screenshot, highlighted the seller's ID and turned to Tanner. 'To the same person.'

'Don't suppose you've got a name and address?'

He shook his head, searched and clicked. 'No way round Data Protection with this stuff, but I've got the name they use online.'

Tanner leaned in closer to see the online profile of the buyer.

ScreenSiren (63 *★★★★*)

Feedback 98% Positive

Lives in: Hastings. UK

'I managed to access her purchase history,' Chall said. 'Presuming it *is* a her ... which tells me that not only did she buy the same number of handsets a few months ago, but a few days before she bought this latest batch, she also splashed out on a multipack of these.' He clicked and bought up another screen-shot, shrank it and set it next to the buyer's details.

100ml Clear Plastic Spray Bottle/Atomizer

Tanner was smiling as she read the description. '"Uniform mist spray" ... very nice. "Ideal for water, mouthwash or perfume."'

Chall nodded. 'Yeah, and probably comes in pretty handy if you, I don't know, wanted to spray liquid Spice on to a letter from home or a kid's drawing.'

Tanner reached across and dropped a hand on to Chall's shoulder as she went back to the buyer's profile.

'Hastings,' she said.

'The seaside,' Chall said.

Thorne was praying for death when Tanner knocked.

He was ten minutes into a conversation with a technician from the computer team, having been out of his depth for all but the first few moments, and the update from the operation's comms

317

manager half an hour before had been no less difficult to follow. Like trying to understand someone talking in a foreign language on a badly tuned radio. He tried his best to take in everything he was now being told about proxy servers, VPNs and disposable accounts. He grunted politely once in a while, only because he had nothing more useful to offer, but the headache had begun to build well before this second one-sided conversation had even started.

He said, 'Yes?' and enthusiastically beckoned Tanner in when she put her head round the door. He rolled his eyes then closed them as the IT expert continued his verbal download.

Guerrilla Mail, profile generators, online reputation management.

Thorne knew how important this stuff was, of course. He understood that the groundwork currently being done by the techies was vital to the operation's success, and he was well aware that the communications network in use on the day would be far more complicated than anything he was used to, but still.

He just wanted to tell them all to shut up, to stop talking gibberish at him for a second or two, so that he could ask the only real question to which he needed an answer.

When?

'Be careful what you wish for.' That's what Brigstocke had said, quiet and unsmiling, when news of the operation's approval had come through three days before. 'All I'm saying, Tom.' He had been talking about possibilities far more unpleasant than the tedium of technical briefings, obviously, but still, Thorne could only hope that this was as bad as it was going to get.

A couple of aspirin would get rid of the headache.

He held up a hand to let Tanner know he was almost done.

He was trying to think positively, to be anything but the glass-half-empty doom-monger Phil Hendricks often accused him of being. This was his stupid idea, after all. Even so, these last few days he'd found it hard to shake off the memory of Trevor Jesmond's nauseating smile in that meeting room, or that moment of fury etched on the face of the Deputy Assistant Commissioner.

'Listen, something's come up,' he said. 'Can you put all of this in an email?' As the man-child on the other end of the phone was telling him that wouldn't be a problem, even before the promised email *pinged* into his inbox a matter of seconds later, Thorne was regretting it; knowing that reading this stuff would be even more tortuous than listening to it.

'I wish you were doing this,' Thorne said, when he'd finally hung up. 'Or translating it, at least.'

'Like I haven't got enough to do,' Tanner said. 'I *am* still working another major inquiry, you know. Those two murders, remember?'

Thorne rubbed at his temples. It felt only as though he were massaging the pain deeper into his skull. 'Yeah, sorry. You don't need to remind me that I've not been a lot of help.'

'You sure? Because I'm happy to.' Tanner saw the pained expression on Thorne's face. 'It's fine. I know you've been up against it.'

He wasn't going to argue. Even before the kick-bollock-scramble that was now underway, the hunt for Aiden Goode had been full-on, though it had yielded little in the way of results. Almost a fortnight's covert surveillance on Tracey Goode had revealed nothing beyond the fact that the F1 magazine Thorne had spotted belonged to one of her husband's mates, who was clearly providing services that her Rabbit was not capable of. The carefully placed stories in newspapers and on TV had not prompted any of Goode's friends and associates to make contact with him, even discounting the one who might be reluctant because he was currently 'comforting' the man's wife.

A lot of effort, and expense, and they were still nowhere.

'Actually, I think we might have had a break,' Tanner said. 'On the Jandali and Sykes murders.'

'Right.'

319

Adnan Jandali . . .

Thorne was suddenly struck hard by the realisation that, in recent weeks, it was not a name that had passed through his mind as often as it probably should. While Tanner – with a modicum of help from Thorne – had been preoccupied with arrangements for Andrew Evans and finding the woman who had worked as a go-between for the gang responsible for framing him, the first victim himself had perhaps got a little . . . lost in the shuffle. He remembered the stirring speech he'd made in front of the team after the Alice Matthews murder. Yes, he had 'turned it on' a bit for the troops, pointing at pictures and urging them to remember who they were working for, but those words had come from somewhere.

He had felt it.

He understood that Tanner wanted to get Andrew Evans back to his family, that she desperately wanted to find the woman who had supplied him with drugs in prison. But he also knew she felt equally passionate about catching the man who had shot a helpless refugee to death on his doorstep in broad daylight. That she wanted justice for Adnan Jandali, and for two boys who were now orphans. He knew how badly she wanted it, and that she would want to give Kieran Sykes's family their day in court, too.

'You remember I asked Dipak to do a spot of online shopping?'

Thorne pretended that he did, even though it actually took him a few seconds. The headache seemed to ease a little as he listened, and when Tanner had finished telling him what Chall had discovered, and what she was planning to do with the information, he said, 'Count me in.'

'You sure?'

'Well, there's nothing useful I can do while they're setting all this up, is there? Spare prick, really. This technical stuff does my head in, anyway.'

'OK, then,' Tanner said. 'Get yourself a bucket and spade and we'll see if we can make a day of it.'

FIFTY-SIX

Though Brigstocke had made sure that Thorne did not forget what was owed, this was the first time they'd managed to get together in the Oak since the plan they'd presented at Scotland Yard had been approved. It was time for Thorne to settle up. It promised to be a long and expensive evening, made even more irksome by a predictably interested onlooker, who had been unable to resist coming along to marvel at Thorne's having to put his hand into his pocket.

Repeatedly.

'I might record it,' Hendricks said, when he arrived. 'Send it to one of them stupid shows on Channel 5. *Weird Happenings* or whatever. *Great Unexplained Mysteries.*'

Thorne carried the beers across to the table as hands were rubbed gleefully together. It was clear from the look on his friend's face that Hendricks was fully intent on enjoying himself.

'Your life must be even more shallow and empty than I thought,' Thorne said, laying down the glasses.

'You can't begin to imagine.'

'You know, if you're willing to come all the way up here just to ponce a couple of free drinks.'

'More than a couple,' Brigstocke said.

The pathologist touched his glass to the DCI's. 'Cheers.'

'Why should I pay for you, anyway?' Thorne asked.

Hendricks mock-spluttered his first mouthful. 'You serious? Years' worth of favours, mate, *years*. If I was to cash them all in, we'd clear this place out of ale.' He took another drink, said, 'Tell you what, I'll get a couple of bags of nuts in. How's that?'

For twenty minutes – and two pints each – or so, Hendricks held court with a fresh batch of dark yet hilarious work-related stories. A successfully suicidal vicar with a hitherto secret Prince Albert. A partially decomposed woman found after neighbours were alerted by the barking of a *very* well fed wire-haired dachshund. He finished with a story about a young man with mental heath issues, who had hit himself so much, and so violently, that the bruises had formed blood clots which had found their way to his lungs and suffocated him.

'Jesus,' Brigstocke said. 'Couldn't his family have done something?'

'Probably.' Hendricks's lips curled slowly into a smile at the rim of his glass. 'Still, no point anyone beating themselves up about it.'

Thorne and Brigstocke laughed, as they had done a good deal since Hendricks had started. Barring the occasional sarcastic comment, though, or the drawing of attention to an empty glass, neither had spoken much directly to the other. Thorne could not help thinking that, as much fun as they both seemed to be having, there was an awkwardness between him and his boss, a tension even. He guessed it was down to how and why the drinks had been earned in the first place.

Their beautifully presented example of modern, proactive policing.

After returning to the table with the third round, Thorne decided it was time to at least acknowledge the elephant in the room.

He said, 'There's no guarantee we'll crack this first time, Russell.'

Brigstocke looked at him.

'I'd be gobsmacked if we did, to be honest.'

'The ACC quite specifically sanctioned a one-time operation.'

'Yeah, I know,' Thorne said. 'But surely she'd do it again.'

'Don't bet on it.'

'She must think we're in with a chance, at least.'

'Doesn't matter what she thinks if there isn't the money.' Brigstocke clocked the scorn washing across Thorne's face. He set his glass down hard and leaned across the table. 'Look, I know things like budgets don't keep you awake at night, but I've seen the figures. It's an arm and a leg, mate.'

'He's killed five women, Russell.'

'I know how many women he's killed, all right?'

'Sorry—'

'I'm the mug who helped you get this signed off, remember?'

They drank in silence for half a minute.

'So, what's likely to happen if we don't get a result first time?'

The DCI downed what was left of his drink. 'Well, off the top of my head ... that pointless arsehole Jesmond gets to say "I told you so" and one of us had better start thinking about spending a bit more time with his family.' He waggled his empty glass on the tabletop. 'Oh, and it's not going to be me.'

Thorne nodded and stared into his remaining inch or so of Guinness.

Be careful what you wish for ...

'Well, this is fun,' Hendricks said. He looked from Thorne to Brigstocke and back. 'Listen, I've got a cracking story about a toddler and a cement truck. You know, if we need to cheer things up a bit.'

'You should come down for a few days.' Frances Coombs tried to keep the nervousness from her voice. She was trying

323

not to sound too keen, either. That never worked. 'You'd like it, love.'

'Yeah, maybe.' As usual, her daughter made rather less effort to disguise the way she felt. 'Looks a bit boring.'

So she'd looked. That was a start, at least. 'It's sunny.' Frances laughed, a twenty-a-day crackle. 'Well, sunnier than Hackney, anyway.'

'I've got things on.'

'What things?'

'Seeing mates, whatever.'

'I'm only talking about a few days. There's a smashing pier . . . a lovely new art gallery. All that modern stuff, I think.'

'Since when did you care about art?'

'Nice day out, that's all.'

Her daughter sniffed. There was music playing in the background, urgent and angry as she was.

'I'm just saying, Nat . . .'

Six years of this, and Frances couldn't even remember how it had happened. Not the details, the hows and whens, but she knew it was all her fault. Back then, it had been hard to hide what she was doing from a nosy teenager, all her business things laid out in the front room; the phones in their boxes, the spray bottles and the Mars bars.

The smell of what was in those little plastic wraps.

Easier to recall how she herself had got into the business, of course. She'd known what her late husband had been up to, how he'd topped up his monthly pay packet from the prison. When he'd gone, it had all been there on his phone, the details of the people he'd been working for, and, a couple of calls later, she'd stepped into his shoes. She'd kept it in the family, but that hadn't meant she'd wanted her daughter to have anything to do with it.

Maybe she could have tried harder to keep it from her little girl, but what was she supposed to do? She didn't have the room, and besides, nobody with any sense was ever going to think she was an Avon lady, were they? It didn't matter much now, she supposed, exactly how her daughter had got into this mess. Somebody dropping merchandise off at the flat one day, a flirtatious conversation Frances couldn't do much about, and the next thing, Nathalie's getting a discount on the harder stuff, because her mother's on the payroll.

Mates' rates.

All her fault, but no point crying about it, and ever since she'd been doing the only thing she could: putting the money away and waiting until there was enough to get her daughter into one of those programmes. Get her cleaned up. She hadn't thought much about *how* she'd do that, how she was going to persuade her to go. She'd cross that bridge when she came to it, drag the silly little mare there if she had to, but the first thing was to get enough money put by, and her pension wasn't going to do the job, was it? She'd been scared to death after that business with Andrew Evans, when everything got put on hold, but now she was back at work and that nest egg could start growing again.

There was a fair bit already, but she knew she was going to need more.

She'd need to get her nut down, maybe offer to start making visits a bit further afield. Take a few more jobs on. There were a couple of Young Offender places that were only a bus ride away . . .

The irony wasn't lost on her. How could it be? The fact that she was turning those poor souls behind bars into junkies, in the name of helping the one she'd given birth to.

'So, what do you reckon, then?'

'I said. I'm busy.'

'I'll send you the train fare.'

'If you want.'

Frances regretted the offer immediately. She knew that her daughter would not come as surely as she knew what the money would actually be spent on. 'I haven't seen you for ages, love.'

'Christ, don't start that.'

'Start what?' Frances strained to hear her daughter's voice above the music.

'The shit about how much you worry.'

'Well, I can't help it, can I?'

'Have you any idea how much that stresses me out?'

'Sorry—'

'Drives me *mental* . . .'

Frances stared down from her window at the darkened street. Another one of those hideous seagulls was pecking at something in the middle of the road. A young couple sat with cans of something on a low wall. 'It's what parents do, isn't it? Who knows, maybe one day you'll have kids of your own and then you'll know exactly what I'm talking about.' She watched as the girl sitting on the wall lobbed her empty can at the bird, which hopped nonchalantly away. 'How's it going with that bloke you were seeing, anyway? Dwayne, is it?'

But her daughter had gone.

Thorne called from outside the pub, the fresh air welcome, though that did not stop him gratefully sucking in the cigarette smoke that was drifting across from a group gathered a few feet away and chatting noisily.

He said, 'I just wanted to let you know it's looking like a late one.'

'OK,' Helen said.

'Russell's making me pay, you know?'

'You're not driving, are you?'

'Don't be stupid. Probably do a few people a favour if I did and got done for it, though.'

'So, I'll see you in the morning then.'

'Are you all right?'

'Yeah, just tired, that's all. Alfie was a sod tonight.'

'Just, you sound a bit . . .'

Helen grunted a laugh. 'And you sound a bit . . . too.'

'Jenny say something, did she?'

There were a few seconds of silence, broken only by the bray-ing of the group smoking nearby. Students, Thorne reckoned, or maybe newbies from Colindale station. It was hard to tell the difference, sometimes.

'No.'

'We need to deal with it, you know. Or *I* need to deal with it. God knows—'

'I haven't spoken to Jenny in days, all right?'

'You said once she used to have a go at Paul too, remember? So, maybe it's just because she doesn't think coppers should be together, like it's not healthy or something. Well, good news, because she might not have to worry about that for too much longer.'

'I'm going to bed now, Tom—'

'She'll probably find something else to bitch about, mind you.' Thorne drew in a long breath and, in a rush of clarity, he real-ised that he was taking his bad mood out on her. It was exactly what he'd accused Helen of doing. 'Phil suggested I pay for a hitman.' He forced a chuckle, to highlight the fact that he was being comical, that he'd let it go. 'To take your sister out. What do you reckon?'

'How many have you had?'

'A few,' Thorne said. 'Not enough.'

He watched one of the smokers flick their fag-end into the gutter and, for a few moments, he toyed with the idea of stepping across and arresting the snotty little toerag for littering. Maybe, while he was at it, he could nick the rest of them before they had a chance to do the same. That was nice and proactive, wasn't it? Wouldn't cost a great deal either, so he wouldn't be laying his career on the line, placing an unnecessary drain on resources.

Win-win.

Helen said, 'Don't fall asleep on the Tube.'

FIFTY-SEVEN

The young man sitting opposite her had been all smiles when he'd first come in, of course. Pleased to see her, and why wouldn't he be, but now that he'd got what he came for he was obviously keen to be on his way and get stuck into what she'd brought him. He didn't seem comfortable with chit-chat.

'Keep smiling,' the Duchess said.

'What?'

'You're very happy I'm here, remember?'

The boy did his best, like he was posing for a photograph.

'Much better,' she said. 'And keep talking.'

'How much longer, though?'

Skinny, in T-shirt and sweats, he was fifteen, but he looked even younger, and that sulky tone was one she was all too familiar with. Nat had never grown out of it. 'It's a full visit, OK? Everything needs to look normal, that's the whole point. Especially if I'm going to be coming back to see you again.' She reached forward and patted his pale hand. 'Like we've got a relationship of some sort, Tony.'

'What sort of relationship?'

'Like maybe I'm your gran or an auntie or something. Or just one of those do-gooder types who likes to pop in and keep your spirits up.' She cast a glance towards the nearest prison officer, who was not paying much attention to anything beyond what he was trying to extract from his nostril. 'They're not allowed to ask, so it doesn't matter which. But if I just pop in for five minutes and leave again, it might start to look a bit suspicious, don't you reckon?'

The boy shrugged.

'Tony?'

He smiled again, just his mouth making the necessary shape. He said, 'How old are you, anyway?'

'A lady does not disclose her age,' the Duchess said.

Old enough to know better.

'Suit yourself,' the boy said. 'Just a bit freaky, that's all.'

First time here and it had all gone very nicely. She'd been told which officers were happy to look the other way, same as her old man had used to do, and which cameras to avoid. The people she worked for always had good information. She'd gone straight to the vending machine to buy the chocolate bar she'd switch for the one in her bag, and passing the moody one across hadn't been a problem. The boy had carefully eaten as much as he'd had to, then made the necessary move to hide what was inside like he'd been doing it for years.

The new ones got taught fast enough.

'I've brought you a letter from your mum,' the Duchess said.

The boy looked confused for a second or two, then nodded.

She reached into her handbag for the letter she'd prepared the night before, smiled as she slid it across the table.

'Cheers,' the boy said.

'No.' She shook her head, stopping the boy as he moved to put the letter into the pocket of his tracksuit bottoms. 'Read it.' She leaned closer, smiling, and dropped her voice. 'It's a letter from home, OK? Aren't you happy about that? Try to look like it means something and you aren't just desperate to tear it up and smoke it.'

The boy nodded, clearly a little scared of her, which she thought was no bad thing. He mouthed the words as he read the letter, slowly.

'Now, smile and put it away, there's a good lad.'

The boy did as he was told, stole a look at the clock mounted high on the far wall.

'So, why are you here, Tony?'

He looked at her.

'There's plenty of time to kill.' She sat back. 'So we might as well make the most of it.'

'I nicked a car.' He folded his arms. 'A smart one.'

'That's not too bad, is it?'

'Yeah, well. I did a bit of damage as well. Hit some bloke in his stupid little Vauxhall Astra, and it wasn't even like it was my fault.'

'Was he OK?'

'A week in hospital. A *week* . . . and I get eighteen months. Like that's fair.'

'It'll go quick enough,' she said. 'Especially if I'm coming in to see you nice and regular.'

'Shit.'

'Well, it's entirely up to you, but—' She stopped, aware now that the boy was looking past her. She glanced round to see a prison officer approaching fast; a man and a woman close behind him who did not look like staff. She turned back to the boy, whose head had already dropped, but not before seeing that everyone else in the visiting area was watching the group as they walked towards her table. It was evidently clear to anyone with an eye for such things that they were not here to visit anyone.

'Mrs Fleming?'

By the time the woman at the table looked up, Tanner and

330

Thorne already had their warrant cards out. Tanner told the woman who they were.

Thorne raised a hand, waved. 'Sorry to interrupt.'

'Would you mind coming with us for a quick word?'

'This is an authorised prison visit,' the woman said.

'Really?' Thorne nodded down at the boy, who had not raised his head. 'He doesn't look too thrilled about it.'

'Or we can just arrest you right here,' Tanner said. 'Nice and loudly. I suppose it depends on how quickly you'd like the people you work for to find out about it.'

The Duchess looked up at her, across at the onlookers on every table. She carefully lifted her handbag from the floor and pushed her chair back.

'Good choice,' Tanner said.

Thorne pointed to the boy and to the empty Mars bar wrapper on the table. He nudged the prison officer next to him. 'There you go, mate. Might be rubber glove time, I reckon.'

The prison officer looked less than thrilled.

'Oh, come on,' Thorne said. 'Don't pretend it's not a perk of the job.'

FIFTY-EIGHT

He was getting careless at work, making silly mistakes, and it wasn't like him. Not that he never did anything wrong. Now and again, he let his attention wander a little; he was no different from anyone else, in that respect at least, but unlike most people he knew why these things were happening so frequently. He knew it was because he was getting itchy.

He knew he was ready.

Browsing was all a necessary part of it, of course, eliminating those who, for one reason or another, would not be suitable, whittling down the likely looking candidates. He enjoyed that stage of things, no less curious than anyone else when it came to other people's lives, enjoying how much of those lives he was secretly privy to. That he could observe and document, unseen. Often he would sit down at the laptop after dinner and root happily about, lost in it, until such time as he would glance up at the clock and realise that five or six hours had gone by. Even when he finally turned in for the night he would lie awake, still mentally putting pictures together: her with him, him with her, this or that location. It was absorbing.

But prepping was not doing, was it?

It was time to make a final choice, to get out there and do what he did, because nothing could compare with that. Fun as it was getting all those ducks in a row, nothing came close to the moment when he finally came face to face with the subject he'd selected with such care and skill. Elated after her dream date or licking her wounds after a disaster, it didn't much matter. Only a second or two, obviously, because there were usually screams to stifle, but those moments would see him happily through the long days and weeks afterwards, back at his computer every night as he clicked and scrolled and put the next adventure together.

When he got itchy again.

He finished his coffee because it was time to get back to work, but even the fact that the fancy new Nespresso machine hadn't arrived couldn't spoil his mood. Tonight, he would go home and get busy. He would cross his 't's and dot his 'i's. He would make his choice from the remaining faces printed out and pinned up on the wall above his desk. The final three contenders. He would stare until those eager faces were imprinted on his mind, and close his eyes and ... yes, it was silly, because there was nobody there to see it, but he would milk the moment a bit, like they did on those TV talent shows.

And the winner is ...

That done, the discards forgotten for now, he would check to make sure that arrangements hadn't changed at the last minute. Because it always paid to be thorough and didn't women have an annoying habit of changing their mind at the eleventh hour?

Actually, I think I prefer Italian.

Sorry, can we try that new wine bar instead?

There would be some Googling to be done then, maps to be studied and routes chosen. There were layouts of restaurants or pubs to memorise and the best vantage points to be selected, but that took no time at all really, because he had one of those brains, and it was always easier learning stuff when the subject in question was one you enjoyed.

When you had a knack for it.

Then, when it was all done and dusted, and only the creeping hours until his date lay ahead to frustrate him, he would go to bed; calm and content.

To sleep better than he had done in a long time.

FIFTY-NINE

From the moment they had escorted the woman calling herself Rita Fleming out of HMP Warren Park, a young offenders' institution between Hastings and Folkestone, things had gone much as Tanner and Thorne had expected.

Unfortunately.

The 'Duchess' had not spoken during the two-and-a-half-hour drive back to London. Other than to confirm her real name and address, she had said nothing once they'd arrived at Colindale station and booked her into the custody suite. She'd clearly talked plenty during her subsequent phone call however, as within the hour a smartly dressed and no-nonsense solicitor had breezed in, calling the shots. After the compulsory disclosure of evidence – a number of fake ID documents as well as phones and drugs already discovered during a search of premises in Hastings that was currently taking place – there was a ten-minute consultation with his client. The solicitor then proceeded to sit in silence throughout a twenty-minute interview, while next to him Frances Elizabeth Coombs was once again struck all but mute, saying only what her solicitor had instructed her to say.

Those two predictable words.

An hour later, back at Becke House, Thorne watched Tanner prowling back and forth between the walls of his office. She shook her head, then stopped to aim a gentle kick at the leg of his desk.

'That's not going to do any good,' Thorne said. 'Why don't you go home and kick the cat? Much more satisfying.'

She looked at him.

'Why are you surprised?'

'I'm not remotely surprised,' Tanner said. 'Doesn't stop me being pissed off, does it? All the time it took to find her.'

'Maybe they'll find something at her flat. She's obviously in regular contact with the people who had Jandali and Sykes killed, so somewhere there's going to be a name or a number. I mean it's probably not going to be on a note pinned to her fridge or anything, but who knows?'

'Did you see how scared she was?'

'You're very scary,' Thorne said. 'You've got a touch of Rosa Klebb, sometimes.'

'Who?'

'*From Russia With Love*. She had a knife in her shoe.'

'Scared of her solicitor.' Tanner sat down. 'Couldn't you tell? Whenever he looked at her she flinched.'

'Well, she's got every reason to be, because he's obviously on the same payroll she is. He almost certainly called them before he showed up, made it very clear what was expected while they were consulting.'

'Yeah, well unless anything changes she's not going to be any more use to us than Andrew Evans.'

'She's guilty,' Thorne said. 'Evans isn't ... well, not guilty of very much, anyway. That's something.'

'So, we stop a few phones going into a few prisons. A bit less Spice. It's not going to help us catch whoever killed Jandali and Sykes, is it?'

336

'Probably not,' Thorne said.

'And who knows what might happen to her if we put her away? They'll have plenty of people inside who can do them a favour. Make sure she never says anything. That's what Evans was frightened about.'

'You can't worry about that.'

'Can't I?'

Thorne sat back, drummed his fingers on the desktop. 'I'm thinking I might open a shop.'

'What?'

'When this Aiden Goode operation goes tits up and I'm out on my ear.'

'Won't happen,' Tanner said.

'Records, maybe ... or vintage clothes. What about fruit and veg? People always need fruit and veg.'

'I can see you've given it a lot of thought.'

'Why don't you knock all this on the head and come and run my shop with me? We'd have a lot less to worry about.'

Tanner was still smiling when a civilian member of staff knocked and put her head round the door.

'They just rang through from Colindale,' she said. 'The old woman in the cells over there says she wants a second interview. Without her solicitor.'

Tanner stood up and waited for Thorne to do the same. She said, 'Maybe I'll pop in now and again. Pick up a cauliflower.'

SIXTY

'Déjà vu,' Tanner said. She pushed the piece of paper across the desk, as she had done several hours earlier in the same interview room. A photocopy of a passport, recovered from the visits office at HMP Warren Park. 'That's you, correct?'

'Yeah, that's me.' Frances Coombs had barely glanced at the document, then, seeing that Tanner was not yet satisfied, she took wire-rimmed glasses from a tatty leather case and put them on. She stared down. 'I've looked better.'

'Oh, I don't know,' Thorne said. 'I think the auburn suits you.'

'You think?'

Thorne nodded. 'Takes years off.'

The truth was that, despite the make-up and the dye job, the woman in front of them looked every one of her sixty-nine years. Her cheeks were hollowed and mapped with veins, the skin sagging from her neck like tired crêpe. She did look younger in the pictures, and from everything they'd heard from witnesses, her turns in visiting rooms were those of a somewhat more energetic middle-aged woman. Clearly playing a role of some sort had a rejuvenating effect, and though she was acting now, affecting an air of poise and confidence, the performance was not doing the trick on any level.

Tanner slid three more pieces of paper across. 'And these are all you, too, yes? The passport in the name of Sophia Crawford. The driving licence in the name of Audrey Davis.'

'All me, yeah.' The old woman pushed the papers to one side. 'Look, you know why I'm here. You're not stupid.'

'No, we're not,' Thorne said.

'So why are we wasting time?'

'Somewhere you need to be?' Thorne asked. 'Not keeping you from the bingo, are we?'

Coombs looked at Tanner, pointed at Thorne. 'Does he think he's funny?'

'We need to do things properly, Frances,' Tanner said. She turned a page in her notebook, while Thorne smirked next to her. 'You used these and other fake ID documents to gain entry over several years to a number of prisons, including Maidstone, Pentonville and Warren Park YOI?'

'Yes.'

'You pretended to be a visitor.'

'Yes.'

'This was in order to smuggle various prohibited items to a number of prisoners.'

'You know it was.'

'Drugs, including Spice.'

'Yeah, Spice mainly. Coke once or twice, speed ...'

'Anything else?'

'Mobile phones. I took in a lot of them.'

'Those dinky little arse-friendly ones,' Thorne said.

'You'd know about that, would you?'

Thorne feigned shock and looked at Tanner. 'Does she think she's funny?'

'These prisoners you visited ... did they include Graham French, Kyle Mason and Andrew Evans?'

'I visited a lot of people, love.'

'Yes, but you must remember Andrew Evans,' Tanner said. 'He was one of those you saw after he came out of prison, too. We're not talking very long ago.'

'Come on.' Thorne tapped the side of his head. 'I'm sure it's in there somewhere.'

Coombs placed the flat of her hand against her hair, dabbed delicately at it. 'Yeah, I remember him.'

'You delivered more drugs to him,' Tanner said. 'Made sure he knew exactly how much money he owed. You put him in touch with the people he owed money to.'

'The people you work for,' Thorne said.

At the mention of those who had so helpfully supplied her with a solicitor, who had furnished her with the necessary merchandise for so long, the woman's façade cracked a little. She took off her glasses and rubbed her eyes. The skin tightened just a little in that saggy neck.

'Do you need a drink of water, Frances?'

Coombs shook her head, and when she looked up it was clear that she had rallied a little, or at least reminded herself of the part she had come here to play. 'Can we talk about what I want?'

'What you want?'

'Why I'm talking to you. Like I said, you're not stupid, so you know why I didn't want my brief here.'

Thorne leaned across the table. 'What makes you think you're in a position to ask for anything?'

'You're happy, are you? With me?' Coombs picked up the papers, the fake IDs, waved them at Thorne. 'With this?'

'We're easily pleased.'

She turned to Tanner. 'What happened to Andrew Evans?'

'I'm afraid I can't tell you that.'

'Well, you've obviously got him stashed away somewhere, but I can tell you right now that, with him on his own, you'll be lucky if you can charge anyone with loitering, let alone anything you could get excited about. Nothing's ever going to court, because he knows bugger all.' She smiled and fussed at her hair again, then laid one liver-spotted hand on top of the other. 'This kind of business, see, the fewer people know anything, the better. That's how the people who run the business prefer it. But when you've been close to it for as long as I have, you can't help but pick up a few bits and pieces. Well, you do it without meaning to, even when you're supposed to be looking the other way, because you've lived a bit, and you're not a stupid kid any more. Because you know that one day, if things aren't going quite so well, those bits and pieces might come in handy. A few names and numbers, maybe the places the people with those names might be every so often.' She gave Tanner a good look at her shiny dentures. 'When you look at it that way, how useful those bits and pieces might be to the likes of you, it doesn't sound like I'm asking for very much, not really.'

'There you go again,' Thorne said. 'Wanting things. I want Spurs to win the Premiership, but I'm not holding my breath.'

Tanner waited a few seconds. 'If, as I understand it, you're offering to co-operate fully with us, and if your information leads to an arrest in connection with the murders of Adnan Jandali and Kieran Sykes—'

The woman sat forward suddenly. 'Now hang on, I don't know anything about murders.'

'Really?' Thorne looked astonished. 'That sort of stuff never come up? Never been one of your bits and pieces?'

'I've never even heard those blokes' names,' Coombs said. 'What was that first one again? Sounded foreign—'

Tanner raised a hand. 'All right. Just help us find the people who fitted up Andrew Evans and that'll probably get us close enough.'

'Good.' Coombs stabbed a red fingernail against the tabletop. 'Because I'm not here to talk about anything like that. About murders.'

'Understood.'

'So.' She looked at Thorne. 'Can we talk about what I want now?'

Thorne folded his arms, considered it. 'Well, we can talk about what we might be able to offer,' he said. 'Why don't we run that up the flagpole, see where we are?'

'I need protection.'

'Of course you do.'

'Me and my daughter. It has to be both of us. She's . . . struggling a bit and I can't leave her on her own.'

'I'm filling up,' Thorne said.

Coombs looked at him, like she was ready to push those nice red fingernails into his eyes.

'We'll see what we can arrange,' Tanner said. 'Best I can do at the moment. A new identity shouldn't be a problem, and it's not like that isn't something you've had plenty of practice at. There are measures we can put in place.'

'Mind you, if you're thinking about a new life in the Bahamas you're probably pushing your luck.' Thorne watched the woman nod, happy enough, and he saw the tremor which momentarily narrowed the dark bag beneath her right eye. He said, 'I hear Wolverhampton's very nice.'

SIXTY-ONE

It had been Susan's idea to name the cat Mrs Slocombe and, as far as Tanner was concerned, it had been funny for about five minutes. She'd got tired of explaining the pussy joke to anyone not old enough to remember the awful sitcom it had come from and it wasn't exactly the sort of name she'd ever felt comfortable shouting out loud. *Saying* out loud. Standing in her dressing gown and rattling a box of cat treats outside the back door late at night.

Whispering it, while the bloody thing skulked out there in the dark and ignored her.

The cat had always preferred Susan anyway and Tanner had been happy enough to be as standoffish in return as the animal was. That had all changed when Susan had died and the cat had become more than just something to be fed and taken to the vet. Something which, since the fire, Tanner would simply have been unable to live without.

After Mrs Slocombe had saved Tanner's life.

She lifted the cat up and set it on her lap. It watched her, maintaining its balance as she shifted to kick off her shoes, then leaned down to place them neatly next to each other. She lay back on the sofa and picked up her phone as the cat padded up her body, settling down to knead at her chest while she waited for the call to go through.

She gave the duty officer at Long Barrow Manor the pre-arranged code word then waited. She listened to the man's footsteps on the wooden floor fading as he walked away. The pinpricks of the cat's rhythmic clawing had quickly become annoying and she had just reached down to deposit it back on the carpet when Andrew Evans came on the line.

'What's happened?'

'It's fine,' Tanner said. 'Paula and Sean are fine.' She heard Evans exhale. 'It's good news. We found the Duchess.'

'And?'

'She's talking.'

'Well, she was always good at that.'

'So, we're getting there, you know?'

Evans said nothing for a few seconds. Tanner could hear chatter in the background. 'Don't suppose there's much point asking when you're likely to actually get there, is there?'

'Well, we need to get as much out of her as we can.' The cat began clawing at the edge of the sofa and Tanner waved it away. 'Especially because there's been another murder.' She waited, but Evans said nothing. 'The same people that killed Adnan Jandali had a drug dealer called Kieran Sykes shot to death in Tottenham.' She heard Evans sigh. 'Look, you knew these were dangerous people, Andrew.'

A grunt. 'Yeah, well. I suppose they're just as likely to top me for going against them on one murder as they are with two. So it doesn't change much.'

Tanner was happy that Evans had taken the news so well. She had been afraid there might be a degree of panic, that he might decide he no longer wanted to co-operate. But he was right to realise that, as far as the men they were after were concerned, he was already as committed as he was ever going to be. 'We have to get what we can from the Duchess and build up enough to make some arrests, to bring charges against whoever killed Adnan Jandali and Kieran Sykes. That's got to be done properly, then obviously there's a court case to prepare and that doesn't happen overnight. We will still need you to be a witness.'

'Even if you've got her?'

'We're not a hundred per cent sure she'll testify,' Tanner said. 'But what's really important is the information we can get out of her. I mean, I'm hoping she will, but either way, you'll be part of the prosecution's case. The attempt to fit you up for the Jandali murder.'

'So I shouldn't start packing just yet, then?'

'No, but ... look, we know it's happening now. There's an end point, OK?'

'So what are you going to do with her? If she's grassing them all up, I mean? Christ, she's not coming here, is she?'

Where to put Frances Coombs during the next stage of the investigation had been the subject of much discussion. There were a number of safe houses mentioned but, in the end, they had opted for a small hotel near Alexandra Palace. She would be escorted to and from the hotel daily by armed officers. She would wear a panic alarm at all times which, if activated would alert the Met's Central Communications Command who, in turn, would immediately contact Tanner or Thorne. 'No,' Tanner said. 'She's not coming there, because she doesn't have any addiction issues. Besides which you're both witnesses, so you need to be kept apart.'

'Lucky for her,' Evans said.

'Right.'

'I'd like to smack the old cow.'

Tanner had not been expecting Andrew Evans to react as if he'd won the lottery, she had known his major concern would be about the timescale, but all the same, some ... appreciation would have been nice. She could easily have ignored the story he'd told her weeks before in that cell and fallen back on the evidence she already had. She could have talked to the CPS, charged Evans with Jandali's murder there and then and put a major case straight to bed. Instead, she'd gone out on a limb.

She could almost hear Tom Thorne telling her that she didn't do this job expecting to be thanked and that anyone who did was an idiot.

She said, 'This is good news, Andrew.'

Evans let out another noisy breath. Said, 'Yeah, I suppose. Definitely the best news I've had since I came here.'

'I think you're forgetting you've got a baby on the way.'

Evans laughed. 'Shit, yeah.'

'Look, I can't promise anything, but if there aren't any major issues I don't see any reason why you shouldn't be there when Paula gives birth.'

'What . . . six and a half months?' Evans said. 'Some of these murder cases can take longer than that, can't they? Years, some of them.'

'Sometimes.' Tanner caught movement from the corner of her eye and turned to see the cat spring on to the window ledge. She watched it raise its tail and slink behind a framed photograph of herself and Susan. 'I can promise I'll do whatever it takes, OK? To make that happen.'

'Yeah, OK,' Evans said. 'That'd be great, obviously.' There was a hiatus, a change in sound as if he were moving the phone from one ear to the other. 'Thank you.'

On his way back towards the communal sitting room, he walked past Barrett, the lanky copper he'd struck up a decent relationship with over the previous couple of weeks. Evans's father would have called him a lanky strip of piss, but the bloke was friendly enough. A Chelsea supporter, but nobody was perfect.

'Good news, Andrew?' Barrett asked.

Evans looked at him.

'Bit of a spring in your step, that's all.'

'I'm getting out of here,' Evans said. 'I mean, not tomorrow or anything, but hopefully soon.'

The officer smiled; flat, automatic, like he couldn't be bothered to pretend he cared much one way or the other. A few more guests had arrived in the last week or so and it wasn't as if one less junkie trying to cut a deal was going to make a great deal of difference. 'Nice,' he said.

'Back in time for the baby with a bit of luck.'

Barrett grunted, nodded around. 'Best make the most of all this then, mate. It'll seem like a holiday once you're changing nappies and not getting any sleep.'

'You got kids?'

'Teenagers,' Barrett said. 'I can't wait to come to work every day.'

Evans walked on to the sitting room and found one of the recent arrivals watching TV. A stocky lad in his early twenties, tattoos and a dirty tracksuit; he'd dragged a chair up close and sat craned forward, his face no more than a foot from the screen. He did not look up when Evans came in.

Evans said, 'All right?' and was not surprised to be ignored.

He walked slowly across the room towards the French windows, one eye on the lad, who sat, as though transfixed by some seemingly endless and noisy car chase. Stock-still, save for the small, elaborately inked hands which slid rapidly back and forth across his knees.

Evans stared out across the grounds through a curtain of drizzle. A pair of squirrels chased each other around the fountain, then tore off across the lawn. He watched the tops of the trees behind the perimeter fence bend with the wind, and listened to the desperate scratch-hiss of flesh against polyester, and he wondered if he had been that bad a month or so back when he'd arrived.

347

Worse, probably, he decided.

His foot bouncing against the floor, like he was in fucking *Riverdance*.

He still saw Call Me Rob for an hour every day, but now it was more or less just chatting. He had begun to look forward to it. They talked about the kind of job Evans might look for when he got home, about Paula and the baby.

Normal stuff.

There were still moments – flashes of hunger, a desire to lash out – but the last one seemed like days ago and, even before Tanner had called, he had started to believe that whoever killed that refugee and fitted him up for it had actually done him a favour. Him and his family. It hadn't felt like that at the time, of course: dragged away from Paula and Sean; sitting in that cell wondering what the hell was happening; spirited away to a weird old house in the middle of nowhere and pumped full of pills.

Now, those things felt like stories he'd heard about another person.

Now, he could sleep, and they didn't have to change his sheets every morning because he'd sweated so much it was like he'd pissed the bed.

Now, he could go back to his new baby, clean.

He turned away from the window and took a step towards the wall. He leaned so that he could get a better look at his fellow guest, who was still glued to the TV. The hands were still going nineteen to the dozen, rubbing and rubbing, but now Evans could see that the lad wasn't actually watching anything; that both his eyes were screwed tightly shut.

SIXTY-TWO

Alfie sat playing with Helen's old iPad at Thorne's feet, while Thorne flicked through the documentation sent to him by the computer team. As he had suspected, it was no more comprehensible in black and white than it had been over the phone, but he was doing his best; telling himself that he didn't need to understand how it worked, as long as it worked.

'Yes!' Alfie said. His little fist clenched in triumph, another jewel or chest or zombie chicken collected or captured or blown up.

'Got one?' Without a clue what was going on, Thorne leaned down to watch; amazed, as always, at how frighteningly adept the child was with the technology. At how kids could play games like this before they could read, could open apps and navigate screens before they could manage joined up writing. He remembered Alfie, eighteen months younger than he was now, trying to swipe the picture on the TV and announcing loudly that it was 'rubbish'.

'Eaten a *massive* snake.' The boy raised the iPad to show him.

'What are you playing?'

'Slither,' Alfie said. 'Look how big I am now.' He pointed and tried to explain that he was a snake that got bigger every time he swallowed another snake, but that if he was too greedy he would explode and then another snake would come along and eat all the bits.

'Right.' Thorne didn't understand a word of it, but it was very obvious which one of them was having the most fun.

Helen was sitting at the kitchen table, working on a report. As DI on a Child Protection Team, she was almost certainly enjoying herself least of all. She looked across. 'Any the wiser?'

'Well, the bit about snakes eating snakes sounds a lot like some senior officers I could mention,' Thorne said. 'But apart from that, no.' He sat back, waved the sheaf of papers as if he were about to throw them across the room. 'Still makes more sense than this, though.'

'Maybe you should ask Alfie to have a look.'

'I think he's a bit busy.'

Helen smiled, looked back down at her report. 'So, who's doing it? On the night?'

'Who *isn't* doing it? Mind you, I had to turn Christine Treasure down.'

'Why? No reason two women wouldn't work, is there?'

Thorne thought about it. 'I suppose not.'

'Everything you've said about this bloke, how he sees the women on these websites, it might actually be a good idea.'

'Got another one,' Alfie said. '*Huge* one.'

Helen looked across at Thorne. 'That kind of mindset, you know? He might think a woman going out with another woman is as desperate as it gets.'

'You might be right.' Thorne was annoyed that he hadn't considered it, when perhaps he should have, but it was too late to change the arrangements now. 'Still not sure Christine would be the right choice, mind you. I've seen her get stuck in come closing time, but I'm not sure how she is on jobs that need a bit more ... you know?'

'Finesse?'

'Good a word as any.'

'Are you absolutely sure that *you* should be doing it?'

Thorne looked up, saw Helen's sarcastic grin and returned it with interest.

'Doing what?' Alfie asked.

'It's just a job that Tom's got,' Helen said. She looked over at Thorne again. 'A very tricky one.'

Alfie did not bother looking up from his screen. 'What does finiss mean?'

'Finesse.'

'What does it mean?'

Helen stared at Thorne, but he just held up his hands. *Over to you.*

'It means ... doing something very carefully.'

'Skilfully,' Thorne said. 'Without making too much fuss.'

'Like being sneaky?' Alfie asked.

'Yeah ... sneaky.'

Alfie nodded, getting it. 'How I catch the other snakes,' he said.

Helen's phone rang.

Thorne watched her glance down at the screen, pick up the phone and walk towards the door without answering. It might have been a work call, of course, demanding conversation she would not want her son to overhear. But Thorne had recognised the look on Helen's face when she'd seen who was calling.

It wasn't Alfie she was worried about.

Jenny.

After half a minute or so, Alfie stood up and clambered on to the sofa, pushing Thorne's legs roughly out of the way. He settled back and said, 'Do you want to play?'

Thorne glanced at the file of technical notes he was still clutching.

'It's good fun. You can be a red snake or a blue snake. Any colour, really.'

Thorne dropped the notes and wondered if the boy was as good at reading people's moods as he was with technology. He said that he would very much like to play, and opted for something stripy.

'You could be black and white.' Alfie laughed. 'Like Spurs.'

Thorne could hear Helen murmuring in the bedroom.

It was only a shame that Alfie was still too young for some of the more violent shoot-em-ups, because at that moment there was someone Thorne could easily imagine as a target.

It would have been so easy to miss it. To miss *her*.

He could have gone straight back to those three pictures, pinned up on the wall above his maps and charts with printed biogs beneath.

Sarah (53) likes mountaineering and fine wine.

Jo (41) is always there for her friends.

Karen (26) doesn't like to argue but she's not a pushover!

The last three candidates he had so carefully selected over previous weeks, pored over and pried into, moved up and down the running order as the mood took him. He could just have ploughed on and made his final selection, no real reason not to, but experience had told him that a last look was never a bad idea. Checking that each of those final three was sticking to the arrangements they'd made with their dream dates, that there hadn't been any last minute changes.

Times, places, all that.

Cold feet or a better offer.

It had not taken him long to see that there had been no emails between the six interested parties to get concerned or annoyed about. No reason to change his plans because they hadn't changed theirs. Tick. On we go. But still, a voice in his head that he had come to trust had told him to wait, to bide his time just a little longer.

Had said, *You never know.*

So, just in case, he'd gone back to the site for what he'd guessed would be a cursory scan of the fresh arrivals, the eager new clients. A five-minute browsing session which, if he was lucky, might throw up another candidate to think about and perhaps get to know better a little further down the line.

It was not a half-bad selection.

A physiotherapist who thought she was 'warm and intelligent', a consultant (whatever that was) who had 'so much to do and so little time', a property manager who could not live 'without smiles and hugs'.

Then, there she was.

Her photograph, leaping from his screen, and London-based too, which was always handy. He wasn't sure how long he'd stared at her pictures for. By a boat, leaning against a car, with a man who looked enough like her to almost certainly be her brother. Then he'd scrolled down through her personal profile. What made her laugh, how she spent her leisure time, what her one wish would be. It was the section of the site headed *Neuroticism* that he enjoyed the most, as always.

All of us have the ability to feel intense emotions. This is perfectly normal. We all experience fear and elation, sadness and rage, as well as shame and envy. But to what extent do we control these emotions? Does your prospective partner have their emotions under control, or is it those very emotions that control them?

He almost laughed out loud.

According to the site's Christmas cracker graph, *she* was quite stable emotionally. Well, thank heavens for that.

He got up and wandered into the kitchen, his mind racing. He poured himself a glass of wine, downed half of it in one go then carried the rest back into the smaller bedroom, the one he used as an office. He barely glanced at the three pictures above the desk as he sat down.

Sarah, Jo and Karen would have to wait a while.

He stared at her picture.

353

Yes, he had made amendments before now. A different choice of venue or the date being knocked on a week because the woman had a 'work thing' or the man was having a minor operation. There was one occasion when the happy couple had not been able to keep their hands off each other and had driven back to her place without even bothering to order dessert. No point him paying that randy little bitch a visit, was there?

But abandoning a plan before he'd even begun and rethinking, that had never happened.

He had simply never come across anyone who demanded it.

No woman had ever been worth that.

But this one was.

SIXTY-THREE

Tanner groaned as she listened to her phone message. She shook her head and cursed under her breath as she put the phone back on the table afterwards.

'Look, I know I'm not really your type.' Thorne leaned close to her. 'But I think you should at least *look* like you're enjoying yourself.'

'I know, but—'

'Nice and calm, OK? Happy.'

Tanner kept her voice as low as Thorne's. 'Frances Coombs's panic alarm was activated.'

Thorne nodded, as though entranced by some personal anecdote of his companion's. He said, 'Tell me, but keep smiling.'

'It could be worse, I suppose.' She picked up her wine glass and Thorne leaned across to touch his own to it. 'She was complaining about pains in her chest. Heart palpitations or some nonsense. They've taken her to hospital.'

'No need to panic, then.'

'I wouldn't trust her as far as I could spit her,' Tanner said.

'How do we know who she's been talking to, what she's cooked up? Maybe they've made her a better offer.'

'Whatever else that woman is, she's not stupid,' Thorne said. 'So, just try and relax and remember how much fun we're supposed to be having. I don't think we need to worry that he's able to hear us, but we have to at least assume he's watching.'

'I do know what we're supposed to be doing, Tom.'

'*Alan*,' Thorne said. 'Alan, the recently divorced landscape gardener. You like the fact that I work outdoors, remember?'

'Well, it wouldn't have been anything else, would it?'

'Food's pretty good, isn't it?' Thorne reached for one of the crostini on the plate between them. 'And remember to hang on to the bill for expenses. I presume we're going Dutch.'

They were seated at a corner table in a smart Italian restaurant on the outskirts of Watford. At the same time, at an Indian restaurant in Bromley, Yvonne Kitson was dining with Russell Brigstocke, while Dipak Chall and a DC named Charita Desai sat in a wine bar in Hayes; all within twenty miles of central London. Six fake profiles posted over the previous week on the Made In Heaven website. Six new email addresses, online histories and social media identities, each carefully created and monitored by the operation's computer team.

The team which had confirmed that their suspect had illegally accessed the Made In Heaven website again, late the previous night.

Two further officers had been posted undercover inside each meeting place, as fellow diners or members of staff, with several more on surveillance at carefully chosen positions outside. High speed pursuit vehicles stood ready close to each location, with firearms units on standby at the vacant properties which were 'home' that night for the three women who might be targeted. Thorne, Tanner and the others on bogus 'dates' made up no more than a fifth of the officers on operational duty that evening.

As Jesmond has suggested, it had been a big ask, but they had put it all together remarkably fast. Now, they simply had to hope that the man they were aiming to tempt would take the bait. Three desperate single women to choose from, three single men who lived alone and would struggle to find an alibi, and, if the geographical profiler was right, all on dates close to where the killer was based.

They'd made it nice and easy for him.

The waiter brought their main courses and asked how they were enjoying their meal. He topped up both glasses. There had been careful liaison with management and staff in the days leading up to the operation and the waiter did not seem concerned that he was pouring grape juice from a bottle of Pinot Grigio.

He rather seemed to be enjoying the subterfuge.

Thorne took the opportunity to check out the people sitting at adjacent tables. Would the killer really be that close to them? There was no reason why not, he certainly wasn't lacking confidence, but Thorne could see no single men. It struck him suddenly that they had never considered the possibility that the killer might be on a date himself. It was a perfect cover, after all. He might be sitting with a woman unaware of his real motives or he might be there with an accomplice. Thorne took another look at the couples eating nearby. There had been nothing to indicate that the man they were after was working with anyone else, but perhaps it was a theory that should have been looked into. The operation had been put together quickly, because it had needed to be, but now, at the eleventh hour, Thorne could not help worrying that rushing might have caused them to miss something.

He could not help worrying about all sorts of things.

They ate and talked, and Tanner, her back to the wall, took her own chance to look at the restaurant's other customers. She leaned close. 'Single man at the bar. Came in just after we sat down.'

Thorne did not turn round. 'Age?'

357

'Fifties. Greying hair, six one, maybe taller. It's not Aiden Goode.'

'Spotting Aiden Goode would be a bonus,' Thorne said. 'But we can't be certain he's who we're looking for.'

'And we can't be certain that the man we're looking for is even in here,' Tanner said. 'Or in the curry house, or the wine bar. He doesn't need to be. Easy enough for him to be watching the place from outside. He just needs to see that the woman he's after leaves on her own.'

If so, there was every chance that the surveillance team had already spotted him. Thorne would not know about that until he was outside, in his car and in radio contact with the rest of the team.

'Which I will,' Tanner said. 'Sorry, but I'm not really sensing a connection. There's no spark.'

'I'm doing my best,' Thorne said.

At ten o'clock, Thorne asked for the bill, knowing that in Hayes and Bromley, as arranged, their colleagues would be doing exactly the same thing. He finished his coffee and watched Tanner finish hers; a welcome shot of caffeine as they approached the business end of the evening. He handed over a credit card, thanked the waiter, then stood and helped Tanner on with her jacket.

A final chance to get a good look at those around them.

A glance at the officer working undercover on the door.

Clocking the man's hand signal indicating that he had no concerns.

They walked out together and along the main road to the car park. It was a dry evening and the Friday night traffic would work to their advantage too, with any car they might need to pursue unable to get anywhere terribly fast.

'All set?' Thorne asked.

'Oh Christ, yes,' Tanner said. 'Ten minutes from now I'll be at home to visitors.'

358

'Let's hope you get one.'

They walked to their cars, which had, with the same meticulous eye for detail the logistics team had applied to every other aspect of the operation, been registered with the DVLA in the names under which they'd signed up to the Made In Heaven website. Both looked like bog-standard saloons, but each had been upgraded and was capable of outrunning almost anything else likely to be on the road.

Thorne leaned in to kiss Tanner on both cheeks.

'I'm on the other end of the radio if you need me, OK?'

'I know,' Tanner said. 'I *was* there when this was being put together, and if anything kicks off I think SO19 have got it covered.'

'Just saying.'

'Let's see how desperate and needy *he* feels when my front door opens and he's got a Glock 19 in his face.'

A minute or so later, Thorne's Skoda followed Tanner's Volvo out of the car park. He drove slowly away in the opposite direction, keeping Tanner's tail lights in the mirror until she was out of sight. He took the first turning on his left, bumped up on to the pavement and picked up the radio from the front seat.

'All units. Tanner is on her way home ...'

In Hayes, Charita Desai was on the road, as was Yvonne Kitson, driving towards a carefully selected property within ten minutes of the restaurant in Bromley.

The officers inside the wine bar and the two restaurants confirmed that no other customers had followed the couples from the premises on foot.

Thorne reminded them to stay in position and report back every few minutes.

The three mobile surveillance teams outside had nothing to report. No vehicles were following from any of the date locations.

Thorne gave them the same order.

It was possible, of course, that the killer had not tracked his victims directly from the location of their dates; that he had picked them up somewhere between restaurant and home, well aware of the routes that they would be taking.

He spoke to Desai and Kitson. Neither was aware of any vehicle that appeared to be following theirs.

'Couldn't say one way or the other,' Tanner said, when he spoke to her. 'Lots of traffic . . . and he's probably good at this.'

Thorne had no doubt of that. Whatever Hendricks had to say about stupid, over-confident criminals, five dead women were ample testimony to the killer's capabilities.

To his skill and preparation—

'*Unit three, Watford.*'

'This is Thorne. Go ahead.'

'Individual leaving car park in red Toyota Corolla.'

'What? Did he come from the restaurant?' Thorne had heard nothing from the officers inside.

'Negative. He walked in off the street . . . not sure where he came from, to be fair. Suspect vehicle now turning right, that's *right* onto the High Street towards Exchange Road.'

The same direction as Tanner.

'Description?'

'White male, forties. Medium height, dark hair . . .'

Goode.

'We are in silent pursuit. Repeat, in pursuit.'

Thorne threw the Skoda hard into a three-point turn, radioed Tanner as he straightened up and pushed into traffic on the main road.

'I heard,' Tanner said.

'I'm not far behind you.'

'I hope you're wearing your seatbelt.'

Thorne talked to all units in Hayes and Bromley, ordered them not to stand down until instructed. Then he spoke to the senior firearms officer on call at the address in Watford they were all now heading for.

'Put your team on immediate standby.'

'Pleasure,' the man said.

'ETA five minutes.'

SIXTY-FOUR

The A&E department at the Whittington Hospital was as crowded and miserable as might be expected on a Saturday night. Not quite the ninth circle of hell, but in the top two or three.

'Couldn't have picked a worse time,' one of the coppers had muttered on the drive over.

'Be a bloody zoo in there,' his mate had said.

The plods were not the friendliest of company, but still, there was nothing like having a police escort when it came to jumping a queue. A quick word with the woman on the reception desk, and there was barely time for the coppers to get coffee from the machine in the corner before Frances Coombs was called through.

'We'll be here,' one of the coppers said.

A man with a wad of bandage pressed to his eye, who had been watching since they'd come in, stuck his leg out as she tried to walk past. 'How come you get to go in before me? I've been here for hours.'

Frances pushed the leg aside. Said, 'Life's not fair, is it?'

She sat in a cubicle waiting for a doctor.

362

She pressed a hand to her chest and tried to take deep breaths. She could feel it in her throat as well.

The curtains were pushed aside and a man stepped in. He asked what the trouble was, and Frances told him.

To be honest, she hadn't felt right in herself for a while, not since that cocky pair had come bowling into the visits area at Warren Park. It had been a lot worse the last few days, though. Holed up in that crappy hotel. She'd been allowed to make one call to let Nat know she was all right, and that had been a waste of time and effort, as her daughter hadn't seemed particularly bothered one way or another, but since then she'd just been sitting around doing nothing, picking food from a delivery menu and watching TV. Trying to sleep while her heart was going like billy-o and waking up trying to catch her breath. That daft alarm thing hanging round her neck, same as they gave coffin-dodgers in old people's homes, like she was helpless.

Not that she wasn't glad of it now, mind you. They'd got her in here pretty bloody quick, to be fair.

'Does it feel as though your heart's racing?' the doctor asked. 'Or does it feel like it's skipping a beat?'

'Both,' Frances said.

'And your chest feels tight?'

Frances nodded.

The doctor sat her on the bed and listened to her chest. He asked if Frances drank a lot of coffee, if she smoked, if she suffered with anaemia or diabetes, if she'd ever had thyroid problems.

'Yeah, diabetes,' she said. 'Had it for years, though, and never felt anything like this.'

'Right.' He took her blood pressure and told her it was a little high, but nothing to worry about. 'Well, if none of those conditions apply, the most common cause of an irregular heartbeat such as yours is usually simple stress or anxiety. Would you say you've been under a lot of stress recently?'

'Definitely,' Frances said.

'So, what's causing that?'

Frances remembered how she felt in that interview room when they were telling her about the refugee who'd been shot in the neck; the scary-looking sod in the bike leathers with the blacked-out visor; the voice on the other end of the phone when she'd called needing fresh supplies. She thought about those names she'd given to Thorne and Tanner.

'Oh, just normal things, you know? Work, family . . . '

The doctor looked at her, nodded. 'Well, I'll prescribe some anti-anxiety medication, but I'm going to run some blood tests while you're here, and we might as well do a chest X-ray to be on the safe side.'

'Are they addictive? These tablets? You hear all sorts of stories.'

'Well, there can be side effects, but hopefully this will all go back to normal fairly quickly.' The doctor slung his stethoscope round his neck, like he was in an episode of *Casualty*. 'The best advice I can give you is to try and deal with whatever's making you stressed, and to take it easy. Get out in the garden and go for long walks. Have you got a dog?'

She said that she hadn't.

'Swimming's good . . . '

Forty-five minutes later, Frances walked back towards reception with a week's supply of Diazepam in a paper bag. What with the painkillers she was taking for her arthritis, the ones with the unpronounceable name for her acid reflux and the statins for her cholesterol, a few more pills weren't going to make a lot of difference, whatever the side effects might be. To be honest, she already felt a lot calmer than she had when she'd come in, and, things being what they were, getting hooked on tranquillisers was the least of her worries.

SIXTY-FIVE

Thorne did his best to move through the traffic without driving too recklessly, confident that, as yet, the suspect did not know he was being followed. Five minutes from the destination he still did not have the target vehicle in sight. But the high speed pursuit vehicle ahead of him did and they had already run the Corolla's plates.

'Car is registered to a Brian Mulhearne. 15.6.72. An address in West London.'

Not the man whose photograph was pinned up in the incident room.

Unless Aiden Goode had become someone else.

'No criminal record. Not so much as a speeding ticket.'

He followed the one way system on to the A411 and drove south, touching fifty past the Palace Theatre, the branded façade of the Intu shopping centre. A short stretch of dual carriageway gave him an opportunity to make up some ground and he took it; accelerating hard past cars in whichever lane was easiest, flashing a van ahead of him until it grudgingly gave way. Not overly concerned that he might be the one getting a speeding ticket.

Via the radio on his passenger seat, Tanner was reporting her progress as regularly as the pursuit vehicle was describing the Corolla's.

'I'm turning left on to Grosvenor Road.'

Half a minute later: 'The suspect's vehicle is making a left on to Grosvenor Road.'

'Right on to Stanley Road.'

The Corolla took the same turn.

There could be little doubt that the suspect was tailing Tanner's car. Four vehicles, by now within no more than half a mile of one another and all heading for the same destination.

Tanner. The suspect. The pursuit vehicle. Thorne.

As Thorne made the same manoeuvre into a narrow street lined with terraced housing, a familiar voice crackled from the radio. DCI Russell Brigstocke, calling through from Bromley.

'Tom? A status report would be nice.'

Thorne told him as quickly as he could then cut him off to talk to the firearms commander.

'ETA three minutes.'

They rapidly ran through the prearranged strategy for the neutralisation and arrest of the suspect: the deployment of the vehicles, the movements of the armed officers both inside and outside the address.

'ETA two minutes,' said an officer in the pursuit vehicle. 'That's two minutes to target address.'

Everyone's voice was suddenly cranked up a little higher; a tightness in the throat and, almost certainly, in the gut.

'Left on to Gladstone Road,' Tanner said.

This was the road on which the woman Tanner was pretending to be lived.

Now she was nearly home.

Thorne waited, the cars parked on either side of the road making it impossible to overtake a four by four. He leaned on the horn, willing someone, anyone to let him know that Tanner had arrived, that she was safely inside the house.

'Nicola? You there yet?'

The next voice belonged to an officer in the pursuit vehicle, confirming that the Corolla, which had clearly made up ground on Tanner's Volvo, had taken the same turn.

Thorne was approaching the road himself, grateful that the four by four had carried straight on.

'I'm at the house,' Tanner said. 'I'm inside.'

'Suspect vehicle is pulling over . . . parking a few cars down.'

'I'm almost there,' Thorne shouted. 'Go, go go . . .'

Ahead of him, at the far end of the road, an unmarked car screamed round the corner and pulled up inches from the Toyota, at almost exactly the same time as the pursuit vehicle stopped alongside. The front door of a house opposite opened moments later and armed officers tore down the front path and along the pavement, until they were lined up on the passenger side of the vehicle.

'Hands on the dashboard,' one of them shouted.

By now, two more armed officers had jumped from one of the cars and had their weapons trained on the driver's window.

'Hands on the dashboard . . .'

Thorne stopped in the middle of the road, got out and waited. Now this was a firearms operation, so he hung back and watched as one of the officers from the pursuit vehicle shone a torch into the car. He looked for Tanner, but could not see her.

An officer moved cautiously forward and opened the door of the Toyota.

'Step out nice and easy for me.'

The driver did as he was told and was instantly spun round and slammed against the car. Once he had been patted down and handcuffed, the officer stepped back and the firearms commander took his place. He removed his helmet and signalled for Thorne to come forward.

'What's your name?' Thorne asked.

The man looked terrified; eyes wide, his face even paler than

367

it would normally have been in the torchlight. He shook his head as though he'd momentarily forgotten who he was. 'Brian Mulhearne.' Nodding now. 'My name's Brian Mulhearne.'

'Where've you come from tonight, Brian?'

'I had a drink in town.' He was breathing hard. 'Just a quick drink, that's all. Jesus, what's—'

'Where?'

'The Black Horse. On Clarendon Road.'

'So what was your car doing parked at an Italian restaurant?'

'It's free.' He attempted a shrug. 'I always leave it there.'

Thorne pointed towards the Volvo. 'Why were you following that car?'

The man looked. 'I haven't been following any car.'

'So, why are you here? This isn't where you live, is it?'

'It's where my mother lives.'

Thorne felt as though someone had punched the breath out of him. He glanced across to see that Tanner had appeared in the doorway of the house from which the armed officers had come. 'Your mother?'

The man pointed to the house next to the one Tanner was standing outside. At that moment, its front door opened and an old woman peered nervously around it. Her voice was high and unsteady. 'Brian . . . ?'

The man waved. 'It's fine, Mum . . . I'm fine. Go back inside.'

Thorne was already on the way back to his car. He got to the open door in time to hear the rather less tremulous voice of Russell Brigstocke booming from the radio inside.

'Tom? What the hell is going on?'

SIXTY-SIX

There were even more people gathered in reception by the time Frances Coombs walked back in from the treatment area. The man with the bandage was still waiting. She smiled at him, but he just glowered then went back to his phone.

Her escorts were sitting near the doors. They stood up as she approached, making hard work of it, as though they'd been enjoying a quiet chat while she'd been wasting valuable NHS resources.

Like she was wasting valuable Met Police resources.

'Right then,' one of them said. 'Back to Fawlty Towers.'

His mate fished car keys from his pocket. 'Tell you what, I wouldn't mind living in a hotel. All your cleaning done, bed made every day, meals on tap. Sounds like a total doss.'

'You try staying there,' Frances said. 'Not allowed to talk to your family, not even allowed to tell them where you are. Just like one of your cells, only with room service.'

The copper jangled his car keys. 'Suits me.'

His mate placed a hand on Frances's back to guide her forward. 'You haven't met his missus.'

369

They stopped outside the sliding doors. There were a group of people smoking and chatting on a bench, the oldest of whom was attached to what looked like an oxygen tank. The copper who was driving announced that he would go and fetch the car and jogged off, leaving his colleague to lead Frances across the pedestrian concourse towards Highgate Hill.

'How's the palpitations?'

'No need to pretend you give a toss,' she said. 'I know you think I'm putting it on, anyway.'

'Just making conversation,' he said. He didn't bother making any more until they'd reached the street, when he nodded down at the paper bag she was carrying. 'Give you some happy pills, did they?'

Frances heard it then, like an angry wasp close to her ear.

'Could do with a few of them myself, if I'm honest.'

She didn't take it in, because she was already looking down the hill and watching the single headlight getting closer. The noise grew louder, *angrier*, and she flapped for the copper's arm, grabbed at his sleeve.

'What?'

The copper looked too, then, but the bike was already coming quickly; accelerating towards them with a furious whine and only slowing at the last, crucial moment, when the rider held out his arm.

'Christ . . . '

The copper stepped across her and tried to turn away.

Frances staggered back and shouted again as she raised her hands, some strange part of her racing brain randomly telling her, in those final few moments, that whether or not the man on the bike was Romanian or Polish, he would surely understand what 'no' meant.

The paper bag of pills hit the pavement a second before the first shot.

SIXTY-SEVEN

He'd watched from outside for a while, content to enjoy a drink in the bar opposite, eyes on the restaurant car park until the eager singletons had met up and gone inside. For tonight, he'd only wanted to watch them arrive, that was all; to get a look at the man his chosen woman had been matched with, see how things were shaping up.

The fun would come later. A very different kind of fun this time.

He'd arrived first, 'Alan', the 'landscape gardener'. Ten minutes early and looking every bit as surly as he did in his profile picture. Looking nervous, but determined. Looking exactly like what he was.

Back at home now, a takeaway pizza on the desk in front of him – Italian, in their honour – he smiled as he imagined how this first date had gone. He always did, telling himself each time he rang a doorbell, as he wrapped his hands around a neck and squeezed, how much misery he was ultimately saving them both – but this date was extra special.

What had they talked about?

Was there a chemistry?

Would they see each other again?

He grinned and lifted a slice of pizza from the box, tore at it hungrily and looked up at her photo, now the only picture pinned above his desk. He'd chosen the one of her standing by the boat, because he liked the way her hair had been moving in the wind. Longer then, flying behind her. She didn't look awfully happy, though, which was a shame. Probably just one of those people who didn't like having their photograph taken, but all the same, it wasn't doing her any favours. He might say something to her about how she should smile more, next time he saw her. A bit pointless, he supposed, because it would also be the last time and she certainly wouldn't be feeling much like smiling then, but he'd tell her anyway.

Because she deserved to hear it.

She had such a lovely smile.

They'd opted for the Skoda Thorne had been driving and were halfway back to Colindale when Tanner took the call.

Before then, there hadn't been a great deal said, the mood predictably subdued, Tanner making sporadic, if unsuccessful, efforts to lift Thorne's spirits.

'Nobody ever thought we'd crack it first time,' she said.

'No.'

'They've got to let us run it again, surely.' She leaned back and turned her head towards the passenger window. 'They're not going to put that much work into setting all this up, then just pull it because we didn't get a result straight away.'

Thorne said nothing, swallowed down garlic and onions. Acid. He knew exactly what the result would be.

An urgent inquiry. The brass, blowing hard.

'Could have been worse,' Tanner said.

Thorne looked at her.

'You know it could.'

Tanner was right, but that didn't mean he particularly felt like acknowledging it. When that many officers were involved, when pursuit vehicles and weapons were deployed, the smallest mistake could prove horribly costly: he'd seen it happen. Could cost lives, careers.

'No shots fired. No harm done.'

'Oh yeah, it was textbook.' Thorne stared ahead, the low drone of the engine moving through him, white line after white line sucked beneath the wheels. The terror and confusion on that man's face and in the old lady's voice as she called his name. 'Full marks all round, definitely. Everyone did their job, whole thing went like clockwork, and if the object of the exercise had been to waste a shedload of time and put the wind up some accountant from Acton bringing his mum a birthday present we'd all be heroes. As it is . . . '

'What did Russell say?'

'That,' Thorne said. 'More or less. He got a bit more worked up when he started talking about the conversation he'd need to have with Trevor Jesmond, but that's fair enough.'

Tanner shook her head. 'He won't throw us under the bus. He's part of this.'

'Well, he's wishing he wasn't.'

'He got a free curry out of it.' Then Tanner's phone rang, and, for her at least, an evening which they would all be doing their best to forget got substantially worse.

Thorne heard most of it, so didn't need to ask too many questions when the call ended. 'Doesn't sound good,' he said.

Tanner was looking out of the window again. 'Coombs is dead, and one of the officers who was with her is in surgery.'

'Fuck.'

'A motorbike.' She slipped her phone back into her handbag. 'I should get down to the Whittington.'

'What good's that going to do?' Thorne asked. 'I mean, if they're operating—'

'And I need to call Andrew Evans. Give him the bad news.'

'Really?' Thorne still found it hard to understand the sympathy Tanner appeared to feel for the man at Long Barrow Manor. As though she owed him something.

He put his foot down and moved into the outside lane. They said nothing for half a minute. He could sense that, next to him, Tanner was still processing the information and struggling to plan a useful route forward; buzzing with the compulsion to do something and infuriated at not having the first idea what that should be.

Thorne was somewhat less conflicted.

He was exhausted, with little beyond sleep to look forward to, at the arse-end of an hour which had seen two separate operations turn spectacularly to shit.

He had no desire to go home.

'Why don't we just go back to your place?' he said. 'Open whatever the hell you can lay your hands on and get thoroughly hammered? Seriously, I can't think of a better idea.'

Tanner closed her eyes for a few seconds, as though she was thinking about it. Her hand drummed against her thigh.

She said, 'Drop me off at the hospital.'

PART FOUR

THE
NECESSARY
STEPS

SIXTY-EIGHT

Thorne decided that it was because of what had happened the previous weekend: the operations in Watford, Bromley and Hayes, the modus operandi of a killer they had tried to draw out, yet were no closer to catching. It almost certainly explained why he was sitting in a bar in Camden, studying the woman he was drinking with and asking himself whether he was single and they were meeting in very different circumstances, this could feasibly have been a date that might lead somewhere.

Did they have much in common? Well, one thing, definitely.

Was the conversation interesting? It would end up being . . . memorable, he'd have put money on it.

Did he find her attractive?

He told himself to stop being ridiculous.

The dating connection did not however explain the singularly more inappropriate thoughts he'd briefly entertained weeks before, sitting in that wine bar with Melita Perera. Why he'd been hoping the psychiatrist might call to see how the case was progressing. Why he'd considered calling her again and suggesting that they catch up over yet another drink. Or dinner.

The fact that neither call had taken place was probably for the best.

In the same way it was best to avoid picking at scabs or biting into mouth ulcers, Thorne was doing his best not to think too much about soulmates or romantic meetings. Besides which, the woman on the other side of the table was his girlfriend's sister.

'Helen said that things were a bit tricky at work,' Jenny said. 'For you, I mean.'

'Did she?' Thorne hoped the smile was convincing. It seemed as though his attempts to put the case out of his mind, even temporarily, were doomed to failure.

'This big case you're working?'

'Right.'

'Nothing specific, obviously.'

Thorne nodded. He knew Helen would never discuss the details of a case with her sister, but he was nevertheless irritated that she'd even mentioned it. An intrusion on private grief.

The fallout from the failed operation a week before could not have been much worse. Tanner had hoped that the financial investment already made might have merited the continuation of the operation, but Thorne had not underestimated the alacrity with which the likes of Trevor Jesmond moved to distance themselves from anything even remotely tainted. Best to get out now, before any more money was wasted, then line up those who could easily be blamed for the cost incurred thus far, and swiftly punish them.

The buck passed, the arses at Scotland Yard covered.

An inquiry had quickly been launched into the fiasco in Watford and, if that weren't enough for the likes of Thorne and Brigstocke to worry about, there was the small matter of the case being brought against the Met by Brian Mulhearne for the mental anguish caused to himself and his aged mother.

Thorne had been assigned other cases to be getting on with. He had been shunted unceremoniously into a dull and dusty

378

operational corner, where he couldn't do any damage. Where all he could do was sit and wait for the axe to fall; trying to pretend he didn't care, while meetings were held in those brightly lit conference rooms and jokes about a new job selling fruit and veg were not quite so funny any more.

He said, 'I don't really want to talk about work.'

'Suit yourself.' Jenny reached for a glass of wine, her second in ten minutes.

Thorne looked at her. She *was* attractive – there was no harm in acknowledging that, was there? – but she couldn't hold a candle to her elder sister. 'It's not the reason I called.'

The half-empty wine glass was placed carefully back on the table. 'Yes, I was wondering when we'd get to that.' She sat up straight, concerned suddenly. 'Helen's all right, isn't she?'

'Helen's fine,' Thorne said. 'No thanks to you.'

'Sorry?'

Thorne took a second or two. This was the speech he'd been running through in his mind since he'd called Helen's sister from work two days before; had rehearsed on the drive up from Tulse Hill, having told Helen he was meeting Phil Hendricks. 'For whatever reason, you've clearly got a major problem with me. I really couldn't care less about that, but it's making a problem for *us*. For me and Helen, and I'm sick of it. Whenever she sees you or you call, you bitch about me to her . . . I'm too old or I'm too miserable, she can do better, whatever it is—'

Jenny cut him off. 'Is this how you interview suspects, Tom?' There was an attempt at lightness, but she could not look at him. 'You sit them down and give them the hard-man act? I've seen all that nice copper/nasty copper stuff on TV, and there's no need to guess which one you are, is there?'

Thorne was determined to finish, to say his piece. 'Look, I've had enough, simple as that. Helen loves you, course she does, but I don't. Truth is, I probably dislike you every bit as much as you dislike me, but we need to sort this out for everyone's sake.

379

Because I'm not going anywhere. I'm not going to let you drive a wedge between us, so it would really help me if you said what the hell I've done to piss you off and why you've got such a stick up your arse.'

Jenny tucked a loose strand of hair behind her ear and reached for the wine again.

'Is it just because I'm a copper?'

She shook her head.

'You think Helen would be better off with a nice sales rep or a teacher or something?'

'No . . .'

'Because the way I hear it, you weren't any different when she was with Paul.'

'I liked Paul.'

'Really?'

'And I don't *dis*like you.'

'So I'm just imagining it, yeah? Like I must have imagined that stupid smile on your face when you tried to talk about how "tricky" things were for me at work. Like you weren't enjoying it.'

Helen's sister shook her head. She downed the contents of her glass, then looked at Thorne good and hard for the first time in several minutes. She said, 'You're being ridiculous.'

'Am I? Because—'

'I'm *jealous*, OK?' She caught the eye of a waiter and held up her empty glass to let him know she wanted another. She leaned forward and tried to smile. 'Happy now? I'm jealous of Helen.'

SIXTY-NINE

Tanner drove past Turnpike Lane tube station, heading north towards Wood Green. She glanced at the clock on the dash and saw that she was going to be late for the appointment. She winced. Punctuality was something that she normally set a good deal of store by, was part and parcel of an ordered, *tidy* life, but for once her irritation was no more than momentary, because the truth was she didn't much care.

There were far more important things to worry about than downsizing.

The Jandali/Sykes case had stalled, perhaps permanently. Frances Coombs had been their only direct link to the men responsible for the murders of the refugee and the drug dealer, and now that she had been eliminated Tanner had no idea where to go next, how to pick up the thread.

Meanwhile, Andrew Evans was in limbo.

Tanner remembered the long silence when she'd called Long Barrow Manor to break the news about what had happened to the Duchess. The anger and then the resignation when he'd finally spoken and her own hollow attempts at reassurance.

'We start again,' she'd said. 'We'll find someone who's willing to talk.'

'Oh, yeah. Because after the Duchess got a bullet in her head they'll be queuing up, won't they?'

Tanner had said nothing, because she'd known he was right.

'Well, maybe I'll make it home for my new kid's first birthday.' Tanner could hear the crack in Andrew Evans's voice. 'I'll hang on to that, shall I?'

The conversation with Paula Evans had not been any easier. With the police presence outside ramped up after the Frances Coombs shooting, she and her son were now virtually detainees in their own home and the strain was clearly beginning to tell.

She had choked back tears. Said, 'It was easier when he was in prison.'

Tears too, plenty of them – while Tanner could do no more than dig tissues out of her handbag – from the wife of the officer shot outside the Whittington Hospital; the only glimmer of good news since that awful night being his transfer from the critical care unit two days earlier.

One less worm of guilt.

The failure still weighed heavily enough though, and not just on Tanner. Chall and the rest of the team had been mooching around all week like they'd had the breath kicked out of them. As if they were marking time until something more urgent came along; a case that might actually get them a result.

Ten minutes or so later, she turned into a short road that ran parallel to White Hart Lane. She smiled. Though the Spurs ground was not quite on her doorstep, she could think of one person at least who would be happy if this turned out to be her new address. The smile quickly faded as she thought about the nightmare of parking on match days.

Tom Thorne might well end up disappointed.

The street was nice enough, though. Newer builds on one side and an older, two-storey terrace running the length of the other.

A small park at one end. There was nothing to get too excited about, but the truth was that she was only really doing this to take her mind off other things. Besides, the estate agent was nice enough and had been happy to organise viewings around her shifts.

She recognised his car and pulled in behind it, then got out and stared at the house.

It sat in the middle of the terrace; in reasonable nick, Tanner thought, and painted white, which she approved of, with a small tiled canopy above the front door. Nothing screamed 'home' at her, but the price was right, so it was probably worth twenty minutes of her time to take a look.

She walked to the door, pressed the bell for the ground floor flat and was buzzed in. Junk mail had been piled up on a shelf above the meters and a bicycle leaned against the stairs that led up to the first floor. She peered along the hall, then decided that she'd check out the communal garden afterwards.

The door to the ground floor flat was open and she put her head round.

'Simon?'

'In here.'

She stepped inside and turned left into a decent-sized living room. She looked at the modern fireplace, which she immediately decided would have to be torn out, then walked through a dining area into the kitchen. The appliances were top of the range and she liked the marble worktops, but it was a little small.

'Ms Tanner?'

'This kitchen's not exactly huge,' she shouted.

'Come and have a look at what they've done to the bathroom.'

The estate agent's voice was muffled, as though he were speaking from behind a door or with his head inside a cupboard. Tanner walked back across the living room, passed what she guessed was one of the bedrooms and nudged open the door to the bathroom.

The estate agent was lying in the bath.

At least she presumed it was him. She recognised the suit, the shock of dark hair, but nothing else was normal. She struggled to take in the duct tape fastened around his hands and the pool of blood beneath his head, livid against the white enamel.

She was leaning down to look for signs of life when she heard a noise behind her and spun round to see the man who had presumably stepped out of the bedroom opposite.

He nodded past her. 'They certainly earn their commission, don't they?'

Tanner could only blink for a few seconds. The surge of adrenalin left her dry-mouthed and dizzy as she wrestled with the picture, willing it to make sense. She knew exactly who he was, of course, but he should not have been here.

'What are you—?'

Then she saw what was in the man's hand and the moment of clarity punched through the roaring in her ears. Left only terror. She understood how stupid she had been – they had all been.

The man lunged forward suddenly, his hand reaching towards Tanner's hair. Instinctively, she retreated, until the backs of her legs were pressed against the bath. She tried to breathe.

He said, 'That picture doesn't do you justice.'

SEVENTY

Thorne sat back as the waiter opened a bottle and poured what was definitely not grape juice into a fresh wine glass. He watched Jenny take her first mouthful, shaking her head; eyes closed, as though regretting what she had said or simply steeling herself for the conversation to come. He wrapped his hands around the single bottle of beer he had been nursing since they'd arrived.

She was jealous?

This was something Hendricks had suggested once, but no more than jokingly . . .

He looked at her.

'Not like *that*,' she said. 'I'm afraid you're not my type, Tom.'

'Obviously. I didn't think that's what you meant.' He smiled and felt the tension diffuse a little. 'So . . . ?'

That strand of hair had come loose again, but she ignored it. 'It's not like it's something I'm particularly proud of. I mean, I should want my sister to be happy, shouldn't I? That's what any normal person would want. I should be pleased that she is.'

'Yeah, I would have thought.'

'Right. But the truth is I'm only ever pleased up to a point, which is actually not very pleased at all.'

'You're jealous of Helen being happy?'

She nodded. 'Pathetic, isn't it? I was jealous because she was happy with Paul and I suppose I'm jealous now that she's happy with you. Don't get me wrong, that's still a bit of a mystery to me.' The smile was tentative, but she appeared to be doing her best. 'She could do better.'

'Nobody's arguing,' Thorne said.

'So.' She reached for her glass. 'There you are then.'

Watching her drink, Thorne decided to keep her company and lifted the bottle. 'And you're jealous of Helen being happy because you're not?'

She stared at him. 'Hello? Have you *met* my husband?'

Thorne laughed, because she was inviting him to. Tedious Tim. A man whose soliloquies about the delights of angling or detailed descriptions of car maintenance could render most people comatose within moments and whom Thorne had rarely seen without a golfing sweater. More important, Thorne could not recall ever witnessing a tender or solicitous gesture, or even a kind word from a man who played the put-upon husband in public, but almost certainly insisted on being deferred to behind closed doors.

It was hard to see how the woman who was married to him could have been even close to happy. And it explained the drinking.

'So, why don't you leave? Or get him to leave?'

She shrugged. 'Usual stuff. Kids. Settling for what you've got because you're too scared to make that jump.'

'Still.'

'I know. You're right.'

'Talk to somebody. Talk to Helen.'

She scoffed. 'That'd be a bit rich, don't you think? Asking my sister for help with my shitty relationship after I've been doing everything I can to sabotage her good ones?'

Thorne did not know what else to say. The limits of his marital advice had already been stretched. He stole a look at his watch and saw that he needed to leave. 'Listen, I've got to shoot off.'

Jenny nodded.

'But thanks for coming . . . and thanks for clearing everything up. First decent result I've had in a while.' He looked at her, worried for a moment that, considering what she had just confessed, he might have sounded insensitive. She did not seem offended.

'Don't tell Helen,' she said. 'I want to tell her myself. Say sorry.'

Thorne nodded and reached for the leather jacket that was draped across the chair. He said, 'I'd wondered if it was anything to do with what happened in Polesford. The stuff with you and Helen.'

She let out a long breath and stared down at the table. 'That makes it all so much worse, doesn't it? Everything she did back then, protecting me from . . . all that, and I behave like this.' The glass was in her hand again. 'Like a complete bitch.'

'You're not,' Thorne said, but she wasn't listening, her head back as she polished off what was left of the wine.

Thorne left a twenty pound note on the table and walked away towards the exit. He turned at the door to see Jenny waving at the waiter. She didn't look happy, far from it, but seemed content enough, in the circumstances, to sit there and drink away what was left of the afternoon.

SEVENTY-ONE

Tanner sat motionless on a chair, her back to the fireplace; knees together and arms held stiff at her sides, eyes fixed on the man sitting directly opposite her a few feet away. She tried to blink as little as possible. She forced herself to stay looking at his face and not to let her eyes drop, not even for a moment, to the weapon in his right hand.

She did not want to show fear.

She understood – or hoped she understood – enough about the man who had killed Alice Matthews, Patricia Somersby and the others to know that weakness was what he thrived on; that need, of any sort, was what marked someone out as a potential victim.

She knew what provoked this man to kill.

And now, for all the good it was likely to do her, she knew what his name was.

Graham French, who Tanner had last seen waving from the door of his overpriced beauty salon, leaned slowly left and right, studying her. 'I meant what I said.' He nodded, confident in his expert appraisal. 'Sorry to say this, but you looked a bit . . . frumpy, if I'm honest. In those pictures you posted on the website, or someone posted for you, I should say. Obviously your hair's looking a lot better now – he said immodestly – but you just seemed as if you couldn't really be bothered, and trust me, I looked at those photographs a *lot*. I mean, what sort of smile was that? Hardly much of an advertisement if you were looking for a match. Mind you, that was never really the idea, was it?' He shook his head, as though amused. 'I have a sneaking suspicion it was me whose eye you were trying to catch.' He tut-tutted, enjoying himself. 'Didn't say anything about being devious in that blurb of yours, and that's just dishonest! More than one bogus date that night, I'm guessing, because there were a couple of other matches that didn't smell right.'

He waited, but Tanner said nothing.

'I so wish you could have been there the first time I logged in and saw your face staring back at me, the first time I read your profile. It was priceless, I promise you. Yes, a bit of a shock, obviously . . .'

He raised his hands and waved them in mock-terror. Tanner did not let her eyes move upwards as the weapon rose.

'. . . you know, that I'd been *rumbled*.' He let his arms drop down and shrugged. 'After that, though, it was just . . . hilarious. The idea that you thought I could actually be fooled by any of it. By some computer tricks and a spot of dressing-up. A few coppers playing make-believe. I was actually laughing out loud, I kid you not. In fact, it was almost as much fun as thinking of you all running around like the proverbial chickens trying to find my old friend Aiden Goode. I wonder what happened to *him*?' He leaned forward, as though sharing a nugget of gossip. 'Newsflash. You were *seriously* wasting your time.'

He sat back and the smile slid from his face as he began to spin the scissors around his index finger.

'Did you honestly think it would be that easy? Do you think I'm stupid?'

'Absolutely not,' Tanner said.

French seemed pleased that she'd finally spoken. 'Actually . . . I believe you. I mean, how could anyone in their right mind think that? You don't get to be sitting where I am, to have achieved as much as I have, without plenty going on up here.' He tapped, once, twice, at the side of his head. 'I'm not saying I'm Stephen Hawking or anything, but I'm not a mug.'

Tanner allowed her eyes to drift to the scissors and watched them spin. It might just give her an extra second or two, she thought, the blades being open like that. Perhaps she could get to him. To stab, he would need to move his finger, would need to close the blades and form a fist. He could easily fumble. Yes, he was probably stronger than her, but she might be able to get past him.

She scanned the room quickly, looking for something to use as a weapon.

'I should have taken a bit more off at the front,' he said.

Tanner looked back to him and saw where he was staring. 'Really?' She lifted a hand, very slowly, and moved fingers through her hair.

A sorrowful nod. 'Stupid, because I remember thinking that at the time and I never said anything, and now look at it.'

'It's great,' Tanner said.

'Almost.'

'I love what you did—'

'No.' He stopped spinning the scissors. He slipped out his finger and closed the blades. 'It's already getting too shaggy. Normally, I'd tell you to get it done again as soon as possible, but I can't see much point in that, can you?'

Tanner felt something cold curling in her belly. She swallowed and said, 'So, what happens now, Graham?' She had been struggling to remember anything she'd learned on the three-day hostage negotiation course she'd completed a few years before. She didn't even know that she *was* a hostage, she didn't know anything . . . but had there been something about repeating what

390

the hostage-taker said? *Including* them? She definitely remembered that using their first name whenever possible was a good way to establish trust.

French thought about her question for a few seconds. 'Honestly? I'm not altogether sure. I mean, I'd be kidding if I didn't say I've got a *rough* idea how things are going to pan out. For you, at any rate. But this is all a bit impulsive for me. I'm a planner ... well, you know that. Obviously, as soon as I saw you up on that website, once I'd finished laughing, I knew I'd have to change tack, but even I was surprised when I came up with this. Whatever this is. I suppose I just thought it was important for you to know how stupid you'd been.' He jabbed at the air with the scissors to make his point. 'To show you who you're dealing with. You know?'

Tanner lowered her head.

Studied the weave of the nice new carpet.

'Nicola?'

The tone of his voice, and the telltale clicking beneath it, were more than enough to bring Tanner's head back up sharply. She could only watch as he rapidly opened and closed the blades of the scissors.

A practised, professional display.

Snip, snip ...

He said, 'Right. Let's get busy, shall we?'

SEVENTY-TWO

Obviously, Thorne had not failed to notice its proximity to the Field of Dreams, but on first glance at least, he doubted this latest property would be Nicola Tanner's cup of tea. Not that he was altogether certain what her cup of tea was. Whatever the place turned out to be like inside, he could certainly think of any number of ways he'd rather be spending a Saturday teatime.

Watching Sky Sports, sleeping, removing his eyeballs with a teaspoon ...

This would be the debt paid, he decided.

Pushing through the front door as he was buzzed in, he thought about calling Helen as soon as he managed to get away, seeing if she fancied asking Jenny to babysit and going out to the pub. Or maybe they could try that new Cuban place in Herne Hill they'd spoken about. Then he remembered how he'd left Jenny, who had looked as if she wouldn't be calling it a day any time soon, and decided they might not be leaving Alfie in the most capable of hands.

Perhaps a quiet night in with a takeaway was a better idea.

He heard Tanner call his name from the other side of a door.

He leaned against it and stepped into the room.

Froze.

Tanner was bound tight to a chair with silver duct tape. She was gasping for air. A man Thorne recognised, but could not place, stood next to her, the tip of the scissors in his hand pressed against her neck.

'Sorry,' Tanner said. She stared at him, helpless with fury.

Thorne said, 'It's all right,' though it clearly wasn't. Her eyes were wide and wet and her face was streaked with snot and tears. A few thin trails of blood snaked down her forehead.

And Christ . . . her hair.

The man pointed casually with the scissors. 'Shut the door, will you?'

Thorne did as he was told then turned back, still struggling to take in what he was seeing.

What was this man doing? Who was he?

The man lifted a flap of duct tape and fastened it back across Tanner's mouth, then saw where Thorne was looking. 'Oh yes, *that*.' He took half a step back to look, though he kept the scissors close to Tanner's neck. 'I've done better work, no question.'

Tanner moaned against the tape.

'Shush,' the man said, moving the scissors back against her flesh.

Then Thorne knew exactly who he was. The ex-con Tanner had spoken to when she was trying to track down the Duchess. Thorne had only seen a picture of the man once, passport-sized at the top of Tanner's report.

He was the one who had told her about the cat killings at Maidstone prison and given them Aiden Goode's name. The one who had been so very helpful.

Now it was clear why.

'You're the barber,' Thorne said.

'Hairstylist, please.' He lifted the scissors and teased aside a strand of Tanner's hair. What was left of it.

393

Thorne's first thought had been that Tanner's hair had been cut by a madman and now he saw that it had. There were places where it had been randomly shorn back to the skull and others where it had simply been hacked at; patches where just a few tufts or longer clumps remained. There were bald spots; pink, livid, and pitted with cuts still oozing blood.

'Graham French.'

'Yes, indeed.' The man smiled. 'And you're the less-than-convincing landscape gardener, of course. I hope you enjoyed your meal the other night. Bit of a shame how all this has turned out, really, because the pair of you made such a lovely couple.'

Thorne said nothing, as unable to move as Tanner was.

French . . .

He'd seen the name before and now he realised what else he'd missed.

French had been the prisoner Aiden Goode had been heard talking to about disappearing once he'd been released. The name had been there all the time in Goode's IIS file which Thorne had seen at Maidstone prison. Another piece of Tanner's puzzle slotted into place. French had known exactly what Goode had got planned, his notion of disappearing, and he had almost certainly helped to arrange it when the time was right.

Taken him off the grid permanently.

It had been clear from the beginning that the killer they were after had planned things carefully, but Thorne was only now beginning to see just how far in advance those plans had been hatched.

In the same way that French had provided police with convenient suspects in the shape of the men with whom his victims had gone on their dates, he had found in Aiden Goode an ideal candidate to be the killer who was setting the whole thing up.

'Just out of interest, did you have to pay for that meal yourself, or do you get it back on expenses?'

Thorne looked at Graham French and made a few more educated guesses.

394

He'd done computer classes with Goode, even though he was already highly accomplished. The fraud he'd done time for had probably been computer-based. Whoever had actually butchered those cats at Maidstone, once French was out and committed to killings of his own, it had suited him to spread the word that Aiden Goode had been responsible.

As skilled at manipulating people as he was with computers.

'The Met paid for all of it.' Thorne looked at Tanner, saw the fear in her eyes, but also caught a glimpse of something more determined. 'Watford and the others. I mean, obviously you'd worked all that out.'

French nodded. 'Like I told your girlfriend, I'm not daft.'

'Never thought you were.'

Thorne considered his initial thinking about the cat killings. He was no longer convinced the cool-down theory made any sense, but whether he'd been right or not didn't really matter now. He was only sure that he needed to keep the man talking until he had a better idea. *Any* idea . . .

'Tell me about the cats.'

'What about them?' French asked.

'Why?'

'Seriously? After sad little Alice and poor, desperate Leila and the rest of them? After all that and considering where we are, you want to talk about a couple of dead cats?'

'More than a couple,' Thorne said.

French said nothing. He cocked his head slightly, and the look of confusion that passed momentarily across his face was one Thorne would only understand much later.

'Was it Goode? Those cats at Maidstone?'

'Oh, probably,' French said. 'He was certainly capable of it. The important thing was that you believed it was and that you believed he'd moved on to rather more serious things. That you'd waste your time looking for a man you were never going to find. Mind you, he's no more of a loss than any of those women.'

Thorne nodded, as though grateful for the information. 'Just so you know, I *am* considering it.' He took half a step towards Tanner and was relieved to see that French did not seem too concerned. He had no reason to be, those scissors still so close to Tanner's neck as he fussed gently with her hair. 'Where we are, I mean. And the way I see it, there's no way this is turning out well for you.'

French peered at him. 'For *me*?'

'Well, you're not walking out of here, are you?' He pointed at Tanner, was sure to make eye contact. 'You make a move to hurt my colleague, I'll be on you.'

'Really?'

'Or you could decide to try and get me out of the way first.'

'Yes, I could.'

'That's definitely another way to go.' Thorne was trying to sound unruffled, but he could barely suck up enough spit to talk. He still blamed himself for the fire that had almost cost Tanner's life, and making the wrong call now could finish the job. 'The Met don't just shell out for Italian meals, you know; they pay for all sorts of stuff. Like armed combat training ... how to handle frontal assaults with knives. Or scissors.'

'Thanks for the heads-up. That's good to know.'

'I'm just saying, you should probably bear all that in mind. Weigh up your options and maybe think about just putting those scissors down.'

Tanner was staring hard at Thorne, but he couldn't be sure what, if anything, she was trying to tell him.

Was he doing the right thing?

Was he pushing French too hard?

French puffed out his cheeks and took a few seconds, as though he was considering what Thorne had said. The choices available to him. He said, 'Yeah, I can see what you're saying and it's tricky, no question, and I really should have thought it through a little bit more. Not like me at all, but now we're all here

396

I suppose I'll have to do *something*. So, I reckon I should probably just *pop* ... ' he jabbed at the air, 'these into Detective Tanner's neck, in and out, then take my chances with you.'

'I would seriously advise against that,' Thorne said.

French seemed distracted, suddenly. 'I don't know ... '

Thorne took another half-step towards him.

'To be honest, it's hard to think straight when ... ' he looked down at Tanner and shook his head, 'a job's not finished. I mean come on, it's hardly my fault, because she never said you were coming, did she? She was being devious, again. So I had to stop before I was finished. *Look* at it. You can't ... I mean, I can't leave it like that, can I?' He moved behind Tanner and leaned down. 'The back's all over the place. Shapeless. Now, obviously I haven't got a mirror, so you'll have to trust me, but I really need to do a bit more back here.'

He began to cut, and Thorne watched as Tanner flinched with every snap of the scissors.

She winced and grunted behind the tape.

Her fists clenched and the muscles tensed in her neck, but her eyes stayed locked on Thorne's.

'Better,' French muttered. 'Much better ... '

He bent even lower, his mouth close to her ear as he whispered and snipped. Thorne looked fast at where the scissors were, then turned his eyes back to Tanner's. He gave a small nod, and Tanner screwed her eyes shut and threw her head back hard into French's face.

Thorne launched himself across the space between them.

Tanner's head did not quite make the full-on contact she had intended, but it was enough to send French reeling backwards, to make him bring the hand clutching the scissors up to his face.

It was all the time Thorne needed.

While Tanner tried to rock the chair away, Thorne grabbed French's wrist and twisted until the scissors fell to the floor. He smashed his own head down on to the bridge of French's nose, took a firm hold of the man's jacket and threw him across the room. He was on him again almost immediately as French struggled to sit up, kneeling across the man's chest and using one hand to push his head against a radiator then the other to punch him until he was unconscious.

It might have been seconds or it might have been minutes after Thorne crawled away before he felt as though he could get to his feet without falling over. He shivered and spat. The pain in his hand was excruciating and he'd torn a muscle at the top of his leg.

He thought he was going to be sick.

Tanner cried out and cursed when he tore the duct tape from her mouth.

'Sorry,' Thorne said. He picked up the scissors and began to cut away the tape around her arms and legs.

'Have you got handcuffs in your car?' Tanner asked.

'Yeah, but—'

She nodded towards French's body. Said, 'Get them.'

Thorne handed her the scissors then ran outside to fetch the set of cuffs he carried in the glove compartment. By the time he returned, Tanner was out of the chair, just a few shreds of duct tape still clinging to her clothes. She stood, a little unsteady on her feet, staring down at the clumps of hair on the polished wooden floor. Thick brown hanks, some streaked with silver, lying like fake extensions on display, a few with small gobbets of flesh still attached.

She had begun to cry again.

Thorne went to the kitchen and fetched a cloth, which he gave her to wipe away the blood from her face and the top of her head. Then he walked across to where French lay, heaved the man up to a sitting position and handcuffed him to the radiator pipe.

'We should call this in,' Thorne said.

'I suppose,' Tanner said.

He took his mobile phone from his pocket. 'And we should get you an ambulance.'

'I don't need an ambulance,' Tanner said. Her voice was small and she spoke in a cracked monotone Thorne did not like the sound of. 'But you should probably call one anyway.' She nodded towards the bathroom. 'In there.'

Thorne ran to the bathroom, pushed the door open and found the estate agent lying in the bath. He knelt down and removed the tape from the man's mouth. The man moaned and tried to turn over, and despite a nasty-looking head wound Thorne could see that he seemed to be breathing easily enough.

He called an ambulance, told the man that help was on its way. He was about to call for police back-up when he heard a noise from the living room. Not quite a bang ... more like someone stamping on a box of eggs.

He ran back into the living room and saw immediately what the noise had been. French was now lying slumped, his head at an awkward angle against the base of the radiator.

What was left of his head.

There was blood spattered against the radiator and leaking from his ear. Thorne turned to see a fat drop fall from the poker in Nicola Tanner's hand.

Her face was grey, immobile.

'Jesus ...' Thorne looked around to see where Tanner had acquired the weapon, saw the set of decorative irons beside the fireplace, the gap next to the brush and shovel where the poker had been standing. He rushed across to feel for a pulse in French's neck, knowing even before he'd failed to find one that there was little point. 'The hell have you done?'

Tanner dropped the poker.

She walked slowly across to the chair and sat back down; knees together, arms by her sides.

Thorne got to his feet.

He knew it was only a matter of minutes until the ambulance arrived.

He tried to control the panic, to think.

'Call it in,' Tanner said.

Thorne looked at her. 'Seriously?' He pointed at French's body, the blood still running down his white shirt. 'You've just bludgeoned a man to death while he was handcuffed to a radiator. While he was *unconscious*, for Christ's sake.'

Tanner said nothing.

'That's not just suspension, it's not just your career fucked here, you're looking at a murder charge ... involuntary manslaughter if you're lucky.' He stepped quickly across and crouched down next to the chair, took hold of Tanner's arms and shook. 'We're talking about prison, Nic ...'

She turned her eyes to his, flat, unblinking, and shrugged as if it were no more than a triviality. But Thorne knew exactly what was at stake, and that, as things stood, Tanner had a damn sight more to lose than he did.

Thorne stood up. He had made the decision and now he was thinking through the first and easiest option. 'Did anyone know you were going to be here?' He waited. '*Nicola?*'

She casually waved a hand in the direction of the bathroom. 'I sent Simon an email to confirm the time.' Another wave towards French. 'It's how *he* knew I'd be here, I suppose.'

'OK, so we can't just take our chances and leave.'

Thorne was on his feet and moving around; talking the scene through, working through the necessary steps.

'Right. The first thing we need to do is get rid of these.'

He knelt down and removed the handcuffs, stuffed them in his jacket pocket. He checked to make sure that there were no marks around French's wrists, which there would have been had he struggled, had he been conscious when Thorne had put them on.

'Now ... the blood spatter's here and there's nothing we can do about that, so this is where it happened, OK?'

400

'Where what happened?' Tanner still spoke as if she were just waking up.

'Where you did what you had to. Where you took appropriate action to prevent me getting seriously injured or killed.'

'That's not how it was,' Tanner said.

'You just need to shut up now and *listen*. OK, Nic?'

He looked hard at her until she nodded. She looked scared, suddenly; staring at the poker, then at the body on the other side of the room, as though she had only just realised what one thing had to do with the other. That she had been responsible. Seeing the shock start to break across her face, Thorne began to understand why she had done what she did. Why she had snapped. It hadn't been about Graham French, at least not completely. It had also been about Susan and about the fire that had destroyed so much of what had been left *after* Susan.

In his painful humiliation of her, Graham French had unlocked a rage that Thorne guessed neither of them could have imagined was in there.

'It's going to be fine, all right? We just need to cover the basics.' Thorne was pacing, working out relative positions. 'I thought French was unconscious, OK, but he clearly wasn't . . . I didn't pick up the scissors which he dropped on the floor *here* after we struggled.' He walked across to Tanner. 'I should have picked them up, but instead I came straight over to see if you were all right and helped you get free . . . which is when *he* picked up the scissors and I went back to try and disarm him.' He turned and pointed. 'We struggled again and you thought I was in danger of being stabbed, so you grabbed the poker.' He picked up the scissors from behind the chair and went back across to the radiator. He sat down next to French's body. 'Prints aren't a problem because all three of us touched the scissors at some point, right? You picked them up after it happened.'

Tanner stood up, still looking dazed and wobbly, and followed Thorne across. 'After what happened?'

'After he attacked me with the scissors and you hit him.' He looked down at the scissors in his hand, the fine hairs still clinging to the blades. 'It's not going to be good enough, though.'

'What isn't?'

'You took aggressive action against the suspect because you genuinely believed I was going to be seriously hurt, that I was going to be killed. You understand what I'm saying? You didn't mean to kill him, but your first thought was to save a fellow officer's life, and that's ... understandable.' Thorne was sucking in breaths fast, gearing himself up, because he had already decided what needed to be done. 'They need to see that ...'

He turned the scissors around in his hand and held them towards Tanner.

She shook her head.

'There's an ambulance that's going to be here any minute.' He forced the scissors into her hand. 'This is what's going to clinch it, all right?'

'I can't.'

Thorne held up his right hand, palm towards her. 'A defensive wound, that's all. It happened when I put my hand up to shield my face, when he was on top of me. That's when you grabbed the poker.' He watched her kneel in front of him then stared, waiting. 'Hurry up.'

'How can I—'

'Just fucking *do* it.'

'*Where?*'

'There's no time to worry about that, there just needs to be some blood—'

Tanner stabbed him.

'Jesus ... *fuck.*'

Tanner dropped the scissors, got up and bolted into the kitchen. Thorne was still shouting as he leaned across and transferred a convincing amount of his blood on to Graham French's neck, the collar of his shirt. He put his hands around the back of his head, rubbed his bloody palm against the man's thick black hair.

For the second time in five minutes he fought the urge to throw up.

Tanner came back with a tea towel which Thorne took and wrapped around his injured hand. 'Does it hurt?'

'Of course it fucking hurts.'

Tanner sank down next to Thorne and took his other hand in hers. She leaned against him and closed her eyes, the two of them bleeding and shaking.

'Now we can call it in,' Thorne said.

SEVENTY-THREE

A fine morning in late June and the sunshine was soft against the house's crooked, honey-coloured walls. With a huge variety of plants and shrubs now providing a riot of colour, the carefully tended gardens of Long Barrow Manor looked lovelier than they had at any point since he had arrived more than two months before.

Andrew Evans stepped out through the French windows and stared at the lush lawns and the line of flowering horse chestnuts beyond. The squared-off banks of marigolds and the rainbow of hydrangeas on three sides of the fountain.

He might as well have been looking at paint-daubed metal shutters.

'I know there's been a setback,' Call Me Rob had told him. 'But it's important to get past that.'

'A setback?' He had no idea how much the counsellor knew, the investigation that was now going backwards, but he was certain that, despite the suit and the framed certificates on his desk, the man had little idea about what his longest-serving patient was now going through. The crash and the emptiness.

'Especially when you've already come such a long way.'

Right. One step forward and God only knew how many back. Back to uncertainty that made him feel like he was drifting through the days and to nights that had become sleepless again. Back to a prison where the food was slightly better and those you loved were always absent. A wife who needed him and a baby he would not see born.

He had let everyone down so badly. He could not forgive himself, so could easily understand how they might feel the same, *should* feel the same.

'You need to man up, Andrew. I'm sure you've been in worse places than this. In every sense.'

He walked down to the fountain because he could think of nothing better to do; taking little in, until he spotted a new girl sitting on one of the benches. She had a book on her lap, but her head was thrown back, her face to the sun.

She jumped when he sat down next to her and reached to stop the book tumbling from her lap.

'Sorry,' he said.

'No worries,' she said.

God almighty, she looked a state. Probably worse than he had when he'd first arrived. She'd piled her hair up like she was Amy Winehouse or something, but it just looked ratty and was thick with grease. There were whiteheads clustered at the corners of her mouth and he'd seen more black holes than teeth when she'd tried to smile.

'What's your name?' she asked.

Evans said nothing. He stared at the ornamental fountain and thought how good it would feel to take a sledgehammer to it, to climb in afterwards and lie down in the water.

'Suit yourself.'

'We're not supposed to talk.'

'Yeah, they said.' The girl took out a tobacco tin, opened it and began to roll a cigarette. 'But, you know, balls to that.'

Evans looked across and saw the police officer, Barrett, watching from beneath a tree. He waved and Barrett waved back, before walking away along the perimeter. 'I'm Andrew.'

The girl nodded, but seemed too engrossed in her roll-up to bother reciprocating.

'Just got here?'

She nodded. 'Seems all right.'

Paula would be getting big now, Evans thought. He remembered what she'd been like with Sean, the fun and games when the hormone fairy arrived.

'A lot posher than what I'm used to, anyway.'

He wished they'd let him have his phone back, just for five minutes so he could look at those pictures. The ones his mum had taken after Sean had come along. The three of them squeezed on to that bed, him messing about with the gas and air . . .

'Hoping I won't have to be here that long.' She looked at him. 'Fuck you crying about?'

Evans shook his head; wiped his eyes and watched as the girl took a good look around, then pulled a small bottle with a dropper top from her jacket pocket. He knew exactly what was in it.

'How the hell did you get that in here?'

'How do you think?'

'Jesus . . .'

She smiled. 'Don't worry, I've given it a good wipe.'

Evans's mouth had gone dry and he could feel a sheen of sweat on the back of his neck that had nothing to do with the sunshine. He watched her transfer the liquid into the roll-up; just half a dozen drops evenly spread, but it was more than enough. His blood was jumping, sensing it, and he was rooted to his seat.

The girl licked and rolled expertly, checked again to see that nobody was watching as she took out a lighter. She looked at Evans, then nodded and held out the joint. 'Here you go, mate. I reckon you need this more than I do.'

Evans stared; could barely breathe. He knew that he should

406

walk away, that he should alert one of the officers then go and tell Rob all about it.

'Come on, you want first crack or not?'

I promise, everything's going to be fine.

You swear?

He knew exactly what he should do.

I'll be home soon and I'm going to be different.

He snatched the joint, jabbed it between his lips and leaned towards the flame.

Then he stopped, because something in the girl's expression was not quite right. A hunger he'd not seen before, certainly not when someone else was about to get all the benefit. A junkie letting someone else have first hit was weird enough, especially a complete stranger, but she looked ... *desperate* for him to get into the stuff. Far too desperate.

He leaned away, breaths coming faster. He took the unlit joint from his mouth and held it towards her. He said, 'No, you.'

She shook her head, irritated. 'Just fucking light it, will you?'

'I don't think so—'

And the girl was on him immediately, throwing her weight, such as it was, across his chest and pinning him to the bench, spitting and clawing at his face. Turning his face away as blows rained down on his head and neck, Evans saw the copper, Barrett, running up the slope towards them.

'My name's Nathalie and this is for my mother, you prick.'

The girl might have been skinny as a stick, but her fury had given her far more strength than she looked capable of. Evans could only shout and struggle, eyes squeezed shut as she reached for them, blood running into his mouth.

'This is for Frances Coombs—'

Then suddenly it was Barrett she was lashing out at, when the police officer heaved her off the bench and manhandled her on to the grass.

'I paid you, you fucker.'

'Not for this.' Barrett pushed her away, raised his arms to shield his face when she flew straight back at him.

'I *paid* you . . .'

Pushed back even harder, she ran back towards him and aimed a kick which only half connected. She immediately tried again and roared in frustration when the officer stepped back to avoid it, a hand held towards her in warning. Breathing heavily, she turned for a few seconds to glare at Evans, who was sitting up, fingers dabbing at the wounds on his face, before she wheeled away and sprinted towards the treeline.

Evans and Barrett said nothing as they watched her go.

She ran screaming and weeping into the trees, then crawled through the hole that had been cut in the perimeter fence and out on to the single-lane track where the car was waiting.

SEVENTY-FOUR

Having already consumed far more than he should have, and unable to get up and join in even if he'd wanted to, Thorne sat at one of the large round tables with Tanner and Treasure, picking at leftover chocolates and watching those even drunker than he was throwing themselves around the packed dance floor. Ties had been loosened, jackets and heels removed. The singing got even louder suddenly and a flurry of arms punched the air as the chorus of 'Sex On Fire' kicked in.

Thorne sang along tunelessly.

It was his first gay wedding, but aside from a welcome absence of awkwardly posed photographs, a cake with Catwoman and Batgirl figures perched on top and a predictably filthy speech from Treasure, it was much the same as any other he'd attended over the years. Someone had thrown up in the Gents and he'd already seen a woman crying on the stairs. He was fully expecting one of the children to slide across the dance floor on their knees at any moment, and having met Treasure's brother and his mates he wouldn't be surprised if there was a fight come chucking-out time.

Treasure leaned into him and together they stared across at the woman she had just married, dancing; screaming with excitement as the DJ mixed into a Black Eyed Peas track. She had barely left the floor for the last hour, since she and Treasure had kicked proceedings off, smooching to 'At Last' by Etta James and reducing a good many of their friends and family to tears.

'Done all right for myself, don't you reckon?'

Thorne looked at her. A tailored black-and-white pinstripe suit, her wife's initials freshly inked on her wrist and a grin that had not slipped from her face all day. 'Yeah, she's gorgeous,' he said.

'You're gorgeous, too,' Tanner said.

Treasure's grin got even wider.

'So, I can only presume you've got something on her ... or maybe you're secretly hugely wealthy.' Thorne leaned away, bracing himself for the inevitable punch. Instead, Treasure pulled him back towards her and kissed him on the cheek.

'As it's you, I don't mind if you think about her every once in a while. You know, when you're knocking one out.' She nodded, winked. 'I mean, obviously you'll have to use your left hand.'

Thorne looked down at the palm of his right hand. The scar was still evident, though it had already begun to fade a little and there would still be plenty of physio to do before he got full movement back. Next to him, Tanner adjusted the stylish black trilby she'd chosen for the event. Beneath it, Thorne knew, her hair was growing back; still fuzzy to the touch, though it would soon be long enough to hide her own scars.

'I think I'll manage,' he said.

It had been three weeks since the incident at the flat in Wood Green. A death that had inevitably required investigating, but had not necessitated the involvement of Internal Affairs. A search of Graham French's flat above the salon in Wembley had turned up more than enough evidence to prove that the dead man had been responsible for five murders and that more had

410

been planned. They had also been able to establish that, before being sent to prison, French had been involved in a brief relationship with Sandra Cook, the book-keeper at Made In Heaven. Though there was no reason to suspect that the woman had any knowledge of his activities, she had almost certainly given French enough information about the website to convince him it was ideal for his purposes.

The final piece of the puzzle.

A case closed.

Despite the fervour with which Tanner had thrown herself back into it, there had been no such progress on the Jandali investigation. No fresh leads on the man in the motorbike helmet who had killed Adnan Jandali, Kieran Sykes and Frances Coombs, or rather, no fresh leads that had led to anyone who wasn't inexplicably struck dumb when questioned. A police officer suspended pending further investigation after a serious breach of security at Long Barrow Manor. A cigarette containing liquid Spice laced with rat poison, and a girl believed to be the daughter of Frances Coombs being sought in connection with an attempt on the life of Andrew Evans.

A man who would not be reunited with his pregnant wife any time soon.

And two more Spice-related deaths in the last week.

'Who wants another drink?' Treasure stood up, dancing on the spot.

'I'm good,' Thorne said.

Tanner shook her head.

When Treasure had moved away towards the bar, Thorne said, 'Nice day.'

'First in a while,' Tanner said.

They had made separate statements at the time, of course, but had not spoken since that ambulance had arrived; not about what had really happened. What had been done to make it look like something else.

411

'All good?'

'Fine.'

'Sure?' As was standard practice, both had been offered counselling after the event. Each had declined the offer, though Thorne had been quietly hoping Tanner might see the benefit in it.

She had rather more to live with than he did.

'I think I'll probably call it a night,' she said. Thorne moved to lay his good hand on her arm, but she was already getting to her feet; adjusting the hat again. 'Better go and say my goodbyes.'

Thorne watched her walk away and caught the look she exchanged with Phil Hendricks as he stepped from the dance floor with Helen and Liam. Hendricks looked at Thorne as the other two peeled off towards the bar, then walked across and dropped into a chair next to him.

'Knackered,' he said. 'Your missus has worn me out.'

It was the first time Thorne had seen him since Hendricks had carried out the post-mortem on Graham French. Since his report confirming that the cause of death had been major head trauma, while also pointing out that French had possessed an abnormally thin skull.

'I don't know where she gets the energy from.'

'Question is . . .' Hendricks leaned in, 'is she wearing *you* out?'

'I try to keep up.'

'Seriously.' Hendricks was amiably pissed, talking slowly, the Mancunian accent even broader than usual. 'Nice to see you two, you know . . . firing on all cylinders again. No more trouble from little sister?'

'Little sister's behaving herself,' Thorne said. He watched as Tanner embraced Christine Treasure at the bar, one hand pressed firmly to the trilby to hold it in place.

'How's Nicola doing?' Hendricks asked.

'Hard to tell.'

'Well, you know her better than I do.'

'Not sure about that.' Thorne watched Tanner as she disappeared towards the cloakroom. 'Do you reckon she knows?'

Hendricks appeared to sober up quickly. 'No idea. Maybe.'

'I saw her look at you a minute ago.'

'Well, she's not daft, is she?'

'Not the way you mean it, no.'

Graham French would not be missed; there was no reason to pretend otherwise. Certainly not by the friends and families of the women he had murdered.

Alice Matthews.

Leila Fadel.

Patricia Somersby.

Annette Mangan.

Karen Butcher.

Not by their children and grandchildren.

Thorne kept telling himself that.

He emptied the bottle from which he was drinking. 'Just out of interest, how thin *was* Graham French's skull?'

A shrug. 'No thinner than anyone else's.' Hendricks spoke quietly with no trace of slurring. 'A bit thicker than normal, if anything.'

They stopped talking as Liam and Helen came back to the table with more drinks. The moment they had set them down, there was a thunderclap, and the opening strains of 'We Found Love' kicked in. Liam and Helen shouted and cheered, keen to get back on the floor. Hendricks jumped up, equally enthusiastic, and he and Liam hurried away to dance.

Thorne watched them go, still thinking about Nicola Tanner and the conspiracy into which he had now drawn his closest friend.

'Come on, you.' Helen beckoned him with a finger and a sexy smile.

Thorne shook his head, as though he barely had the energy to do that.

'Surely you can manage one dance?'

He looked up at her. The repetitive thump of the bass rang through him and it felt as though his bones were rattling.

'I'm not the man I was,' he said.

EPILOGUE

She was always amazed at how easy it was.

Not all of them, of course. There'd been plenty who didn't want to know, however hard she tried; whatever treats she tempted them with. But eventually she could always find one that could not resist what she had on offer. One was never going to do the trick, certainly not by the end of it, but it wasn't like there was any shortage, was there?

Millions of them running about, sniffing and spraying.

One for every six people, she'd read that somewhere. Might even have been in one of the stories she'd read about herself. The things she'd been busy doing with her bits of chicken and dangly toys and those shears she took care to keep nice and sharp.

They'd covered it in the local paper first off, and then the nationals, for heaven's sake. She enjoyed reading about what she'd been up to, the horrified reactions from the sad and the sickened. The pictures of the stricken owners, which was just ridiculous, and *nobody* getting the irony of the whole thing, because these oh-so-precious, fluffy little bastards were killing machines. Rats and mice, that was fair enough, but baby rabbits?

415

Songbirds? Not even eating them most of the time either, just tossing the tiny corpses around like it was all fun and games.

Best of all, though, looking through the coverage, was the wit and wisdom of the crackpots; chipping in with comments and half-arsed opinions right, left and centre, because they'd seen some film or other. Because they'd read one of those stupid true-crime books and that made them an expert.

It's what they always do.

It's how they always start . . .

Now, the forces of law and order were moving up a gear, too. Under all sorts of pressure to get a result, apparently. Well, that was fine, because it was just about time for her to stop anyway.

To stop *this*.

It was a shame, because she'd enjoyed being out and about. Especially this time of year, with the nights as mild as they were; blossom on her boots when she got in, and gutters free of damp, dead leaves. She enjoyed the fresh air on her face and hands as she walked the streets, though not her hands at the end, obviously, when the gardening gloves had needed to come out if she wasn't going to get scratched to ribbons. Well, they could be put away under the stairs for a while, because she'd need to trade them in for a pair of those nice thin ones. Like the forensic bods wore on the telly. She'd best get a few, she decided, because you could get fingerprints off human flesh these days, she'd seen that somewhere; off a woman's neck, certainly.

It was exciting, the thought of what lay ahead, but that didn't mean she wouldn't miss being out and about after Tibbles and Smoky and Blackie and the rest of them. The long, quiet nights of walking. The thinking time. The special moments when the headlights of a passing car would pick out those telltale pinpricks of orange; on a wall or in a shop doorway. The stillness then and the breath held.

The will she/won't she?

Here, puss-puss . . .

Now things would be different for a while, but that was OK, because different was good.

Spice of life, all that.

Now, it was time to take that step up.

AUTHOR'S NOTE

The series of cat-killings fictionalised in this book is based on a real and disturbing case, that, at the time of writing, remains unsolved. The Metropolitan Police began their investigation in 2015, after concerns were raised by the South Norwood Animal Rescue and Liberty charity (SNARL). Originally dubbed the Croydon Cat Killer and later the M25 Cat Killer, the individual thus far responsible for the deaths of up to four hundred pet cats, as well as a large number of squirrels, rabbits and foxes, is now simply referred to as the UK Cat Killer, with offences committed as far away as Gloucestershire, the West Midlands and the Isle of Wight.

The animal charities PETA UK and Outpaced are offering a £10,000 reward for intelligence leading to an arrest and conviction. Anyone with information should call the police and quote Operation Takahe.

Further information can be found at: snarl.org.uk or on Twitter (@SNARLLondon)

Mark Billingham, January 2018

ACKNOWLEDGEMENTS

I am hugely grateful to the police officers (serving and retired) who were able to provide helpful information about Operation Takahe, and current lines of enquiry in the ongoing hunt for the UK Cat Killer. The Macdonald Triad is genuine, but the leap made by Tom Thorne as to what the other activities of this individual might be, is – thankfully – purely fictional. Thanks to the real-life Christine Treasure (cheers, Terror) for making the connections and I hope I did your wedding justice.

Thanks as usual to Wendy Lee, who misses nothing, and to Tim Marchant for sorting me out tech-wise. To Chris Brookmyre who knows far more about computer hacking than he should and to Lisa Cutts for endless patience in answering my stupid questions about police procedure.

With each book I am reminded just how lucky I am to work with the amazing team at Little, Brown. Ed Wood is a remarkable editor (those lunches at Nando's have made the book *so* much better) and, from first draft to bookshop, my scribblings could not be in safer or lovelier hands than those of Emma Williams, Catherine Burke, Sean Garrehy, Thalia Proctor, Tamsin Kitson,

Robert Manser, Sarah Shrubb and (praise be) Laura Sherlock, who is quite simply the best publicist *ever*.

I am equally in debt to their opposite numbers at Grove Atlantic, US: Allison Malecha, Morgan Entrekin, Deb Seager and Justine Batchelor. Thank you, and I'll try and keep the Cockney rhyming slang to a minimum.

Thanks, of course, to my amazing agent Sarah Lutyens and to Juliet Mahony and Francesca Davies at Lutyens & Rubinstein.

A big shout-out (don't worry, I'm stepping back from the mic) to my fellow Fun Lovin' Crime Writers (Val McDermid, Stuart Neville, Luca Veste, Doug Johnstone and Chris Brookmyre) who have made the last year so much more enjoyable than it might otherwise have been. Long may we continue to murder songs for fun.

The biggest thanks, as always, are due to my wife, Claire. Let me stress, again, that my registration on that dating site was done purely in the name of research. Not that anyone was interested . . .

3